BEASTLY MANOR

ALEX HALL

MADISON PLACE PRESS

Madison Place Press

Cover art by Katherine Davis 2022

ISBN: 9780692627815

THE CHEESE MONGER'S LAD

"The rose and the thorn..."

—Saadi

CHAPTER 1

Once upon a time in a faraway land, a very wealthy merchant lived on a good piece of property just west of the hamlet we now call Littleton. The merchant was blessed with luck and guile, strong bones and sharp eyes, a pretty wife who had both wit and a gentle spirit, and four healthy children. He was called Jean de Beaumont, after his father and his grandfather both. His wife liked to call him Roux for the color of his hair. To his three daughters, the merchant was always Papa, but his eldest child and only son always called him simply Da.

Like many of the tenant farmers subsisting on squares of land just outside Littleton proper, de Beaumont dedicated his time and talents to the making of good cheeses. The native soil was made rich with salt from the nearby sea, and that fragrant earth produced a grass greener than the king's most rare verdigris dyes. Black-and-white cattle grew fat in the fields. Their milk was thick and sweet, suitable for drinking straight from the pail or churning into butter. More importantly, this milk was the very key to the family's survival, for de Beaumont poured it into great bowls and set it aside to curdle before molding. The milk turned into cheese, the cheese now called Camembert.

Camembert was not so rare around Littleton. But de Beaumont, being a clever man with a head for experimentation, began to add an extra ingredient to the cheese: a special brandy his wife made from the apples collected from the trees growing wild among the hedges. Only she knew how to correctly prepare the brandy, and only de Beaumont knew when to add the sweet-smelling liquor between curdling and molding, and then again before he sealed the cheeses in wooden boxes and set them aside to age. The recipe was a family secret kept only in de Beaumont's head. As word of the unusual and delicious Camembert spread so did demand, but de Beaumont was canny and never increased production. He raised the price for a wheel. His fortune was made in a matter of years, while Corbin was still a babe not yet out of his cot.

They say there are still wheels of de Beaumont Camembert laid aside in the king's cellars, held back for a special occasion. If this is true, the king is a very lucky man, as by all accounts de Beaumont's special cheese exists nowhere else. It is possible the merchant meant to teach Corbin the recipe once the child came of age, so that as heir he could pass the secret on through the generations, ensuring the family's continued fortune. But God plays tricks on a man, gives with the right hand and takes with the left, and like de Beaumont's pretty little farm and charming family, that magical strain of Camembert is nothing more than a distant memory, a lingering taste on the tongue of good fortune, a fleeting recollection of pleasure.

IT CAME to pieces all at once, in the late summer of Corbin's tenth year, when the boy's mind was turned toward nothing more pressing than how he could escape the house and his books and run off to swim in the sea, or wile away long hours beneath the apple trees hunting rabbits in the hedge or digging up garden snakes with which to torment his little sisters. Corbin could swim like a fish. He knew all the paths up and down the cliffs above the beach. He had a knife of his own brought back from the king's favorite blacksmith—likely in exchange for a wheel of cheese or a flask of Mother's brandy—and he used it to skin the game he sometimes caught. Three times he employed it in boys' brawling, although never for more than threat. That summer there was a new litter of kittens in the cheese cellar, and Corbin had just recently coaxed their protective mum into letting him stroke her babies.

Corbin's own mother adored him. His sisters worshipped or hated him at a turn. Da whipped him only when he could not first reason Corbin's redheaded temper away, while Nan said the boy was a thorn in her side even as she bound his various cuts and scrapes, made up an ointment for his bruises, and kept him fed and clean.

All summer long, Corbin ruled as a prince in his own kingdom, but now as he stood outside the family cottage to see Mother and Da off with the dawn, it was time for him to be a man. Like most young people forced into responsibility, he both resented and rejoiced at the opportunity.

"See to the cattle first every morning," Da said. His hand was warm on Corbin's head. It was the same instruction he'd repeated every day of the year, but Corbin nodded gravely as if it were the first time. "Remember to poultice Daisy's teats; she'll need them eased at least until I come home. No shirking, Corbin. It isn't fair to her."

Corbin grimaced but nodded. "Yes, Da."

Daisy was the oldest of the de Beaumont herd. Her udder tended to crack winter and summer. The poultice Da used to ease her teats was a greasy mixture of fat and herb. It stank, and Corbin hated the feel of it between his fingers, but he wouldn't shirk his duty.

"Look after Nan and your sisters," Da continued. Corbin tried not to shuffle his feet under the weight of Da's regard. His three sisters stood in the door of the house, sniffling as they peered sleepily around Nan's skirts. Mother crouched at their feet between the two great pink-and-blue hydrangeas. She whispered into Faith's small ear while Beauty giggled and Hope sulked. "Help Beauty with her letters, lad, and sing Hope to sleep at night. She'll have nightmares without your mother about."

"Yes, Da."

"Help Nan with Faith's nappies, Corbin, and remember to watch the apple trees. The blossoms are turning. I'm counting on you."

"I will." Corbin did shuffle then, wishing Da would get on with it. The cart horse, called Snip for the white on his nose, stomped a hoof in shared impatience. The gelding was hitched already to a cart heavy with boxes of Camembert. It was only a day's ride west to Caen where Da would do his twice-yearly business with the merchant marine, but a good portion of that was through the black forest—a dangerous endeavor even if one wasn't loaded down with boxes of heavy cheese. Corbin wasn't worried. Da's travels were part and parcel of the business that kept the little farm prosperous, but this was the first time as far back as Corbin could remember that Mother was making the journey as well.

"Good lad." Da removed his hand from Corbin's shoulder and strode to the cart. Mother took Da's place, squatting in front of Corbin as she had his sisters. Her face was wet as she kissed him and then ruffled his ruddy curls. Corbin had to swallow hard past a lump in his throat but refused to sniffle in front of Da.

"Fine little man." Mother smelled of apple tree and smoke off the hearth. The simple jet earrings Da had given her on their wedding day sparkled in the morning. She pulled Corbin close. He buried his nose in the crook of her neck, inhaling comfort. Then Da called, and she let Corbin go, rising to her feet and dusting off her skirts. "Six days and then we'll be back. On the sixth day, there will be sweets and new shoes. If you are very good, mayhap a wooden sword for your practice."

The promise gave Corbin something to hope for. He nodded, mouth watering in anticipation of chocolate and macaroons. He trailed Mother across the small front garden, bees not yet waking to test the lavender or Mother's beloved white roses. He stood beside Snip as Da boosted Mother up onto the running board. There was room for only one on the cart. Da would walk the entire way, Snip's long reins in one hand. He wore a long sword on his back. The sword was old, the pommel decorated in whirls and swirls. Corbin hoped to have it for his own one day, but he knew first would come long lessons on the wooden sword Mother had promised.

Corbin bit the inside of his cheek and hoped the six days would pass very quickly.

Then Da clucked his tongue and shook the long reins, and Snip walked on. The cart's wheels rolled easily on cobblestones, but soon enough the road would give way to a mud track, and Snip would have to pull hard. Silently Corbin wished the gelding strength and haste.

Mother turned to wave once before they rounded the first hedge. Da didn't look back. Baby Faith began to wail. Hope furiously bid her hush, but it was Beauty who plucked the toddler from the ground and soothed her with a hug. Corbin knew this all without looking away from the empty road because it was a routine witnessed over and over again. Every member in the family knew their role and played it well. Corbin found it all very boring, the mummery of daily life. As he stood there in the dawn among lavender and roses, he wondered if he could chase Da's cart all the way to the edge of the forest without once being seen.

"Corbin," Nan called sharply, as if she knew exactly what he was considering. "Go now into town and fetch back some bread from Henri," she said. "I'm out, and we'll have porridge and toast for supper I think."

Corbin turned, a protest half-formed, but Nan speared him with a look. Standing still in the threshold, she looked very much like Mother, but the neat plait of her hair was the color of steel instead of wheat, and her eyes were a muddy blue like Corbin's, not violet like Mother's and Beauty's and Faith's. Da used to say Mother's eyes were the color of the sea beneath the moon, but Corbin's were like the Seine on a clear day. Secretly Corbin wished for eyes green as Da's, green as the grass that fed their cattle.

"Corbin!" Nan shook her skirts. "Stop woolgathering and go. The lasses are hungry. Get on now! Go!"

So Corbin sighed and went, setting out on the west road toward the forest and walking east toward Littleton.

CORBIN'S DA was well liked in Littleton. De Beaumont seemed a godly man, generous with both his wit and his wisdom. He was envied for his gracious wife. Corbin was aware of his family's influence and not above making occasional use of Da's good name, but he was equally well liked simply because he was Corbin. The village matrons believed him an affable lad, quick to call hello or lend a helping hand with an afternoon's washing or a long evening with the butter churn. The farmers knew him for his burgeoning skill as a shepherd and as a source of sturdy labor at harvest. Littleton's maids treated Corbin as they might a young lamb or eager puppy, awarding him pets and treats and, on the laziest of afternoons, vying to comb his red curls.

Corbin's peers fell to frank worship, but not because they were impressed by Da's wealth or Corbin's role as village helpmate. In the way of youth, Littleton's children recognized Corbin for what he was: a natural flirt with an honest smile and loyal heart. He was slow to anger but vicious of temper once he kindled. He knew how best to charm the baker free of half an apple tart, how to talk himself out of a whipping when he fell asleep during Father Mercy's Sunday sermon, and how to spit an apple seed twice as far as the nearest champion.

By age ten, he'd already kissed his first lass behind the waterwheel. It was a dull and disappointing experiment that earned him points for hubris rather than technique.

He had his small jeweled knife while most of the other boys had to make do with secondhand dirks. He had a fine old pony that he shared with Beauty and Hope, and he lied when he told Littleton's gang of wide-eyed pups that he often rode that pony through the forest to the sea and back.

The other children loved Corbin. He enjoyed their regard. But the only one of the pack whose affection he returned was a motherless urchin called Nell. Nell was older than Corbin by two or three summers, taller than Corbin by half a hand, and could spit apple seeds better than any other lass. Her father worked a plot of land on the northernmost edge of town. It was said in Corbin's family that the dwarves had got Nell's mum one especially cold winter, but Nell never spoke of her, and Corbin never dared ask.

Nell didn't pet Corbin's hair or offer him sweetmeats and kisses behind the waterwheel. She wasn't afraid to call "bollocks" when he was acting like a little lord. She didn't know Corbin adored her with a passion usually reserved for summer sausage and apple pies. Corbin intended to keep that secret to the grave for fear Nell would laugh herself breathless if she ever discovered the truth.

Corbin hated being laughed at.

NELL WASN'T LAUGHING when she met him halfway into town. Corbin heard her coming before he saw her, the swish of her skirts and the slap of her sandals in mud. Her family's third field was left black and fallow against the boundary wall, last season's chafe burned to the ground in hopes of a healthier planting come fall. Nell's father would be up and working in the second field, cutting wheat before the day grew too warm. Midday would see Nell sowing kale for winter in the field closest to their home. That first field was always Nell's to work, and she treated the crop with pride, managing to produce a fine bounty two years out of three.

As he watched Nell run toward him along her father's fence line, Corbin was secretly grateful his family had chosen the raising of cattle over the coaxing of bounty from the earth. Livestock could sicken and die, spring babies might be born breech or too small, but at least a man knew how best to ease a suffering calf or foundered cow. Plants were mysterious and fragile things, far too dependent on the whim of weather and soil.

"Corbin!" Nell waved as she raced close. She bundled the hem of her skirts in one fist, scrambling deftly over the rough stone wall separating her father's field from the road. "*There* you are. Stopped in to find you, but Nan said your mum and dad had ridden away early, and you were off to Henri's shop for toast."

"They've gone," Corbin agreed, feeling very much the man of the house. "I'm to be in charge until they return: Mother said so." He lifted his chin just a little, but even then he wasn't quite as tall as his friend. Corbin was one of the taller village lads, but Nell had legs like a stork, all knobby knees and thin shanks. Corbin could see her kneecaps now, what with her skirts hiked up. Her legs were dusted black from the burned field. Beneath the layer of soot, her kneecaps were scraped and bruised as any boy's. Nell kept no truck with housekeeping when she could run wild under blue skies instead.

Nell drew her wool skirts up between her legs and tucked them in a loop of thick rope she used as a belt. Her sleeves were rolled up past her elbows, her arms as grubby as her legs, but when she curled her fingers in the crook of Corbin's elbow, it was with the grace of a titled lady.

"Didn't follow after then?" she mused, disappointed, as they continued side by side along the road. "I suppose it's too late now."

"Nan was keeping a weather eye." Corbin shook his head. "Hope, too, I wager. She's deathly afraid of the forest and supposes the trees will eat any soul that comes beneath the edge of the canopy. She'll have nightmares tonight and every night until Mother and Da come home."

Nell hummed in sympathy, ruffling the dark fringe that hung always in her eyes. "Poor mite. Can't say I blame her. I used to dream of the forest and its monsters when I was a wee lass."

Corbin wondered if his friend was thinking of dwarves, but as they rounded the last muddy bend in the highway and Littleton came into view, Nell tapped her fingers restlessly on Corbin's forearm. She pursed her lips.

"There's been wolves seen out again," she said, hushed. "Old Man Cooper says he chased a mated pair from around his barn just last week when the moon was high. He had to bring out sword and torch before they'd leave his henhouse be. And father's Auntie Grace says she's heard them howling in the night. Dad thinks they're hungrier than usual this year because game's sparse."

Corbin pictured the fat cows trundling in the field behind his cottage and shuddered. Nell's fingers grew still on his arm. She giggled.

"Not that you need worry, for your Angus is frightening enough to keep any monster at bay."

Corbin snorted in loud agreement. Angus was the family's stud bull and very ferocious when he was stirred to take notice of the world past the tip of his muzzle. The bull tolerated Corbin, for it was his responsibility to bring the old stud oats once in the morning and once before bed, but he had no patience for Hope or Beauty, and in fact had once split Nan's lip with a solid whack of his heavy tail. Corbin couldn't help but think Nell was quite right; Angus would use hooves and horns to keep his pasture clear of hungering wolves.

As Corbin and Nell drew close to town, the road changed, growing straight and wide. Weathered boards lay across the deepest ruts, the oak worn smooth by foot traffic and wagon wheels. Low stone walls gave way to thick hedgerows taller than Corbin's head. The vegetation provided natural boundaries between small village plots. Corbin could see thatched roofs and stone dormers above and past the thorny tangle, but the homes themselves were mostly hidden. Those rare souls who could afford to live inside Littleton proper valued their privacy. Corbin supposed he couldn't blame them, but he did often wonder what treasures might lie hidden beyond the hedgerow. Even a wealthy merchant's son couldn't quite grasp the extravagance of holding land for the sake of simply keeping it and not farming it.

Nell glanced sideways, smiling. "Flowers," she offered, guessing the direction of his thoughts. "Masses and masses of red and yellow flowers brought from over the sea and planted in groups. Not like our roses. These are delicate with long stems, and a single bulb is more expensive than a flagon of good wine, says Auntie Grace, and they open and close with the rising and setting of the sun like magic, and they smell like rain."

Corbin looked up at the nearest hedge and decided Nell's auntie seemed to know a lot of interesting things for a woman who rarely left her hearth. Many of the houses were kept empty during the cold winter months, their occupants gone up to court, but now at the heart of fine weather, he could sometimes hear laughter or singing through the natural walls. He wondered what it would be like to throw open your windows and see flowers even in midsummer.

Nell let go of Corbin's elbow and hopped from buried cobblestone to muddy plank, placing one sandaled foot in front of the other, both arms spread for balance. Mud lay deep over cobblestones between. The sun warmed Corbin's head. The day was turning very pleasant quite early on, and the bit of his heart that regretted Mother and Da's departure lifted toward cheerfulness. Littleton looked like a pretty hamlet in the early morning light, white stone shining. Corbin, who was still learning his numbers but had just the day before impressed Mother by counting to fifty without using his fingers once, knew that there were six solid structures in Littleton—seven if one counted the mill and waterwheel crouching over the sleepy Alevins.

"I smell fresh bread," Nell announced. "Henri must have just put it up. Your nan will be pleased. We're quick enough to get the best of the lot."

"We?" Corbin challenged, less kind than he could have been. "You've no money for bread, Nell."

But Nell was already looking ahead toward the center of town where Henri's bakery waited just out of sight. At three stories, Henri's holding was both the fattest and tallest of all

Littleton's buildings. It served as the baker's shop and home, but also sometimes as the village inn.

"Your nan gave me coin for a heel." Nell flounced a little as she tossed her head. Her sandals squished in the mud, but her skirts, still bundled safely in her belt, remained clean. "In trade for my fish."

"Fish?" Nell had lengthened her stride, cajoled by the smell of new bread, and Corbin had to trot to keep up. "What fish? You haven't hooked any fish in *days*."

"That's just it: my bit of news, what I stopped in to tell you," Nan called back over her shoulder. "Hurry, Corbin, the day's already half-wasted!"

Corbin was inclined to disagree with Nell's assessment. As far as he was concerned, the morning was still fresh. He was well used to waking before sunrise to help Da with chores. He didn't need the fancy little carriage clock Da had commissioned a foreign jeweler to make for Mother's last birthday to know the day had barely begun. The clock had come all the way over the sea in a crate stuffed with horse-hair and not suffered any damage at all. It had taken a full two years to build the timepiece. Da sometimes remarked to no one in particular that the clock kept better time than any of the king's own.

Corbin, who could tell time by the position of the sun in the sky and the length of the shadows on the field, was in no hurry to return home and help Nan with nappies, but Nell's impatience was catching, so he trotted after his friend. The perfume of warm bread grew heady as they reached the center of town. The line outside Henri's shop was already three deep. Nell danced on the toes of her sandals while Corbin folded his hands behind his back and studied the group of women waiting on the stoop for Henri's wares. The women were gentry, clothed in a finer quality of wool than even Corbin's Da could afford. They wore ribbons in their plaits and carried woven baskets for bread. They chattered like bright little birds as they waited for Henri to finish opening shop, pretending not to see Nell and her dirty, scraped knees. Corbin they smiled at, whispering and pointing first at his curls and then at the sparkle of his knife on his belt. When Corbin showed his teeth in a scowl, they tittered nervously, turning their backs.

Henri finally opened his shop with a flourish, throwing open the wide painted door and bellowing good mornings. The baker was a lean man for all that he sampled his wares. His yellow beard was neatly trimmed, his hair kept close to his head under a white kerchief, and he was always impeccably dressed but for the sprinkling of flour he wore like a second tunic. Corbin distinctly recalled bouncing on Henri's lap one evening before he could yet walk and the yeasty smell of the man as he bent to kiss Corbin's cheek.

Now Henri bowed and scraped to the three impatient women before leading them into his bakery. Nell trotted after, shedding dried mud onto Henri's clean boards. She ignored the women's aghast chirping. Henri only winked at Nell and Corbin, gesturing at them to wait. Nell circled the cool, dark space Henri used as his showroom. One of the beribboned women said something very rude about Nell's breeding. Corbin opened his mouth on an equally scandalous correction, but Henri caught his eye and shook his head in warning, and immediately after that Corbin's attention was caught and held by a row of still bubbling mincemeat tarts. He licked his lips, regarding the tarts in despair. He wished Nan had sent along enough coin for both bread and a sweet treat.

Outside the bakery, Littleton's streets were slowly filling. Men returning from the fields for a second breakfast talked quietly among themselves as they brushed soil from their trousers. Women and children bustled about on private errands, while the morning's first travelers split the village as they galloped through on the highway. Corbin caught sight of two separate riders wearing the king's blue livery. The horsemen paid little attention to Littleton's own residents, ignoring shouts of greeting or calls of query, sparing no sympathy for pedestrians forced to scramble out of the way of flying hooves. The soldiers would follow the highway through the forest, but unlike Corbin's parents, the cavalry had crossbows strapped across their broad shoulders and wore long knives on their belts.

Henri clicked his tongue. "Bit early for riders. They've been coming more frequently of late, flying back and forth along the highway like great birds. They say the king's building a new ship, don't they, tall as two houses and bristling with artillery. Caen is a busy city this summer, but I suppose you'd know that already, what with your father on his way back north, Master Corbin?"

Corbin looked away from Littleton's cobbled streets. He met the baker's curious stare, surprised. "I suppose so," he allowed doubtfully. The three women had moved on while Corbin was busy admiring blue livery. Nell had a small heel of bread stuck already in her mouth and was gnawing on the hard crust like a squirrel with a nut.

Henri smiled. "Come, Corbin. Here's bread for your nan and three *pain au chocolat*: one each for Faith, Hope, and Beauty." The baker wrapped his wares in paper, tying the bundle deftly with a bit of string. "And what is it that strikes your fancy this morning, lad?"

Corbin hesitated. He had no extra coin on his belt. Da kept a running tab with the baker and the cooper, with Littleton's seamstress and farrier, and even with several of the roaming tinkers who traveled between hamlets. De Beaumont always paid his due, and he was a very careful bookkeeper. Nan had required bread for toast, nothing more.

Corbin thought the croissant would be forgiven; Mother always said little girls were meant to be kept in lace and sweets, and Da rarely refused his daughters any treat. Corbin was expected to eat porridge and toast and be grateful for a daub of honey or a wedge of cheese because strong lads were never coddled, even strong lads with their very own jeweled knife and fine old pony.

Henri waited expectantly. Nell had already separated her coins onto the baker's battered counter. Corbin thought of Nan, who would be angry if he spoiled his breakfast on a tart. He thought of Da, who would eventually take accounting of the baker's tab and then ask Mother about mincemeat tarts. Mother would have to walk into town and speak to Henri, and eventually Corbin would be found out and sent down into the cheese cellar for a whipping because Da would say ordering up a treat without first asking Nan was *cheating* and good men never did.

Corbin could see it all in his head exactly as he knew it would happen. He could almost feel the lashes from Da's belt on the back of his thighs, almost hear Mother's disappointed sigh. Faith would cry. Hope would shake her head in disappointment, and Beauty would berate Corbin for being a selfish fool. Nan would have a firm word with Henri, and the baker would look askance at Corbin forever after.

"Corbin?" Nell prompted with a mouthful of bread. "I haven't got all day. Hurry up. I want to tell you about the fish."

"Two tarts, please," blurted Corbin. "Mincemeat, both. On account, thank you."

Henri smiled. He secured two scalloped tarts in little cups of folded paper, placed them in a woven bag, and then carefully added Nan's bread and the croissant. He handed the bag to Corbin.

"Enjoy, young sir," he said. "And good day to you both."

Back out on the cobbled street, Corbin dug both tarts free. He passed the first to Nell. His friend took the offering with greedy delight, tucking in immediately. Nell smacked her lips, savoring pastry and mincemeat. She cleaned spilled filling from her fingers with a swipe of her tongue.

Corbin felt suddenly tall as a man twice his age. It was worth a future flogging to please Nell. When she grabbed his hand to pull him along as she ate, her sticky fingers entwined with his own, Corbin's ten-year-old heart leaped in his breast. He'd never felt happier.

Days later, of course, as he lay on his cot in the dark and listened to Da's muffled weeping, Corbin couldn't help but wonder—as a child inevitably will—if the thing that had happened to Mother was all his fault, if maybe God was punishing him for taking two mincemeat tarts, on account, without permission.

For *cheating*.

CHAPTER 2

The Alevins is one of our Orne's lesser known tributaries. Wide, brown, and fenny, it flows in a westerly direction along Littleton's northern boundary before crooking gently again and cascading into Bretons Sea. The fall there is locally called *Chute de Cadavre*—Dead Man's Drop—and even the most foolhardy know better than to linger long near the edge. There are stories of unwary wanderers being taken by the water and pulled over the cataract. Everyone in Littleton can recall for you in a hushed whisper the family legend of a grandparent, an uncle, or a great-nephew lost near Dead Man's Drop to the otherwise tranquil Alevins.

Some swear the falls are cursed. They are not, but they are indeed very, very dangerous.

Away from sea and closer to Littleton, the Alevins has become muddy and shallow, so much so that the old mill once used for grinding wheat is now abandoned. The water-wheel sags. Even before Corbin was born, production had stopped; flour comes instead in bags east from the king's capital or south from Honnefleu.

Ten-year-old Corbin always only knew the dilapidated mill as a favorite place to nap in rain or heat. The water around the base of the wheel was calm enough and safe enough to make the perfect swim hole. The long grass around the mill made a comfortable bed.

That second evening without Mother and Da Corbin finished his chores early, tending the cattle properly but with haste, parsimonious of pats between the ears and kisses on damp noses. The milk cows forgave him his hurry, but Angus snorted over grain spilt on the ground and not in the trough. He threatened Corbin with his long horns. Corbin apologized and scooped as much of the lost feed out of the pasture and into its proper place, but Angus continued to snort and sigh until Corbin's conscious stung. So he paused long enough to stroke the bull's stifles and tell him what a lovely animal he was, how strong and how clever.

Once Angus had calmed, Corbin ran to check the cheeses in the cellar. Da's work appeared exactly as it should be, stinking and ripe. Corbin stuck a thumb into one of three large bowls and determined the curds soon ready to be turned into molds. A flask of Mother's brandy stood stoppered and waiting for Da's return. Corbin knew better than to bathe the Camembert himself. Hope had tried once when she was still too young to know better and ruined an entire batch of cheeses in the process. Da hadn't shouted or struck Hope—she had been barely old enough to lift the brandy and had got more of the precious liquid on her smock and on the floor than in the molds—but his disappointment had lingered about the cottage for days afterward, chill and frightening.

After assuring himself that the cheeses were sound, Corbin ran back up the cellar steps and dashed across the front garden. The day was long enough that the bees, absent at dawn, were still busy among the flowers. The cottage door was propped open to the evening breezes. Corbin stuck his head over the threshold.

"Nan!" he hollered, dancing from foot to foot. "I'm off!"

"Hsst, Corbin. What is this shouting?" Nan came around the corner of the house, Beauty caught in her wake. Nan carried a basket of fresh-plucked herbs. Corbin could smell crushed thyme and mint. Beauty was holding a second smaller basket filled with hens' eggs. She swung the basket as she trailed Nan's skirts, endangering the eggs, and she smiled at Corbin.

"I'm off, Nan." Corbin hopped off the front step. "Nell's going to show me her new fishing hole, remember?"

"I do," Nan said gravely. "And have you finished your chores?"

"Yes, yes." Corbin bounced on his toes while Beauty made faces behind Nan's back. "The herd and Angus and the cheeses and Daisy's teats. Also, I've locked the pony in his shed. Nell says there've been wolves ab—"

"Hsst!" Nan said again, this time making a warding sign with the fingers of her left hand. Beauty ceased making faces and grew intent. "Don't scare your sister, Corbin. We haven't had wolves out of the forest since your granda died, and that won't change. The creatures of the forest have better things to do than bother the likes of us." She brushed past Corbin toward the open door. "Off you go then. Back before dark. Bring us a fish if you're lucky. Come, girl."

Beauty looked at Corbin as she slipped by, brow furrowed. He wished he'd thought to keep the wolves to himself. He opened his mouth to apologize, but Beauty slammed the cottage door in his face. Corbin hesitated on the front steps for only six heartbeats. Bees on lavender buzzed busy contentment, then lifted from the blossoms in surprise as Corbin took flight himself, leaping over the low shrubs as he raced back around behind the house. He didn't bother with the king's highway. There was a more direct route through farmland to the old mill. The shortcut was not without its difficulties, but Corbin was used to scrambling over the walls dividing field from field. The hedgerows were more dangerous. Corbin knew the secret ways between stone and bramble, gaps wide enough for a boy to slip through, but it was impossible to completely avoid the sting of nettle across the back of his hands. Four times long wicked thorns pulled at his tunic, threatening to snag the wool until Corbin was forced to stop his forward scramble. He paused long enough to carefully disentangle himself from the greedy barbs before racing ahead.

By the time Corbin reached the river, he was out of breath and scratched bloody in more than a few places. He squatted on the sandy bank. Cupping his hands, he scooped cold, sweet water over his head to cool his sweaty brow before bending again to drink deep. The shore sloped gently away beneath the water before dropping into the depths. The shallows were clear as the glass face on Mother's clock. Corbin could see pebbles and other debris sparkling beneath the water. Tiny fish ghosted back and forth between the submerged rocks, bellies scraping sand. The fish were too small to make a meal, naught but skin and bones. They were but snacks for the bigger creatures that swam in darker waters. Sometimes Nell used their like to bait her hooks.

Corbin shook water from his hands. He stood and followed the curve of the river away from the sea. High grass tickled his elbow as he walked between field and river. The nearby crop was only half-cut for hay while the land across the water had been recently scythed, leaving behind swathes of golden stubble. Corbin caught up a long blade and stuck it between his teeth, chewing thoughtfully as he judged the sun's height in the sky. By the length of the shadows on the river, he had a few hours yet of freedom, but even during summer season, night seemed to fall all at once, with no time spared for twilight.

Corbin clamored over one last low wall. The mill seemed at first a part of the land, so worn and sun-bleached were the stone walls and crumbling foundation. Grass grew out of cracks in the neglected mortar. Vines climbed skyward along old timber toward the partially collapsed roof. The walls were crooked, buckling gradually inward. The mill had been in danger of falling for as long as Corbin could recall, kept in place only by the grip of stubborn vegetation. The wheel had sunk deeper into the water than it was ever meant to sit. Corbin knew the axle was long disintegrated. Most of the paddles were rotted away to nothing. What remained of the wooden skeleton beneath the water was grown over with iridescent moss stretched into long flags by the pull of the current. Corbin liked to dive and swim through that gleaming forest, pretending all the while that he was a sea serpent guarding distant shores.

Nell was singing when Corbin approached the mill. She lacked a minstrel's true talent, but she was gifted with a knack for remembering a song after listening only once. She made even a rough soldiers' anthem sound sweet against the rush of the river. Corbin blushed to hear the vulgar chorus sung so prettily. He couldn't help but wonder where Nell had picked up the bawdy tune.

"You'll scare the fish away with words like that," he warned, scrambling over the remains of the axle toward his friend. The mill cast a long shadow over wheel and river, and also over Nell and her fishing poles. She stopped singing and turned her head. Briefly gloom obscured her face beneath the cowl she sometimes wore.

Corbin shivered. He laughed uneasily. *"Mon Dieu,* Nell!

You look almost like a goblin crouched in the shade like that. Come away into the sun where it's warmer!"

"There are no such things as goblins, Corbin," Nell replied. She sounded solemn. "Don't be afraid."

"I'm not!" But he strode close and bent to make sure it was his friend under the cape and cowl. Nell lifted her chin. She smiled at his scrutiny. Corbin let out a small breath he hadn't realized he was holding and relaxed.

"Sit," Nell ordered, patting the ground at her side. "Don't knock over my poles. I've got them arranged just so."

There were four poles stuck in the grassy bank, each fashioned from salvaged windfall. Corbin knew Nell preferred apple wood because the fallen branches were easier to prune back into a single rod, but she would sometimes make due with sycamore for its flexibility. The four poles were of varying lengths—Nell was constantly experimenting in her war against the fishes—but each was sharpened to a vicious point at each end, one to sink into the ground and keep the pole in place while Nell fed out her lines and the other to use as spearhead. Softhearted Nell preferred to put her catch immediately to death, piercing each fish through the eye before the creature realized it was dying out of water.

"That's a new one," Corbin declared, pointing at the fourth and final rod as he stepped gingerly along the bank to his friend. Close by Nell looked more like the muddy urchin he knew. "What is it, briar wood? Not as good as the last, the apple I helped you prune. Briar wood's too fragile, Nell."

Nell shrugged. Her attention was focused again on her lines and lures. The lines were made of pilfered tail hair plucked from a cow or horse and then woven together in twos or threes for strength. Nell's lures were magical things crafted from bits of trash and treasure: shiny buttons, grubs or insects caught in the field and preserved in a jar for the hook, or pieces of the smallest river fish sliced into enticing chunks.

"What are you using today?" Corbin demanded. Nell startled as if she had forgotten he was there. Mortified, Corbin turned to leave her be, but Nell reached out and caught him around the wrist.

"No, stay," she said. With her other hand, she pushed the cowl off her head, baring rosy cheeks and sparkling eyes. There was a smudge of dirt across the bridge of her nose, just visible in the false dusk. "Look, this is what I wanted to show you. See how they race to eat, the hungry things!"

Nell let go of Corbin's wrist. She pointed into the river just below her perch. Corbin crouched, looking into the water. Here between the mill and the crooked waterwheel the river was black and sluggish, more pond than cataract. Nell's lines, all four, drifted clockwise in the lazy current. Corbin could see the shapes of her lures as clear as day, although shadow made detail indistinct. It was impossible to tell with what Nell had baited her hooks, but whatever temptation she'd chosen was an undeniable success.

"I've never seen so many!" Corbin said, gaping. "And so big!"

"Oh, yes," Nell agreed softly. "Those are the old men of the river, Corbin. The grandfathers and great-grandfathers, and look how greedy they are!" She grinned. "They can't resist my treats, can they? It's why I had to fashion another pole so quickly. I'd have stripped another five had I the time. Look!" Still watching the school of gigantic river fish circling closer to her lures, Nell shrugged a shoulder sideways. "Look how many I've caught already, there in the bucket."

Nell's bucket was one of Old Man Cooper's castoffs. It was probably intended as a washerwoman's tub; it was too large for cheeses but too small for butter churning. Fashioned of good oak, the bucket had nevertheless somehow developed a wide split between two staves. Nell had stuffed the crack with wads of grass, bits of cloth, and daubs of sap. She used the bucket for everything from hauling apples and kale to pressing table grapes.

The bucket wasn't perfectly repaired. As Corbin approached it, he could see the slow sweat of water through the patch. Still, the liquid inside would hold as long as Nell needed. Corbin counted six river fish submerged gills to fin in the bucket, kept cold by river water. They were quite dead, each pierced through one eye. They were also each fat enough to feed three hungry men, far larger than any fish Corbin had seen in Nell's bucket before. Any one of the six would fetch a pretty penny in town.

"*Mon Dieu,*" Corbin breathed a second time. He looked from the bucket to his friend and back again. "How have you managed this? The grandfather fish *never* bite! Everyone knows they're too clever for the hook."

Nell shook her head. She started to reply, but at that moment, one of her poles began to vibrate and bend, the horsehair snapping taut. Corbin stared wide-eyed as the rod pulled free of the earth, dragged forward by the fish on the other end of line. Nell scrambled after on hands and knees. She grabbed, managing to wrap all ten fingers around the butt of the pole and save it from the river. She sat on her heels and pulled hard, and something silver shifted beneath the surface of the water.

"Corbin!" she cried as she scooted backward in the mud on her skirts. "The other one!"

Corbin swung around just as a second rod bent toward the water. He lunged, managing to save the rod. The unexpected weight of the fish on the line made him stumble, but he held tight.

Nell shouted, "Pull!"

Corbin tried. He was a strong lad. The fish on his hook seemed impossibly stronger. Out of the corner of his eye, he saw Nell land her catch. The fish flopped at her feet, spraying mud and water, until she stabbed it neatly with the end of her pole. She moved to take Corbin's rod then yelped as the briarwood pole flew directly from the bank and into the water with barely a splash to mark its passing.

"Shit," she said succinctly. Corbin felt shock flush the back of his neck but was too busy fighting his own battle to spend the energy on a reprimand. Besides, the last two poles were vibrating in tandem. Nell whirled away again.

By the time it was over, they'd lost another rod and gained two more gigantic fish. Corbin's wrists and shoulders hurt from playing tug-of-war with the river. There was blood on his tunic because his particular fish was spiny in places Corbin was sure it wasn't supposed to be. He'd gashed his thumb trying to free the hook.

Nell's two monsters filled the bucket to the very top, causing water to overflow. She nibbled at her lower lip as she regarded her catch. Corbin sucked blood from this thumb, awestruck.

"Never seen such a thing in my life," he said around a mouthful of salt and iron. His whole hand throbbed. "How?"

"Good luck," Nell replied with a shrug, but Corbin heard the hitch in her breath and saw the wrinkle on her brow. "Just good luck, I suppose."

"I suppose," Corbin echoed doubtfully. He glanced down at his catch, cataloguing thin, curling feelers and fins sharp as knives. The dead fish's jaw hung wide. Its teeth were almost as large as Corbin's own, pointed as if for tearing flesh. It had silver scales like the rest, but along the tail and fluke the silver was mottled rust.

It was nothing Corbin would want on his dinner plate and nothing he wanted to encounter again.

Nell said, "That one's bad. Throw it back."

So Corbin did.

CORBIN AND NELL carried the fish together across the fields toward Littleton. The bucket was heavy. Corbin had to clench all his fingers around the iron handle and walk sideways to keep his end up. Nell puffed, switching the weight back and forth between her hands. She'd had to leave her remaining three poles behind out of necessity, and she wasn't happy. The bucket dripped down Corbin's thigh. He grimaced in disgust, thinking they must look like a very unhappy pair for all that they carried a river catch between them.

His suspicion was confirmed when their path between the hedgerows intersected that of two soldiers on horseback. Nell caught the flash of a blue cape before Corbin. She set her bucket down with a thud in the tall grass, causing Corbin to stop and look up. When he followed the direction of Nell's gaze, he couldn't help but whistle soft appreciation.

"Always the finest coursers for the likes of them," he said, letting go of the handle. He flexed smarting fingers. "Why, the bay would make five of my pony; the crop is barely past his hocks. And look at the crossbows on their backs, Nell! I wager those would kill a man a furlong distant!"

"Look sharp, Corbin," Nell warned. She eyed the crossbows. "They're coming our way." She stepped in front of the fish, folding her arms across her chest.

To Corbin's surprise, Nell spoke true. The men were riding away from town, holding their mounts to an easy canter as they made straight for the two children. Corbin could hear the susurrus of grass falling beneath the horses' hooves and then the high-pitched barking of eager hounds.

"Huntsmen," Corbin realized. "Out in the evening for sport."

"So long as they're not out for our fish." Nell unknotted her skirts. She smoothed them carefully down over her legs then pushed back her cowl. She ran her hands through her hair, but her braids had become wild with the day's adventure and her shaking fingers only made the tangle worse.

"They'll not dare," Corbin asserted. He placed himself in front of both Nell and her prize. "I won't let them."

Nell didn't reply. The men drew near. Corbin could see the hounds now, long-limbed and graceful as they ran alongside the horses. They'd grown quiet, perhaps warned off by their masters. Night's paintbrush was finally turning land and horizon gray, but the horses' tack sparkled even in the failing light. The men and the coursers and the hounds were beautiful, and Corbin wished with all his heart he might someday grow as brave and strong.

The men pulled their mounts to a halt in front of Corbin and Nell. Their hounds, tongues lolling, continued to snuff about in the crop but did not leave sight of their masters. Both coursers shook their heads impatiently. Tiny silver bells sewn into the horses' bridles jingled when they shifted. One of the two soldiers smiled down at Corbin. His bearded companion squinted at Nell.

"Late home, are you, lassie?" He arched two brows bushy as his beard in dramatic concern. "It's coming on dark, and the fields after sunset are no place for children."

"I'm not a child," Nell replied. "I work these fields. I know them. And I'm not scairt of anything in them, day or night."

"Sirs," Corbin prompted in a whisper. It wasn't Nell's fault she didn't know her manners, but the soldiers wouldn't care that she didn't have a mother or that her father would rather grub in the soil than teach her how to speak properly to her betters.

"I'm not scairt of anything in my fields, *sirs*," Nell repeated.

The bearded man pursed his lips. His companion shook his head.

"Wolves," he said. "We've heard talk of wolves come out of the black forest at dawn and dusk, hunting farther afield than any farmer can recall."

"Oh," breathed Corbin, delighted. "Have you come to kill them, sirs? Have you come to hunt them down and shoot them dead?" Wolves, Corbin knew, were not easily slain. They were tricky animals, especially those out of the nearby forest, fleet of foot and unusually large. But these two men carried sturdy crossbows on their backs and wore the king's insignia on their shoulders. "I bet you could, with bows so fine as yours. Shoot them quick before they even realize you're about."

"Corbin!" Nell hissed. Corbin recalled his friend's soft heart too late. Nell, who couldn't stand to see the river fish suffer out of water, who sometimes sang to the bees in her garden, and who often managed to coax wild starlings and sparrows to eat from her hand.

"Quick, I said, Nell," he hurried to reassure. "They'll kill them quick, good and dead, no flopping about in the dirt."

The bearded man snorted. The other shook his head again.

"Not the wolves," he said with emphasis. "We've come for the king's due: hind and buck."

The hounds, grown bold, were beginning to show interest in Nell's bucket. They circled closer to Corbin and Nell, tails wagging. They wore wide, spiked collars around their necks—hunting hounds' collars, used to protect a vulnerable throat from tooth, claw, antler, and dwarven spears.

"What have you in the bucket?" inquired the bearded rider. He stood in his stirrups, looking between his horse's ears, intrigued by his hounds' enthusiasm. "What, trout?" He urged his courser forward to get a better look, nearly trampling one of his eager hounds in the process. "*Jésus*, Alain, look at this. I've never seen one fish so big, and they've a bucketful."

The man called Alain looked down his nose. It was difficult to tell in the fading light, but Corbin didn't think he was impressed. Alain shifted in his saddle then snapped his fingers.

"Come, Luc, we're losing time. We've work to do. I'm not eager to face *Capitaine* if we return home empty-handed. I gave him my word we'd make headway."

Without waiting for reply, he kicked his courser hard in the sides, spurring it sideways into the crop and then away over the field. He whistled as he went, a piercing call. The hounds immediately abandoned their snuffing to race after. The bearded man lingered a moment longer.

"Hurry on now," he urged. "Your parents will be looking for you at dinner sooner rather than later." He shook his shaggy head. "Although they'll not begrudge you the time once they see your bloody great catch."

Stiff and mute, Nell grabbed her side of the handle. Corbin hurried to help. Cold water dripped on his shin as the bucket swung between them. Nell would have marched off without another word, but Corbin remembered courtesy.

"Good hunting, sir," he called as Nell did her best to drag him forward.

The soldier laughed. "Thank you, lad."

Then he wheeled his courser and galloped after his companion, quickly disappearing into the gloom.

Corbin and Nell walked the rest of the way home in silence. Corbin was busy watching his step in the darkness, while Nell continued to quietly fume. It wasn't until they had reached her father's cottage—a ramshackle affair nearly as sullen as the old mill—that she spoke again.

"They lied. Trying to spare our feelings, I wager, and believed us naught but foolish children. Wasn't deer they were hunting, not with dogs like that."

"No," Corbin agreed carefully. Nell shoved the cottage door open with one foot. Together they hoisted her bucket up over the threshold. A single fat candle burned on the hearth. The fire was banked low. There was no sign of Nell's father.

They set the bucket next to the candle. In the flickering light, the fish appeared even more monstrous than before. Their jaws gaped, showing sharp, white teeth, and their flat eyes reflected flame like tiny mirrors. They stank more of the salty sea than fresh water.

"That's a lot of meat," Corbin marveled. "You've some work ahead of you, Nell. Will you pickle them whole?"

"One or two." Nell's mouth was still pulled flat. There was a wrinkle of displeasure between her eyes. Corbin knew it wasn't the chore that pricked her temper. Nell never disdained any work that filled her coin purse.

"The rest for stew, I think," his friend decided. She shrugged out of her cowl and spread it across the cottage's one chair to dry. "I'd best wash up and start. Come back tomorrow, and I'll send some pickled in a crock for your family to put by."

Corbin nodded. He yawned, surprising himself. Nell's expression softened. She flapped her skirts just like his Nan, which made Corbin giggle, and chased him out into the night.

It was true dark now, the moon not yet risen but the sun

well down past the horizon. The air had grown cooler, pleasant. A dog howled in the distance, plaintive and lonely. Corbin knew it for the cooper's old half-blind bitch; she often sang mournfully after dark. Still, he shivered. He brushed a hand over his knife, reassured by the weight of it on his belt, and his heart raced when he imagined brave Alain and Luc hunting wolves near the forest.

CHAPTER 3

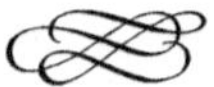

Six days later, Corbin's parents still had not returned from Caen. He was not alarmed, but he was displeased. He'd become weary of playing the man of the house. The summer afternoons grew impossibly warmer. As a result, the milk cows were both lazy and irritable, more willing than usual to step on Corbin as he prepared their feed and to kick at his hands as he pulled their teats. The lush grass suffered in the heat, becoming dry and brown almost overnight. Beauty caught the croup from one of the lads in the village. Her cough drove Nan to distraction and kept Corbin from sleep at night. Hope complained it was too warm to eat. She would not touch even Henri's special pink cakes.

Only the baby seemed unaffected by the torrid weather. Of Corbin's sisters, Faith was the sunniest, content to toddle after Nan or sit quietly in Beauty's lap while the older girl struggled over needlework. Hope took solace in the baby's enthusiastic kisses even as she compulsively checked the road for sign of Mother and Da and Snip. In the evenings, Corbin played charades with Faith before Nan took her away to bed. No matter how sour he felt at day's end, Faith's snorting amusement and funny faces managed to soothe his mood.

So when on the ninth day the baby erupted into sudden shrieks of rage while helping Nan tend Mother's white roses, everyone was surprised. Nan, thinking perhaps Faith had run afoul a bumblebee or biting spider, checked tender flesh but found no puncture or sting. Faith sat among the lavender and kicked her small feet. She only screamed louder when Hope tried to appease her with a length of hair ribbon. Wounded by the rebuff, Hope broke into tears of her own and fled back into the cottage.

Beauty, sitting on the stoop with a book on her knees, frowned. "It's a tooth," she diagnosed. "Mother said she was due to cut one. It must be. Corbin, go and get her a bit of crust to gnaw on."

Corbin glowered. "Get it yourself. Nell's waiting on me at the mill."

Beauty's eyes widened. "You can't go swimming now, Corbin. Mother and Papa will be home anytime! Nan, tell him! He mustn't go *now*."

Nan had her fingers in Faith's mouth, muffling the baby's angry cries. "Not a tooth, not that I can feel," she decided with a sigh. "Mayhap just colic or the lurgy coming on." The old woman touched her cheek to Faith's. "We're all flushed in this heat. Corbin"—she lifted the sobbing child in her arms—"take her down the road for distraction. Go on."

Corbin started to protest, but Nan held firm. She nudged Faith in his direction. The baby hesitated, sobs dwindling into hiccups, before toddling resolutely toward Corbin, chubby hands outstretched.

"See now," Nan said, pleased. "She just needs a little brotherly attention. Go and look out for your father's cart, Corbin. They'll be here anytime."

It was that promise that propelled Corbin off the grass and onto his feet. Ignoring Beauty's doubtful expression, he hoisted Faith up and onto his back. Her hands locked tight around his throat, making him cough, but once he settled her legs around his ribs, the baby relaxed her grip. Her pointed chin stabbed his shoulder. Her mouth pressed damp against his ear.

"Hyah!" Faith cried, kicking her heels against his chest. "Pony, hyah!"

"Like Snip, Faith?" Corbin asked, snorting air through his nose. He bounced Faith on his back then pretended to gallop through the garden, circling lavender and rosebushes before trotting through the gate and onto the highway. Faith squealed in delight.

"Snip, Snip!" she caroled, tears forgotten, as Corbin danced in place, tossing curls glossy as any courser's mane.

Beauty rose from her seat on the stoop, book forgotten. She rolled her eyes at Corbin's antics before calling a warning. "Don't go far, brother! She'll want her nap before long, especially in this heat."

Corbin pawed the tip of one shoe against cobblestones before cantering in wide circles. "No time for sleep, Beauty! We're off to find Mother and Da and their most courageous stead, Snip Fleetfoot!"

Faith's giggles puffed in Corbin's ear, drowning Beauty's halfhearted protest. Corbin grinned and tossed his mane one more time before taking off west along the highway. His legs easily ate up ground. His feet were steady on the cobblestones. Faith felt light on his back. If he squinted, he could pretend they were galloping in truth, liveried all in king's blue and perched on the back of a coal-black stallion, hunting wolves, crossbow in his hand, flying over and around the hedgerows and between the apple trees.

The weight of the angry sun caught in the back of

Corbin's throat, and he was finally forced to slow to a jog as he puffed in the heat. Sweat trickled into his eyes and down the bridge of his nose. He licked his lips, tasting salt, as he swallowed great gasps of humid air. Faith was quiet on his back, her nose pressed against the nape of his neck, her feet flexing against the palms of his hands.

"Down?" Corbin suggested. He could feel the baby's sweat soaking through his shirt and mingling with his own. The slow trickle made his spine itch. "Walk?"

Faith nodded. She squirmed over Corbin's hip and slid down his legs, clinging like a squirrel until her toes touched the cobblestones. Then she trundled forward, head wagging side to side as she scanned the dwindling farmland. Corbin shortened his stride. He clasped her sticky fist in his own. When she stumbled on uneven stone, he held her upright until she found her balance.

"At least the sun's baked away all the mud," Corbin said. He used the edge of his shirt to wipe his face. Faith stumbled again. Exasperated, Corbin snagged her collar before she could fall. "Or I'd be rescuing you from every puddle, and Nan would be insisting on a bath at the end of it."

Faith looked up at him from beneath white-blonde lashes. "No," she said, disgusted. "No Nan."

Corbin couldn't help but grimace in agreement. Nan tended to favor steaming water and enthusiastic scrubbing when it came to bathing. Despite Corbin's insistence that he was a grown lad of ten and could wash himself, she often threatened to clean behind his ears.

"Mother will be kinder." Recalling that Da had left the baby and the state of her nappies in his charge days earlier, Corbin scanned Faith covertly from head to toe before shrugging. "You've got strawberry preserves on your nose and knots in your hair, but you don't stink. You'll do."

Faith babbled agreement then stopped in her tracks. "Snip!" she cried, pointing.

Relief made Corbin's scalp prickle. He turned eagerly, expecting the cart and the weary gelding and Mother's fond smile. His heart sank.

"That's not Snip, Faith. That's Gaffer Julian's old plow horse. She doesn't look at all like our Snip."

Julian's field was the last before the rolling hills gave way to wild brush. There were no more cultivated hedgerows past Julian's boundary wall. Unclaimed briar and shrub and wild rose ruled the land on both sides of the road. The forest's edge was visible from Julian's back porch. The old gaffer delighted in telling anyone who would listen tales of the things he'd seen come out of the trees in the night: not just wolves and dwarves but pheasants large as cattle, tiny winged serpents with scales the color of banked embers, and two-headed pigs with tusks as long as a man's arm.

Everyone in Littleton knew the gaffer had a wild imagination and a taste for potent drink, but no one ever dared make mockery of his anecdotes for fear he spoke the truth.

Corbin glared at Julian's cart horse. The mare—slender, chestnut, and not at all similar to Snip—swiveled her ears forward as she regarded them across her pasture. Corbin groaned aloud at the absurdity of the world in general and his littlest sister in particular.

"You can't call every horse Snip, Faith," he lectured. "That's like calling every boy Corbin."

"No!" Faith heaved a sigh that rivaled Beauty's most petulant groan. Her little body strained with effort as she stood on her toes. "Snip!"

The baby's insistence gave Corbin pause. Her unhappy mood was quickly returning. Her lower lip puckered in a deepening pout, and her round cheeks were flushing again in distress. She thrust one finger stubbornly in the direction of the curious mare.

Corbin suffered a pang of regret. He crouched in the highway to better meet Faith's fretful stare. "I'm sorry, birdie," he said, using Mother's nickname for her smallest chick. "I didn't mean to laugh at you. It's hot, and you're miserable, and I'm a horrid big brother, only I don't see Snip. That horse is the wrong color, Faith, and it's a *girl* horse at that."

Faith looked from Corbin to the gaffer's chestnut. Then she took Corbin's face in her hands, pressing her damp palms to his cheeks, and bodily adjusted his line of sight until he was staring not into the field but past plow horse and hedgerow at the slice of darker afternoon where the king's highway disappeared under the forest's nearest boughs.

"Snip," she repeated solemnly.

Corbin regarded the regiment of trees. They stood still in the heat, undisturbed by any breeze. Thick green ferns grew against the trunks and roots, bowing over the edge of the road. Their spreading fronts were each three times the width of Corbin's palm and longer than his arm. The deep shade beneath the forest canopy should have been inviting on a midsummer afternoon. Corbin knew better.

"No." Corbin let go of the baby and stood up. "No Snip, not yet. We'll just have to wait. Come on, Faith. I'll give you a ride back. Gallop?" Faith's lower lip stuck out like a shelf. Tears welled, overflowing. Corbin smothered a sigh and reached to swing her up into his arms.

As he clasped her up against his chest, small skull beneath his chin, a horse's scream split the air.

Corbin jumped. The baby squeaked protest. In the gaffer's field, the chestnut mare pinned her ears and wheeled, kicking up clots of mud as she fled away toward Julian's cottage. Her tail flagged as she galloped. Corbin had never before seen the old horse move so quickly.

"Snip," Faith said miserably into the hollow of Corbin's throat. She fisted her small hands and pressed them against her ears.

"*Merde*," Corbin breathed. He took a step forward. He thought distantly that he was moving in the wrong direction, that he should turn around at once and take Faith back to Nan. The forest was no place for a baby, even its very edge. There were things in the trees that would find a baby tasty: hungry creatures beyond the wall of ferns and trunks.

Wolves, Corbin thought, even as he took a second step toward the trees and another. Then he was running, not back toward Nan and safety but ahead toward the slice of shade. Faith was rigid in his arms. Corbin thought he could feel her heart beating against his chest, too fast. His own was pounding against his ribs.

They were past the boundary of Gaffer Julian's pastureland. The highway dipped through a wide patch of bramble before rising again. The forest loomed, close enough now that Corbin could smell the rich earth that made Littleton's fields so fertile, sweet, and damp beneath reaching ferns. His feet were still moving in the wrong direction, despite the threat of *wolves, wolves, wolves* rolling frantically through his head.

Miniscule hyacinth grew along both sides of the highway where the road slipped into forest shade. Mother's garden hyacinth had withered and faded in the summer heat weeks earlier. Corbin knew the little purple flowers were impossible so late in the season, as were the Mary's stars: tiny white blossoms shining silver in the gloom. Vines grew like yellow snakes up tree trunks, wrapping around low branches, their pale pink flowers gaping. Fat bees drifted from flower to flower, made indolent by the forest's false shade.

Corbin stood on the edge of light and dark. He gripped Faith too hard against his front, but the baby didn't complain. He knew Nan hadn't meant him to come this far down the highway. He knew Mother would scold and Da would be furious if they discovered he'd dared pass the gaffer's land.

"Snip," Faith whimpered, still insistent.

"Quiet," Corbin whispered back. "Listen."

For once the baby did as she was told. Corbin muffled his panting in her soft hair. Slowly noises coalesced past panic. He heard the chirrup of a busy squirrel. Birds fluttered high in the canopy, stirring twig and leaf. The sleepy bumblebees buzzed as they took their supper. Behind and seemingly far distant he could just catch the voices of busy villagers lifted in song as they worked the fields. The afternoon seemed just the same as any other; nothing untoward disturbed nature's languid dance.

"We should go back," Corbin decided, still whispering. It seemed impossible that he'd imagined that animal sound of pain and terror. He knew he hadn't. The screams had set the gaffer's mare to galloping. But the rest of the world went about its business as if deaf to the scream. A brown starling straddling a spray of pink flowers cocked her head inquisitively, regarding Corbin and Faith with one calm black eye.

Corbin exhaled. He loosened his grip on the baby, swapping her to his hip, and was relieved when his body recalled obedience. His arms ached as tension left his muscles, but his feet didn't argue when he silently ordered them home.

He was half-turned, flowers still bobbing out of the corner of his eye, when the starling took flight, shaking free a shower of pink petals. The bird rose straight up out of the shadow and into the blue sky, making Corbin pause and

Faith squeak. As if its sudden flight was a signal, the bees went quiet and the squirrels in the canopy froze.

When Snip broke from the forest, narrowly missing Corbin and Faith, he flew almost as fast on four legs as the departing thrush had on wings. Corbin had the fleeting wild thought that the only thing keeping their loyal gelding pinned to the highway was the awkward weight of the empty cart he dragged behind.

NAN SENT Corbin running into Littleton. Henri rang the alarm on the church bells. Nell's father marshaled men from the field. The men gathered with pitchforks and scythes in hand. They carried burning torches although the sun was still proud in the sky. Littleton's women flocked about Corbin's home in clouds of distraught wool and ribbon. They wrung their hands and cossetted Corbin's white-faced sisters as Nan served out plates of Camembert and brandy. Nan's face was set in the expression she wore midwinter when she'd gone weary of too much cold. She scolded Nell and Corbin for being underfoot in such a crowd. Eventually she sent all five children back out behind the cottage in a bid to coax Snip from hiding.

"But don't go far," she warned sharply. "Not past the apple trees, do you hear? If that old animal hasn't the sense to come in for his grain, I'll not have you risking your skins over it. Your mother would never forgive me."

One of the village women gasped and began to weep into her handkerchief. Nan's flinty expression turned sour. Corbin quickly ushered Nell and his sisters out of the cottage and into the pasture beyond. Beauty and Nell jogged Faith between them while Hope trailed disconsolately behind. Hope's eyes were red from weeping, but Faith was finally quiet, her earlier tantrum dissipated.

The day was cooling as afternoon waned and evening approached. Corbin scrubbed both hands through his curls, lifting the weight of hair off his neck. He looked across the pasture to where his pony stood at the edge of the field. Past the hedge, Mother's little group of apple trees stood proud against the blue sky. Pony stared past bramble at the small orchard. Corbin couldn't help but do the same.

"Did he really run all the way home only to fetch up in the apple trees?" Beauty scoffed. Her lower lip trembled, but her face was as stony as Nan's. "Stupid old gelding. However did he get through the orchard with the cart still harnessed to his back?"

Corbin swallowed.

"There wasn't much of it left to begin with," he admitted. "Just the wheels and the running board, that I could see." He shrugged. "Probably Snip wasn't paying much attention to anything but getting away. It was mashed up. Da will be furious."

"Stupid old gelding," Beauty repeated at the same time Hope asked in a thin voice: "Getting away from what? Where are Mother and Papa? Corbin?"

Corbin glanced away and accidentally caught Nell's sympathetic gaze. He scrubbed his hands through his hair a final time before reminding himself he was still the man of the house and owed his sisters answers. If he couldn't join Henri, Nell's father, and the rest of the party bearing blade and flame, he could at least bring Snip home.

"I don't know." He straightened his shoulders. "But I'm sure they'll soon be found. Let's go get Snip before the wolves do."

He hadn't meant to say that last thing about the wolves. Hope went white. Either Nell or Beauty clutched Faith's hand too tightly, and the baby squeaked. Corbin clenched his own fists at his side as he strode toward the apple trees.

Cattle glanced around, curious, as he hurried through their pasture. Daisy was due a milking soon. The cheeses needed tending. If Da didn't return soon with his magic touch and secret recipe, the latest batch would be ruined.

The pony sighed as Corbin and the girls approached but didn't look around. He was a stout animal, round as a barrel. Corbin generally thought him very handsome and quite brave, but at the moment, he was caked with dried mud, the hair on his withers drying into sweat-sculpted curls. His nostrils flared, showing pink velvet. He didn't look away from the orchard when Corbin patted his rump in greeting.

"Ho, Pony," Corbin murmured. "Is Snip away there with Mother's apples? Why doesn't he come home?"

"Bet he's got the sense scared right out of him," Nell decided. "Or he's just got hisself stuck in all them close trees."

"Apple," Faith suggested as Beauty and Nell lifted her through the hedgerow.

Corbin's laugh felt gritty against the back of his throat. Last season's apples were mostly rotted. It was too early for the fall crop, but Snip did have an uncanny nose for treats. Mayhap the old gelding really had stopped mid-flight for a snack.

As he climbed over stone, Corbin caught a flash of flame on the road and smelled smoke. Standing atop the hedgerow, he watched as Littleton's bravest advanced down the road toward the forest. They looked like a small knot against the spreading canopy. Corbin's mouth went dry.

"I should be there," he said, speaking his anguish aloud. "I should be with them."

"You?" Hope scoffed from the other side of the wall. "Corbin, you're just a little boy with a fancy dinner knife. You don't even have a *wooden* blade of your own. What good would *you* do?"

"Hope!" Beauty hissed. She let go of Faith to shake Hope's arm in warning. "Stop."

"But it's true." Hope sniffed. She prized Beauty's fingers off her sleeve. "The wolves have got Mother and Papa, and they'd get Corbin, too, if he went in the forest. They'd gobble him right up! He's just a little boy."

Faith began to howl. Nell scooped the baby up, pressing her face soothingly against grimy wool. Beauty and Hope stood locked in a silent contest of wills. Corbin didn't see what the difficulty was.

"If the wolves have Mother and Da, I'll kill them," he said with certainty. "Using my knife or a wooden sword. If the wolves hurt Mother and Da, I'll kill them all, every single one."

THE GELDING WASN'T difficult to follow. The smashed cart left a trail behind even Faith could follow. They chased it over flattened pasture and up a gentle hill into Mother's orchard. Pieces of wood littered the ground. When Nell swooped and came back up with a shattered wheel spoke, Corbin felt sick.

Snip wasn't snacking on late season windfall. They found him at the center of the orchard, still tethered to the remains of Da's cart. The cart was a skeletal thing—hardly more than an axle and leather harness. It lacked all but one wheel. Mother's driving bench was smashed right down the center, the backboard little more than a nest of jagged splinters.

The axle and one wheel were caught up against a gnarl of exposed tree root. In the resultant struggle, Snip had managed to snag the driving reins around an especially sturdy yearling apple tree. White froth stained the horse's muzzle and dripped from between his legs. He quivered where he stood, head hung low, well and truly trapped.

"Oh, poor Snip!" Hope cried. She'd always had a special fondness for the gelding. She ran ahead of Corbin, making calming noises as she ducked between apple trees to Snip's front end. The horse shuddered when she touched his shoulder but didn't raise his head.

"Corbin," Beauty said, eyes wide as saucers. "We have to cut him free. Poor thing. He looks done in."

Corbin dragged his attention from the broken cart. He'd noted the great scrapes and scores on what wood remained. He didn't think they were the work of errant branches. He'd seen similar marks before, on the corpses of cattle lost overnight and recovered days later, and on the outside walls of a chicken coop that stank of wolf piss.

"Claws," Nell agreed quietly. She stood close to Corbin, Faith on her hip. "And teeth. Something attacked your da's cart, Corbin. Something big."

Corbin didn't answer. Instead, he took his knife from his belt and approached Snip. Hope whispered reassuring words into the gelding's drooping ears while Corbin took hold of one tangled rein and began to saw. Beauty tied her skirts neatly up between her legs away from the brambles and branches. She sidled up to the shattered cart and began picking through skeletal remains.

"The cart will have to stay here," she said. "It's ruined. But Mother and Papa will want whatever we can salvage."

Corbin wondered if grief had driven his sister mad. Beauty must have caught his dubious expression because she huffed loudly.

"You're forgetting," she admonished. "Use your head, brother. Mother's treasure."

"Oh," Corbin said. He *had* forgotten. It was a family joke: Mother's treasure. Short hand for the tin money box Da kept secured beneath the running board, close at hand yet carefully hidden by the fall of Mother's skirts when she sat atop the cart.

"Is it there?" he asked. He didn't think it could be, with Mother's seat split in two.

Beauty squirmed over the axle. She stuck her head between pieces of running board. Her hair fell forward over her face, obscuring her eyes, and she made a sound of annoyance. Corbin, still wielding his knife against leather, swallowed past the lump of affection clogging his throat as Beauty muttered and patted about under the running board.

"It's here!" She popped back upright, triumphant. "It's still here, wedged up tight! Corbin, toss me your knife!"

"I'm using it." Corbin sawed with more energy. The first tether split reluctantly beneath his blade, causing Snip to shift uneasily. Hope patted the gelding's muzzle as Corbin attacked the second rein.

"Poor Snip," Hope repeated. "Look, Corbin. His knees are all over bloody. He must have fallen."

Corbin glanced down and saw that Snip's knees and ankles were indeed splattered a darker red. More streaks of gore painted narrow swathes on the horse's wide chest. Corbin felt goose pimples break along his forearms. He paused in his work to stroke shaking fingers along the gelding's bony topline.

"He's not bitten, anyway." Beauty squirmed out from beneath the running board. She ran a knowledgeable eye over Snip's underbelly and hind end. "Could be it's not his blood. Could be he gave the wolves something to think twice about, brave Snip."

Which meant Beauty had noted the marks on the cart as well, Corbin realized.

The final tether pulled apart and fell from Corbin's grip to the dirt. Snip startled. The gelding would have run but for Hope's hand on his bridle.

"Ho," she said. "Ho, brave Snip. Corbin, shall I take him back? He needs tending."

"I'll help," Beauty said quickly. She shot Corbin a pointed look. "Corbin will get Mother's treasure. Don't spill the box, Corbin. It feels full." She laced her fingers through Snip's long mane. "And don't be long, or Nan will worry."

Corbin watched them go. When he turned around again, Nell and Faith were regarding him solemnly from the other side of the ruined cart.

"What was that?" he asked blankly. "Beauty never helps with anything, if she can help it."

"Hope's sensitive, not like the rest of us," Nell replied. She bounced Faith absently, not meeting Corbin's eye. "Beauty didn't want her to see."

"See what?"

"There, under the running board." Nell used her chin to point. "Stuck deep in the wood by the coin box. Beauty and I saw it at the same time, I think. Faith won't understand, but I think Beauty didn't want Hope to know."

Fine little man, Mother had said as she'd left Corbin in charge. More than anything he didn't want to duck under the broken bench and see what Beauty and Nell thought would send Hope into a fit of nerves. More than anything he wanted to shut his eyes and wait until he woke safe in his bed from whatever strange nightmare he'd fallen into.

He looked under the bench.

He recognized the fine old sword at once, even stuck so inelegantly between slats and smeared hilt to blade with dirt and other debris.

"It's your da's, isn't it?" Nell ventured when Corbin couldn't speak. "I mean, I thought—I've seen it only a few times before, but—"

"Yes," Corbin interrupted. He squatted until splinters

brushed the top of his head and wrapped both hands around the pommel. "It's Da's."

The boards let the blade go without protest. The sword came away in Corbin's grip, heavier than he recalled. He overbalanced, sitting down hard on his tailbone, but he didn't let go of his prize.

"He wouldn't have lost it." Corbin laid the sword lengthwise on his legs. "He kept it with him, always. He wouldn't have let it go, not if he could help it."

There was a short piece of yellow vine caught in the hilt. Corbin plucked it free.

"You can cry now," Nell said after a moment. "It's just me and Faith. You can cry, if you like."

Corbin shook his head. He stood up, holding the heavy blade carefully off the ground. Then he took Da's sword out of the orchard and down to the cottage.

CHAPTER 4

On the day Corbin turned seventeen, he strapped his da's sword across his back, snugged a carefully wrapped bundle of cheese and bread into his journey pack, and bid his three sisters good-bye. Hope wept bitter tears, Faith petted Corbin's unruly curls into a semblance of order, and Beauty pinned a dried sprig of Mother's lavender to the collar of his shirt for luck and remembrance. Nan watched from the hearth, arms crossed beneath her breasts. Corbin knew she wanted to speak her disapproval aloud but wouldn't dare do so in front of Da, hadn't dared cross her son in anything since the day he'd stumbled alone from the black canopy, half out of his mind with fever and grief.

The fever had passed, but the grief and madness lingered still six years later. Sometimes, as he lay awake in the night listening to his family sleep, Corbin allowed himself to think it might have been better if Jean de Beaumont had perished on the forest floor alongside his wife. The ravaged skeleton who sat in Da's place at the supper table, who slept in Da's bed and used Da's familiar gruff tones when he bothered to speak at all was not the man Corbin remembered before that last ill-fated trip to Caen.

That man, while often cold, kept room in his heart for love.

His replacement thought and spoke only of revenge. The cold glint of mania never left his eye, even when he gathered Faith on his lap and sang to her the Picardy hymns of his childhood or when he plaited Mother's silk ribbons in Beauty's hair. Hope, being Hope, couldn't reconcile the new Da with the old and often blamed him loudly for Mother's loss. Da never disagreed, and Hope grew increasingly distant.

"You'll want this." Nan left the hearth. She swept Da's old traveling cloak from its place on a hook by the cottage door and held it out to Corbin. "It's cold. Winter will be here sooner rather than later."

Corbin glanced past Nan at his father. Da, sitting on the edge of his cot, shrugged.

"It's well made," he said. "And I've no use for it. Take it. *Bon anniversaire.*"

So Corbin unstrapped his sword and hung it from his hip instead. Da's cloak wasn't the blue cape he'd dreamed of wearing as a child, but the dull brown wool was lined with ermine. It was heavy and warm: a rich man's cloak.

"It looks like it was made for you." Da nodded before pinning Corbin with a shrewd. "You've the letter I wrote? Don't lose it. Thomas Chevalier is expecting you. Show his man my signature. You won't be kept waiting."

"Yes, Da." Corbin kissed Hope a final time. He disentangled Faith from the folds of his new cloak and put one of her small hands in Nan's for safekeeping. Then he turned and let himself out of the cottage.

Beauty followed after, even though she was meant to be helping Da with the milking. They had only one cow left on the farm, one of Daisy's daughters. She'd been bred to one of

Nell's bulls and birthed a fat healthy calf in the spring. But now her calf was sold at market, and her milk was slowly drying up. She'd have to be bred again soon if Nan was to be kept in dairy through the winter, but Da had put it off too long. A yuletide calf often rarely lived long enough to see spring, and even with Nell at hand to help with a winter birthing, too many things could go wrong.

"Have Nan buy milk from Henri through the cold months," Corbin said, stopping on the stoop as Beauty pulled the door shut on Hope's muffled sobbing. "It's costly, but less so than a new heifer come summer."

Beauty rolled her eyes. "Papa won't. You know he won't. And Nan won't go behind his back."

"Speak to Nell," Corbin decided. "She's plenty to spare, and she knows I'll send good coin back once I'm settled."

"We can't rely on Nell forever, brother," Beauty said, disapproval plain in the set of her jaw. "She's her own land to look after now. Not to mention the babe."

Corbin clenched his teeth, equally annoyed. "It's not mine, sister. I've told you so one hundred times at least."

"It—*he*—has your hair."

"I'm not the only man in this town with red hair, Beauty."

"None so bright as yours. And the babe has your curls."

"Jean Robert has curls. And so do half the lads come down the highway on the king's business. The babe isn't mine, Beauty. Don't go borrowing trouble where there is none."

Beauty stomped a foot on stone. She shivered convulsively in the cold. "A babe's not trouble, Corbin. A babe's a blessing."

Corbin stared. Beauty chafed her arms, relenting. "Fine," she said. "But are you sure you don't have any message—"

"No."

"Not even—"

"Tell Nell I'll send coin for the milk. I've already said everything else that needs saying. And, Beauty," he warned, "keep your nose clear of my business."

"Your business and my business are forever intertwined," Beauty retorted as if Corbin needed reminding. "I'll keep my whiskers clean, brother. But if that child's eyes darken to Seine blue, Corbin, I'll be writing you at once."

Corbin shook his head. Then he bent and kissed Beauty between her eyes.

"Write me anyway," he said, "blue eyes or no."

"I will," Beauty said. "Travel safely, Corbin. Don't do anything foolish, if you can help it."

Corbin smiled. He pulled the hood of the fine cloak up over his head, enjoying the brush of soft ermine against his ears. His breath puffed like smoke in the air as he walked through Mother's garden, asleep now as winter approached. It was a beautiful day for an adventure, and he was eager to get on with it.

It's a pleasant walk between Littleton and Honnefleu. A rider on horseback can do it in a day; a man on foot will take two. Corbin was expected in three and so intended to take his time. He'd been rooted to Littleton all of his life. He was past ready to venture into the world and make a name for himself. He didn't dare dream of freedom—not with the weight of Da's sword always at hand—but young Corbin was an optimist. As he walked away from Littleton, he had it in his head to sample every joy city life had on tap before time ran out.

He did think briefly of Nell, whom he'd neglected to bid farewell. He wished he'd thought to stop at Henri's for a pastry and an embrace. The baker was getting frail. It was possible he'd be in the ground when Corbin returned.

Corbin allowed himself a pang of anticipated sorrow before banishing regret with a shake of his head.

As he'd drilled Corbin in the ways of the blade, de Beaumont had also schooled his son in the intricacies of revenge. A man trained to vengeance has no room in his life for remorse. He must quickly set his worries aside before they become an albatross about his neck.

So Corbin whistled as he walked, cheerful even in the cold. His breath puffed white in the morning, but he was warm enough in his ermine cloak. His boots and leather gloves were secondhand, got off a tinker in the summer. The boots were snug but serviceable. The gloves stank heavily of goat when they got wet, so Corbin kept them dry. His shirt and trousers were new, a birthday gift from Nan and his sisters. Hope had developed a real talent with the needle, and the local mercer was soft on Beauty; the two girls had done Corbin proud, even if his shirt was just a smidge too tight about the chest. His new trousers didn't chafe, and that was a blessing.

Past Littleton, the king's highway branched east toward the capital and north toward the Seine. Corbin took the northerly arm.

As soon as he stepped onto the new road, he felt a swell of something not unlike vertigo. His head spun as if he'd spent the morning indulging in perry instead of saying his good-byes. Heat spread across his chest and up his throat until it broke in a sweat across his brow. Corbin shoved back his hood and gulped air, stretching one hand forward as if he hoped to steady himself on a swathe of blue morning. With his other, he scrabbled against the silver clip at his throat until it loosened wool. He shrugged Da's cloak from his shoulders.

The road's rocking slowly steadied. The dormant fields and hedgerows stopped revolving overhead and found their usual places on the horizon. Corbin's panting eased to ragged inhales and exhales, while the flush ebbed away, leaving his new shirt damp.

"*Mére Marie.*" Corbin gasped. He was thankful the highway was empty. There was no one about to witness as he sank onto the cobblestones alongside the discarded cloak. He rubbed his eyes, brushing away stinging salt, before stripping off his gloves in baffled disgust.

He sat in the middle of the road until he began to shiver. The sword and scabbard on his belt scraped on the cobblestone when he reached into his pack for bread. He'd missed breakfast over the business of packing and the excitement of leave-taking, and he had the hopeful thought that he was suffering the rather extraordinary pangs of a neglected stomach.

It couldn't, Corbin told himself as he took a savage bite of good bread, *be a fit of nerves. I'm not Hope. I don't fall faint when a dog barks in the night or take to my bed when the wind rattles the roof.*

But the bread stuck in his throat, and he couldn't help but wish for a dram of wine to wash it down. He set his chin on his knees and schooled his stomach to calm.

Eventually Corbin had company on the road. The king's highway is a hardly a lonely place even in the off-season. There are quicker routes from Caen to Honnefleu, but never as safe. Armed men in blue livery might brave the ride across wild country, but the average person has better sense. The king's road is at least patrolled regularly by soldiers whose sole intent is to keep travelers safe. A man on the highway might think to guard his purse, but he knows it is unlikely he need fear for his life.

It was the sound of hooves on cobblestone that first alerted Corbin. He shoved his impromptu breakfast back into his pack and hastily stood up, relieved when the road stayed steady. But his surge upright was unfortunate. Even the laziest donkey will spook if a body springs up under his nose.

"Woah!"

The jennet was a pretty illustration of her breed. Her master—a lanky, barefoot fellow dressed in a black cassock—was less so. He had a beaklike nose and two large dark eyes beneath wild gray brows. His balding head was marred with bumpy freckles.

"Woah, mule!" He yanked hard at the donkey's mouth, causing her to halt in place and sit back almost on her haunches.

"Dom." Corbin swallowed back amusement. The two made a foolish pair. The jennet sat so low the monk's bare feet were planted flat on the road. "Apologies. I didn't see you there."

The Benedictine cocked both bushy brows. "Nor I, you. You've given my Jenny quite a fright." He slapped a large hand on the donkey's neck, regarding Corbin suspiciously. "Why, lad, were you crawling about on the ground?" The monk made a show of scanning the cobblestones around Corbin. "Have you lost something? Mayhap your senses?"

"No, Dom." Corbin refused to squirm in the face of the man's mockery. He sorely wished he could walk away, but he knew better than to rebuke one of God's chosen, even if God's chosen had an unkind eye and cruel hands. "I was only resting."

"In the middle of the road?" The monk dismounted his donkey simply by swinging one leg over her quivering haunches and then rising to his full stature. With the man's beak on full display, it was a bit like watching a stork stir and shake, and Corbin had to bite back another unkind giggle. The Benedictine, perhaps sensing Corbin's derision, took two angry strides in his direction.

Corbin's right hand settled on the pommel of Da's sword.

"Ah," the monk said. "Stupid and dangerous. And younger than I thought, despite your size. A ginger boy, the devil's flames in your hair." He muttered in Latin under his breath before looking again at Corbin. "What're you called, lad?"

"I'm not a lad. I'm a man grown," Corbin replied. His fingers flexed on the hilt of Da's sword, but he pasted a smile on his face. "And I'm not devil-touched. I'm Corbin de Beaumont, and I'm off to Honnefleu on business."

The Benedictine stilled. The donkey climbed laboriously back onto all four hooves. She took herself to the side of the road where she lipped at brown grass, dragging her reins on cobblestones. Corbin noticed a bit of embroidery gleaming on her saddle blanket.

"*Le Saint-Michel.*" Corbin couldn't contain his surprise. "You've come from the island abbey."

"And you've come from Littleton. I know your father." The monk snorted. "Hardly out of town and already 'resting,' are you?"

"The monks of Saint-Michel are disbanded," Corbin said, ignoring the man's jibe. "Scattered far and wide."

When the Benedictine smiled, there were gaps where he lacked teeth. "Not all of us," he said. "A few stubborn souls remain yet near the *mont,* waiting upon the archangel's pleasure. We're left in peace so long as we keep to ourselves and don't linger overlong inside the abbey's walls."

"But how do you know my da?" It seemed very unlikely to Corbin.

"I know his *cheese,*" the monk said. "Who in this duchy does not?" He scratched his chin. "There is also the story of de Beaumont's pact with the demon in the forest, of course. That's a famous tale, that is; tasty as the Camembert, in its own way. Many times upon the boards I've heard how Jean de Beaumont traded his eldest daughter's future to the lord of the black forest in return for his own life."

"Child," Corbin corrected.

"Eh?" The monk blinked. "Pardon?"

"Your donkey is getting away," Corbin said with relish. The jennet, having given up on her human companion at last, was making her way carefully through an adjoining field toward a copse of trees. "Best catch her, Dom."

The monk shouted. Grumbling, he darted off into the field after his ride, black robes flapping about his tall figure like tattered crows' wings. When the man was well out of earshot, Corbin at last allowed himself a fit of giggles. He couldn't help wishing Nell were about to share his merriment. Nell held little truck with the church.

The donkey had no intention of letting her master put her back to work. Corbin silently wished the animal luck with her escape then went on his way, the fit of hunger or nerves already forgotten.

THE REST of the day's walk was as pleasant as Corbin had hoped. As Littleton disappeared behind him, the scenery changed not at all. A farm half a day's stroll from Corbin's home appeared from a distance no different than those he had labored on as a child. He passed four small villages, each hardly more than a cluster of houses around a small stone church. None were as large as Littleton.

As the sun rose in the sky, the highway filled with fellow travelers. A family of tinkers overtook him from behind, their covered wagon rattling cheerfully behind two laboring oxen. Corbin had never before seen such large cattle. The breadth of their horns was as long as his reach from thumb to thumb and wide as his forearm. Each horn was capped with silver sharpened to a dagger point. Corbin charmed the family matron with his easy smile and earned a ripe pear for his trouble. Her husband was less friendly and seemed to take great pleasure in explaining to Corbin the damage his trained oxen would do to any brigands who dared set upon his wares.

The tinkers had three children, a boy and two girls. They ranged in age from three years to seven and were prepared to talk Corbin's ear off without ceasing as the morning stretched into afternoon. From them, he learned that the weather was expected to remain clear and cold for at least another fortnight, but then would follow a great and blinding snow. They knew this from the bones their father threw alongside the fire at night, and also from the paths of the migrating waterfowl, and finally from the pattern of the winter coat growing on the oxen.

"It's Honnefleu until the snow passes," the matron explained in heavily accented *d'oïl*. "They are kind there to travelers. And business will be good, if the weather closes the roads in. Come an unexpected storm and every house finds itself low on candles or lamp oil."

Corbin thought her plan very clever and said so. The children urged him to stroke the oxen about the neck to feel the growth of coat for himself. The oxen tolerated his hand without protest and kept walking on even as he gently fondled their fuzzy ears.

"Are you a soldier?" the head of the family inquired, nodding his head at Da's sword. "Have you lost your blue cape?"

"No."

"A blade-for-hire then." He was impressed. "You're young for it."

"Not that, either," Corbin said. "I'm taking my da's sword to Thomas Chevalier in Honnefleu to learn how best to kill a man."

"To kill a man?" the matron inquired, looking concerned.

"A monster in the shape of a man," Corbin clarified. He didn't like to scare the children who looked at him now with puzzled expressions.

Soon after their mother shooed them up into the wagon, and her husband urged the oxen to a faster pace. Corbin saw them go with regret. He distracted himself with the business of watching for migrating waterfowl overhead.

By late afternoon, the road bustled with traffic. People of all kind trod the cobblestones. Many were in a hurry, calling and shoving as they dodged their less fleet companions. Many more appeared in no great haste. They laughed and chatted together as they went about their business. Corbin kept his blade hidden beneath the folds of his cloak to avoid further interest.

He marked more blue livery. As the sun fell low in the sky, the king's soldiers became more numerous. Some rode on horseback while others walked the perimeter of the highway. They seemed a jovial group, exchanging pleasantries with travelers and stopping to help when a cartwheel got stuck in a rut or a babe—near naked in the cold weather— began to scream. It took two men to push the mired cart free but only one to give his cape to the frozen infant's mam for shared warmth. Corbin watched as soldier and mother wrapped the babe tightly in swathes of blue. He recalled how he'd once dreamed of wearing the king's color. The fantasy now seemed to Corbin a child's naïveté.

Even so, he felt a throb of jealousy as the infant, snugged in the cape, let out a huff of relief.

The traffic on the road thinned when evening fell. Most of Corbin's fellow travelers turned off the highway onto smaller lanes toward home. Those journeying farther afield peeled off one by one or in groups, seeking a night's safe sleep in the nearest holding or farm. Corbin hadn't the coin to waste on a straw bed in a barn and so kept walking even as the sun disappeared behind the horizon, and the king's patrol fired lanterns to light their way.

It wasn't until his weary legs called a halt that Corbin realized his mistake. The night was moonless, dark as pitch, and increasingly cold. He was well in between villages, and if there was a homestead near, it was shuttered and invisible. The soldier he'd been shadowing continued on along the road, lantern swinging. Corbin frowned after the receding light. He debated walking on, but the next village might be a good distance, and his legs were gone unreliable with overuse. His feet were throbbing sharp protest, and he was sure he could feel blisters forming on his heels.

Corbin had been raised among farmers' children. For all the little luxuries that came with his da's wealth, he knew how to survive off the land. Surely, he decided, one night alone in the dark alongside the king's highway would be—if not exactly pleasant—no more difficult than sitting through a midnight calving.

The soldier and her lantern were but a waver of candlelight on the road ahead. Before that final illumination could fade, Corbin shook his aching body into action. He stepped warily off the cobblestone and found himself standing on rich, recently tilled soil: a field, newly put to bed for winter. The ground, when he set his palm to it, was frozen. He sighed. There'd be no danger of setting fire to an entire field, but starting a flame in the first place would be difficult, and to Corbin's mind, the only thing worse than sleeping on frozen ground was sleeping in the rain.

He trudged farther away from the road for safety before

reaching into his pack. It was full dark, the soldier and her lantern no more than a memory. But he'd packed his provisions himself, with care, and didn't need light to dig out what he needed. His fingers easily found both the flint and a small bundle of Normandy peat. He had cut the peat himself and wrapped it in linen to keep it from crumbling. Beauty called the little packets "shepherd's stars" for their initial bright flare and long-lasting warmth. She'd insisted Corbin pack four of the peat bundles, and now Corbin was glad he'd listened.

Blind, he struck the blade of his jeweled knife against the flint. His hands worked knife and flint until sparks leaped from the stone to the linen char cloth. As soon as the cloth caught, Corbin used the tip of his knife to drape the burning cloth over the brick of peat. Soon he had the quick, hot blaze of a perfectly made shepherd's star to keep the night at bay.

The peat fire didn't give off as much light as a lantern. What it lacked in brilliance it made up for in heat. Corbin glanced around long enough to be sure he was indeed away from any haystack or bramble copse before rolling himself tightly in Da's rich cloak and curling around the small fire. He doubted he'd warm enough to sleep but expected a few hours of rest would refresh his legs and calm his blisters. It was far too cold to shuck his boots and check for bleeding.

Blisters, Corbin reminded himself as he cinched his hood around his face until only his nose poked into the night, became calluses, and calluses were a traveler's best friend.

The fur cloak kept the cold at bay and made the frozen soil seem less hard. Corbin was surprisingly cozy. He congratulated himself for not wasting coin on a bed in a hayloft. His stomach growled mild complaint, but he had no intention of sticking a hand out into the chill in search of bread and cheese. Stars glimmered overhead: miniscule diamonds set in distant black velvet. Corbin tried to count them all, and in doing so, he fell asleep.

It was again the jennet that woke him, the sound of her ponderous hooves first on cobblestone and then on frozen ground. Corbin was on his feet, cloak tossed back and blade drawn, as soon as the donkey stepped off the highway. Later he'd claim the donkey saved his life. Probably he wasn't wrong, for as he rolled from ground to standing, the Benedictine's own weapon sliced the soil where he had been sleeping.

Corbin blinked at the vicious little hand ax in the monk's hand.

"You weren't supposed to wake," the Benedictine complained, snatching his ax before Corbin could react. "Easier for us both if you'd slept on."

"You're no man of God," Corbin accused, incredulous. His muscles wanted to shake in cold and shock. He held them firm. "To murder a person in his sleep."

"I'm but doing God's work, getting rid of one such as thee." The monk shifted his ax from hand to hand, testing its weight. "Ginger lad, too pretty to be natural, and his sire clasps hands with the devil? There's no good to come of you. God will thank me." Then he shrugged, a shifting of black robes against blacker night. "Not to mention I'm near starving, haven't had a bed to call my own in months, and as de Beaumont's heir, your pouch there's likely to be rattling with coin."

"You're a thief!" Corbin adjusted his own blade. He bent his knees to keep them from locking.

"And a sinner." The monk laughed. "Mayhap you're right, ginger. Mayhap I killed a lonely Dom along the road, stole his cassock and his donkey, put on his priestly guise. Or I'm a

Benedictine in truth. Either way, you and your family are a stain on God's good land, better wiped out than left to prosper. I'll not regret my ax in your throat, lad, but can *you* kill a man of God?"

Corbin retreated as the thief advanced. He thought he could best the man in combat. For all his size, the fellow was thin near to frailty, and there was stiffness in his gait and reach that spoke of the ague. Corbin was young, strong, and quick, and he had spent the last many years learning his weapon. Corbin was not encumbered by a monk's unwieldy cassock or forced to go barefoot on frozen ground. He had every advantage, and he knew it, but his brain was muddled by the shock, his reflexes slowed. When the thief struck out, Corbin barely managed to parry the ax away from his knee.

The Benedictine grunted. He swung again, this time at Corbin's head. Corbin dodged sideways, raising Da's sword across his chest in defense.

"Someone's taught you the dance, ginger. You've got a modicum of talent, I see. But I can tell you've not yet taken first blood."

Killed a man, he means, thought Corbin.

And it was true. Of course it was true. Wasn't that why he was being sent to Honnefleu, to Thomas Chevalier? Because he needed to learn how to fight a man and mean it. Da was spending the last of his fortune to ensure Corbin blooded his first man in a practice yard under a good knight's tutelage and not in the middle of a fallow field under a starry sky.

"*Merde*," Corbin said, the strongest word he knew, and one that would surely make Mother roll over in her forest grave.

The thief only laughed. "Life's shit, ginger," he agreed. "Cold, hard, unfair, and full of pain. You'll thank me for taking yours." He threw his ax.

Corbin ducked but not quickly enough. The ax struck

him not across the face as the thief intended, but in a glancing blow across his temple. Corbin saw flashes of light that had nothing to do with stars. Pain and heat burst across his brow. He staggered, nearly falling. Only terror kept him standing. If he fell, he knew, he'd die.

The Benedictine had lost his first ax in the night. He drew a second from beneath his cassock. The jennet began to shift and snort. Corbin knew she smelled his blood as it ran hot over his eyes and into his mouth.

"You're sturdy. I'll give you that."

Somehow the lanky monk had slipped too close. Corbin could see the flash of the man's smile in the faint light of burning peat. He backed away, knees shaking. The Benedictine followed, murmuring again in Latin. Corbin recognized the cadence. The thief was giving him the last rites—*may God pardon all your sins*—and Corbin, who until that moment had felt only terror, became angry instead.

"No!"

He circled away, tucked the toe of his boot under the shepherd's star, and flipped the burning peat at the thief. Sparks showered orange. The donkey squealed. The Benedictine laughed quietly. He threw his second ax at Corbin's gut.

Just as they'd remembered how to build a fire and strike a flint, Corbin's hands recalled swordsmanship. Da's blade flashed up, stopping the ax before it could bite flesh. The fine old sword blade came down again on the thief as he reached to retrieve his fallen weapon. The Benedictine screamed. He rolled on the dirt, clutching his arm to his chest, then rose to his knees and tried to scramble out of sight. Corbin followed. His boots pinned a trailing fold of black cassock to the ground. The thief tugged, shouting, then stopped struggling and sat up. Corbin couldn't see his face, but he thought the man was still laughing.

"You've more daring than I supposed," the Benedictine said, panting. "You've taken half my hand, ginger." He shifted, groaning. "Well? Have you the balls to finish it?"

Corbin tasted blood. He turned his head and spat into the night. His brow felt like it was on fire. It took all his fortitude not to reach up with his free hand and probe the wound.

"If I spare you," he asked, "will you go and leave me be?"

"My word as a man of God," the thief promised, the lie plain in his mocking tone.

"Stand up!" Corbin ordered. He stepped off the Benedictine's heavy cassock, at the same time setting the point of Da's sword against the man's chest. "Slowly."

The scattered peat sputtered small patches of light. It was difficult to tell, but Corbin thought the thief staggered as he rose, one arm still clutched tightly against his chest. His breathing was harsh in the otherwise quiet night.

"Turn around."

"So you don't have to look in my face when you cut me down?" But he turned obediently, wincing as he did. He hunched his shoulders away from the threat of Corbin's blade against his spine.

They stood without speaking while the cold numbed Corbin's face beneath the pain in his skull. Wind moved in the trees on the other side of the king's highway: Corbin could hear twigs snap. The jennet stamped uneasily. The Benedictine sighed.

"What fools we are to stand bleeding in the night. Are you waiting to see who will drop first, ginger? I wager it won't be me. Make your move and be done with it."

Da's sword listed in Corbin's hand. He tried to steady the point, but it was too late. The Benedictine seized his moment. He whirled, ducking beneath Corbin's sword arm, and plucked the little jeweled knife from Corbin's belt. He clutched at Corbin with two perfectly good hands, locking the first around Corbin's wrist while with the other he set the point of the knife to the pulse point in Corbin's throat.

"Drop the sword," he said. "Quickly now."

Corbin loosened his fingers and let Da's sword slip from his hand. Blood dripped into his eyes, stinging, and down his cheeks. It felt warm as tears on his flesh. Shame burned a knot in his gut.

He waited for the thief to cut his throat. He felt the instant the other man clenched for the kill. At the last moment, he hadn't the courage to keep his eyes open, so he squeezed them shut against the stars. Just as he did, the Benedictine shrieked.

Corbin jerked. The knife fell harmlessly from his throat. The thief was still screaming from somewhere near Corbin's feet. There were other terrible sounds: the jennet's frightened bellows and the distinctive snarl of wolves near their prey.

Corbin took one step back, deeper into the sleeping field. He took another and another. He tripped and fell. He landed on hard soil, scrabbling. His groping hands encountered a familiar curve of decorated metal pommel. A wolf howled. The Benedictine's cries turned to mewling before they trailed into silence.

Corbin snatched up Da's sword. He lurched to his feet and ran.

WHITE HILL

"Many have said of alchemy, that it is the making of gold and silver. For me such is not the aim, but to consider only what virtue and power may lie in medicines."

—Paracelsus

CHAPTER 5

"We do what we can," said the soldier, squinting to get a closer look at Corbin's scalp. The sun was just rising pink over the field and road. "But this stretch of the highway is rife with brigands. It's no place for any traveler after dark. Poor lad. Someone should have warned you."

"'Twasn't brigands," Corbin repeated for the third time. He sat on a log in what he saw in the dawn was an impressive square of scythed grassland. The soldier's companion, a sturdy farmer to whom the land belonged, poked thoughtfully at Corbin's wound. Corbin hissed. "I told you, it was wolves."

"No wolves around these parts since I was a boy," the farmer said. Upon finding Corbin collapsed just off the road he'd taken it upon himself to wake the lad with a bucketful of well water before calling for help. Corbin had come around slowly and not before the farmer and newly arrived patrolman had discovered the Benedictine's mutilated body.

"Pack of wolves wouldn't savage a man only to leave good meat behind," the soldier added. He watched with interest as the farmer tipped mead from his flask onto a dirty handkerchief then pressed the sodden mass to Corbin's wound. Corbin yelped.

"Head wound like that, no wonder you're dreaming up wolves." Ignoring Corbin's involuntary shudders, the farmers cleaned his wound with gentle hands. "It's a sharp slice to your noggin. If you're lucky, it'll heal without a scar." He glanced at the soldier. "Dead man's got sword marks on him, too. Left thumb's chopped clear off."

Corbin peeked across steaming soil at the black-and-red huddle that was the Benedictine's corpse then wished he hadn't.

"It was wolves," he insisted. "I heard them. I grew up near the black forest. I know the sound of feeding wolves. Sir."

"The black forest, is it?" The soldier studied Corbin with renewed interest. "Your sort don't often travel so far afield. Bit of a shy group, aren't you? Prefer to stick close to home."

The farmer pulled forth the edge of Corbin's new shirt. Before Corbin realized what the man was about, he'd ripped the hem clear off. Corbin gaped. The farmer grinned.

"Better binding your head then about your middle," he explained. "And you've a nice thick cloak to keep the rest of you warm. Funny thing, a boy like you dressed in a lord's cloak. Good living near the cursed forest, is it?"

Corbin shook his head then wished he hadn't. He put a hand up, but the farmer batted it away. Whistling softly, the man bandaged Corbin's brow with a deftness that might have impressed even Nan. The soldier hummed respect.

"Seen a piece of the war before I turned to working the land," the farmer explained. "Patched up more than a few bloodied men in my time. You'll do," he told Corbin. "I'm sorry about your friend. Has he kin? Our soldier here will want to take his body into Honnefleu for inquest. King's law."

"He wasn't my friend," Corbin corrected. "He tried to kill me. Before the wolves attacked. I don't know about kin. He was a Benedictine, I think."

The soldier exchanged a veiled look with the farmer. "One of the order, you say? And he tried to kill you? Not very likely." He gave Corbin's shoulder a sympathetic pat. "What about the donkey?"

Corbin knew he was doing his best impression of a lackwit, but he couldn't stop himself from goggling. He followed the line of the soldier's index finger. The thief's jennet, shed of blanket and saddlebags but still dragging her reins, lipped calmly at the frozen dirt in a fruitless search for winter grass. Her long ears swiveled back and forth.

"Jenny?" Corbin said in disbelief. The donkey swished her tail but didn't look his way.

"Yours, then," the farmer deduced. "Too bad. She's a fine specimen. I wouldn't have said no to her if she needed a new home." He smiled genially. "Animal like that, there's no chance she'd linger near a wolf hunt. She'd be long gone by now, lad. There's all the proof you need it was brigands."

Corbin knew the man spoke the truth about the jennet. He recalled how the black forest wolves had driven old Snip mad. The gelding had never completely recovered. Afterward, even the scent of a wandering village dog would send him into frothing, staggering fits of remembered terror. The poor horse's mind and body had finally given out only a year after Mother's death. He'd simply stretched out among the lavender one spring afternoon and not got up again.

Hope had insisted on planting wolfsbane on the gelding's grave. Snip's violet flowers bloomed profusely every autumn after.

"She's mine," Corbin decided. It didn't make sense to claim her. It also didn't feel quite like the lie it was. If she'd stayed by Corbin's side through the night, he wasn't going to rebuke her affections. He would return her loyalty as best he could.

"There'll be a wagon soon to take the corpse to Honnefleu for inquest," the soldier said. "Would you want to be riding alongside, lad? Not with the body, of course." He made a small moue of distaste. "But with us nonetheless."

"No!" Corbin protested. The soldier frowned, and the farmer shook his head, but Corbin forged ahead. "Thank you, sirs. But I'm expected in the city. I'll need to be off immediately."

"Are you certain?" the farmer fussed. "You've had quite a fright, no to mention bled on my field. If you're not feeling it now, you will very soon."

But Corbin was already up off his log. He approached the jennet, hands spread in supplication. Jenny ignored him. The farmer and the soldier, after exchanging another puzzled look, pretended not to see the unusual sword and scabbard hung from Corbin's belt.

"Jenny!" Corbin cajoled softly, speaking in the low tone dogs, cattle, and horses seemed to prefer. "Time to go. There's a lass."

The jennet rolled an eye. Her nostrils flared. Corbin realized he must stink of blood. He expected her to bolt. She didn't. When he was close enough, he grasped her trailing reins, disentangling them from a knot of bramble. Then she was his; she abandoned her grazing and let Corbin lead her across the field.

"Where's your blanket got to?" Corbin wondered quietly. "And your panniers?"

Jenny had no answer for him. She balked when they approached the monk's body, digging her hooves into the soil and threatening to sit. Corbin couldn't blame her. He knew the smell of butchered meat and fresh stuffed sausages. The Benedictine's corpse gave off the same ripe stink plus something worse that Corbin suspected was punctured bowel. He pressed his sleeve against his nose and mouth.

He stole a peek at the last moment, and what he saw made him retch up bile and bread. The vomiting made his head pound and his eyes water. The farmer and the soldier looked on with the amused sympathy of hardened men.

"When you get to the city," called the soldier as Corbin tugged Jenny in a wide half circle past the corpse toward the highway, "stop at the Blue Goose Tavern before you sleep. My mum works the taps, and she'll give you a draught of spiced wine to help the head and keep you from nightmares. She knows all about the bad things, does my mum, and how to fix them. Just say it was Jack who sent you."

"Thank you," Corbin replied without glancing back around. He wanted to leave the place as quickly as possible. If her eager stride was any indication, Jenny felt the same.

"Don't forget now!" the soldier insisted. "It's the Blue Goose! Mum'll do you good."

Corbin waved a hand in acknowledgment before slinging himself onto Jenny's back.

HONNEFLEU TODAY IS A SOMBER TOWN. The Black Death lingers inside shuttered buildings and in crooked alleys. The streets are quiet while Saint Stephen's Church fills with mourners. The Seine is like glass, and Honnefleu's sister port, Harofluet, is host to ships forced into quarantine, their cargo left to rot. Carrion birds pace roofs and walls; their raucous cries split the air.

Honnefleu when Corbin first set eyes upon it was prosperous. Recovering from one war and not yet started on the next, the city's maritime trade was flourishing. Spirit of commerce held sway. New homes were going up alongside their older cousins. Caen stone was plentiful, and the stink of chalk used for building competed with the Seine's own perfume. The people of Honnefleu were happy in their good fortune, blissfully unaware of sorrows to come.

There are always sorrows to come.

CORBIN RODE JENNY into Honnefleu without fanfare. The donkey was tired. Corbin's wound was afire, and every jostle sent agony through his head. Dried blood stuck the farmer's bandage to Corbin's skull. He knew he should be grateful that he was alive and mostly whole and that he'd reached Honnefleu without further incident and before full sunset, but it was difficult to feel much of anything other than the pain and exhaustion.

Honnefleu at dusk was lovely. Flames danced in cressets outside shops and homes and along the meandering streets. Young men carrying long torches hurried to and fro, setting fire to cold baskets, trying to outrace darkness. They laughed and called to one another before disappearing deeper into the city. Corbin and Jenny followed more slowly. The jennet's hooves slipped on wet cobblestone. The air was thick in Honnefleu, humid and heavy. Corbin's curls ran riot. The hair on Jenny's coat curled in dark gray whirls.

The damp, Corbin decided, must explain the abundance of green plant life. Despite the season, lush vines and colorful flowers still bloomed in window boxes and on stoops. There were no garden walls in Honnefleu; one small yard fell into the next. Neighbors shared patches of kale and autumn lettuce. Pear trees spread their branches wide, brushing against two houses at a time. And the homes themselves were beautiful, much taller than any cottage Corbin had ever seen, lit from within by candlelight and cheer. The coming dusk reflected purple off the stone.

The streets grew less steep as they approached the Seine.

Shops outnumbered homes. Corbin glimpsed the Blue Goose, its sign painted to resemble a giant indigo egg. He passed it by. There were other taverns as well, and many inns and stables. Corbin ignored them all, looking instead for the shine of the river. Eventually the twisting lane spat them out onto a wide, sandy road, and the water of the port's famous basin spread at their feet, full of sails large and small.

Corbin was duly impressed. He slid off his sagging mount, looped her reins around his wrist, and led her into the mass of people hurrying along the water. The press of bodies was tighter here than on the king's highway. Corbin kept Da's sword tucked close to his thigh. Nan knew plenty of stories about Honnefleu's talented pickpockets: light-fingered boys and girls who would slit the bottom of a man's bag and relieve him of his coin while he went on about his business all unaware.

"Make a noise if you see trouble," Corbin whispered into the donkey's closest ear. Jenny sneezed, frightening a child in pantaloons. The child looked around in surprise, stared past the donkey at Corbin's bandaged head, and gaped with a gratifying amount of disgust.

"Which way is Le Château?" Corbin asked.

"Which?" The child had a charming lisp and plump mouth sticky with the remnants of pastry. "*Grand ou petit?*"

"Big or little?" Corbin scratched beneath his bandage. "It's Thomas Chevalier I'm meant to see."

"*Grand,*" the child said. "You're going the wrong way. Turn around. Past the broken ship. You'll see the pennants, all blue and silver."

It took a great deal of maneuvering to turn Jenny against the masses. The tired donkey didn't want to reverse, and the busy crowd didn't want to part. Corbin managed to pivot Jenny partway around before she got stuck between a fish-monger's cart and woman with tallow candles slung from a stick across her shoulders. Soon they'd caused a bottleneck on the street, and people began to take notice. The chandler swore, poking Jenny's flanks with the end of her stick. The fishmonger more sensibly tried to clear space on the road for the donkey to complete her rotation. The commotion only encouraged travelers to pause and gawk. Corbin had never seen so many people in one place before in his life. They were a veritable river all on their own, of color and sound and shape, rival to the Seine running sluggishly alongside.

"Here now." Someone wrapped an arm around Corbin's waist, keeping him from falling. "Pass me the reins. That's right. You're pale as milk, friend. And what happened to your head?"

Corbin blinked. His rescuer smiled genially back as he took stock of Corbin through the thick lenses of wire-rimmed spectacles. The lenses made his brown eyes look large as walnuts, too big for his thin face. A pointed hat set atop his dark curls made him appear elongated and strange, but his grin was infectious.

"You're early," he scolded without censure. "We didn't expect you until long after dark." He guided Corbin around, tugging Jenny after. The crowd parted in front of him like water before oil, making space enough for Corbin to remember how to breathe properly again.

"Of course, we thought you were walking in," the remarkable young man continued in a pleasant chatter. "If I'd know you'd have a horse—"

"She's an ass," Corbin managed.

His companion snorted. "Four hooves, long tail, not a cow: looks like a horse to me. Either way, if I'd known you'd come *mounted,* I would have been up the hill to meet you earlier."

"To meet me," Corbin echoed. "No one was meant to meet me. Da said I was to present myself and his letter at the château and hope Sir Thomas Chevalier would honor his pledge as promised."

The young man paused to give Corbin an arch look over the top his spectacles.

"Sir Thomas always keeps his promises," he said. "And he's not the sort of man who waits to greet his guests at the gate. You'll learn that soon enough, Corbin de Beaumont, if you don't die on me first. By all the fishes in the sea, is that a sword cut to your temple? What's happened? Was it highway robbery?"

"It was a thief in monk's garb," Corbin said. "He tried to kill me for my coin and the color of my hair, but I cut off his thumb before the wolves finished him off."

To Corbin's great surprise, his rescuer nodded, accepting the explanation as truth.

"I've never seen a wolf," he said. "Well. In books, of course. And Thomas has a skin in his bedchamber. You'll tell me all about it, won't you? As soon as we get you home. Best hurry now. Hold tight to me. I won't let you fall."

"What's your name?" asked Corbin.

"David."

"If we're in a hurry, David, I think you'd best help me back onto my donkey. I can't feel my legs."

WHEN PRESSED LATER, Corbin couldn't remember the ride from bay to château. It's safe to assume he was unconscious for most of the short journey. At the time, the *Château de la Colline Blanche*—White Hill Castle—was crouched on an outcrop of land overlooking both the Seine and Honnefleu below. It was an extraordinarily large and beautifully constructed château. Some say Philip the Fair had it built for one of his loyal barons. Others say the castle was raised entirely from the ground by an alchemist who used the Seine as the base of his universal elixir and whose mad wife was confined to a windowless tower room for the entirety of their long, turbulent marriage.

The château was certainly a delirious extravaganza of towers and turrets. The roofline was jagged as any mountain range. There was no lack of chimneys—ovens are an alchemist's most important tool—or gardens. In truth, it was the carefully considered home of a Renaissance mind, but no one who lived there when Corbin was carried in a faint through its gates knew exactly what to do with the place. Thomas Chevalier, while a talented swordsman and a successful knight, was no Renaissance man.

But Sir Thomas knew enough to have Corbin put to bed beneath a pile of his warmest furs. He ordered a fire kindled and sent David in search of the Honnefleu's best surgeon. Then he sat down with a bowl of hot water and a bottle of whiskey and sponged loose Corbin's bandage himself. The gash ran straight as a pin one hand's width back from above Corbin's right eyebrow. The wound was deep but not deadly. The edges were clean. Thomas thought it would leave a scar but not an ugly one. He also recognized the wound for what it was: the mark of a Picardy hand ax.

He filed that unsettling snippet of information away in the back of his head for further examination at a quieter time.

Corbin stirred only once beneath Thomas's ministrations.

"Welcome to White Hill," the chevalier said when Corbin's lashes fluttered. "Now drink."

He managed to get several fingers of whiskey down Corbin's throat before the lad passed out again.

When the wound was cleansed and Corbin made warm as is possible in a drafty château in autumn, and there was nothing to do but wait for David's return with the surgeon,

Sir Thomas set aside the bowl and sponge and sorted through Corbin's belongings.

He examined the sword first, admiring its length and quality. Despite the wearing on the hilt he knew the elegance beneath. He recognized the distinctive nautilus curves on the grip, the singular etchings on the knuckle guard, and the Saracen blacksmith's stamp on the pommel. It was a sword meant for killing afreets and would do for executing the devil in the black forest, so long as a lad was wedded to his task. Sir Thomas had seen two of the sword's sisters in the king's treasury. There were supposed to be four in the set, all told.

Sir Thomas couldn't help but wonder how a cheese merchant, no matter how wealthy, had managed to get his hands on such a weapon.

The fire leaped in the grate. The brocade curtains around Corbin's bed stirred in a draft. A door banged. There were hasty footsteps in the hall beyond: David and the surgeon. Sir Thomas hung Corbin's sword on a hook on the wall, safely out of the way. He plucked Corbin's journey pack from the floor, taking it with him to a bench in front of the fireplace. When David, the surgeon, and the surgeon's assistant hurried into the bedchamber, Sir Thomas was busy sorting through Corbin's small collection of valuables.

The surgeon went at once to Corbin's side. His assistant —Sir Thomas knew the young woman for the man's spinster daughter—threw off her wrap and began rolling up the sleeves of her chemise. She called for more hot water and clean clothes. David ran off again.

"It's not mortal," the surgeon diagnosed after a moment of concentrated poking and prodding. Corbin muttered but didn't wake. "It needs sutures, and he'll have a bad headache for several days yet. Who is he?"

"Village boy, come to learn proper swordsmanship." Sir

Thomas liberated some bread, an apple, two bundles of peat, a piece of flint, and a sprig of dried lavender from Corbin's pack. He set them in order on the bench for further consideration. "I owe his father a favor."

The surgeon grunted acknowledgment. He set his doctor's case on the foot of the bed, unsnapping a pair of metal latches. The case had a hinged spine. The wings on either side were deeply padded, the tools within scrupulously organized. Sir Thomas had been the surgeon's patient regularly since he'd settled on White Hill, and each time the chevalier was further intrigued by the man's tools.

"Stitching the skin together is a new and dangerous trick," Sir Thomas said as David returned, Sir Thomas's butler and two young page boys dogging his heels. The page boys each carried a bowl of fresh, hot water. The butler bore the château's best silver candelabra and a box of beeswax candles. David held a delicate glass bottle almost hidden in one hand. The bottle was mottled green and blue, the glass etched to resemble snakes' scales.

"Two drops, no more," David cautioned, holding out the bottle. "Injuries to the brain are tricky, and he's insensible as it is."

The surgeon's daughter accepted the bottle on her father's behalf. The surgeon looked at David with distaste.

"I'm familiar with opium," he said, affronted. Sir Thomas hid a smile behind his fist. He rose from his bench by the fire and crossed the room, pretending to study the contents of the surgeon's case, recapturing the man's attention.

"David's opiate mix is unique." Sir Thomas chose a pair of forceps from the surgeon's tools and examined them idly. "Very potent and yet without the usual side effects. A family secret, I'm told. Best pay him heed." He set the forceps atop the bed furs and reached again into the doctor's case, this time dragging forth a short, blackened poker. "Sutures are prone to infection. Cauterization seems the better choice. The old ways are often the best ways."

Sputtering, the surgeon plucked the poker from Sir Thomas's hand.

"Cauterization will leave behind a scar and possibly numbness. You don't want the lad to lose the use of his eye."

Sir Thomas scowled. "Is that likely?"

"No," said David. "But the honorable physicker is quite right. The cut is deep but not wide. Stitch the edges together, and your new apprentice will keep his looks. The poker is unnecessary and will leave a scar for certain."

David had a knack for taking control of a situation seemingly without effort. Sir Thomas enjoyed watching the trick. It was one of many reasons he kept the younger man close at hand. The butler paused in the middle of lighting the candelabra to watch David charm the surgeon while the two page boys goggled outright, entranced by the obvious enthusiasm on David's mobile face and by the light, quick gestures he sketched in the air as he spoke.

"Sutures then," Sir Thomas decided, interest waning. It was getting cold in the room, and he needed to be about the business of delayed supper. David, he suspected, was late to evening ablations and prayer. "And no more than two drops of the opiate." He nodded at his butler. "Build up the fire. Come and find me when it's done. David, off you go. Too many hens clucking about spoils the laying."

David would have resisted, but Sir Thomas brooked no argument. With a snap of his fingers, the chevalier cleared the sickroom but for the surgeon and his daughter. For the moment, he dismissed de Beaumont's heir and the afreet sword from thought. Time enough, Sir Thomas assumed, to deal with that puzzle in the morning.

CHAPTER 6

$\mathcal{C}$orbin dreamed of Da and Beauty. It was a pleasant dream, full of sunlight on spring fields and fat white clouds speeding overhead in an afternoon sky. Da was telling Beauty about the calves he'd raised to adulthood on Normandy grass. He knew the bloodlines by heart, knew which cows did well by milk for cheese and which birthed the strongest bull calves for breeding. Da thumbed his ebony walking cane on the ground for emphasis as he named off cattle. His frail form shook with emotion.

Beauty sat in the grass at his feet, plaiting lavender and roses into a flower crown. She'd pricked a thumb already on the thorns but seemed not to care. She sucked casually at the puncture whenever blood welled up. Corbin knew from her fixed smile that she was only pretending to listen to Da's recitation.

Beauty only wore that particular expression when she was dreaming of places beyond Littleton.

"But, Papa," she said, interrupting gently. "The cows are gone now. The pasture is empty but for Corbin's vicious pony. Why must I memorize bloodlines if they don't matter?"

Da paused midsentence. He blinked at Beauty in astonishment.

"Don't matter? Of course they matter! It's all I have left of my fortune—the knowledge and how to use it! You must listen and remember, daughter! Soon our luck will change; I know it!" Da rocked back and forth, pointing his cane at Beauty. "I won't live forever, child. Age takes me and breaks me. Your nan is but a pace from the grave, God save her. Faith is too young, and Hope has no head for numbers. You're all I have left, Beauty. It's for you to redeem the family name and rebuild the business. And to do that you must recall the old bloodlines as you know your own heart."

Beauty's face fell. She raised the completed flower crown from her lap and set it on her head. The white roses and blooming lavender enhanced her loveliness and made her look like a spritely queen. She paid no attention to the thorns pricking at her temple or the blood running in increasing rivulets through her hair.

"I do know my own heart," she said. "And it's not here in backward Littleton it lives, Papa. I want something more than this! More than cows and cheese and lads who court me only for my land and my own breeding and *bloodlines*. Papa, I want more." The false smile fell from her mouth. Anger turned her mien unseemly. "It's me you should have sent away to live in the forest, not Corbin. Beastly Manor may be horrid, frightful, full of spiders, and worse, but I've met the Beast, Papa, and he's anything but *dull*."

Corbin sat up. Pain lanced his skull. He clapped his hands to his head in groaning objection. What he felt there made him gasp.

"Careful." Fingers gripped his wrists, pulling his hands

down and away. "It will be tender for a while yet. Here now. Open your eyes. Look at me."

Corbin opened his eyes. He stared past flickering candle flame into a long face and wide brown eyes. His head throbbed. He groaned again.

"David," he said. "You've misplaced your spectacles."

"Ah! Good! You remember." The other man set his candle aside. His smile was sympathetic, and his strange hat crooked. "Excellent, that's excellent. Sometimes, after a blow to the head like you've suffered, recollection is foggy. How many fingers am I holding up?"

They were bony fingers. Ink stains darkened the tips.

"Two," Corbin replied. "Where am I?"

David retrieved his spectacles from a small bedside table. The same table held several burning candlesticks, a silver flagon, and a stoppered glass vial. As Corbin's vision slowly adjusted, he saw that he was in a large bed situated in the middle of a narrow chamber. The bed, with its fur-heaped mattress and canopy, was much too large for the room. Walls pressed in on either side, leaving barely enough space for a man to squeeze between mattress and stone.

Drab tapestries hung on the far wall, presumably covering windows. The chamber was still very cold, in spite of the merry fire burning in a grate unsettlingly close to the bed.

"Don't fret," David said. "No one's ever burned alive in this room. It's tight but safe. The old magician saw to that."

"Magician?" Corbin put tentative fingers to his chin. He felt a day's growth of stubble. "Where did you say I am?"

"Sir Thomas Chevalier's single and only first-floor chamber," David replied. He perched on the edge of the mattress, regarding Corbin earnestly. "Previously some sort of parlor, I believe. But that was very long ago. The magician suffered from the gout, you understand, and preferred to avoid the stairs whenever possible."

Corbin walked his fingers up the side of his face, along the curve of his ear, and—cautiously—over his skull. There, also, he encountered a day's growth of bristles.

"My head."

"Shorn," David agreed. "Well. Half of it. For the sutures. You're quite the picture. All amber ringlets on the one side, boiled egg on the other. But how do you feel?"

"Like I've been gnawed all over by a pack of dwarves," Corbin admitted. "How long have I been asleep?" And then, with growing horror: "Where are my things?"

Once again, David took Corbin's hand by the wrist, pulling it away from exploration. He set it in Corbin's lap with a warning pat.

"Your magic sword is hung there on the wall, see? Perfectly safe. I sent your gorgeous cloak out for a brushing. It was covered in blood and soil. The maids will have it back in no time, but you'll not want to wear it about White Hill. No one will like you better for it putting on airs. Thomas went through your pack, but not before I'd removed your pouch of coin, so that's safe as well."

He tossed Corbin's coin purse onto the furs.

"Sir Thomas wouldn't steal my coin." Corbin felt his cheeks heat with temper. The wound on his head stabbed in response.

"Of course he wouldn't. But he's a practical man, Thomas is, and he expects payment for services rendered. He also thinks very highly of himself and so might have decided he was worth all the silver in your pouch, not just the payment promised."

David was smiling, but his words had weight. Corbin heard the unspoken implication. He nodded slowly.

"The sword isn't magic," he said. "It's only a fine old blade."

"Isn't it?" David's smile remained unchanged. He shrugged. "Be that as it may, you needn't fret. The sword is there, safe by, and tomorrow we'll take it exploring, if you like. But for now I can tell by the furrow in your brow that it's another dose of the poppy for you, Corbin de Beaumont." He reached for the glass vial and lifted the stopper. As Corbin watched, he dribbled two fat drops into the waiting flagon.

"Drink," David ordered. "It's good wine, down from the north. Drink it all down and rest. I'll stay to guard you."

Corbin downed the wine without question. It *was* good: a dry, red vintage. He couldn't taste the poppy in it at all. He lay back in the furs, propping his head on a round cushion, and regarded the canopy overhead.

"But I'm safe." He yawned. "Now I've found Sir Thomas. Aren't I?"

"Certainly," David agreed. "Quite safe. Still, I'll sit by you for a while, shall I?"

"If you like," Corbin said. He fell promptly back to sleep.

"LOOK INTO THIS." David held out a small square of silver. "And tell me again you don't want me to take it all off."

Corbin had lost track of the days, but from the light shining through one bared window, it was midmorning and from the breeze still very much early autumn. David had pulled the tapestry away from the window, letting both light and air in, before sitting Corbin in a chair by the opening. He'd draped Corbin in furs from neck to toes, but even then, the change in temperature made Corbin shiver. He didn't care. He was weary of being closed in a small space with no glimpse of the sky. He craned his neck to get a better look through the small window. David, busy stirring something in a small bowl, nudged him with a pointy elbow.

"Corbin. Pay attention, if you please. I've other things to do today besides serve as your barber. Thomas has me searching the library tooth and comb for the old magician's writing on demonology. The magician was a prolific scholar, Corbin. There are a shelves *and shelves* of possibility."

Corbin grunted. He turned the piece of silver over in his hands. Rough etchings decorated one side: flowers and vines. The opposite side was polished to a shine.

"Tilt it," David prompted. "Take a look at your reflection and make a decision."

Corbin held the polished square up in front of his face. He tilted it back and forth before it caught the light and then his reflection.

"*Mon Dieu!*"

"As I said." David sounded grimly amused. "Half-boiled egg, half-amber locks."

"I can't go out like this."

"You can't," the scholar agreed. "Which is why you're going to stop fussing and let me shave the rest of it. This evening you're to have supper with the others. Do you want to be the butt of every joke?"

Corbin flung the piece of silver at the bed. It bounced on the mattress. He clenched his fists on the furs in his lap. It was foolish, he knew, to be so vain.

"It will grow back."

"Of course it will," Corbin retorted. "Do it then. Don't cut me. One gash to the skull is quite enough, thank you very much."

"I have steady hands." David held his bowl so Corbin could see inside. The contents were white as milk and smelled of honey. He'd used a small brush to whip the mixture into froth. "My mother's recipe," he explained.

"Helps the straight blade run true and conditions the skin at the same time."

Corbin couldn't help but glance pointedly at David's ever-present hat. David smiled.

"For the gentry, of course," he clarified. "They paid her handsomely for bottles of her barbering cream. My people aren't allowed a razor. We wear our beards with pride, or like me, trim away the hair from our chin with scissors." He used the little brush to froth the cream further. "I'm surprised you made the connection. I'll admit I'd wondered why you hadn't yet mentioned my head covering."

"My father did business with many Israelites in Caen," Corbin replied. "Before the first exile. He'd bring back stories to Mother of the many people he saw in the city, travelers from across the sea."

"I'm a Rouen-born Jew, Corbin. I've never seen Israel, nor do I plan to. Bow your head, now, and close your eyes. Keep still."

David used the brush to apply his mixture to Corbin's scalp. It felt pleasantly cool except where it gathered about his still healing sutures. There it stung. David swirled the brush about from the nape of Corbin's neck to the peak of his hairline, soaking curls. When the foam threatened to run into Corbin's eyes, David wiped it back with a cloth. Corbin kept his eyes shut and his head dipped and tried his best to hold still even though his scalp had begun to tickle.

Sweet honey perfume saturated the room, pleasant in the drift of cool air.

The small brush clicked against the side of the empty bowl when David set it aside. Corbin heard the unmistakable strop of leather against metal.

"You're shivering," David pointed out. "Are you too cold?"

"No," Corbin said. "Get on with it."

David set his razor against Corbin's flesh and began. He

hadn't exaggerated. He was a more than competent barber. He sheared Corbin's red curls free without hurry, pausing every few strokes to clean and strop his blade. The razor ghosted along the curve of Corbin's skull, never pulling or catching. Slowly, Corbin began to relax. His shivering abated. He tucked his hands under the furs and matched his breathing to the glide of David's hand. By the time the other man finished one complete pass with the razor and began his second, Corbin was almost asleep.

"You're very trusting," David murmured. He set the razor briefly aside and used a towel warm from the grate to blot Corbin's naked skull. "You've known me but a day, I've a wicked blade in hand, and you're languid as a milk-drunk puppy. I'm flattered. No wonder your father is concerned."

Corbin opened one eye. The press of David's fingers through the warm cloth against his head felt wonderful. Outside the window, morning was passing.

"My da is not concerned," he said, too sleepy to put much heat into the objection. "Nor am I. You found me in Honnefleu. You abide in Sir Thomas's château. If for some reason you wanted me dead, you'd only to smother me while I slept the poppy dream. Besides which"—Corbin opened his other eye, grinning—"if you tried now, I'd break your neck before you cut my throat."

David snorted as he gave a final pass with the cloth over Corbin's barbered scalp. "Naive and ignorant both. Well. We'll soon have you well cured of that."

LATER THAT SAME DAY, David rousted Corbin from deep sleep. The scholar tossed a pair of thick woolen hose and a gray tunic on the bed and then added a knit cap and gray cowl. He placed a walking stick lengthwise across the pile.

Corbin sat up in bed and fingered the hose and tunic. The clothes were serviceable but plain.

"Not the quality you're used to, I imagine," David said. "But there's no use complaining. All of our students wear the same uniform. The boots you came in with will do until the cobbler visits. Be careful of your stitches when you put on the cap. Use the chamber pot. We'll be away for a while."

Corbin scowled, and not because the other man sounded a bit too much like Nan lecturing Faith. He reached for the walking stick and dragged it across the furs. It was a simple staff, shod top and bottom with a bit of bronze, but it brought to mind his earlier dream of Da and Beauty and an ebony cane thumping in long spring grass.

"What is it?" David demanded. "Don't tell me you're too proud for the stick? You'll be glad of it by dinner, believe me."

"My legs are fine!"

"That may as well be, but your head is not, and every phsyicker knows a man's brain commands his heart, lungs, and bowels. Two days out of surgery and you shouldn't be leaving this chamber at all, only Thomas has grown impatient, and no one on White Hill dares argue when he's in a mood." David scrubbed a hand over his face. Only when the scholar pulled his bony fingers down his chin did Corbin notice the bruises of sleeplessness lurking behind those spectacles.

"Very well. Step out in the hall while I dress."

David looked as if he wanted to protest. Then he sighed and rolled his shoulders in capitulation. "Don't take long. And wear your sword." He strode out the door, pulling it shut behind him with more force than Corbin thought necessary.

Corbin crawled out from beneath the warm furs. He dressed in the narrow space between the mattress and hearth, grateful for the fire in the grate. The hose were rough against his skin, and the sleeves of the tunic were too short, but the cap and cowl were knit of a yarn soft enough to please even the most discriminating nobleman. Corbin tugged the cap down over the tips of his ears, wary of the sutures along the right side of his scalp. He found his boots behind a fold of bed canopy and reached for Da's sword. It didn't escape his notice when he freed the sword from its hook on the wall that the straps and scabbard had been cleaned. Corbin unsheathed the blade and saw that it, too, had been scoured free of the Benedictine's blood.

The flesh on the back of his neck prickled. It displeased him that stranger's hands had tended his weapon without his permission or knowledge. When he fastened the sword around his waist, he felt as if a forgotten limb was waking again after too long a time gone numb.

He shoved his feet into his boots and snatched up the walking staff. Then he flung open the chamber door and stepped boldly into the hallway.

The corridor was hung with tapestries. Rugs overlapped the stone floor. Candle flame danced in hanging lanterns while uncovered lancet windows on the outer wall let in the evening. David stood beneath a lantern, a book open in his hands. Upon Corbin's appearance, he closed the slim volume, secreted it in his robes, and smiled.

"You'll do."

The corridor was wide and straight. It dead-ended just past the door to Corbin's bedchamber. When Corbin leaned to peek out a lancet, he saw only bare trees beyond.

"This way," David said. He walked quickly down the corridor, short robes flapping around his knees. For the first time, Corbin noticed the ring of keys fastened to the other man's belt. The keys, in all shapes and sizes, rattled quietly in David's haste.

Corbin followed more slowly after David, staff tucked defiantly under one arm. The corridor branched twice to the right, but David ignored the turnings and continued ahead. They hurried past another larger window. It looked out onto a muddy courtyard. Corbin thought he saw the glittered of lights coming up in Honnefleu beyond and below. The port city appeared more distant than Corbin expected. He wished he could remember the journey up White Hill to the château. Then he winced, struck by a guilty thought.

"Jenny! David, what happened to Jenny?"

"Your long-eared mount?" The corridor dropped three narrow steps. David took them in one stride. He stuck out a long arm, preventing Corbin from doing the same. "In the stable. Perfectly content now, although I hear she struck out at Marc when he checked her over for wolf bite."

Corbin shoved David's arm away. "She's not injured. The wolves left her alone."

"Strange, don't you think?" David peered at Corbin through his spectacles. "Wolves being naturally hungry, and horses naturally prey. I must say, Thomas is very interested in your story."

"It's not a story. It's the truth."

"I don't doubt you, Corbin. Nor does Thomas. In fact, he's quite concerned. So much so that he'll award us both a tongue lashing if he sees you tottering about, stick in the air. Do us both a favor and make use of it, please."

Corbin ground his teeth. David waited. Past the scholar's thin form the corridor widened into an archway. Corbin could hear voices beyond the opening: shouts, laughter, and then a piercing whistle. Twilight gathered in the nearest lancet. Another day was coming to a close, and he'd spent too much of it in bed.

Corbin took the walking staff from beneath his arm, gripped one end in hand, and set the other end lightly on flagstone.

"I don't need it."

"Pretend," David suggested. "You'll be doing me a favor. Now." He whirled around. "The dormitories are this way. What you heard was kitchen call. Rooms will be empty for the moment, so you can look your fill undisturbed. Pick a cot and I'll have your things sent over. Come on. Keep up."

The vaulted opening led—not into a first-floor gallery as Corbin expected—but instead into a spacious spiral staircase. A gigantic chandelier hung suspended on a chain made of thick iron links. Large candles burned on branches crafted to look like the horns of a great stag. Streamers of hardened beeswax festooned both the chandelier and the length of chain running through space to the level below. When Corbin leaned sideways and looked up, he could just make out the block and ring bolted to the tower rafters above.

"Rouen pulley," David said with pride. "One of my uncles perfected it years ago. You'll see similar machines on the tall ships now, for pumping the bilge. This stair used to be dangerous, especially in the winter, until I put my mind to lighting it."

Corbin, looking up at the spiral curve and into the empty air between floors, was dubious.

"Even with light, a man could set but one foot wrong and fall to his death."

"Oh, it's not so bad as that." David began to the climb upward, one hand pressed against the curving outer wall. "You'll grow used to it. And you'll grow stronger, running up and down all day. The practice yards are below. You'll see them later. The dormitories are up top, beneath the eaves. It's warmer there, believe it or not. I think you'll find it comfortable."

Corbin was fit as any man his age, more so; he'd spent years training his body to strength and dexterity in a relentless race toward vengeance. Despite of the constant throb in his temple, the spiral staircase was not a challenge. It was satisfying to feel the muscles in his legs wake and stretch after too many days spent abed. He sighed in muted pleasure as they climbed then flushed when he caught David watching him askance.

The other man shook his head.

"You'll fit in here," he said. "Cheerful little soldiers, the lot of you."

"I didn't expect others," Corbin admitted as they reached the top of the spiral. The pulley was now only a man's height over their head. The chandelier hung below their feet halfway between the floor and ceiling. "Da said only that Sir Thomas had a reputation."

"For turning promising young lads and lasses into members of the king's most specialized guard, yes." David threw open the wooden door at the top of the stair. "He's also earned a bit of a name for himself as a slayer of monsters. In you go. This is the lads' dormitory. Lately it smells of rotten apples. I've no idea why. You'll grow used to that, too."

The room was square and simple, tucked up beneath a peaked roof. The walls were the same Caen stone that ran throughout the rest of the château. The floor was uneven wood slat. There were no windows. A forest of mismatched cressets kept the shadows at bay, burning merrily and unattended. Corbin wondered if the magician had spelled his attic against fire as well. As David had promised, the space was warm. Six identical horsehair mattresses lined the walls, three to each side. Four of the six looked as if they were claimed from the state of personal odds and ends strewn over stuffed horsehair and on the floor.

"The door across the room leads to the lass's room," David said. "Thomas has only three for the nonce. They keep to their own space for the most part." He walked between the mattresses, casting a thoughtful eye over the detritus on the floor. "You're provided a blanket and a chamber pot. I'll have those sent up as well." He stopped in front of the final two mattresses. "One cot is much the same as another, I suppose. Do you have a preference?"

Corbin had been more deliberate in his walk across the floor.

"That one," he said, indicating with his staff.

"Why?" Intrigued, David looked from Corbin to the mattress and back again.

"It's been more recently stuffed," Corbin declared. "You can tell from the seams. It's on the inner wall, not the outer. Thus: cooler in the summer and warmer in the winter. Farthest from the staircase, which could be good or bad, depending. That one's neighbor"—he jerked his stick at the mattress he'd passed over—"is a restless sleeper. Look at the state of his blankets. He's got rosemary and rue tucked under his pillow. Nightmares then. I've a sister who's the same. I don't need to be disturbed midsleep."

"Marc's nightmares disturb all of White Hall," David said. "Luckily for us he's off to don the blue come the new year."

"He'd do better to swap the rosemary for garlic," Corbin replied. "Which leads us right round to this." He laid his stick across the cot he'd chosen and dropped to his knees at its head. "Look. This is why I want it."

The marks on the floorboard were very faint, scratched along the edge of one wooden slat by knife tip or thumbnail. Corbin traced it with one finger. David, bent so that his chin almost brushed Corbin's shoulder, exhaled in surprise.

"Is that what I think it is?" He huffed again, this time in disgust. "Rotted apples."

"No." Corbin reached for his knife and came up empty. He frowned. "Do you have a blade handy?"

David's knife was utilitarian but well kept. Corbin slipped the point under the floorboard and pried up. He was rewarded when the end of the slat popped, revealing a hidey-hole beneath. Roughly square and very shallow, the compartment had been carved into the joist beam beneath the floor.

"Not an easy job." Corbin flashed a grin over his shoulder. "And it would have taken some time. I wonder how long that's been there?"

David's spectacles had slipped down his nose. He pushed them up with his thumb, bemused. His warm breath tickled Corbin's neck.

"No idea. It was Parks who had this cot last and doesn't have the patience for the task, I assure you. He did, however, have a taste for good cider."

"Mystery solved." Corbin had to crook his wrist to reach the flask cached under the floor. A simple leather jug with a wax stopper, it was sticky to the touch. "Fermented not rotted. Leather's improperly tanned. It's got a slow leak, hardly more than ooze. Not enough to damage the boards, just enough to stink."

"Powerfully," David agreed. "And this is the space you want?"

"Toss the flask, stuff a few rags in the hole to blot the drip, and now I've got the perfect hiding spot for those coins you seem so worried over. And anything else I want to keep safe." Corbin hesitated. "You won't say anything?"

David's cap wobbled when he shook his head. His knees popped when he straightened. "No," he promised. He reached down a hand, helping Corbin to his feet. "You found it; I suppose it's yours to use as you like. How *did* you find it?"

"Wasn't difficult." Pleased with himself, Corbin leaned on his staff. "I have three sisters. Fellow will do what it takes to keep nosy siblings out of his treasure. Mine was a piece of loose stone beside the hearth." Absently he returned David's serviceable knife. "I've no reason to believe my collection of stones and pressed flowers aren't still there, waiting upon my return."

"Pressed flowers?" David's brows rose beneath his curly fringe.

"Littleton violets are among the most beautiful in all the world," Corbin retorted, but he couldn't help flushing and looking away. "Or so Mother always insisted. Some things are too lovely to let go, she used to say."

"She's quite right." David squeezed Corbin's shoulder. "True beauty's a rare and precious thing. Come. Put the board back. I think it's time you met the rest of our lads and lasses."

When it came to his son's tenure on White Hill, Da hadn't supposed it necessary to share with Corbin more than the most basic details, and Corbin hadn't bothered to think much past the letter of introduction in his pack. If Da thought Corbin had skill enough to catch the retired knight's interest, Corbin didn't question the assumption. Da had just enough coin to pay for a year's tutelage on White Hill, so Corbin presumed a space was waiting. It never even occurred to him that things might go awry.

Part of this naïveté was an innate innocence that lingered in Corbin, unspoiled even by family machinations. A greater piece was the force of Jean de Beaumont's personality. The cheese merchant was not an easy man to live with even before his wife's death. Unlike his famous Camembert, he didn't improve with age. To this day, only one of his remaining three children can speak of the man without flinching, and that's only when she's well into her cups.

Between the ages of ten and seventeen, Corbin was for all intents and purposes the sole focus of Da's attention. De Beaumont lived only for vengeance. Corbin was the weapon he intended to wield. No true swordsman himself, de Beaumont believed the best blades are hammered in the hottest fires. It's no wonder the boy found it difficult to look too far ahead.

The real surprise is he didn't hang himself from one of Mother's apple trees before he turned twelve.

"YOU SAID LADS AND LASSES," Corbin muttered. "I see grown men and women."

"From what little I've seen, you do a fine impression of a grown man yourself," returned David. "When you're not gaping like a fish. Close your mouth and be brave. First impressions matter in this household."

"I hate being laughed at," Corbin complained. He'd managed the spiral staircase again without difficulty, but the throb in his head was growing worse, whether from exertion or panic. He hadn't expected an audience when he bent the knee to his new master.

But here he stood on the threshold of a sizable chamber, five somber faces turned his way.

"Then don't do anything laughable," David suggested without sympathy. "Onward, Corbin de Beaumont. It's time to prove your worth."

He led the way into the room, clearly expecting Corbin to follow. Corbin did, fingers gripped tightly around the cap of his staff. It was clear the chamber was meant for dining. Several broad wooden tables were placed slantwise in front of a large cook hearth. The earthen floor was strewn with rushes. Although the space was at least one level too low for windows, thick rugs hung edge to edge on the walls. A large iron pot steamed over a banked fire on the hearth next to a rack of toasting rolls. The room smelled deliciously of fish and potatoes and fresh bread. Corbin had to bite his tongue to keep from drooling. Three days on nothing but an invalid's diet of broth and porridge left him feeling hollow.

A man sat on a bench near the hearth, feeding bits of dried meat to two spotted cats. The cats vied for his attention, circling his legs and digging sharp claws into his leather trousers. The man wore a jerkin in the king's blue. The matching cape on his shoulder was pinned with the starburst sigil that meant he had the king's full faith.

"Sir Thomas." David ignored the rest of the people in the room and went straight to his master. Corbin kept his gaze on the back of David's neck because it was easier than looking side to side. He heard the scrape of wood against dirt: the chevalier's students rising from the dinner boards upon David's arrival. Corbin knew he was being thoroughly scrutinized. He could feel the weight of their curiosity between his shoulder blades and was desperately glad of the knit cap covering his shorn head.

"Sir Thomas," David repeated, drawing the man's attention from the greedy cats. "Here he is, sir." He stopped two paces in front of the bench, essaying a quick bend of the knee. "Just in time for dinner."

Sir Thomas raised his head. He looked at David. Corbin thought some unspoken challenge passed between them. The knight's mouth tightened, and a muscle in his throat jumped, while David clasped his hands in front of his gown, knuckles white.

"Good," the chevalier said after a moment of silence broken only by the purring of his cats. "Much longer and I would have grown angry. You know I hate to wait for dinner." He stood.

A compact man corded with hard muscle beneath his togs, he wore a princely forked beard clipped close around his chin. His dark hair was bundled atop his head in a soldier's knot. When he smiled, baring crooked teeth, it was with real warmth. The weight of the chevalier's attention was heavier than that of anyone else in the chamber, so much so that Corbin found himself bowing his head and bending his knee at once.

"You've manners." Sir Thomas sounded pleased. "And grace. A promising foundation. Can you use that sword you wear as well as your father boasts?"

"Yes, sir." Corbin kept his gaze down. One of the spotted cats came to wind her tail around his shin. "Better. Da—my father—is sometimes parsimonious with his praise."

"We'll see." The fingers of Sir Thomas's right hand tapped against his leather-clad thigh. "I'm to teach you how to kill a man, is that so?"

"Not a man." Corbin lifted his chin and met the chevalier's narrow stare. "A monster. They call him lord of the dark forest, or sometimes just the Littleton Fiend."

Sir Thomas nodded minutely in recognition. "There's a story going around how this monster murdered your mother."

"It's true," Corbin retorted. Then he remembered to whom he spoke and lowered his voice. "Da was there, sir. He saw it happen."

"That's part of the story," Sir Thomas agreed. "How the forest Beast, in the shape of a wolf man, tore Jean de Beaumont's bride to pieces before supping on her blood. De Beaumont couldn't bear to live on without the love of his life, so he threw himself at the monster, sword drawn, meaning to fight unto death."

"It's true," repeated Corbin.

He heard the shift and sigh of the students behind him. Before Mother's death, he'd enjoyed a good story, a frightening tale of dwarves or ghosts or of the tattooed blue cannibals from overseas. He understood grisly fascination. Still, he hated that his family's embarrassment was being trotted out like nothing more than a bedtime story to frighten children. He took a shallow breath, forcing temper back.

Sir Thomas's mouth curled knowingly. "As de Beaumont is more cheese monger than swordsman and our demon long ago made a name for himself as the cleverest of predators, the story should have ended there, with the Beast using your father's bones to pick his teeth. But it didn't."

The pot on the hearth began to bubble over. A kitchen boy appeared, iron hook in hand. His shoulders strained visibly beneath his tunic as he lifted the pot from the fire. It looked a difficult chore, but the boy spilled nary a drop.

"Why didn't it?" The question came from behind Corbin. "Why didn't he die, your father?"

Sir Thomas lifted one of his spotted cats from the floor. Cradling the delighted creature in one arm, he used the other to wave Corbin to standing. Corbin staggered a little as he rose. His sutures ached. Hunger knotted his stomach. He was angry, but he knew better than to let emotion show. When the chevalier motioned for Corbin to turn around and face the boards, he did so without hesitation.

At first glance they looked no more unusual than any family waiting on dinner, politely attentive. They sat in small groupings around the tables: young men and women dressed identically in the same simple uniform of gray hose and tunic. Each of them looked older than Corbin, although not by as much as he'd first thought. It was composure that aged them, a stillness he'd seen before only in Littleton's most venerable residents.

Two of the lasses looked close as sisters or cousins; they had the same shining black hair and ruddy cheeks. One of the lads had burn scars across his face and down beneath the collar of his tunic. Another carried his right arm in a sling and sat on the bench with the stiffness of a fellow nursing broken ribs as well. He grinned when Corbin looked his way, turning his solemn expression sunny.

"They're an inglorious crew," Sir Thomas rumbled, "but they're mine. And it's they who'll decide if you stay or go. Affrodille, step up and repeat the question, if you please."

Affrodille had yellow hair bundled into a messy braid and a full mouth Nell would have insisted was made to drive men mad. Unlike the rest of Sir Thomas's students, her otherwise drab tunic had decoration: delicate red embroidery around the cuffs and hem. At her master's call, she stepped from the floor to a bench to the middle of her table, there standing at attention between cups and cutlery. Corbin didn't miss the clasp of her hands in front of her tunic. It was David's stance repeated exactly.

"I only wondered," she said in a high, clear voice from atop the boards, "what convinced the demon to let this boy's father live. Even as far as Paris we've heard of the fiend. He delights in disrupting the trade routes. There's a reason the king's soldiers go armed through the black forest. If he's not stealing from the royal coffers, he's making a meal of men. It's said His Majesty's put a bounty on the demon's head, enough coin to set a person up for life, plus good land and a title at court."

"Oh, la!" The lad with the broken ribs clapped his free hand against the boards and winked at Corbin. "Do it right and you'll come out of this story a lord."

"Laurie," Sir Thomas chastened. "Wait your turn. Affrodille?"

"Well." The kitchen boy was serving out toast and potted fish, taking trencher from table to hearth and back again. He worked around Affrodille, reaching past her booted feet to set out a brimming trencher and a fresh flagon of wine. Affrodille ignored him. "The Littleton Fiend never lets anyone go unharmed. He only ever sends back bits and pieces as warning. What did this cheese merchant do to keep his life?"

"My father spent ten days trapped alone with the Beast in his manor," Corbin said through his teeth. "You may as well say when he came back he was returned in 'bits and pieces' as he's never been of sound mind since."

Distress thinned Affrodille's beautiful mouth. "I'm sorry," she said. "I don't doubt he's suffered. But he lived to tell the tale while so many haven't."

Corbin realized he'd taken to leaning on his stick. He deliberately straightened before answering. "The Beast took an interest in companionship. I don't know why. Mayhap even demons grow lonely after centuries alone with stolen treasure and old bones. Da is a clever man. He can sing and recite poetry and read. He knows politics and philosophy and the art of war. He can wield the sword and the bow, and he knows how to tend the land. He kept the Beast entertained for a while."

"And then?" David asked quietly. He'd moved from the hearth to Corbin's side. Corbin spared him a glower.

"When Da ran out of more worldly material, he told the Beast stories of home and family. Of Littleton and Mother and my sisters. Mayhap he wanted the monster to feel guilty for the lives he'd ruined—all our lives. We were happy before. The Beast ruined everything. Da thought he would soon be dead. He couldn't help but grieve aloud about what he'd lost."

The boy with the puckered scars on his face raised a hand. "I wager the devil was only playing a game from the beginning, sir. It wasn't the merchant it wanted at all. Poor man was just a means to an end."

"Well done, Marc," Sir Thomas praised. "Stand up and explain."

Marc climbed from bench to tabletop. He arranged

himself between a plate of rolls and a tall candlestick. When he clasped his hands together, Corbin saw they were as scarred as his face.

"Even the youngest of devils are prone to boredom, we know that. They're not dwarves to be satisfied with hunting or succubi with raping, we know that, too. Perhaps it wanted companionship, but I believe it's more likely the Beast knew exactly who this man was, knew the ins and outs of the nearby village far better than his poor prisoner. Sir, I think it's possible this unlucky cheese merchant had somehow come by something the fiend wanted or needed. It killed the wife in front of the husband as a display of strength and cruelty, then kept the poor fellow by in its lair until he was ready to strike a bargain."

He studied Corbin with pity. "These sort of devils enjoy a good game. They're full of tricks and traps. Your father is a tradesman. He crossed through the forest regularly?"

Corbin admitted, "Yes."

"The Beast would have known that certainly. I think it's fairly obvious the family has something the devil wants, sir. I mean no insult to your father, monsieur, but unless he was very comely, I don't see why it would choose an old man for companionship. Those type are more often attracted to youth and beauty."

Corbin jerked, making the end of his staff rattle on the floor. Marc would surely have guessed the answer from the rising heat in Corbin's cheeks, but Sir Thomas had chosen that moment to walk forward, inserting himself between Corbin and his students. A spotted cat rode his shoulder, tail held low for balance. Sir Thomas turned in a small circle, letting Corbin see the glint of unexpected humor in his eye before turning blandly back Marc's way.

"Close," he said. "Very close. Sit back down."

Marc hopped from the table and seated himself again on

a bench. Only Affrodille remained on the boards. Corbin had forgotten her. When Sir Thomas turned her way, Corbin saw his mistake. Affrodille had been watching everything from her perch on high. While he'd been distracted by Marc's musings, she'd been making note of his unease.

"Affrodille?" Sir Thomas prompted.

She heaved a small sigh. "Marc had it but thought too hard. Young man, you mentioned sisters. You're not hard on the eyes. I suppose they're not either?"

"Oh," gasped Marc. He thumped a fist on the table in irritation. "I'm an idiot."

Corbin had let go of the stick. Only David's quick grab kept it from falling in the rushes. Corbin's own hand was on Da's sword, in warning and in fury. Sir Thomas eyed him up and down.

"Manners are good. Temper is not," he said. "Although it bodes well de Beaumont didn't manage to beat all the spirit out of you—"

Corbin moved. The sword moved with him, ringing quietly as it pulled free of the scabbard. David backed away.

"*En garde*," Corbin said, moving into position. Da's sword felt heavy in his hand, perfect.

"Infant," Sir Thomas chided, but he plucked the cat from his shoulder, dropping it gently to the floor. "I saved your life, and now you want to die over my supper?"

"I won't die," Corbin said. "I'm good. Everyone says so." He shifted his stance, letting candlelight glint across the tip of his blade. "Apologize. What you said about Da and his fists, that's none of your business. Apologize now or I'll teach *you* manners, cut you where you stand, no matter if it's your home and supper."

"Oh, lad." Sir Thomas sighed. "The apple doesn't fall far from the tree. I bet you're quite like him. No wonder he had to send you to me. Much longer, I imagine, and one or the both of you would have ended up dead."

Corbin lunged, but David struck faster, landing a sharp blow to the back of Corbin's sword hand with the end of his stick. Corbin's fingers went numb. Da's sword fell from his hand and spun across the floor to fetch up against a bench. Corbin wheeled on David, but the scholar held up the staff in warning.

"Enough," he said. "Finish it, Thomas. The lad's angry, exhausted, and embarrassed, and the rest of us are starving and stroppy with it."

Sir Thomas had the grace to look abashed. "Laurie," he barked. "Speak!"

Laurie didn't bother to lift his battered body from the benches.

"Fairly straight forward, really," he said with regret. "Merchant had three pretty daughters. Demon's decided it needs companionship, probably a concubine. Goes about acquiring one in the usual way. Violence, threats, promises. De Beaumont barters his life and, no doubt, also the lives of his remaining family, the people of Littleton, mayhap all of Normandy, who can know? In trade for his eldest daughter. Really, Marc. It's hardly a new gambit. You should have seen it straight out."

"Child," Corbin muttered.

"Pardon?" Laurie blinked.

"In trade for his eldest *child*. I did tell you. Da's a very clever man. The bargain was: Jean de Beaumont's eldest child or a curse of death upon his entire family."

Marc began to smile. "You're—"

"The first of four children."

"Meant to knock on its gate as concubine?" Laurie covered the bottom of his face with his free hand. "Will you disguise yourself in skirts then?"

"Meant to kill the Beast, in skirts or trousers, it makes no difference, so long as he lets me get close enough." Corbin wasn't sure how the staff had made its way back into his hand, but he was past the point of pride. He let the stick take some of his weight, closing his eyes halfway against the pain in his skull. "So long as I present myself at the manor's gate before my eighteenth birthday, I fulfill Da's bargain and keep the rest of my family safe from the demon's curse."

"Only if you kill it quickly," one of the matched girls pointed out. "Even if you've kept to the letter of the bargain, it's going to be very angry once it realizes the trick."

"I'm not afraid," Corbin replied. "I'm good now, and I have time to get even better." He glowered in the chevalier's direction. "I've got the coin, sir. You promised Da you'd take me on."

"Unlike your father, I'm not irrevocably bound by a hastily made bargain. Besides which"—Sir Thomas tilted his chin at the boards—"it's not entirely my decision. We're an egalitarian household. Affrodille?"

"Aye," the yellow-haired woman, still standing atop the table, proclaimed. "It's a sad story, and God knows I've no love for the Littleton Fiend nor his kind. The boy's not wrong; he's quick with the sword. I'll not say we can make him a hero, but there's a chance we can teach him a thing or two about slaying demons. The rest is up to him."

She sprang from the boards, vaulting lightly over a bench. After landing in front of Corbin, she held out her palm. "Welcome to White Hill. Much good may it do you."

Corbin clasped her hand. It was rough as his own, calloused by the sword. "What about...?" He cast a puzzled glance past Affrodille at the others. "Don't they get a vote?"

Affrodille laughed. It was a hearty, belly-deep guffaw, and it refreshed Corbin immensely.

"By 'egalitarian' Sir Thomas meant himself and David and

the ranking student, which is me. Sir Thomas decided 'aye' when he saw the weight of your father's coin. David decided 'aye' when he heard your tale of the wolves and the Benedictine on the highway. And me? Well, you've got a pretty face and a fine body, and I like the way you wield your weapon, Corbin de Beaumont. So it's 'aye' from me as well."

Laurie hooted around a mouthful of bread. "Don't let it go to your head, Corbin. She says that to every lad, even the ones ugly as poor Marc."

"It's true," the burned man said easily. "She told me I had a voice like sunshine and a poet's way with words."

The matched girls shook their dark heads in fond amusement. "Wait till she gets you on the practice yard," said one. Her sister finished: "Affrodille doesn't waste time on flattery when she's wanting to box your ears."

"The twins," David said, appearing once again at Corbin's elbow. "Marie-Louis and Dot. Fraternal not identical. Time to eat. You've gone the color of cream again. Here. Thomas is bringing you a trencher. Marc, fetch Corbin's sword from under the benches, if you will."

Corbin sat between Dot, who made room, and Marie-Louise, who refused to budge over. Sir Thomas placed bread, fish, and potatoes at Corbin's elbow and a cup of wine in his hand. The chevalier held a goblet of his own. He thumped his fist on the boards before lifting the drink in a toast.

"To the cheese monger's lad," he said. "And now you're one of our own. *Bienvenue*, Corbin. May you thrive in my care."

"*Bienvenue*, Corbin!" shouted the inglorious crew, raising their glasses one by one in blessing. "Welcome!"

CHAPTER 8

*I*t was Marie-Louise who first approached Corbin about Da's sword. By all accounts, Marie-Louise was the more cautious of the matched sisters, which may explain why she waited until Corbin had been a member of Thomas Chevalier's household a good eight weeks before she pulled him aside one snowy afternoon when they were meant to be sparring.

It was cold and windy outside. The snow came down in swirls, covering the already slick courtyard flagstone in weak drifts. Corbin was grateful for his knit hat. His hair was growing in nicely over the thin pink scar on his scalp, but it wasn't yet long enough to cover the tops of his ears, and winter was in with a vengeance. Wherever the wind touched, his flesh grew pink.

Marie-Louise wore a matching hat, but her dark hair was long enough to braid and coil about her head. Her cheeks were mottled red. Tears ran unnoticed from the corners of her eyes. Her hands, like Corbin's, were wrapped in strips of linen. They'd been boxing long enough to be out of breath and sweating beneath wool, even in the freezing temperatures. They were equally sufficient when it came to fisticuffs, although Dot was far better than her sister and was in fact responsible for breaking Laurie's ribs in the autumn. Today she was holed up in the château library before a warm fire. Affrodille and Marc were busy helping Sir Thomas with something in the stable, and David was secreted in his tower room away from the miserable weather.

Marie-Louise had been kind enough to sham she wanted Corbin's tutelage, but she'd already almost blackened his nose twice, and she wasn't pretending any longer that she couldn't dance under his longer, slower reach.

"You're lucky demons aren't fond of boxing." She smirked through the falling snow at Corbin. She bent with her hands on her knees as she gasped for breath. "You're really not much good. It's like you haven't the heart to put the all of your weight behind the release." Struck by a thought, she regarded him suspiciously. "You're not pulling your punches because I've not got a cock and balls, are you? Mind, demons aren't fond of boxing, but they adore shape-shifting, and who's to say the Littleton Fiend might not decide it'd do better dueling you in a skirt and bosoms?"

Corbin's lungs felt like they were on fire even as he was positive the tip of his nose was frozen solid. "I don't care if they've got bosoms."

Marie-Louise stomped her booted feet on the flagstone to warm her toes. "You'd do better to focus on learning the ways of your blade. I don't know why Sir Thomas insists I teach you boxing or makes Dot school you in fletching. If you were meant to join the king's army, that would be another thing. But you're not. And you're no more likely to kill your fiend with a shaft through the eye than a punch to the gut." She blew on her fingers. "I appreciate your enthusiasm, but it's filthy cold out here, and you're wasting both our times."

Corbin stuck his fists in his armpits and jogged in place to keep from turning into an icicle. Snow stuck to his lashes. "David says a workout in the cold only improves bodily humors. And I know my sword, Marie. I do just fine against Laurie's straw men. You're the one who needs bladework." The last came out with more bite than Corbin meant.

"Pah!" The young woman turned her head and spat onto the ground. Her sputum beaded on the flagstone. "You're an idiot. There's no need for magic against straw men. That sword's got demon-killing enchantment writ all over the hilt, but everyone's pretending you'll slay your devil with strength and wit. You won't." Marie-Louise wasn't precisely delicate, but she was shorter than Corbin by a head. Still somehow she managed to make him feel small when she poked a thumb against his chest. "You need to stop pretending you're training to wear the blue. Your sire may have dropped you in the shit hole, but he handed you the shovel you need to dig yourself free and a bag of good coin to make sure you were trained up right. So pull your head out of your ass and go and make Sir Thomas and his flighty magician teach you how to use it."

Corbin frowned at Marie-Louise's stubby brown thumb jabbed against his sternum. He must have stood unmoving a heartbeat too long because all at once she jerked her hand from his front and used it to grab his chin instead, roughly tugging his face down and close. The playful smirk she wore flattened to dismay.

"Fuck me." She released his chin and turned in circles in the snowfall, hands held overhead in disgust. "Dot said, but I didn't believe it. You've no idea. Do you?"

"No." The cold seemed to have Corbin about the throat. He coughed.

"No." Marie-Louse began to rip the linen binding from her hands in short, furious jerks. "*Mon Dieu. Marie me sauver des innocents.* I don't know what game they're playing or why, but that sword you've got is your only chance at surviving a devil as old and powerful as yours—the rest of us know it even if you don't—so best you go start asking some pointed questions. They've got the answers, believe you me, locked up in one of those chambers they guard so close."

Then she surprised him by reaching up and patting the chin she'd just bruised. "I like you, Corbin. So does Dot, though she'll never admit it. You seem a sound sort. But believe you me when I say you're nothing without that sword, and it's the only reason Affrodille and David agreed to take you on."

Corbin didn't go to Sir Thomas that day or even the next. He avoided the dining hall by claiming a sour stomach and kept to his cot in the mornings until well after the others had left for their studies. Marc and Laurie teased him some about too much sweet pudding but cheerfully carried his excuses to Sir Thomas. Dot and her sister both tossed him furtive glances as they crossed through the lads' dormitory to the château below, forcing Corbin to pull his blanket over his eyes. Affrodille only patted his shoulder and promised to bring him porridge midday.

"Oatmeal and honey," she assured Corbin. "Settles the gut every time."

David was more difficult to avoid. He had his own living quarters and was fastidious about only entering the dormitories when invited. The first several days out of sickbed Corbin had missed the other man's unpredictably timed visits, but Corbin's wound was healing nicely and quickly enough he became accustomed to the business of his new upstairs living quarters. Although he missed David's quiet humor, he quickly grew to appreciate his new roommates.

He saw the scholar at mealtimes and passed him in the halls. Inevitably, David was in the château's extensive library whenever Sir Thomas or Affrodille sent Corbin there on an errand. He often had his nose in a book or his arms full of odd pots and pans and glass vials, but he always stopped to exchange a few kind words or tease Corbin about his fuzzy scalp. About the time Corbin's sutures began to itch, David appeared seemingly out of nowhere in the middle of one of Affrodille's reoccurring lectures on the importance of folklore and proceeded to drag Corbin into the small closet Sir Thomas used as the château infirmary. David snipped away the suture knots with small, bronze scissors then pulled the remaining stitching free of Corbin's scalp. The strange pulling sensation made Corbin shudder, but David only laughed.

"It's healing well, and it will itch less now the binding's out. Let it alone," he scolded genially. "No more scratching at your head when you think no one's looking."

Which told Corbin the other man paid more attention to the rest of the household than he pretended. So it was really no surprise that it was David who grew most suspicious when Corbin took to his bed.

On the first day, David carried Affrodille's promise of porridge and honey up from White Hill's kitchen. He cracked the door and murmured Corbin's name. When Corbin pretended to be asleep, he set the food on the floor just inside the threshold and went on his way. Corbin ignored the porridge, preferring instead to spend the afternoon running his thumb over and over the weathered engraving on the pommel of Da's sword. The food was still sitting on the floorboards when Corbin's companions returned after dinner; Marc stepped in the bowl and complained of cold mush on his boots for hours after.

On the second day of Corbin's self-exile, David was more

insistent. He knocked politely but firmly on the doorframe, repeating Corbin's name between each thump of fist against wood. Corbin groaned and wrapped himself in his blanket and answered the door wearing his best sneer.

"Don't you think it's careless to stand out on the stairs for so long," he snapped. "If you're not wary, someone will push you over the spiral for being a nuisance. Why don't you ever just come in?"

"And risk glimpsing one of you in flagrante delicto? My eyes would never recover, and they're delicate as it is. No, better not to risk it."

"What do you want then?"

"Affrodille said you were suffering a bilious gut. Laurie reports you've been tossing and turning after dark like a flea on a log. And Marc reliably informs me that you abstained from victuals completely both yesterday and this morning, as he's still wearing honey and oats on the bottom of his boot."

Corbin didn't laugh as he supposed he was meant to. David's brows rose above his spectacles. "Are you quite all right?" he asked. "You don't look peaky, not from this side of the door. Is it your head? It shouldn't be. The scar's hardly visible, and it's been weeks, but sometimes these things make a return appearance—"

"It's not my head," Corbin bit out. "Why do they report on *me* to *you* anyway?"

"Would you rather they go straight to Thomas? Besides which"—David regarded Corbin through the lenses of his spectacles—"we're meant to be friends."

"Meant to be?" Corbin, who had gone all of his life never lacking in congenial company, only sneered harder. "It doesn't work that way. You're friends or you're not, and I hardly know you. A few hours shared in a sickroom does not close fellowship make."

"I'd like to be friends." David fiddled with the folds of his short robes. Corbin's attention was drawn to the ring of keys attached on the other man's woven belt. "If something's plaguing you, I'd like to help. You've not been under White Hill's roof long. There's bound to be some adjustment. Often things here are disconcerting, to say the least. It's always nice to have a champion, I think."

It hadn't escaped Corbin's notice that David made "earnest" look like an art form. Nell would have suggested the scholar belonged on a mummer's stage, but Corbin, for all his suspicion, couldn't make himself believe the hopeful tilt to David's mouth or the twist of his hands in the fabric of his robes was anything but genuine. He was a breath away from confession when David shifted on the stairs. The keys on his belt gave another muted jingle, and Corbin immediately had a better idea.

"Mayhap you're right," he said. "This place is disconcerting, what with the twists and closed doors. But you, you turn up everywhere. You know your way around. I bet you've seen every nook and crook of this place."

David abruptly stopped his fidgeting.

"I've had reason to explore," he said. "And time enough to do so."

"*Fantastique!*" Corbin threw off his blanket. He hurried to gather his hat and boots. "A distraction may be just what I need to banish this malaise."

"I thought it was a sour gut?" David ventured. He sounded dry as dust, but when Corbin glanced over his shoulder, the other man's expression was bland.

"Both." Corbin strapped Da's sword across his back. "Show me."

David rubbed his chin. "What, exactly?"

"Everything. I want to see everything."

· · ·

THE SNOW HAD TURNED into a blizzard while Corbin sulked. Although tapestries were pulled tight against every window and the torches burned brightly, Corbin's breath turned to smoke in the air as they descended the spiral staircase. He'd long ago given up his staff, but moisture made the steps slick, and he almost wished for the added balance of a stick in hand. David didn't seem bothered by the cold. Corbin wondered if he'd grown inured to winter in the drafty château. It occurred to him that for all he'd gathered David was Sir Thomas's helpmate, occasional surgeon, and some-times adviser, he really knew next to nothing about the bespectacled scholar himself.

"You've helped Sir Thomas train up quite a few men and women to the blue, have you?" The air grew almost comfort-able as they exited the stairwell into the main hall. The boards were empty, and the open hearth banked for warmth rather than a meal. The chevalier ordered fruit and bread kept on the tables at all hours to fuel his active household, but with the seasons changing, fresh produce was scarce and dearly bought, even in Honnefleu. The few green pears among the toast looked unappetizing even to Corbin's empty stomach.

At home in Littleton, Nan would be bringing up the preserves she had bottled in the summer and stored in the cellar for winter. A sudden wave of homesickness made Corbin falter. Surprised, he swallowed down a lump in his throat. He hadn't yet had time to miss Littleton, nor even Nan and his sisters. Once he'd recovered from the Benedic-tine's attack he'd been kept too busy with schooling to think past the complaints of his hard-worked body.

"A fair number," David answered, recalling Corbin to the present. The scholar paused to fetch a candlestick off one of the tables. He also grabbed two wedges of thick black bread and tossed one at Corbin who caught it easily. "Thomas, of course, was made soldier long before I was born. When he was tasked with this particular holding some years ago, he needed someone who could interpret the old magician's writings." David took a hearty bite of bread, chewed fastidiously, and swallowed. Corbin's mouth started to water in response. "Not all of the throne's requirements are as straightforward as one might suppose. Occasionally, His Majesty may stumble upon a difficulty more…out of the ordinary or odd. Sir Thomas, bless the poor man, has experience in specialized combat. I happen to have an affinity for the odd. Also"—David winked over another bite of bread—"I can read Hebrew, which is the language my predecessor preferred for notes. Together Thomas and I manage to keep the throne supplied with exceptional recruits."

Corbin nibbled one corner of the black bread. It was crusty and sweet. His mouth flooded. He took a more substantial bite. "The inglorious crew," he managed around crumbs.

David smiled. "Yes. We've gained a bit of a reputation here on White Hill. And I've just determined which closed door you should see opened. Come along. Bring your bread."

Corbin was too busy eating to argue or inquire. They left the main hall through a narrow corridor that opened into the kitchen. Sir Thomas's single harried cook paid David and his candlestick no mind. The little maid working flour in a bowl fluttered long lashes in Corbin's direction. She was rewarded with the cook's loud censure. Corbin fled before the cook's ire could spread his way, hurrying after David, an unwelcome blush heating his cheeks.

The corridor ran straight and level. Corbin saw no windows or doors. The walls were smooth stone and clear of tapestry. There were torches set at intervals in brackets at eye level. David lit each one with his taper as he walked. The floor wasn't the packed earth Corbin expected but stone to match the walls. As David's light spread, Corbin saw the rock was smooth. While the rest of the château had been built in the usual way—stone slab upon stone slab—Corbin could find no seam anywhere in the wall, even when he gulped down the rest of his bread and walked his fingers along the surface.

"What magic is this?" It was as if some great worm had tunneled its way through solid bedrock, smoothing rough rock to leave glossy stone behind.

"You've heard of *la Tarasque*?"

Corbin shivered and not from the cold. "The great dragon? Of course. Who hasn't? Mother used threats of *la Tarasque* to frighten us out of our tantrums."

"Yes, well. You'll be glad to know it doesn't live here anymore, hasn't for many generations. But the warren it left behind is one of White Hill's greatest assets."

Corbin eyed the polished passageway with new interest. There were veins in the walls—branches of gold, green, and black. The gold glittered in the torchlight. When Corbin peered closely, he could see shiny flecks of something like miniscule fish scales caught in the striations. He stopped and rotated in place, trying to see the colorful patterns overhead. It was like trying to catch a glimpse of clustered stars on a cloudy night.

"Amazing, isn't it?" David held the candlestick overhead, lighting the ceiling. "Metals in the earth, not unlike humors in the body."

"Beautiful." Corbin was tall enough to touch the curve of the ceiling if he stood on his toes. He stroked the tip of one finger over a wide patch of green. "This is what you wanted me to see?" It wasn't the sort of secret he'd been hoping for, but it wasn't a disappointment, either. He couldn't bring to mind the last time he'd seen anything so striking. *Not since*

Mother died and her roses stopped blooming, he thought. "Thank you."

David didn't respond at once. Candle flame bounced off the lenses of his spectacles, obscuring his eyes.

"Not this," he said after a pause. "Farther on. Follow me."

Farther on, the tunnel dipped downward. Smaller tunnels sprouted in clusters, first on Corbin's left and then on his right. They seemed to come in groups of twos and threes. They were not as wide as the original passage, but they were still as tall as Corbin and broad as two adult men standing shoulder to shoulder. David chose a left hand turning. The torches on the walls were set farther apart. The tunnel, already inclining downward, became steep enough that Corbin felt his ears pop as they descended. He plucked off his hat to tug at his lobes. The air in the tunnels was much warmer than that above, so much so that sweat trickled down the back of his neck.

David paused. Corbin, busy trying to catch further glimpses at the walls and ceiling, almost stepped on the scholar's bootheels. David shoved him gently out of the way then kindled a final torch, revealing the tunnel's termination in an iron-bound wooden door. The door looked out of place against the glossy stone, wholly man-made and crude in the face of *la Tarasque*'s more organic creation.

The door was latched and locked. David passed Corbin his candlestick. Corbin held the light over the lock as the scholar sorted through the keys on his ring. Corbin, who hadn't thought to pay attention in the weeks since he'd made White Hill his home, counted to ten three times over before he lost track of the number of keys in David's care.

The lock was sticky, but David was patient, shimmying the key back and forth until the teeth caught, and the latch released. He secured his ring of keys before opening the door. The room beyond was dark. An unlikely and horrifying vision struck Corbin and made him hesitate—*la Tarasque* lurking in the false night beyond, great maw cracked wide, waiting to strike and swallow him down like so much sweet black bread.

"You first," David urged. "Step cautiously. There's a torch just inside to your right."

Corbin held up the candlestick as he edged into the room. He located the torch and set flame to wick. The torch went up with a whoosh of blue, sweet-smelling flame, throwing the space around Corbin into stark relief. He caught an impression of crooked shelves; books and scrolls piled in corners; a large table and a single chair; and, standing behind the chair, a great horned monster, as tall as three men. The monster leered, wide yellow eyes flashing.

Corbin yelped. The candlestick tumbled from his fingers, snuffing out on the stone floor. He put up both hands in defense and backed directly into David.

The other man sighed. "Corbin. Be calm." As Corbin stood frozen, the scholar retrieved the fallen taper, lit it on the blue flame, and took it across the room to a small cresset that looked as if it had escaped from the streets of Honnefleu.

"See," he said, setting the candlestick on the desk and turning to consider the yellow-eyed horror. "It's only a portrait. Extremely lifelike, I grant you, but still just paint on canvas."

Corbin's pulse pounded in his veins. Licking his lips, he regarded the portrait with consternation. David wasn't wrong: Corbin, who was used to tinker's sketches on bits of tin or parchment or the small likenesses carved into shell Da sometimes brought home to Mother from the city, had never seen such a horrendously realistic painting. Stretched between four long pieces of what appeared at first glance to be bone, the rectangular canvas rose from floor to ceiling, and the monster filled it almost entirely. The great hairy form seemed to suck all color and air from the underground chamber.

Corbin felt light-headed. He put a hand on the wall, seeking steadiness.

"My apologies." David spun from Corbin to the painted beast and back again. "I didn't think. I've grown so used to keeping it company, it never occurred to me to warn you."

"It's him, isn't it?" The beast stood on two legs like a man, but he had the barrel-like chest and jointed limbs of a canine. His loathsome yellow eyes seemed to follow Corbin when he approached. A fat silver moon shone in the painting over the creature's shoulder. The artist had place the beast in a field at night, the suggestion of trees and rooftops in the distance. Corbin gulped. "The Littleton Fiend."

"It's possible, certainly." David walked around the desk. He stopped in front of the huge portrait, fingertips brushing canvas. "This particular example came from an abbey in Ypres, according to the old magician's records. The Dom was reluctant to part with it, I understand, but the abbey was in disrepair, and France paid the price he asked. Philip the Fair had it shipped here for study." David walked his thumb and forefinger along the canvas, measuring the whirls of painted fur with his hand. "The world is full of demons, Corbin. Who knows from whence this devil hails, perhaps even from the artist's own imagination. Even so, he's impressive. Terrible even."

Corbin wished David would step away from the canvas. It was all he could do not to knock the other man's hand from the painting.

"It's him," he insisted quietly. "Da described him over and over. He didn't want me to forget. Again and again he'd tell me. The Beast, fur and fangs and a wolf's tail, but he stands on two legs like a man, *taller* than a man and muscled like a bear. Fast, Da said, very fast and speaking man's tongue one moment, howling like a beast the next. The slavering snout, the horns on his head. Eyes brighter than the summer sun and claws like daggers."

"You're trembling." At last David abandoned the painting. He strode back around the desk and studied Corbin with concern. "This was a bad idea. Here, shall we go?"

"No," Corbin replied. Taking a deep breath, he lifted his chin and met the Beast's laughing regard. "No. I am trembling." He could feel the quiver deep in his bones. "I thought it was *him*."

"It's not." David gripped Corbin's shoulder. Corbin realized he'd come to miss that small gesture, that stalwart reassurance. "Thomas ordered the painting brought up from deeper in the warren after you arrived. The painting and every book on demonology I could find in our collection. To study and plot and plan. This room—it's for you, Corbin. It's your father's coin at work. I thought it might make you feel better to see what's being done for your benefit."

"For my benefit," Corbin echoed. Abruptly, he turned his back on both David and the painting. His flesh prickled to have the beast out of his line of sight, but he ignored the sensation, instead looking around the room.

It wasn't a large space, although the ceiling was higher than seemed reasonable. The chamber was spherical, a bubble left in the earth. Corbin wondered if the great worm *la Tarasque* had once coiled there, dreaming, before turning about once again and burrowing through the ground. The blue flame in the torch gave off a brighter light than any Corbin had seen before, illuminating the space as efficiently as midday sun.

There were shelves against every wall, made crooked by the rounded floor. Books of many sizes were arranged neatly on the shelves. The outwardly facing spines were made of leather or linen; a few were bound in black-and-white horse-hair. Corbin, drifting closer, squinted to read their titles, but most of the symbols were beyond his comprehension, the shapes unfamiliar. He wondered if he was looking at the written language of the Jews, the Hebrew David had mentioned.

Scrolls were piled neatly on the floor between shelves. Bound with pieces of ribbon and leather, many looked dangerously old and delicate. Corbin passed them by, afraid he'd disturb their equilibrium only by breathing too hard. He stopped to examine a small oaken chest sitting on the floor directly behind the painting. The chest was plain, long and narrow, unadorned except for an exceptionally large padlock hanging open on the latch.

"Is that—" Corbin faltered, blinking. "It looks like gold."

"It is," David said. "And a more foolish extravagance I've yet to encounter. Gold is soft and easily bent or broken. Not the sort of metal one would generally choose for a padlock. Still, it's lovely, isn't it? Someone paid a fortune to have that made."

Corbin crouched. The golden padlock was decorated top to bottom with tiny faces. Corbin examined them minutely, nose scrunched.

"Are they laughing or screaming?"

"Hard to tell," David answered. He'd drifted back in front of the canvas. When he spoke, his voice seemed distorted by the painting into something rough and unfriendly. "According to our records, the chest came with the painting, from Ypres."

"What's inside?"

"Nothing at the moment. Open it," David suggested. "Tell me what you think."

Corbin was still young enough not to believe in premonitions. But both his hands shook so when he reached to flip the latch that he paused in trepidation. Frowning, he opened and closed his fingers, clenching his fists and releasing again until the muscles responded as expected.

"Well?" David prompted.

Corbin opened the chest. He looked down onto old velvet the color of emeralds, stretched over padding. Strands of horsehair and down poked through the nap. The case was old and ill used, coming apart at the edges where cushion met wood, but the imprint of sword-on-velvet was startlingly clear, a reverse image pressed into viridian nap, from the edges of the absent weapon's blade to the inverse etchings on the hilt.

"Oh," breathed Corbin.

"I thought so." At last David came around from behind the beast. He stood a respectful two paces away from the chest, but his expression was eager. "Does it fit?"

It did, of course. When Corbin pulled Da's sword from its scabbard on his back and laid it in the chest, it matched the impression perfectly. Velvet embraced the sword's edges and curves, welcoming an old friend. The case made Da's old sword beautiful and turned it into a weapon far more impressive than the battered blade Corbin knew from childhood.

"What does it mean?" he demanded.

David's excitement was palpable in the fluttering of his short robes.

"It means Thomas hasn't lost his eye for treasure. From what little I've gathered, that chest was meant to contain an afreet glaive. The chest came with the painting, as I said, but empty. According to the Dom in Ypres, they'd never seen the missing sword. The chest came to them empty."

"An afreet glaive." Corbin thought of Marie-Louise. Here was proof that she'd spoken true. "A weapon meant to slay demons." Corbin curled his hand on his thigh, hoping the hurt he felt didn't show in his voice. It was childish to feel betrayed, he reminded himself. And he hadn't been a child for years, never mind the two days he'd spent sulking underneath his blanket. "You knew. Why didn't you say something from the beginning?"

"Thomas suspected," David said. "He's an eye for treasure, especially unusual treasure. He noticed the blade immediately, but he didn't want to worry you."

"Worry me?" Corbin exclaimed. "But this is good news!" He felt dizzy with relief. For the first time since Mother's death, he felt real hope. "This is very good news!" When David didn't reply at once, Corbin looked around. "Isn't it?"

"Yes," said David. Then he sighed. "And, though it pains me to say it, also no."

"A blade like that belongs at court," Sir Thomas said. "No matter how your father got ahold of it, and I shudder to think what foolishness landed an enchanted blade on a cheese monger's belt. It's the crown's property. By all good reason, it should already be on the road to Fontainebleau."

He sat with Affrodille and Corbin in the main hall. They'd chosen a corner of the boards closest to the hearth and were warming their hands over flagons of hot cider. Angry winds rattled the château's turrets, sneaking through gaps in the roof, snuffing torches and making cressets all but useless. Layers of snow settled in the corridors, blown in through lancets. Page boys hurried about the halls, trying in vain to tack battered window tapestries back in place against the storm.

Laurie and Marc played a quiet game of dice one table over. They hunched together beneath blankets carried down from the lads' dormitory. Both wore their cowls tucked around their throats and over their faces like highway robbers. Marc was blessed with a pair of fingerless flannel gloves sent from his attentive mother in Caen. The gloves were soft and toasty warm; they also covered the scars on the backs of his hands. Laurie teased Marc mercilessly about his "mittens" even as his own fingers turned purple in the cold, but Marc only laughed as he tossed the dice. From the sound of things, the burned man was well ahead in the game.

The matched sisters were nowhere to be seen, and David had vanished immediately after delivering Corbin to his master.

"I warned David he should let it lie," Affrodille said in disgust, leaning close, as if the howl of the wind against stone didn't already muffle their hushed conversation. "If he had just let it alone, we'd still be safely speculating. But now he's gone and shoved the proof in front of our noses."

Sir Thomas hummed. "David always has his own reasons. Could be this time his reasoning is sound. Corbin deserves to know what he has."

"What he doesn't have!" Affrodille thumped her knuckles on the boards, making cider slosh in Corbin's flagon. The hearth light was unkind to her face, thinning it and putting dark shadows like bruising under her eyes. She had a bruise on her neck in truth, Corbin noted distantly, a red-and-purple blotch mottling the flesh just below her ear, exposed by the tight braid down her back.

"Sword's not his any longer, is it?" Affrodille continued. "It's the crown's, by all rights. Now we know for sure we have to send it on or be hanged for treason. David's gone and lost Corbin any hope he had of surviving Littleton's devil. Might as well just send him back to his daddy with our apologies."

"No," said Corbin. He felt flushed, too hot, despite the shivering of his companions around him. "I'm not going back home. And the sword's mine. Da's, I mean, but mine to use until the Beast is dead. I'm not giving it up."

"You have to." Affrodille's mouth set. "It's part of a set, don't you understand? A very powerful quartet, given long ago to the House of Capet by an important Saracen prince. There are legends about those swords, stories written down in books we have here, in our *libraries*. They're meant to protect the royal bloodlines, not a cheese merchant's son with farmers for family."

"Affrodille," Sir Thomas cautioned. "Not every man is lucky enough to be born into title."

"I know!"

One table over, Marc and Laurie paused in their gaming, then resumed hastily when Sir Thomas glared.

"Don't you think I know, master? But, and I'm sorry, Corbin, I'm not willing to risk my head for the troubles of a backward hamlet. Not even for a chance at ridding the world of an ugly devil. The lord of the black forest has kept himself relatively harmless for generations, and he's hardly a singular occurrence." She picked up her flagon then set it down again, cider untouched. "I'm sorry, but David's forced my hand. The sword goes back to Fontainebleau where it belongs, Littleton looses a few more cattle to wolves, and we keep our heads. And if Corbin's got any sense, he'll run as far inland as his legs will take him."

"Cattle!" Corbin cried, rising from the bench. "My family is not cattle! My mother was not cattle! Apologize at once!" He knew better than to strike a woman, even a woman with soldiering skills, but his muscles ached with the effort of holding back. Rage made him grind his teeth.

"I'm sorry," Affrodille said, regret clear in the slump of her shoulders. "I didn't think. I only meant—"

"Corbin, sit down," Sir Thomas ordered. Marc and Laurie had abandoned their gaming. They drifted closer. With an impatient gesture, the chevalier bade them to sit as well. "Calm yourself. The sword's staying. Corbin's staying."

"Sir!" Affrodille stiffened. "If word gets out—"

"And why would word get out?" the chevalier demanded. "Who will carry tales of the farmer's enchanted sword to the throne? Who here? You, Affrodille? No, I thought not. You value your life too highly. Marc? Laurie? I wish Corbin de Beaumont and his weapon to remain our secret, at least for the time being. Which of you will betray my desires?"

"No, sir!" Laurie murmured. "Not me, sir!"

Beneath the fold of his cowl, Marc's eyes were grave. "You have my word, Sir Thomas."

"Exactly." Sir Thomas took a swallow of his drink. "And that, Affrodille, is why White Hill continues to survive and thrive at the throne's pleasure. There are many secrets here, many more than you'd like to know, and it's our duty—my duty—to determine which are His Majesty's concern and which are not. The king is a very busy man, and his head should not be troubled."

"Sir." Corbin didn't remember sitting. His right hand was clenched around the pommel of Da's sword, his left gripping the table's edge. "Thank you, sir."

"Don't thank me yet," said Sir Thomas. "You've been here two full turns of the moon, and all I've determined is you're hardly worthy of the blade. Why, David told me you cowered, unarmed, in front of a painting like my own nan in front of my uncle's ghost, and didn't think to reach for your sword at all."

AFTER THAT, Affrodille drilled Corbin mercilessly in swordsmanship. Often Marc and Laurie joined Corbin at his lessons. He took pleasure in their company. Marc had an innate skill with the sword. He was quick on his feet and bold. He knew how to step around Corbin's longer range, ducking beneath his arm or around his hip to tap or slap with the flat of his narrow sword. The blows stung Corbin's flesh and his pride both. Sometimes Marc, like a gnat buzzing unwelcome about a man's ear, succeeded in making Corbin lose his temper. Those contests always ended with both participants bloody and bruised while Affrodille, cussing up a storm, promised if they relinquished control but one more time she'd whip them both until they couldn't sit.

She never made good on her promise, and Corbin and Marc continued to occasionally turn a friendly match into messy brawling. Corbin would never admit it out loud, but he enjoyed having an opponent equal in temper and bravery. Dueling a living man was much more satisfying than striking Da's straw targets or parrying the ebony cane. The practiced attacks and defensive stances Corbin knew by rote were of no more use than dance steps when the burned man came at him in a fury. Corbin's body knew the battlefield waltz, but the buzz of anticipation in his blood and the threat of real danger to life and limb turned everything he thought he knew about swordsmanship on its ear. Following a good bout, as he washed grime and blood from his battered body with water warmed on the cook fires, he was grateful for the pain and the split flesh. He cataloged them as lessons learned, each skirmish survived fresh knowledge in his growing arsenal against the Beast.

If Marc taught Corbin how to use his body to its best advantage, Laurie schooled him in bravery. No one mentioned Corbin's mortifying reaction to the painted fiend, but he couldn't doubt his fellow students had taken his embarrassment to heart. He'd been miserable and ashamed until Laurie sat him down and proposed an antidote.

"Reflexes," Laurie insisted, grinning at Corbin's reddened cheeks. "A good soldier needs fantastic reflexes. Things happen very quickly in battle, unexpected things, frightening things. The trick is not to think, but to react, and to react correctly. There's no way you could have learned the way of it before now, unless you'll tell me the famous Camembert took to attacking you on molding day."

Corbin rolled his eyes. "Of course not."

"Well, then." Laurie slapped Corbin's thigh. "Don't be so hard on yourself. Reflexes. We'll fix them right up. I know exactly what you need."

Corbin tried not to let wariness show. "And what's that then, Laurie?"

The other man's puckish grin grew wide. "It's simple. Didn't I just say? *Reflexes.* We need to wake them up!"

CORBIN NEVER LEARNED how Laurie procured all the props for his newfound entertainment, but he came to suspect David had a hand in many of them. The plate-size spider, certainly, must have come from somewhere in White Hill's warrens. Corbin didn't scream when Laurie and Dot dropped it on him from the main hall rafters, but it was a near thing. The arachnid corpse landed directly atop Corbin's head, soaking his cap with pickling fluids, before flopping to the flagstones, pincers dripping. It happened late after dinner when Corbin, exhausted from a day spent battling Affrodille's blade and fists, wasn't at his clearheaded best.

He'd never been afraid of spiders before, but he'd never seen one so large, not even in the briars closest to the black forest. The thing was heavy enough to smart when it crashed into his skull, and years after, he would swear to any who listened the corpse moved, skittering back and forth on the stone floor, green eyes wheeling. He didn't scream, but he did stomp the thing to ichor and mush beneath his bootheels, snarling all the while. Only Dot and Marc and Mary-Louise together kept him from doing the same to Laurie.

In the shock of it all, he didn't remember to draw his sword. Which, as Laurie pointed from a safe distance away, only proved the point.

The next morning Sir Thomas's cook, a genial woman who preferred working to speaking, handed Corbin his breakfast trencher with a smile, then proceeded to assault him with her favorite ladle. Gobsmacked, Corbin spilled eggs and toast all down his front. By the time he'd gathered enough sense to dodge the cook's barrage, the woman had managed to land several enthusiastic blows about his arms and shoulders. Corbin got Da's sword out in time to block her next swing and retained enough sense not to run her through. The cook went back to work, and Laurie smiled at Corbin through a mouthful of eggs.

"Sometimes enemies look like friends," he said. "It's said the Beast can change form. Better distrustful than dead."

"From man to wolf and back again!" Corbin shouted, massaging bruises. "I'll not go about drawing blade on every old woman who looks at me sideways!"

Laurie, still chewing, only shrugged.

It became entertainment in the dreariness of winter: the château's new favorite sport. No place on White Hill was safe for Corbin. Page boys leaped at him from behind tapestries on his way to breakfast. Chambermaids popped up in the library from seemingly nowhere during his studies and tried to clobber him with the thickest tome at hand, giggling all the while. Marc appeared once in the armory garbed head to toe as a lumbering bear while Corbin was digging through the racks for a dirk to replace his jeweled knife. Corbin, now used to unpleasant surprises, laughed like a madman but not before he'd cut the ursine mask to shreds and bloodied Marc's nose in warning.

Marc didn't jump out at him again. Corbin wasted time

searching for signs of hidden passageways behind the château's walls. He never found any. The ridiculous feints continued off and on through yule, waxing and waning in frequency, until Corbin walked always at the ready. Da's sword came to his hand even when Laurie let go a sack of living bog serpents on his bare feet as he bathed, shivering, in the lads' dormitory one cold morning. Six of the venomous serpents met their fate skewered by Da's sword. Three escaped into the château. Sir Thomas gave Laurie a severe dressing down, everyone on White Hill jumped at shadows for months after, and it wasn't just Corbin who learned to sleep with one eye open.

As Christmas approached, the château became a merry place. Sir Thomas ordered swathes of fir and holly brought up from the city below and hung from the rafters. The boughs made the château smell like a forest, and the holly, with its glossy green leaves and bright red berries, brightened White Hill considerably. Dot and Mary-Louise gathered pieces of dropped greenery and used them to make a kissing ball. They sang quiet hymns as they wove holly and fir together, voices as well matched as their faces. Marc found a bit of ribbon somewhere in the warren, the sort of silk embellishment meant to adorn a hat or tunic, and used it to suspend the festive decoration from a beam in the middle of the main hall. Marc promptly claimed kisses from both sisters as his reward. Mary-Louise and Dot complied with enthusiasm. Corbin, watching the flirtation, felt a twist of uncomfortable warmth in his stomach when Marc sighed his pleasure loudly into Mary-Louise's mouth.

"You've gone red as the berries," Laurie said from where he sat on a bench. He'd been struggling over a scroll meant to contain a recipe to cure moon madness, muttering as he did so, but now he smiled at Corbin in sympathy. "Far too long since you've had a woman, I imagine."

"I—yes. No!" Corbin blinked. He thought involuntarily of Nell and her infant.

Laurie chuckled. Under the kissing ball, Dot pinched Marc's ass. The burned man smirked, obviously enjoying the attention, and slung an arm over Mary-Louise's shoulder, whispering in her ear, making her laugh. Corbin knew he shouldn't stare, but he couldn't quite tear his gaze away.

"Sir Thomas is usually such a stickler," Laurie rambled on. "Not that it isn't his right. We're here to work not play. But we're red-blooded men and women, and he knows it. One or twice during the year, he give us leave to visit Honnefleu's most interesting street, if you know what I mean."

"Of course I do!" Corbin crossed his arms over his chest. He stared at the toes of his boots so he wouldn't have to see Marc swagger from the hall, both the matched sisters in tow. "Littleton may be small, but we're not lacking in whores."

Laurie twitched on his bench. "Best not call them that to their faces. Honnefleu's prostitutes are practically nobility. Hey, now." He nudged Corbin's ankle with his foot. "Christmas is a fine time to ask the master for leave to go. I've a particular house I enjoy. It's clean and safe. I'll take you, if you like. I'd say you've earned it, after the cock-up with the serpents."

"No." Corbin squeaked. He hadn't thought it was possible to turn any redder, but it felt as if his blood was boiling in his cheeks. "No, but thank you." He marshaled his courage and peeked at Laurie, expecting scorn, but the other man was looking away and across the room. David had wandered into the hall, cap crooked atop his curls, nose buried as usual in an open book. The scholar leaned, groping for and missing a slice of smoked meat off the nearest boards, before shifting sideways under the sphere of holly and fir. David's spectacles had slid halfway down his nose. A small furrow creased his brow. As Corbin and Laurie watched, he reached up and rubbed the curls at the nape of his neck, mouth pursing in concentration, snack forgotten.

Laurie puffed out a breath. "Now there's a sight. Right under the bloody ball, like he's done it on purpose. I'd try it, too, but that one's not for kissing or any of the rest of it. Lads or lasses, doesn't matter, I hear he's rebuffed anyone who dared try. That includes yours truly, and I'll have you know, there's not many who say no to *me*. I've got a reputation."

Corbin tried to keep shock off his face, but Laurie rarely missed anything.

"Oh," he drawled. Then he cackled, making David close his book and glance their way. "That's a new one on you, is it? None of Littleton's whores the bearded sort? Oh, well. Don't look so alarmed. There's all sorts of people in this world, Corbin, and that's what makes it interesting."

The warmth in Corbin's gut and the fever in his cheeks had spread to burn in a painful knot behind his rib cage. He coughed, trying to dislodge the constriction around his heart. Laurie kicked him in the shin again.

"Breathe, friend," he said. "You look like you've swallowed your tongue. Breasts or beard, it makes no difference to me. Come down to Honnefleu after Christmas, and we'll find something you like."

"Thank you," Corbin managed stiffly. "I appreciate… thank you, but no. I mean to say: not just yet. Or rather, the truth of it is, I'm not one for wh—prostitutes." The last word ended on an undignified squeak.

Laurie's pale brows rose. He looked as if he wanted to say more, but Corbin fled before he could formulate a response. He marched beneath the kissing ball, past David and a blatantly eavesdropping page boy, and up the spiral staircase to the lads' dormitory. There he kicked off his boots, unbuckled Da's sword, and threw himself onto his mattress. After pulling his blanket up past his nose, Corbin squeezed his eyes shut and tried to marshal his frantically galloping heart into some semblance of calm.

Laurie's unique battle schooling proved itself worthwhile two days before Christmas in the most unexpected of ways. Sir Thomas, busy in his library with David, sent Affrodille into Honnefleu to retrieve a package just come into port aboard a ship from across *la manche*. The morning was clear and beautiful, and the sky was purple above the muddy Seine. Snow sparkled on the ground, and for once, the perpetually angry wind was quiet. Corbin was at loose ends and suffering pangs of homesickness and boredom. When Affrodille hunted him down and suggested he accompany her into port, he accepted her invitation with acumen.

It was mild enough that Corbin would have liked to walk the road into town, but Sir Thomas desired his mysterious package as soon as possible. When they reached White Hill's small stable, Jenny was bridled and waiting patiently while Affrodille's mount—a large black gelding—seemed intent on trampling the stable boy attached to the other end of its reins. Jenny's big ears swiveled toward Corbin in what he hoped was recognition. He'd visited the donkey once or twice since they'd arrived together at the château, always with a treat in hand, but for the most part, he'd been too busy to give her the attention she deserved. He was glad to see she looked glossy and fat. When he swung a leg over her back, her girth was considerably wider than he recalled.

Affrodille cowed her ride with a word and a glare before launching herself from the stable boy's hands into the saddle. The horse danced in place, sawing its head back and forth against the bit. When Affrodille clucked it forward, it kicked out at nothing before breaking into an up and down canter. Corbin was glad of the snow on the ground. Jenny was sure-footed as any of her kind, but if they'd been battling bare ice on flagstone, Affrodille could have been in real danger. He'd once seen a horse go down atop its liveried rider on the king's icy highway between Littleton and the black forest. In its thrashing, the fallen animal had crushed the soldier's legs and pelvis. Too broken even to attempt a wagon ride back to Paris, the soldier had lingered for several agonizing days in the room above Henri's shop before finally succumbing to sepsis.

"Be careful!" Corbin called after Affrodille, the old memory making him shake his head. He kicked Jenny into a trot. "There may be ice under the snow!"

Affrodille, laughing, turned her horse in a circle on the road. "He's barefoot. Only city folk are stupid enough to shoe their horses come the first freeze. He won't fall. Save your concern for your donkey. She looks like she's likely to fall into a doze midstride."

Corbin made a rude gesture he'd only recently learned from Marie-Louise. Affrodille reined the gelding alongside Jenny. The big horse gnashed its teeth, whinnying protest. Jenny flicked an ear.

"She's an unusual specimen," Affrodille puzzled. "I've never seen one with a mane quite that light in color. The stable boy calls her Dame Polie, did you know? He says she's the only animal in the stable that doesn't call and fuss at graining time. Someone taught her manners."

"Not the Benedictine," Corbin decided. "If he was a Dom to begin with. Whoever he was, he didn't know horses. He pulled on her mouth and was cruel about it."

Affrodille grunted thoughtfully. "She's better off with us then, I suppose. Come now, Dame Polie, try to keep up. The master is depending on our haste."

"Do you know what it is?" Corbin asked as they left the château behind. "The thing we're to retrieve?"

"I used to try and guess," Affrodille said. "When I first joined the master's house. But you'll see errands into port are frequent enough—especially in spring and summer when sailing is good—as to become common and boring. Once I thought it was a crate of chicken eggs I was carrying up the hill." She snorted, making her gelding balk. When she'd got the animal back under control again, she winked at Corbin. "Turns out it was a crate of basilisk eggs instead. Only my good luck they didn't decide to hatch halfway through Honnefleu. After that, I stopped wondering and concentrated instead on delivering quickly."

"Basilisk eggs?" Corbin suspected Affrodille was teasing him but couldn't be sure. Beneath the edge of her hood, both her eyes and her lovely mouth were smiling. He didn't think she was laughing at him or making mock of his naïveté. She sat her mount with a confidence that made the difficult gelding look easy, surveying their surroundings with professional enjoyment. "What happened to them?"

"Believe me when I say I don't want to know and I didn't ask. Once I passed them over they became Thomas's problem or David's, and good riddance." She lifted her chin, sniffing appreciatively at the crisp air. "But now you've reminded me: this is your first time off the hill since you joined us?"

Corbin nodded. The farther along the road they went, the more excited he became. The château loomed on the rock at their backs, sunlight gleaming on the turrets. There were pennants flying from two of the tallest pinnacles, undulating blue and silver. Corbin had known the colors were there but had not paid them much attention during endless hours of swordplay in White Hill's courtyard. They were impressive even from a distance, brilliant against the blue sky. He could hear the snap of fabric when they were caught in an occasional high breeze.

The road wrapped once around the hill, sheer stone against Corbin's right shoulder and a slant of snow and pine to his left, before shooting wide and straight toward Honnefleu and the Seine. Four more pennants, much smaller and set into the ground by way of tall iron stakes, hung quiet where White Hill's road ended and Honnefleu's streets began.

Affrodille caught Corbin studying the pennants and pulled up to let him look his fill. "The sigil belongs to the château, not Sir Thomas. But White Hill's not old, and the sigil's stamped in books David says are older even than France. No one knows where it came from. Ever seen its like before?"

She seemed honestly curious so Corbin leaned across Jenny's withers and pinched the point of one pennant between thumb and forefinger, unfurling the flag. The blue background and foreground pattern of silver fleur-de-lis was familiar. The escutcheon set center-wise and bearing a silver key crossing a single white feather was not.

"Never." Corbin couldn't help but admire the needlework. He knew talent when he saw it. The embroidery was obviously quite old, but the pattern was still clear and beautiful in its simplicity. "What does it mean?"

"No one's sure about that, either, although David could theorize your ear off. Something about wisdom and innocence or mayhap Saint Peter."

"Saint Peter." Corbin released the pennant. Looking back over Jenny's rump, he stared up the road at White Hill, perched on a spur of stone. He had a vague recollection of Nan teaching Beauty and Hope a parable about Peter and a chapel built atop the highest rock. "Saint Peter and basilisks. You're full of comedies today, Affrodille."

His companion chuckled. "If you say so. On we go. If you're quick, I'll buy you a Christmas pie along the way."

CHAPTER 10

Snow was thick on the ground in Honnefleu, caught in drifts between houses and trees. The flowers and lush vegetation Corbin remembered from his first trip through were now wilted and brown, defeated by frost. Snowmelt turned to mud on the gelding's legs and on Jenny's belly. The sky reflected in the Seine had a dull brown cast. Dribbles of icy water ran like rain off rooftops onto people hurrying past. Winter had finally gripped the port city. Villagers, sailors, and tradesmen alike were wrapped head to toe against the cold. Those who had stopped to enjoy a meal or an exchange of news huddled in groups, warming fingers over Honnefleu's cressets.

It would have been a dreary scene but for the spirit of Christmastide. Honnefleu embraced the season with an extravagance Corbin hadn't imagined possible. Garlands of fir and holly were strung from roof to roof. Colorful wreathes made of citrus, cinnamon sticks, and glossy ever-green leaves decorated windows and doors. Cinnamon was a costly spice, rare in Littleton for all of Henri's wishful missives sent to the merchants in Paris. The baker, had he known the sticks were being used just a few days north as festive embellishment, would likely have dropped dead of an apoplexy over his rolling pin.

There were boys in pointed caps selling roasted chestnuts in bags, and others with trays of mincemeat pies hung around their necks. The miniature pastries steamed in the morning, smelling delightfully of Christmas. Corbin's heart squeezed with renewed homesickness.

"Keep to the right," Affrodille warned. "Foot traffic's on the other side."

As far as Corbin could determine, foot traffic was everywhere, left and right and in between, overflowing the road in and out of shop doors and up the smaller side streets. For safety's sake, he set Jenny's nose to the black gelding's tale and followed Affrodille as closely as he dared. The gelding, contrary to everything Corbin knew about horses, had calmed in the press of people and now trotted forward meekly as a lamb. Corbin understood the animal's reticence. Honnefleu's sheer energy and the roil of new sights and scents and sounds boggled the mind and made Corbin wish for Littleton's peaceful fields and wide, empty streets.

Somewhere up ahead a group of carolers began singing "In Dulci Jubilo." A man walking alongside Jenny coughed miserably and spat, just missing the boot of an old woman clutching a basket of bread to her chest. The woman sidestepped the glob of bloody sputum and disappeared into the crowd. The man, still choking on his own lungs, soon stopped to linger in front of a merry cresset. Men and women around the flames parted to give the fellow plenty of room, averting their faces. In Littleton, Corbin mused, someone would have taken note of the poor man's condition and tucked him up somewhere warm with a healthful posset.

"You're frowning," Affrodille said over her shoulder. "Like

a miss who's just swallowed a lemon when she expected the sweetest orange. City life not for you after all?"

"City living never was," Corbin replied. "I've no interest in the wide world, not since I was a boy with too much time on his hands. My only concern is my family and Littleton."

He wondered if Affrodille looked briefly disappointed. Before he could be certain, she turned off the main street and toward the Seine. The new road was as busy as the previous, but the people were of a different sort. Corbin saw men who reminded him of Da before the Beast: well-heeled tradesmen with a ship to meet or a wagon pointed toward a distant hamlet. Sailors walked alone or in groups, tanned and tattooed and plagued by that drunken gate Corbin knew meant they were not long on land. And there were plenty of soldiers in blue capes intent on the king's business. Several glanced Affrodille's way as she passed, tipping their chins in recognition and quiet respect.

They know her, Corbin realized. *They know she belongs to White Hill. Some day she'll put on the blue, be one of them.*

As they made their way toward Honnefleu's bay—that deep, natural basin on the Seine seemingly made to make a seafaring captain smile—Corbin began to count ships. He glimpsed them first by their masts, but soon enough, he could see their painted hulls. His pulse raced at their magnificence. For all their massive size and frightening creaks and groans, Corbin found the ships fantastic. Their exotic shapes and sizes, so unlike the fishing boats Corbin sometimes spotted off Littleton's cliffs, seemed so unreal as to be ethereal.

"We want *The Golden Borne,*" Affrodille announced, urging her gelding off the road and onto a large pier built along the water on beam and stone. "She's large, with a painted porpoise on her hull, so she shouldn't be hard to miss. Shout if you see her."

Corbin nodded and forebear to mention he didn't know a porpoise from a pincushion. He entertained himself with keeping Jenny from running into the many ropes and pulleys tethering ship to pier. A few of the hulls they rode past were patched and badly weathered. Corbin couldn't help but suppose Da had once laid eyes on the same ships: *The Jolly Mac* or *King Philip's Lass* or an old single-mast cog christened simply *Lady Rose*. Smaller boats bobbed on the water between ships. Most were the one-sailed skiffs used for fishing the river, but there were also rowboats packing cargo to and from the pier. Men shouted back and forth over the water, calling insult or encouragement.

"I see her," Affrodille exclaimed, pulling up. "But she's docked out on the scaffold. We'll have to walk." She swung out of the saddle, put two fingers to her mouth, and let loose a shrill whistle. A lass no older than Hope split from the crowd, jogging forward to take the gelding's reins. The urchin had a rag in her hair and a silver ring in her ear, and she had the grubby appearance of one who washed only twice a year and then in the muddy Seine.

"The donkey, too," Affrodille instructed. "A denier and two pasties if you keep the big black out of mischief."

The child licked chapped lips. "Yes, missus. I will. Thank you, missus."

"Good." Affrodille strode away, gesturing at Corbin to hurry.

Corbin handed Jenny to the little lass, essaying a smile. "What's your name?" he asked.

"Lizzie." Ignoring the gelding's impatient shifting, she patted Jenny's muzzle as she scrutinized Corbin. "Are you from the castle on the hill then?"

"Yes." The crowd was closing behind Affrodille's back, but Corbin lingered, digging in the purse at his belt.

Lizzie wrinkled her nose. "My mum says the castle is

haunted and full of dead people all dressed in white." She took the handful of coins Corbin offered with a somber nod. "Is that true?"

"No," said Corbin. But when Lizzie's face fell, he hastened to add: "Only some of them dress in white. The rest go about in wisps of smoke, rattling chains."

The child squealed in delight, causing Jenny to swivel both ears in alarm. Corbin calmed the donkey with a pat before hurrying on in search of Affrodille. He was still grinning ear to ear when he caught her. She shook her head and rolled her eyes.

"The little pirate charmed you out of extra coin."

"She reminds me of my sister. One of them anyway. Is she really a pirate?" Corbin was delighted.

"Close enough as to make no difference. She's one of the Growler's gang," Affrodille grumbled. Then she pointed across the remainder of the pier. "There's the ship we want, anchored out in the deepest water. How are you at walking the scaffold?"

Corbin eyed the narrow floating walkway with interest. "Are the logs just laid atop the water? What keeps them from sinking beneath man or wagon?"

"How should I know? I'm training to be a soldier not a merchant marine. I get seasick on a mill pond." Affrodille stepped onto the scaffold. The logs were planed flat to prevent a person from slipping. On closer examination, Corbin realized they were lashed together with rope. They rocked gently when Corbin tried his weight, settling in the water, but remained remarkably buoyant.

"*Fantastique!* A road upon the very river!"

"Don't fall in," Affrodille cautioned. "And if you do, save the sword."

Corbin only laughed. Sea birds wheeled overhead, dancing across the blue sky, and the Seine ran beneath his feet, purling away toward the sea. He lifted his brow to the winter sun and felt its tepid caress on his cheeks, a blessing.

The Golden Borne was a very large ship. Anchored at the farthest end of the scaffold, she proudly sported two soaring masts and castles fore and stern. The "porpoise" painted on her hull looked to Corbin like a gigantic trout, although he couldn't help but admire its impressive nose. Her crew dashed up and down a plank running from deck to scaffold, unloading cargo into a series of slim two-wheeled wagons. A man in the rigging played a skirling tune on a whistle. When he noticed Affrodille down below, he broke the melody into three sharp squeaks of warning.

"Hello, the ship!" Forced by the procession of wagons to either stop or swim, Affrodille waved a hand at the deck. "You've a package for Sir Thomas Chevalier, and I've come to claim it."

Several of the sailors looked around in curiosity. One, burned brown, his slight frame corded with muscle, came down the plank in two long strides. He walked on the edge of the scaffold, skirting the line of wagons, lithe as any tree squirrel, somehow managing not to fall into the basin. When he reached Affrodille, he had to cock his head to meet her eye. He did so with a hearty leer.

"I expected Sir Thomas hisself come to claim the tome, but you're a far sight better on the eyes, miss." The Englishman slapped a palm on his thigh. "A women in trews, bless me, and don't you wear them well."

Corbin put his hand on Da's sword, drawing the sailor's attention. Either Corbin's height or the censure on his face made the sailor back up a pace, but his eyes never lost their merry twinkle.

"Sorry, lad," he said. "Didn't mean insult to you nor your woman."

"I'm my own woman," Affrodille said while Corbin was

trying to decide whether he was required to break the little sailor's nose. "I dress for ease of movement not your lecherous glances." Crossing the space between them, she pressed the point of a knife to the Englishman's jugular. Corbin, for all his improved reflexes, hadn't seen Affrodille draw the blade, nor was he sure where it had come from. "The package, if you will. I'd like to be home and in front of the fire before it snows again."

The sailor wet his lips with his tongue. His pulse beat visibly against the tip of Affrodille's knife but not, Corbin thought, with fear. "It's there," the man said, flapping fingers at the line of wagons. "Second cart in, wrapped in leather and stamped with King Edward's wax. I was going to send it up the hill, with the next waif come along needing coin for supper, I promise you. Now will you let me up, lass, before the crew sees their captain brought low by a beautiful woman, and not, I assure you, in the normal way of it."

Affrodille's knife nicked brown skin, drawing forth a drop of blood. The Englishman grunted. His grin became a grimace, but he stood still as stone.

"Corbin," commanded Affrodille, "please retrieve Sir Thomas's parcel before this man is so foolish as to send it away with the next urchin?"

Corbin looked at the narrow strip of scaffold between the wagon and the river. He was much larger than the English captain and lacked the other man's practiced sea legs. Up on the deck of *The Golden Borne*, the crew had stopped their work and instead leaned on the ship's rails, watching their captain's dilemma with amused interest. When Corbin shook his head in resignation and began unbuckling Da's sword to save it from a dunking, the musician in the rigging played a mocking flourish on his pipe.

"No," said Affrodille. "Leave it on. You go into the water with that book in your arms the demon sword's the least of your troubles. Sir Thomas will hang you in the main hall and cut off your balls while you strangle."

The Englishman shot Corbin a look of honest horror. Corbin returned it in equal measure.

"Mayhap," he suggested, "one of this man's stalwart crew, men used to walking—"

"No," Affrodille repeated. "I've decided this man and his 'stalwart' crew aren't to lay their grubby fingers on the master's belongings again. Go and get it. Be nimble."

"Take off your boots," the Englishmen suggested while on the ship his sailors began a slow clapping. "Feel with your toes. Walk quick and keep your eyes up." He blanched as a second drop of blood followed the first down the curve of his throat.

Corbin sat on the scaffold. He yanked off his boots. He knew that he was being observed. He hated the weight of their judgment. When he fell in, he'd be made the laughing-stock. Even Sir Thomas's castigation was preferable.

When he stood again, the floating logs were cold and wet against the bottoms of his feet. The wood felt slimy, danger-ously slick with the remnants of slush. He measured the space between the wagon and the water again, a space no larger than a clenched fist, and knew without a doubt that if he tried to walk the wooden tightrope, he would quickly be swimming in the Seine.

The solution, when it came, was so glaringly obvious Corbin felt the fool for not grasping it at once. He was certain that everyone in sight, from Affrodille and the English captain to the methodically clapping sailors on the ship's deck to the fisherwoman drawing slowly close in her skiff, had set him a test of wits and were waiting with glee for him to fail.

I'd gone so far as to take off my boots!

Berating himself for a knot-head, Corbin hopped straight

up into the first wagon. The scaffolding bobbed under the shift of weight, making Affrodille adjust her stance, but the wagon remained solidly in the center of the floating road. It had a deep belly to make up for its narrow girth and was packed from stem to stern with lettuces. Corbin crawled his way over bunches of kale. When he reached the back of the first wagon, he peered into the second. The clapping overhead had become real applause, the previous buffoonery abated. The piper on the mast played a jig.

"Do you see it?" Affrodille inquired calmly. "Is it there?"

The parcel was just as the captain had described it: the size of a large book, wrapped in old leather, burnished skin stamped with the English king's approval. Corbin had to squirm his way into the second wagon to reach it. He clutched the package in both arms as he crawled back along the wagon line, protecting it from lettuce leaf and newly falling snow. When he clambered back onto the scaffolding *The Golden Borne*'s crew began to stamp and whistle in approval. Their laughter rang unpleasantly in Corbin's ears.

Affrodille released the Englishman. She relieved Corbin of his burden.

"Put on your boots," she said. "It's time to go."

Corbin did as she ordered, rage and embarrassment shivering across his body. The captain, grown wise, disappeared back the way he had come, walking the edge of the scaffold as if it were a simple act and not one requiring preternatural grace.

"Tell Sir Thomas I congratulate him on his household," the man called as he jogged up the plank. "There's hope for France yet."

Corbin shadowed Affrodille back across the scaffold and onto the pier in silence. When they stepped off the floating road onto more solid structure, Affrodille thrust the bundled book back into Corbin's arms.

"One moment," she said. "There's a pie boy there, and I promised the diminutive pirate food."

Corbin bristled. "Was this a joke, a prank? The haste, the parcel, all of it? Just a diversion? 'I've a dull errand to run. Let's see if I can convince Corbin to fall into the Seine'? Or no." He glowered. "It's Laurie again? I thought we were done. He said we were done. He'd tasked you to push me in? See if I kept my balance if you lobbed lettuce at my head?"

Affrodille put her hands on her hips. The knife she'd used to threaten the Englishman had disappeared once again.

"You're furious," she said. "Isn't that interesting?"

Corbin dug his fingers into leather wrappings. He thumb dislodged a piece of wax from the English king's seal. It fell to the pier, a scrap of red, and was trampled by a passing soldier. "You made me your fool."

"It wasn't a joke or a game," Affrodille said. "It was a test. David told me you dislike being laughed at. You're prideful or easily pricked. I don't know which. I've seen it in you some. The master had concerns. The ship"—she waved a hand—"the scaffold and the wagons, that was happenstance. I'll admit, I expected you to fail. As soon as those bastards on the deck started their clap and whistle, I knew I'd see you in the water. You'd flushed up like a tomato and stopped thinking straight, you were that angry. And anger's the deadliest of all weaknesses, Corbin, more deadly even than fear."

Corbin bit his tongue and looked away. Affrodille coughed, regaining his grudging attention.

"But you surprised me. You kept your senses about you in the end. You used your head." She stretched up and knuckled his head, smiling fondly. "You thought beyond the emotion, like a good soldier should. It was a test, yes. And you passed."

· · ·

Lizzie the pirate dropped both pairs of reins when she saw the mincemeat pies Affrodille carried. Luckily neither Jenny nor the gelding seemed inclined to make a dash for freedom. They, too, were eyeing the pasties with interest. When Affrodille broke off a bit of crust and let the black monster lip it from her palm, Corbin understood why.

"Spoiled," he chided before feeding Jenny a bit of his own pie. It was his fourth. He'd wolfed down three on the walk across the busy pier, burning his tongue on the filling. They were delicious. The donkey pricked her long ears forward and scraped the pier with her left foot, begging.

"How do you think I trained him to hand in the first place?" Affrodille collected the gelding's dropped reins and looped them back over his head. She smiled at Lizzie, then indicated a woman making her way in their direction. "That your mum?"

Lizzie, her mouth full of mincemeat, juices overflowing down her chin, nodded. "She has a gift for monsieur."

Corbin, engrossed in the last bites of lunch, glanced up in surprise. Affrodille muffled a snort, tossing Corbin a knowing smirk. "A yuletide gift? Isn't that *thoughtful*. You didn't say you were familiar with the lass's mum, Corbin."

Her implication was clear. Corbin refused to let temper get the best of him twice in one afternoon. He licked his fingers clean and then pasted on his best genial smile just as the woman reached his elbow. When she clicked her bare heels together and spread her skirts in a half curtsy, his pleasure turned genuine. Lizzie must be a pirate's brat for certain, for her mother was exactly as Corbin had always pictured a corsair's bride, from the feathers in her hair to the rings in her nose and ears. Her eyes were lined with kohl, her bare arms inked from wrist to elbow, and her skirts were cut from the same fabric Lizzie wore as a headscarf.

"Monsieur." She clicked her heels again. "A gift for you. In thanks." She held out both her hands, palms up. In her left, she held the coin Corbin had slipped Lizzie. On her right, coiled between her thumb and ring finger, rested what appeared to be a string of yellow beads.

"*Jésus*, Corbin," Affrodille groaned. "There's generosity and then there's stupidity. You'll get us mobbed, people hear you're handing out coin in fistfuls."

"No." Lizzie stamped one foot on the pier, exactly as Jenny had a few moments earlier. She showed Affrodille her slender back, beaming at Corbin instead. "Mum doesn't speak many words *à la français*, but she understands. We'll have full bellies tonight and tomorrow and the next day. Mayhap up till Christmas."

Lizzie's mum nodded so vigorously the feathers in her hair bobbed up and down. She closed her fingers around Corbin's gift then secreted the coins in her skirts. "*Merci*."

Using two fingers, she scooped the string of beads off her open palm and held them up to in display. Several people on the pier stopped their bustle and crossed themselves before hastening on. Their reaction drew Affrodille's attention. She leaned in for a closer look.

"Shark's teeth," she said. "Quite a lot of them. From the same fish, I imagine. Is it a necklace? And what's that strung at the bottom?"

"They look like finger bones," Corbin offered, a sinking feeling in his gut.

"Mermaid's finger," Lizzie's mum said. She thrust the gruesome offering at Corbin until he was forced to take the necklace or risk being struck in the eye. "For protection."

"Protection?" asked Affrodille as pleased as if the strand was made of gemstone and gold. "If I may inquire: protection from what?"

The necklace felt warm and heavy in Corbin's hand. The ridged teeth were as large as the tip of his thumb. The finger bones were bleached dry. They rattled when he shifted.

"From ghosts," he ventured, looking at Lizzie for confirmation. "They've heard about haunts on White Hill, and I, ah, might have added fuel to the fire."

"Shark's teeth to frighten away the angry spirits," Lizzie explained as her mum bobbed and nodded. "Fingers of a mermaid to keep your heart from fear if the teeth don't work. Mum makes charms, for our family and for our friends. She learned from her mum, and her mum before. I'm learning, too, but I can't do protection yet. Just confusion, it's easier. And besides, we haven't seen a mermaid to catch for bones since I was a babe."

Affrodille's eyes were shining. Lizzie's mum poked a finger against Corbin's breastbone, making him twitch.

"For protection," she repeated, then mimed putting the necklace around his neck.

"Put it on," Lizzie said. "It's a gift, monsieur. Kindness for kindness."

"Thank you." Corbin hoped he kept dismay from his face as he settled the string around his neck. The bones fell against this heart. "Is there really such a thing as a mermaid?"

All three women looked at him in disbelief and pity.

"Don't be daft," Affrodille said. "Of a certain there are. Why, it's said William II took one secretly as his wife, and she lived safely hidden in his garden lake until his death. Sir Thomas has seen her portrait."

Lizzie's mum said something very quickly in a language Corbin didn't understand. Seeing his puzzlement, the lass translated: "She says mermaids are beautiful and powerful, very hard to resist. Sea devils disguised as women and difficult to kill. Their bones are also very powerful. You should wear the necklace always in your haunted castle."

"Thank you," repeated Corbin, touched in spite of the gift's grisly nature.

Lizzie and her mum nodded in unison, visibly pleased with the exchange of favors.

"Affrodille," he asked, when the pirate duo had retreated back into the crowd and he was once again astride Jenny's wide back, "what happened to King William's mermaid, the one in the lake, after he died?"

Affrodille shrugged as she pointed the gelding's nose back toward White Hill. "According to legend, she grew legs and walked back to the sea, naked but for the shroud of her long yellow hair."

CHAPTER 11

The dwarves came out of the snowdrift all at once, in an explosion of ice and frozen mud, of tooth and claw. They bellowed as they attacked, rushing straight at the gelding, clinging to his long black legs, trying to pull him down. Blood spattered against White Hill's rocky incline, turning snow pink. Affrodille yelled and reached for the sword on her back, but the gelding, eyes rolling in terror, began to scream and buck, and she couldn't quite get her hand around the hilt.

Jenny stood rooted in the middle of the road, ears flat against her skull, haunches quivering.

Daft animal, she's going to sit instead of flee, Corbin thought distantly as he threw himself off the jennet's back and into the sea of dwarves, sword flashing. *They'll strip her to a skeleton in minutes.*

He felt a twitch of fear for the animal even as he separated a gibbering dwarf from its ugly head. The dwarf's stocky body collapsed sideways, claws still grasping at air, black ichor fountaining in the afternoon. The dwarf's head, its gash of a mouth split in a toothy scream, tumbled off the side of the road into the pine forest below. The dwarf's company, briefly distracted by their brother's demise, turned their attention from Affrodille and her foundering horse. Growling, they advanced on Corbin. Their long gray tongues tested the air. Corbin, sword raised in defense, counted seven of the fetid little horrors. Like all of their kind, they were short—no taller than his kneecap—but preternaturally fast and concerned only with bringing down prey.

"Affrodille?" he queried, not daring to lift his eyes from the approaching pack.

It took her much longer than Corbin liked to answer. He almost gave in to temptation and looked around, but he knew from experience that as soon as he glanced away the dwarves would rush him. They watched him with a predator's intelligence, waiting for any sign of weakness, growling and muttering at the ichor on Da's sword.

"Affrodille!"

"Here." Pain made the word short and sharp. "No, don't turn! Stand your ground, lad. Give me a minute."

One of the dwarves was carrying a knife. It was a crude specimen, the bronze blade pocked and pitted in places. The dwarf held it awkwardly, hampered by the claws on its stubby fingers. Corbin had never heard of a dwarf using tools before. The flash of sunlight off metal looked wrong against the creature's leathery pelt.

"I can't reach my sword." Affrodille grunted. "Bloody bastard bit my leg and unhorsed me against the mountain. Get back on your donkey and ride to the château for help."

Corbin risked a quick peek over his shoulder and was astounded to see Jenny still standing where he'd left her.

"Corbin!"

He wheeled around just in time to turn the dwarf's bronze knife with the edge of his blade before the primitive weapon grazed his thigh. The dwarf shuffled sideways and backward, retreating before Corbin could regroup. Its fellows pressed closer until they stood just outside Corbin's reach, black eyes flat and watchful.

"You're hurt," Corbin said. "Are you hurt? I'm not leaving you, Affrodille. Undefended, your naught but a hearty dwarven supper."

"Dwarves," Affrodille groaned in disgust. "There haven't been dwarves in Honnefleu for a decade, not since Sir Thomas cleaned a nest from beneath the cobbler's shop. Dirty, disease-ridden, infant-stealing vermin. I never thought I'd meet one. What are they doing on White Hill?"

"Dying," Corbin said, resigned. He took a step forward, swinging Da's sword. The dwarves danced out of the way but held their ground in a growling knot. "Tell me you still have the book."

Affrodille's loud and creative swearing made the dwarves bristle and hiss. She swore until the breath caught audibly in her chest on a whimper.

"It went up the hill with Blackheart," she admitted, groaning again. "Fuck me. *My ribs.*"

"The good news," Corbin said, "is that dwarves are common as lice around Littleton, and I've had opportunity, once or twice, to kill three or four." He tested again, this time lunging to his right before slicing left. The group of dwarves bounced out of reach like a many-legged hare.

Affrodille didn't answer. Her breathing was loud and labored.

"Seven seems excessive," Corbin continued. He took two steps down the road. The dwarves scuttled after. He wouldn't be able to chase them away. Dwarves were too dull-witted to know caution and too mindlessly malevolent to abandon prey. They would press until they found an opening, and then they'd do their best to drag him down into the snow and off to their nest.

Just like Nell's mum.

Corbin edged two more strides back toward Honnefleu. He could see Affrodille now, as he'd hoped, slumped against the side of the hill, hugging her gut. Her eyes were closed, her beautiful mouth set in an agonized line. If not for the huff of her breathing, Corbin might have thought her dead.

"Affrodille!" he said with enough force to make the dwarves bare yellow fangs. "Stay awake! I can kill a pack of dwarves, but I can't carry you up White Hill by myself, and I'll not leave you here alone on the road."

"I'm fine!" Affrodille sounded almost as dangerous as the dwarves. Her eyes fluttered but didn't open. "Just get to it. "

Dwarves haven't the brain for language, but Corbin would swear later the little monsters understood the standoff was over. Before he so much as twitched a muscle, they were on him in a flurry of tooth and claw and barbed, venomous tongue. He roared a challenge, dancing in circles, trying to dodge, dislodge, and strike all at the same time. The dwarves clung to his legs like burrs, reaching for his sword arm. Their weight made Corbin stagger. His blade was useless while they tried to climb him, but the sword hilt made a very satisfying crunching sound when he reversed his aim and brought the pommel crashing down on the nearest dwarven crown. The stricken dwarf let go of Corbin's thigh and screeched as it landed in the snow. Corbin stomped hard on the creature's middle even as he crushed another skull with the butt of his sword.

He'd sent four tumbling to the ground, tramping hard on their limbs as they fell, when one of the dwarves managed to claw its way around his waist and up his spine, reaching with clawed fingers for his throat. Corbin wheeled and swatted but couldn't shake himself free. He craned his free arm around, capturing the dwarf's foot and pulling with all his strength, but he earned a gashed palm for the effort, and although he managed to stay the dwarf's climb, his distraction meant its two brothers wriggled farther up his legs, reaching for the softness of his belly.

"*Merde*, fuck me." Corbin released the dwarf's razor-sharp toes and reversed Da's sword again, this time holding the pommel in both hands as he brought the weapon over and down behind the back of his head with as much force as possible.

The blade speared the dwarf neatly from nape to ass bone but also stuck in the twitching corpse. When Corbin brought it back around to his front, he had one dwarf skewered like dinner on his weapon and another poised to rip out his gut. He envisioned his ignoble death between blue sky and white snow: bloody, disemboweled, and brought down by everyday vermin.

Da would rage. Nan would weep. Beauty would suffer the Beast's ire.

Corbin dropped his blade and used both hands to keep ward against the dwarf's seeking mouth.

I'm supposed to be better than this.

Affrodille's first knife took the dwarf on Corbin's thigh through one black eye. The dwarf convulsed and dropped away. Her second pierced Corbin's tunic and almost his finger before lodging in the final monster's side. The dwarf mewled, shuddered, and went limp, coughing black fluid down the front of Corbin's groin. Corbin pushed it off and into the snow before proceeding to retch up lunch all over his boots.

"You were right," Affrodille said. "Three or four you'd have killed easily, but seven is excessive."

Corbin wiped his mouth with a bleeding hand. He straightened, hoping embarrassment didn't show in his face, and regarded Affrodille where she stood in the middle of the road, propped upright against Jenny's sturdy neck, a third dagger poised and ready.

"You're amazing—*mon Dieu*, thank you."

"You're welcome." Smiling small, Affrodille swept Corbin from top to bottom with an assessing eye. She nodded. "Clean your sword. Let's get on with it. You won't have to carry me up the hill, but your donkey may, and it's possible I'll pass out before we reach the top. There may be more of that nest about."

Corbin hurried to do as she ordered. He had to put a booted foot against the speared dwarf's skull and shove before he could yank Da's sword free. Bones cracked while fresh black ichor smoked in the snow.

"Ugh." Corbin shuddered at the stink. "Filthy animals." He sheathed his blade before hastening to Affrodille's side, shaking his head at Jenny as he did so. "And this one frozen in fear again. Someday, jennet, you'll wish you had the wits to flee."

"Your donkey has the heart of a lion," Affrodille proclaimed, groaning as Corbin helped her onto Jenny's back. "She's worth her weight in gold, this one." She slapped Jenny on the neck in fond recognition then clutched at her middle, bowing her head in resignation.

"If you let me fall once I've fainted," she warned through clenched teeth, "I promise you I'll have your hide when I wake."

SIR THOMAS MET them in the château's courtyard beneath darkening skies. He'd obviously just come from the direction of the stables as he had Affrodille's panniers hung over one arm. When he saw Jenny and her burden, the chevalier dropped the panniers. He ran across the flagstone.

"What happened? Is she alive?" Sir Thomas shoved

Corbin out of the way and reached for Affrodille. She roused enough to slap his hand away when he felt for the pulse in her neck.

"Dwarves," she groused, pushing herself upright, one elbow braced against the donkey's neck. "Lurking in the snow, halfway up the hill."

"Where are you hurt?" Sir Thomas demanded, patting Affrodille up and down.

"It's only my—ouch, damn you—my ribs. Blackheart's fault. Came straight home did he, the big bastard?"

"You're all over blood." Gently, Sir Thomas scooped Affrodille from Jenny's back. She hissed but didn't protest.

"Corbin's hand," she explained through pained breathing. "Get that looked at, Corbin." Corbin started to demur, but Sir Thomas turned on a heel and made for the château, forcing Affrodille to roll her head on his shoulder. "And for God's sake, take the book straight up to David."

"Forget the book," Sir Thomas countered. "Find David and get him down to the infirmary. Don't dawdle."

Corbin paused in indecision. His gashed palm bled profusely, but the wound wasn't deep. Jenny was blowing in and out, winded from the run up the hill. And the book in Affrodille's panniers had ended its journey abandoned atop a snowdrift.

In the end, it wasn't a difficult decision. Corbin was more afraid of Affrodille's disapproval than Sir Thomas's wrath. He walked Jenny to the stable, scooping up the fallen panniers as he went. The stable boy pulled a face the state of the donkey and shook his head at Corbin's gory hand but was too clever to speak a word of censure. Corbin awarded Jenny one last pat before running with all his remaining speed for David's tower. The main hall was quiet and empty. As Corbin raced up the old staircase of the eastern turret, he heard Sir Thomas's voice raised in anger from somewhere below. He couldn't make out the words through stone, but the chevalier's unmistakable temper was a relief. Anger, Corbin hoped, meant Affrodille wasn't dying. In his experience, grief was sullen and withdrawn, a muted emotion lurking in eyes and on the tongue, rarely spoken aloud.

Anger sometimes sounded like joy.

David was frozen in the middle of the room when Corbin burst through the door. He gripped a length of black cloth in one hand and one of his curved glass magnifying lenses in the other, but it was apparent he'd been looking toward the stairs in anticipation.

"What is it?" he asked, setting his tools aside. "What's going on?" His dark eyes narrowed, first at the panniers and then at the blood on Corbin's tunic and trousers. "You're injured."

"It's nothing." Corbin curled his fingers over the gash in his palm. "There were dwarves, on the hill. Sir Thomas needs you—I think Affrodille's badly hurt."

"Sit. There." David pointed at a chair by the tower's small oven. He grabbed his spectacles off a nearby table and put them on. "Warm yourself. Don't move. Don't touch anything. I'll be back."

He hurried from the room, leaving the door wide open in his distraction. Corbin took Affrodille's panniers across the circular chamber, dropping them on the floor as he collapsed into David's chair. Despite its size, the old alchemist's oven gave off plenty of heat. Burning logs crackled behind a ventilated hatch. A narrow metal chimney drew smoke up and away through the turret's pointed roof, leaving the air in the close space breathable. Corbin regarded the contraption stupidly as the afternoon's excitement slowly trickled away, leaving him muzzy-headed and dull. He needed to clean the dwarven ichor off Da's sword before it damaged the blade. His hand wanted seeing to; now that he'd stopped moving, the bleeding was slowing, but he knew the wound would need bandaging before the day was over.

Still, it felt very pleasant to do as David ordered and just sit.

The chair was comfortable, wide enough for a man to curl his legs up off the floor against the soft cushion. Corbin knew a chair with cushions was a noteworthy luxury. David's cushions were covered in gray toile and stuffed to bursting with horsehair. Corbin decided the chair was a marvelous nest from which to study the rest of his friend's workroom.

He'd been up the stairs to the eastern tower a few times before, always on an errand for Sir Thomas. He'd never lingered, and he'd certainly never been invited to stay. David wasn't a recluse by any means, but he made it clear to anyone who needed reminding that alchemy was a delicate science, and he considered extra bodies in his chamber accidents waiting to happen. Now, as Corbin stared around the room, he could see that the scholar's concerns were not unfounded. It was difficult to imagine how even one man could move through the space without knocking something breakable to the floor.

Or—Corbin raised an eyebrow at a trio of glass vials filled nearly to overflowing with bubbling silver liquid—*setting something afire.*

The space wasn't untidy. At first glance, it was evident that every pot, scissor, bottle, tong, flask, bird feather, dried herb, scrap of leather, bit of molding bread, and bronze ingot —as well as any of the multitude of tools Corbin could not name—had a place and were in it. But the three square tables of varying height were so cluttered Corbin thought adding even one more glass implement would cause a crash of dangerous proportions. A wide chest of drawers was pushed against the east wall beneath a narrow, tapestry-hung window. Elaborate symbols were burned into the side of the chest. The tapestry on the window above featured an embroidered maiden gamboling beside spring lambs. It was the first Corbin had seen in the château decorated with anything other than fleur-de-lis or birds.

A nine-branched candelabra sat atop the chest. Corbin thought it might be made of honest silver, which seemed impossible. For all its many limbs, the candelabra held only three snuffed white tapers; the rest of the spaces were empty of candles. The harder Corbin stared at the candelabra, the more certain he was it belonged in a king's treasury and not in David's snug tower room. He wondered if it was one of the many odd items David had unearthed from somewhere in the tunnels beneath the château. He was tempted to pick it up just to see if it was solid metal through and through.

But that would mean leaving his padded seat and edging past bubbling tinctures and precariously balanced lengths of hollow glass tubing. A real looking glass lay propped sideways on the closest table against a short pile of books, reflecting a bouquet of multicolored bird feathers, a desiccated apple, and the corner of Corbin's chin and mouth. The looking glass was oval and set in a simple, worm-eaten wooden frame. Corbin watched his reflected mouth pull down as he frowned thoughtfully. The looking glass, like the candelabra, the cushioned chair, and the collection of equipment scattered throughout the space—even the elaborate tapestry over the window—were not the sort of possessions an average Frenchman would ever call his own.

Corbin's gaze alighted on the piece of fabric David had been studying before he was called away. His frown deepened. The cloth was familiar, in color and in weave. The plain, sturdy wool was dyed a deep black. Even from an arm's length away, Corbin could see the fabric was damaged, rent in multiple places. Dried mud caked torn edges. The stains around the tears, black on black, looked more like old blood.

Gripped by a new suspicion, Corbin nudged Affrodille's panniers aside with his food and rose. Gingerly, so as not to disturb anything else on the table, Corbin moved the wool from beneath David's curved magnifying lens. The lens was cool and smooth against his fingers. The torn cloth felt rough in comparison. Corbin ran the wool over his palms and then spread the fabric across his front. In the mirror on the table, he was transformed into a ginger Dom in Benedictine robes that had seen much better days.

"They don't suit you," David said from the doorway. "And it's unlucky to wear a dead man's garb."

Corbin turned, the robes still pressed against his front. "Affrodille?"

"Three ribs broken, at the least," David reported without moving from the lintel. "I think four. A cracked wrist. I've wrapped the ribs and splinted the wrist and dosed her for pain. Thomas is waiting on the surgeon, though I wager there's little more to be done. She needs time to rest and recover."

Corbin exhaled gusty relief. Some of the color came back into the world as if a passing fog had finally lifted. "Thank you."

David came into the room, shutting the door gently. He reached for the black fabric, but Corbin held tight in a tug-of-war. The scholar's brow creased.

"You're bleeding on my robes, Corbin."

"*Your* robes?" Corbin challenged.

To his astonishment, David glanced aside, cheeks pink. He fidgeted, tangling his hands in the front of his scholar's smock before lifting his chin under Corbin's quizzical scrutiny.

"Not mine. Of course not mine *before*. Mine now. I had them sent up from Honnefleu."

"Why?" The wool stank of soil and of death. Corbin released his hold all at once, grimly satisfied when David staggered, catching his foot on a hem. He righted himself but not before a triangle of tattered fabric tore free. David bundled the robes carefully back onto the table. Corbin snatched the remnant from the floor, crushing wool in one fist.

"Thomas wanted to know." David peered into a bubbling vial, pointedly not looking Corbin's way. "You were attacked on the public highway by an ax-wielding thief in Benedictine costume who was then struck down by a pack of wolves. Which then inexplicably left both you and your horse unharmed. Not the usual traveler's tale."

Corbin took the scrap of fabric back with him to the padded seat. He collapsed into the cushions, legs stretched long. With one finger, he smoothed the black wool flat against his thigh. He'd tried not to think too hard on the Benedictine's attack or what it might mean. If not for the scar on his temple, he could almost pretend the confrontation had never happened.

"Is it the thief you don't like to think about?" asked David, turning about. "Or the wolves?"

"Was he a thief?" Corbin returned, hedging. "Are you certain?"

"That he wasn't a man of God gone rogue?" David snorted. He left the table and dropped cross-legged to the floor by Corbin's foot. Tugging Affrodille's panniers into his lap, he unbuckled the topmost flap. "I'm certain. The robes— what's left of them—are genuine, but the man on the governor's slab in Honnefleu definitely is no Dom. He's an ex-tradesman from Caen called Alf with a fondness for games of chance and too much ale. Lost his smithy to the crown for debts unpaid and turned sell-sword to keep from starving. Or rather, that's who he was. Now he's naught but worm food."

Corbin was impressed. "You learned all of that from tattered wool?"

"No." To Corbin's great surprise, David closed one eye in a wink. "Alf had a reputation. The governor's men recognized both his face and his ax." The scholar upended the panniers, dumping the leather-wrapped book free. He smiled when he saw the English king's wax seal.

"Well done!" he exclaimed. "Thomas will be very pleased to hear it's arrived in one piece once he's assured himself Affrodille will come to no lasting harm."

"Now," he continued, setting the parcel aside. "Your hand."

Corbin had forgotten the gash in his hand. "It's nothing." He held up his palm, displaying the wound. "Bloody but not deep. Cleansed and wrapped it will soon be good as new."

David took Corbin's hand in both of his own, turning it this way and that to better examine the split flesh. His fingers were cool, but the gentle puff of his warm breath sent shivers up Corbin's spine. He must have made a sound because David looked up in surprise.

"Did I hurt you?"

"No." Corbin pulled his hand from David's grasp, embarrassed and puzzled both. He was grateful for the heat off the oven to excuse the new color in his cheeks. David seemed uncomfortably close though he hadn't moved to close the gap between them. The scholar's curls, much darker and longer than Corbin's own, fell over his brow and down the back of his neck where they coiled against his shoulder points. For the first time, Corbin looked past the crooked Jew's cap and the spectacles and saw the man: sharp points and long limbs, and the ruddy planes of his face made interesting by a proud nose and a mouth stubborn and tender by turns.

David's lips parted on an exhale or a word. Corbin's heart stuttered, and it had more to do with the fleeting glimpse of David's pink tongue against strong white teeth than mortification. He shot to his feet, nearly knocking toile cushions to the floor in his haste to get away.

This is Laurie's fault, he thought viciously. *Laurie and his talk of bedding for pleasure.* His body hadn't betrayed him so recklessly in years, not since he was a boy just discovering that a cock had more uses than pissing.

"Corbin." David hopped to standing. "What is it? Did I— oh!" His concern vanished, replaced abruptly by glee. "What is this? Why, you beauty. Wherever did you come from?"

For a brief, head-spinning moment Corbin thought for certain his heart had stopped completely. Then David's thumb dipped beneath the loop of tooth and bone around Corbin's neck, tugging.

Corbin blinked down the length of his nose. "That. I'd forgotten. I met a pirate, two pirates, down on the river. They gave me…it's a gift. A charm against, ah. Against ghosts. Shark's teeth and a mermaid's fingers."

"Fingers, certainly." David looked elated. "Mermaids are notoriously difficult to kill and loathe to part with their fingers while still alive. May I?"

Corbin ducked his head, allowing the other man to take the grisly ornament from around his neck. David carried it with him to the closest table, reaching for his magnifying lens. He removed his spectacles and bent over the lens, running the glass up and down the length of the teeth. He had the look about him of a cat in the cream, almost vibrating with enthusiasm.

"It's very well made," he said. "These are complicated knots. A pirate, you said?"

"Two." Corbin drifted near, his body's odd betrayal forgotten in the wake of David's zeal. "The mother claimed she has a talent for making charms. Bit gruesome, isn't it?"

"It's perfect," declared David, trading his lens for a pair of tiny metal tongs. "I've never seen bones strung so capably through the joint. On what? Not cat gut, not thread. I'm afraid to separate them too far for fear of breaking the spell. Protection, you said?" He nattered on before Corbin could respond. "These teeth are from a single mouth, I'll wager. Cracked from the jawbone, all of them in pristine condition. Thomas will want to see this, Corbin. We haven't any charm as finely crafted as this one in our collections. Is it possible —" At last David gave Corbin his full attention. The scholar's eye shone with unbridled excitement. "Would you leave it with me for a little while, just a day or two, so I may take measurements and notes? Sketches for posterity?"

"Keep it," Corbin decided. "I've no need of it, surely. White Hill's not haunted. Any spirits would long ago have been swept out by the drafts."

David laughed and shook his head. "It was a gift," he protested. "A few days of study should suffice." But the look he gave the necklace was full of such desire Corbin felt his stomach flip again in sympathy.

"It's yours," he said hastily. "A gift, yes. From me to you, David. Merry Christmas to you."

"*Chanukah Sameach,*" David corrected, one corner of his mouth curling in quiet humor. "Thank you, Corbin, for the lovely present. I accept." He bowed at the waist before throwing his arms about Corbin and kissing him exuberantly on each cheek. His body was hard, unyielding, his lips soft and dry. The faint scruff of his beard scraped Corbin's heated skin as he pulled away.

Breasts or beard, it makes no difference, Corbin thought, recalling Laurie's boast.

"Corbin," David said in a tone that suggested he was repeating himself and not for the first time. "Are you listening? I said: you're looking green. Go and clean that hand and sup and rest. It's not every day a man is set upon by seven dwarves. It's only natural you're exhausted."

"Yes." Corbin blinked, relieved. "That must be it. I'm exhausted."

David waved a dismissive hand, already turning back to the string of teeth and bone, allowing Corbin to flee with his dignity intact.

BETWEEN SUPPER and sleep Corbin stopped by the sickroom. He'd washed and dressed and tucked the piece of black fabric into the hidey-hole alongside his coin pouch for safekeeping then spent a good hour at the boards entertaining the rest of the inglorious crew with his tale of the dwarves on the hill, embellishing here and there for the sake of his audience. Laurie and Mary-Louise had cheered over the bloodiest bits of the retelling while Marc had worried over what the presence of a dwarf pack in Honnefleu might mean. Dot had examined Corbin's bandaged palm critically and then expressed concern for Affrodille.

"Bones are tricky things to knit," Dot had said, frowning. "It will be some time before she can lift a sword again, much less ride. It's a setback. She'll be furious if it means a delay in training."

Marc seemed less disturbed. "Affrodille won't let something like dwarves set her back. She'll be ready when the king sends for her in the spring."

Corbin left the hall soon after. In spite of Marc's assurances, his concern over Affrodille had grown instead of lessened. For the first time in his life, he struggled with real guilt.

· · ·

"That's quite the long face," Sir Thomas said when Corbin stuck his head into the infirmary. The chevalier sat in the single chair Corbin remembered well, warming his booted feet on the familiar hearth while Affrodille dozed in Corbin's old bed, two spotted cats sleeping entwined on the mattress by her head. "It's late. Why aren't you abed? What's happened now? Dwarves in the kitchen?"

"Sir. No, sir." Corbin slipped all the way into the chamber. "There's nothing. Only, I wanted to see for myself that Affrodille was resting comfortably."

Sir Thomas chuckled. "Nothing is done comfortably with four broken ribs, I assure you. But if you meant to see that she was still breathing then, yes, she is."

"No thanks to your ham-handed surgeon." Sighing, Affrodille opened her eyes. "Or this bloody hard mattress. I don't know how you stood it, Corbin, for so many days. I'll be back in the dormitory tomorrow, or you'll all hear about it."

Corbin grinned. Affrodille lay rigid as if afraid to move, but the spirited set of her jaw and the strength of her glare were reassuring. Beneath the coverlet her chest rose and fell in a steady rhythm.

"I was lucky," she declared, reading his expression. "No punctured lungs. A debacle, but we both came out of it more or less in one piece."

"You saved my life," Corbin said, making Sir Thomas look around from the hearth.

"It was nothing."

"I've never seen knives thrown so well or from thin air like that," Corbin said in heartfelt appreciation. "It was like magic. Who taught you?"

"I taught me," Affrodille said, ignoring Sir Thomas's amused grunt. "It's not magic. They're kept in a special sheath up my sleeve." She hesitated, shrugged against the mattress, then yelped and cursed, clutching at her ribs.

Corbin rushed to seize the flagon of water from the side table, but Affrodille batted it away, annoyed. She wiped tears from her eyes, groaning, and accepted instead the tankard of apple cider Sir Thomas plucked from the floor by his chair. She took a long swallow.

"I'll teach you," she said at last, through gritted teeth. "If you like. The thing with the knives. Nothing says your demon has to be killed with a sword."

"Wrong," said Sir Thomas. "Difficult to pierce a heart with a dagger, unless you go under the arm. Impossible with a dagger thrown."

Both Corbin and Affrodille looked at the chevalier, Affrodille with suspicion.

"What's this about the heart?" she demanded. "What's wrong with a dagger through the eye or up the nose?"

"The book, the English king's book," Sir Thomas explained with barely mustered patience. "The one you nearly lost once into the river and once to dwarves, or had you forgotten already? Honestly, sometimes I don't know how you chicks survive once you've flown my house. Don't you pay attention?"

"Get on with it," Affrodille snapped. "You told me it was a history volume."

"So it is," returned Sir Thomas. He rose from the chair, spine cracking as he stretched. "A history of local devils. A family compilation, if you like." He sauntered to the room's window and edged the tapestry aside, letting cold air in. "I took a gander this evening while you were sleep, and you"— he glanced round at Corbin—"were busy entertaining your peers with reports of dwarven decapitation."

"So?" Corbin had to sit down on the mattress to keep from grabbing the chevalier about the throat and squeezing until the man turned blue. "Was he in it, my beast? What does the book say?"

"About the Littleton Fiend? Not much, but just enough. It's in Latin, or I'd let you read it yourself."

"Thomas," Affrodille cautioned. She'd noted Corbin's fists making mangle of the bedding.

"I'll have David read the passage to you," Sir Thomas relented. "Much of it is useless, flowery description. But the gist of the matter is there, buried beneath romantic notions. There's only one way to slay your beast, Corbin, and that's through the monster's very heart."

"A strike to the heart, is that what you mean?" Affrodille inquired when Corbin couldn't bring himself to speak.

"'A shattered heart will cure Normandy's darkest wood of its last lingering devil,'" Sir Thomas quoted. "Fairly straightforward, that." He let go of the tapestry, closing out the draft. "There's nothing said about an afreet glaive, but the Saracen's enchanted sword will only be to your advantage, of course."

"Of course," Corbin agreed at once, heaving a sigh of relief. He made his fingers unclench. He folded his hands in his lap and summoned every ounce of good cheer. "A strike to the heart. That's easy enough, with practice. Isn't it?"

CHAPTER 12

*D*emon kind was never meant to thrive in the cold places—the land of the Picts and Bretons, the Irisce, and—over the water—the Franks. These damp places have their own spirits, their own monsters and living lore, each one better suited than any devil to existence in fog and sea foam. The afreet prefer the sun, sand, and hot wind of their native deserts. They're a very territorial species, and they'll duel to the death over a singular patch of sand. They're antiquated and averse to change and voraciously opposed to travel over deep water. They're born of an ancient and compelling casting and woefully naive when it comes to the newer magic, oft tricked and trapped and used selfishly by otherwise relatively useless sorcerers.

Any devil living in Europe is not there by design. Look to the gilded cage or the pentagram that keeps it bound. Don't be fooled by fripperies or fancies. A demon away from its desert is likely to do anything in its power to escape captivity, to return home if at all possible, and to simply cease in all ways if not.

In this, Littleton's Beast was at first no different than any other of his species.

AFFRODILLE TAUGHT Corbin how to launch a knife from a scabbard up his sleeve. Corbin practiced every day all winter long, but he never quite executed the perfect throw. The target Affrodille set up for him in one of the less-used practice rooms was peppered around and around with piercings, but the center bull's-eye remained pristine. It became a joke on White Hill. Marc speculated Corbin's vision hadn't survived the Benedictine's ax completely intact. The matched sisters giggled and whispered about Corbin's poor dirk skills while looking pointedly at his crotch. Laurie only laughed and suggested he might do better with a moving target.

Corbin blushed and returned the teasing without rancor. The knife play was a game, a distraction. He wasn't meant to slay the Beast any other way than with Da's sword, and in swordsmanship, he continued to excel. When, in the spring, a blue-clad rider came galloping up the hill, the crown's pennant flying from his saddle, Corbin could handily beat every one of his fellow students in the contest of blade against blade, and even Sir Thomas occasionally fell beneath his onslaught.

"It's all you ever do," David pointed out. They stood shoulder to shoulder in front of his tower window, watching Sir Thomas great the king's soldier in the courtyard below. "It's all you've *ever* done. Of course you're good at it."

"I used to do other things," Corbin retorted. "When I was a lad. Fishing and riding and—" He faltered, searching. Littleton seemed a distant memory lately. "Other things. I wanted to be a soldier, I think, like that one." Down in the courtyard, Sir Thomas ushered the king's man into the château and out of view. His horse, large and bay, farted as the stable boy led it away toward the stable. "Who'll it be, do you think? I've a coin on Affrodille."

"No," David demurred. "I told you once; Marc's the next to go." He sniffed appreciatively at the spring afternoon. "Smell the lilacs. Aren't they wonderful? Last year I started a tincture, but the perfume's very difficult to isolate. Steep the blossoms too long, and it all starts to smell like rotted flesh."

"Ugh." Corbin wrinkled his nose. He'd become used to the scholar's odd notions over winter. They'd spent hours ensconced together in David's chamber perusing the English king's volume on demonology while snow and rain fell outside and winter settled over Honnefleu.

He left the window and paced a circle around the chamber, pausing briefly to inspect himself in the looking glass now hung on the wall above David's chair. The fellow in the reflection was almost a stranger, grown lean and wide-shouldered with constant drilling. He'd taken to keeping his curls cut short for simplicity's sake but spent as much time scraping new ginger growth from his face as he once had combing snarls from his hair. The man in the glass wasn't the lad Corbin remembered reflected in the deep waters of the Alevins. Only the muddy blue eyes were the same.

"Best go down," David said, abandoning his view of the courtyard and returning to his tables. Corbin watched his friend in the mirror. Time spent together in study had fostered an easy companionship, a familiarity that Corbin treasured. Born among sisters, he had often longed for a brother willing to watch his back and share his burdens. David had proved himself to be willing; the scholar seemed as obsessed as Corbin with unearthing any last bit of lore useful against the Littleton Fiend. Some nights Corbin fell asleep on the floor of David's chamber while his friend read or recited bits and pieces of useful demonology from his cushioned chair. When he woke after dawn, David would still be bent over his books, enthralled.

They both knew he was hunting that one forgotten fragment of knowledge that might free Corbin from a lifetime of forced companionship. Corbin was grateful. On that rare occasion when David lost his temper and hurled several glass vials against the tower wall, scattering smashed glass and puddles of colorful tincture along the floor, Corbin didn't ask what David had read that bleached the color from his cheeks and made his hands shake. It was of no matter to Corbin. He'd never intended to serve with the Beast as his master. He'd kill the devil or be killed himself, and that was the whole of it.

Corbin appreciated David's compulsion. And if he sometimes caught himself looking a little too long at the other man's graceful neck or dreaming of that dry mouth against his own—if he sometimes woke gasping on his cot with David's name still lingering on his tongue—those fancies began to fade as their friendship deepened.

Besides, Corbin soon discovered if he worked his body hard enough during the daylight hours he went to bed too exhausted for dreaming.

"Thomas will want you all accounted for and standing attendance." David met Corbin's gaze in the looking glass. "The emissary will require pomp and circumstance. So will Marc, for that matter."

"It should be Affrodille," Corbin grunted as he made for the door. "She's the ranking student. And I'm not here to learn how best to serve His Majesty as a soldier; why should I have to do 'pomp and circumstance'?"

"It won't be Affrodille," David called after, ignoring Corbin's dramatic groan. "And you are His Majesty's subject, even if not meant for his military. Go and make nice."

Corbin galloped down the tower steps. Where once he'd

been able to stand straight in the stairwell, now he had to duck his head to keep from brushing the ceiling. He'd been gangly in the fall and winter. Now he was half a giant. Even Sir Thomas, no small man, had to raise his chin to match Corbin's regard.

Dot met Corbin on the stairs.

"Where've you been?" she complained, out of breath. "Surely you heard the horse. Lord Bellamy is an impatient man. He wants his wine and cheese and a tour of the upper warren, and he can't begin until he's done the inspection."

"Inspection?" Corbin couldn't help but notice Dot looked freshly scrubbed. Her hair hung free down her back, freshly brushed and shining. Her tunic and cowl weren't the tattered everyday set but the lighter, cleaner version reserved for festivals and trips into town.

His own uniform was sweat-stained, the trousers too short. He'd neglected to bathe the night before, and although he'd meant to upon rising, the day had somehow got away from him. He knew with a sinking certainty that he stank.

"Too late now," Dot said. She poked him in the stomach. "Stand straight, don't slouch, and maybe his lordship won't notice the horse shit on your boots."

Corbin, who hadn't had word from home since Christmas and who missed his little sisters terribly, couldn't help but chuck Dot playfully on the nose.

"Maybe he won't notice me at all," he suggested.

Dot puffed her cheeks. "Slim chance of that," she said. "*Everyone* notices you, Corbin. That's the biggest of all your problems."

AGE SAT HEAVILY upon Lord Bellamy. He might have been a handsome man in the prime of his life, but in the sunset of his years, he'd become desiccated and sour. His skin was like leather, tanned by too much time spent outdoors. His long legs were permanently bowed—a cavalry man's affliction—his chest broad above a growing paunch. He wore his blue livery with pride, sweeping it dramatically around as he walked back and forth in front of Sir Thomas's students. The king's favor sparkled as rings on his fingers and medals on his breast.

The inglorious crew stood in a line with their backs to flickering hearth. Lord Bellamy stood before them, head wagging from side to side, expression stern. Corbin felt a trail of sweat slide along the length of his spine.

Sir Thomas, Corbin could tell, thought his lordship a necessary burden. The chevalier waited near the boards, arms crossed behind his back, watching silently as Sir Bellamy examined White Hill's best. Sir Thomas wore a genial smile, but Corbin could see a muscle ticking in his jaw.

"Marc Saulniers." Lord Bellamy paused briefly in front of the burned man before moving on. "Laurent Spare. Affrodille Prive." He strode past Affrodille, hardly sparing her a glance. "Dorothé and Mary-Louise Favreau. You've each blossomed since my last visit. Sir Thomas's talented tutelage at work, I presume."

"Yes, my lord," Dot and Mary-Louise answered in unison. Laurie essayed a small bow while Marc and Affrodille stood still as statues carved from Rouen stone.

His lordship dragged his left leg when he walked. It was only the slightest limp, but Corbin noticed it at once. He wondered if the old soldier had suffered a wound upon the battlefield or if the hitch in his stride was something as mundane as the gout.

"You're gawping, monsieur." Lord Bellamy paused in front of Corbin. They were of a height. Corbin realized with a start that the solider had one blue eye and one brown, like a shepherd's piebald dog.

"I'm sorry, my lord." Corbin tried his best to mimic Laurie's graceful bow. "It's a bad habit of mine, the gawking."

"You are new," Lord Bellamy proclaimed. "And here without my approval. I may be in my dotage, but I'd not forget a great strapping man like you, and redheaded as well."

Lord Bellamy's own hair was sparse and gray. He cocked a brow at Sir Thomas, awaiting explanation.

"Corbin de Beaumont is a special case," the chevalier explained. "A village lad come to learn the hunt. His father paid my price; Corbin's not on His Majesty's payroll."

"Ah. Of course." Lord Bellamy smiled at Corbin. "What are you hunting, de Beaumont? Not the hind nor the hare in this household. More likely a gorgon or sea serpent, am I close?"

Corbin peeked sideways at Sir Thomas. Sir Thomas lowered his chin in assent.

"Demon, my lord. A devil plagues my family. With Sir Thomas's tutelage, I plan to kill him."

Lord Bellamy's piebald stare narrowed. "Demons are tricky things," he said. "And I'll be glad if I never see another in my lifetime. I wish you luck, de Beaumont. Even with Thomas's tutelage, you'll be needing it." He straightened all at once, clapping his hands together.

"I've come a long way. I want good cheese and mulled wine and then bed. Let's get this over with. Affrodille, for all you wear the apprentice's collar, you'll be staying behind once again. Your mother, God bless her, continues to hold sway at court, and she's made it perfectly clear she doesn't want you there so long as you're set on the blue, for all that both your master and myself have spoken eloquently in your favor."

Affrodille, mirroring Sir Thomas's stiff posture, nodded.

"I understand, my lord. Thank you, as always, for your honesty."

Lord Bellamy cleared his throat. "Affrodille," he said fondly. "It's not too late to change your mind. Come back with me to Fontainebleau as my daughter and heir. Your mother misses her child. She's ready to forgive you this escapade, I think."

"Three years on White Hill is not an escapade, Papa," Affrodille replied, dignified. "I'll return for the blue or not at all. And until I have the bunk I deserve in His Majesty's barracks I'm content to stand as Sir Thomas's second." She smiled small. "Blossoming, as you said."

"So I expected." Sir Bellamy cleared his throat. "Although you know I'm sorry to hear it." His limp seemed more pronounced as he paced away down the line. "Then it will be you, Monsieur Saulniers, at last." He extended a hand in congratulations. "No surprise there. I suppose you're already packed? I'll have the blue sent up to your room. Be ready to leave in two days' time."

"Yes, my lord." Marc bowed his head over Lord Bellamy's hand. "Thank you, my lord. The honor is mine."

"The honor is His Majesty's, make no mistake," said Lord Bellamy. "Thomas's students are too few and far between. Which reminds me"—he turned toward the chevalier, amusement making creases around his eyes—"I've brought you another."

"Oh?" Sir Thomas inquired, making a show of glancing about the hall.

"Not a lad or lass, this time." Lord Bellamy's smile stretched. "A man grown. Left him down in Honnefleu, for the time being. He's an odd case. You'll want an interview before you let him over your threshold, I think, but there's no use arguing. His Majesty's set on it, I'm afraid."

"*Mon Dieu.* What's he sent me this time?" Sir Thomas asked, resigned.

"Another from the dungeons," Lord Bellamy replied, brimming with false cheer. "This one for murder. He's a very talented garrotter, I'm afraid. But the interesting thing, you see, is that this man Rob claims he can see into the future using naught but a silver bowl and fresh water."

"Why should anyone believe him?" Intrigued, Corbin forgot to hold his tongue.

"I've asked myself the same." Lord Bellamy wagged his head. "All that really matters is Rob's convinced the king he's a soothsayer and the king wants him kept safe on White Hill, for the time being. Where he can't be used against the crown, you understand."

"Not my student," Sir Thomas clarified. "My prisoner."

"If you like," Lord Bellamy agreed. "Put him down in your warren with the rest of your collection of oddities. Or keep him aboveground and tame him. Doesn't matter so long as I've your assurance he won't trouble the crown."

SIR THOMAS BROUGHT the soothsayer onto White Hill late the next night under cover of darkness. Corbin heard the noise of horses once again from David's tower where he lingered alone in front of the Beast's portrait. Sir Thomas had ordered the painting brought up out of the warren just after Christmas on the premise that Corbin had best get used to the monster's fearsome likeness.

"Repeated exposure lessens fear," the chevalier insisted. "You spend enough time up here rereading the same three pages. Might as well read them aloud to the devil himself."

Corbin didn't say he'd learned every important word in the English king's book by heart. It was easy memorization; the Beast's entry was brief by any standards. By New Year,

Corbin could recite the passages front to back, sitting, standing, or pacing. By first snowmelt, he could do so while standing nose to toothy snout, smiling grimly into painted yellow eyes. Sometimes he put his palm flat against the canvas above the creature's breastbone, a challenge.

"It's only a painting," David would remind him, looking up from his potions. "A very old and rare one at that. Try not to do it damage."

And Corbin, staring up into that wolfish mien, didn't reply.

THE CLATTER of horses down in the courtyard stirred Corbin from his half dreaming, making him look toward the window, but he didn't leave the painting until angry shouts rang out in the night. Then he hurried toward the chamber window, drawing the tapestry aside, hand gone automatically to the sword always on his back. A large cresset and several torches burned below. In their light, he could just make out four horses. Three still bore their riders. The fourth had an empty saddle and was already escaping toward the stables.

A man huddled on the flagstone in the light of the rising moon. He sat hunched nose to knees. His high, wordless bellows echoed off the château walls, bouncing across Rouen stone. There were more shouts from the men on horseback, appeals for help. Corbin, looking down on the courtyard from above, heard Sir Thomas's voice rising from inside the château, demanding explanation.

He abandoned the window and hurried from David's tower, bootheels clattering on stone as he ran headlong down the stairs. The main hall was all but deserted, trenchers of roast meat left abandoned alongside flagons of mulled wine. A lonely kitchen lad, barely old enough to hold a ladle, stood in front of the hearth, breaking fresh bread onto platters.

"They've all gone outside," the boy said in reply to Corbin's inquiring glance. "To see what the fuss is about. Is it a bear, monsieur? It sounds like a bear."

Corbin bit back amusement. "*Merde*, I hope not," he said, wincing as further unearthly bellows echoed against stone. "I wouldn't know what to do with a bear."

"Make a rug out of him, monsieur," the lad suggested as Corbin rushed on. "And stew out of his soft bits."

When Corbin burst out into the night, he found Affrodille lurking just outside the wide entry. She hushed him with a word and a warning fist against his shoulder.

"Flying straight into danger without looking first, and a bloody smile on your face," she hissed. "Haven't you learned anything? Look at that, sword drawn, eager to play. Whom did you intend to cut down first, Sir Thomas? David? His lordship?"

Corbin sobered. He returned his sword to its scabbard on his back. Chastened, he lifted both hands to shoulder height.

"I wouldn't," he promised. "I mean, I wasn't going to—"

"Good," Affrodille said. "Because you'd grieve the first two mistakes and be hanged for the third. Always take stock, Corbin. *Always*."

Corbin saw at once how close he'd come to making a grievous mistake. The light from the torch and cresset managed to reach only the edges of the courtyard; the center was aflutter of moonlit shadow and shifting form. The horses had fled, presumably frightened away by the guttural ebb and flow because Corbin doubted any stable boy would be so bold as to brave the ominous tableau. The man on the flagstones had risen to his knees, head thrown back as he shouted at the glimmering moon. Two figures pressed against him, apparently locked in struggle. Two more stood at attention. Even close as he was, Corbin couldn't make out their features, or he realized in dismay, make any sense out of their garbled cries.

Corbin blinked, waiting for his eyes to adjust, but nothing changed. It was as if the forms beyond the edge of torchlight were caught beneath a deep, dark pond or distorted by thick fog.

"What is that?" He'd heard talk of similar beguiling mists, rising near swamps or other standing water, but never encountered one. The farmers called the fogs hinkypunks and the gentry, pixie pother, and it was said a person so unlucky as to stumble through such a mist was addled forever after.

"Soothsayer tricks," Affrodille answered. "Had a flask of water hidden about his person, I suppose, and someone missed it. If I'd let you charge on into that mess, Corbin, it's possible you *would* have mistaken friend for foe."

A high cloud passed over the moon, snuffing silver light. A loud chime rang out, the shivering boom like a church bell struck once. The man on his knees went abruptly silent while the rest of the people caught in the fog continued to shout and gesture. His shoulders slumped. He toppled sideways onto flagstone limp. The fog collapsed as well, cascading over the ground like black rain, rolling over Rouen stone before disappearing into cracks between, allowing torchlight to once again reach the middle of the courtyard.

"David's doing," murmured Affrodille. "As usual, he's the only one who's managed to keep his head."

Corbin could see Sir Thomas now, standing over the fallen man, dirk in hand. David squatted between the chevalier and his foe, white cap askew, the gleam of silver in his hands. As Corbin moved cautiously in their direction, Sir Thomas sheathed his weapon and held out a hand, hauling David to his feet. The man on the flagstones lay as if dead, but Corbin could see the whites of his eyes rolling in their sockets.

Lord Bellamy and his companion, an unfamiliar young soldier, stood frozen a few strides away. His lordship appeared dazed. He staggered when Affrodille spoke in his ear then leaned without shame on his daughter's supporting arm. The soldier sat down right where he stood, turned his head, and coughed bile onto the flagstone.

"Kill him," his lordship directed, pointing a shaking finger at the fallen soothsayer. "And whoever allowed him near water should be flogged for a traitor."

"His Majesty desires the man alive and contained," Sir Thomas reminded Lord Bellamy. The chevalier cleared his throat. "David has his bowl. He's contained. I won't kill him. He's valuable. As for the water, you left him alone in a city on Seine. What did you expect?"

"He was under guard!" Lord Bellamy roared. The soldier on the ground began to retch in earnest.

"David, see to that young man," Sir Thomas ordered. "Corbin, help me with the soothsayer. He's a big bastard, and thankfully you've more muscle than most."

David nodded mutely, still clutching the soothsayer's silver bowl in his hands. His mouth was set in grim lines. He shot Corbin a worried glance as he hurried away. Lord Bellamy, still blustering, appeared at a loss.

"Get one of his arms over your shoulder," Sir Thomas suggested, frowning down at the twitching soothsayer. "I'll do the same."

"Are you certain?" Corbin hesitated. "Sir, I mean no insult, but you've gone yellow about the gills. Mayhap we should wait a moment."

"I'm not a fish," snapped Sir Thomas. "No man wants to swallow all of his possible futures in a single dose. It's only dumb luck you didn't stumble into the spell yourself, and if you had, I wagered you, too, would be no better than a landed trout. A soothsayer's a dangerous sort even when he's right in the head—which this fellow is not. Now heave, Corbin. Put your back to it."

THEY CARRIED the unconscious man not to the infirmary as Corbin first thought but down into the warren. Down and down again, deeper than Corbin had yet ventured. Rob shook and mumbled but didn't wake. Sir Thomas seemed to gain strength as they descended, which suited Corbin just fine because Rob was indeed a large man. Corbin's muscles, unused to heavy lifting, were beginning to protest. The soothsayer's head lolled on his neck. His feet dragged on the tunnel floor, refusing to bear any weight. The arm over Corbin's shoulder was thick around as a sapling; the man's hands were a farmer's hands, calloused on the thumb and finger pads.

"Here," Sir Thomas directed at last, motioning for Corbin to stop. "Set him down. Against that wall. Carefully."

Grateful for the respite, Corbin did so, squatting to ease the big man half onto the floor, propping his torso upright against the wall. Rob sighed but didn't wake. Corbin looked down into the soothsayer's rolling eyes. He suppressed a shudder. Whatever manner of fit the man was suffering, it didn't look pleasant.

"Almost like he's dreaming with his eyes open."

"Mayhap he is. Fortune-tellers are barely human in the first place, and I don't know of a certain what David did to him." There was a wide door on the opposite wall. Bound in iron and secured with no less than three separate locks, it appeared virtually unassailable.

Corbin frowned down at the farmer. "Will he wake?"

Sir Thomas chose a key from the ring on his belt and unlocked the door. "He's not much good to us if he doesn't."

Instead of opening outward or inward, the door slid sideways into the wall, squeaking protest. The room beyond was furnished with necessities: cot, rug, chair, and chamber pot. It was cheerfully lit not with the usual torch or cresset but with a shrub-size chunk of yellow rock.

"Grab his heels," Sir Thomas said, reaching under the soothsayer's shoulders. "We'll leave him on the mattress for David."

The cot was made for a smaller man. Rob's feet stuck out over the edge. Sir Thomas tossed a thin blanket over his middle while Corbin examined the strange light source. The rock, jagged and striated, grew straight out of the chamber floor. Located as it was in the very rear of the chamber, still it illuminated the entire space thoroughly and softly as an amber sunrise.

"Don't touch it," Sir Thomas warned. Corbin tucked both hands behind his back to avoid temptation.

"Is it dangerous?"

"Not at all," the chevalier replied. "They're in each of the cells, and as far as I know, the crystals are both harmless and impervious. Part of the old magician's repertoire, I'm told. But it's touch that turns them off and on, and I'd rather not be standing in pitch-black alongside a madman and a murderer, if it's all the same to you."

Corbin glanced one last time at the softly glowing rock before following Sir Thomas out into the corridor. The chevalier tugged the sliding door back into place. He didn't speak as he reset the locks. When he turned from the cell, he looked drawn and pale in the torchlight. Corbin felt a pinch of sympathy for the old hero.

"I have a friend called Nell," Corbin said as they made way slowly back up the passage. "She used to tell me we all make our own futures, that nothing's set." Hoping he'd learned the way of reassurance from David, Corbin set one hand on Sir Thomas's shoulder, squeezing. "Whatever you saw in the mist, it doesn't have to be. It's just tricks and possibilities, not truth."

Sir Thomas's shoulder was rigid against Corbin's grip, but his answering smile appeared genuine.

"Thank you," said Sir Thomas. "Your friend is quite right. I suppose she told you that often, did she?"

Corbin nodded. "Every day for an entire year after Mother died, when I despaired of the Beast's curse and the lifetime of servitude I'd be forced to endure to keep my family safe." He stuck out his hand, trailing fingers along the smooth wall, thinking idly of the worm that built the tunnels. "I thought of running away, many times, at first." It was hard to admit. "Nell convinced me that I shouldn't, that running was a coward's way out, and besides, we knew the Beast wouldn't stand for it. Nell's very brave. So we came up with a different plan."

"Kill the Beast. Break the curse."

"It's always been about vengeance for Da, and I always knew it. But for me, it was a way to change the hand I'd been dealt."

"Make a new future." Sir Thomas paused in the corridor, turning. He regarded Corbin with lifted brows. "Unless you're exactly where you were meant to be from the day the Littleton Fiend struck his bargain. All this time, have you never wondered?"

Corbin blinked, taken aback. Sir Thomas's smile grew less pleasant.

"Demon curse on your family, lost afreet glaive on your back. Black forest wolves on the king's highway. Dwarves daring my road. I'd say you're not the only one playing a card game with fate, lad, and you'd best be aware. It's possible—

nay, likely—the Littleton Fiend knows exactly what you're up to, and there's no saying which cards he's backing. An old devil like that's madder than the fortune-teller in my dungeon."

Corbin's heart sank.

"Ah, Corbin. Be wary but take heart." Sir Thomas slapped him on the back with more force than David ever dared. "A devil is no more or less brave than a man. While you struggle under the weight of possibilities, so also does the Beast in his forest lair."

CHAPTER 13

Marc left White Hill without fanfare the following morning. The inglorious crew stood in an early spring rain to see him off. Dot and Mary-Louise whooped when Marc turned solemnly in place, showing off the cut and fit of his new blue livery. The burned man blushed pink but accepted Laurie's overenthusiastic farewell embrace with good cheer. Affrodille bowed her congratulations while Sir Thomas pinned White Hill's silver starburst on Marc's breast. David, awake for once with the sunrise, gripped Marc's arm with genuine affection and declared him well prepared for service in His Majesty's army.

Then it was Corbin's turn to say good-bye, but the proper words stuck in his throat. The king's livery turned Marc into a different man—a stranger capable of weighty deeds. Corbin recalled how he'd idolized the soldiers passing through Littleton and felt warmth touch his own cheeks. Marc, seeing Corbin's agitation, laughed and nudged him in the ribs with an elbow.

"Strange how clothes can make a man seem more impressive," he said. "Underneath I'm still the same fellow who sometimes woke the whole dormitory with midnight terrors and then made you look beneath every cot for Laurie's poisonous serpent."

Corbin grinned. It was easier to suppress emotion if he looked at the starburst on Marc's chest instead of into his face.

"Garlic," he reminded the other man. "And comfrey, in a tea before bed. Don't forget."

"I'll remember, if only for the sake of my bunkmates." Marc stood on his toes to meet Corbin's reluctant eye. "You're not one for writing, I know, but I'll be looking for a note once you've put the Littleton Fiend to rest. Until then, I'll raise a flagon every night to your courage."

Corbin, who never felt particularly courageous when it came to parting ways, swallowed and nodded. Marc nudged him in the ribs one last time. Then the burned man turned away, mounting a red mare the throne had sent for him as a show of good faith. The mare was tall and lovely. Marc, cape darkened to indigo by the rain, looked like a true champion. Sir Bellamy sighed loudly as he climbed atop his own ride. His lordship saluted Sir Thomas with the wave of one gloved hand before doing the same to his proud daughter. Then the two men were off and away down the hill, disappearing quickly around the nearest rocky outcrop.

Sir Thomas didn't allow his students to linger long in the courtyard.

"Back to work," he said. "I've not built a reputation upon the backs of sluggards. You've plenty of loss ahead of you; be thankful you're saying good-bye to the back of his horse and not while he's being planted for good in the ground. Now, off with you!"

. . .

CORBIN SPENT the rest of the morning practicing calisthenics alone in one of White Hill's many empty chambers. The room, located near the château's south wall, was well away from the hustle and bustle of everyday activity. Corbin had found it by accident one night when he'd been unable to find sleep. Looking for distraction and a cure for boredom, he'd taken a single candle with him through the layers of White Hill he'd not yet had reason to explore and discovered in his wanderings that most of the château's backside was—if not neglected—than certainly rarely used. The southern corridors were dark and dusty, untouched by torchlight. The stone floors were bare and smelled damp. Most of the doors he tried were locked, and those few that did yield to his hand opened only to empty cupboards or narrow storerooms.

So he was startled when, behind a door that appeared unremarkable as all the others, he discovered what must once have been someone's spacious bedchamber. The furnishings were long since removed, but when Corbin held his candle overhead, he could see the outline of old rugs left behind on the cold floors. The ceilings were higher than any other he'd seen in the château but hung corner to corner with swathes of what appeared to be velvet. Two large south-facing windows were draped over with curtains instead of the usual simple tapestries. When he stepped farther into the room to examine the rugs, Corbin discovered they were good silk, thick, and soft.

The forgotten room was by far the warmest space on White Hill, and Corbin soon made good use of his discovery. He turned the chamber into a private space for exercise and study, and for quick catnaps in between. The chamber had two chimneys, one at each end of the rectangular space. If Corbin set both hearths to roaring at the same time, the air would grow uncomfortably warm. The heat loosened his muscles and set his heart to pounding, making a long day of repetitive drilling that much more effective. He began to think of the room as a forge. In the chamber's heat, he sweated away fear and hesitation while at the same time he became lean and strong, less the bumbling giant and more the sturdy spear. If only to keep from dropping the sweat-slicked pommel of Da's sword, Corbin developed an economy of movement that was subtler than Marc's hack-and-slash drilling but more forward than Laurie's wait-and-watch dueling dance.

And always, as he battled invisible foes or stretched muscles past the point of pain, Corbin thought, *A strike to the heart, a strike to the heart, a strike to the heart.*

But the day Marc left, Corbin couldn't summon the energy for a hard workout or the ambition for a healthy sweat. He spent the morning practicing Affrodille's knife throw with halfhearted enthusiasm and was just examining the pattern his blade had left in the near wall when David startled him by peeking around the chamber door.

"*Mére Marie!*" Corbin swore. He'd thought he'd managed to keep the forgotten room his secret but now realized he should have known David would suss it out. "You might have lost an eye."

"To your throwing skills?" David smirked. He stepped into the room, looking about with undisguised interest. "Last I checked, you couldn't hit a target if it stood square in front of your nose. I see that hasn't much changed." He shook his head at the knife marks on the wall. "I'll admit your persistence is admirable."

Corbin glowered. It galled him more than it should that he couldn't match Affrodille's artistry. Marc's departure had left him feeling low and not at all in the mood for David's teasing.

"How did you find me?"

Mouth still crooked, David adjusted his spectacles on his

nose. "Do you really need to ask? I make it my business to know everything that goes on in, around, and below the hill. Someone has to. Paying attention to the little things is not exactly Thomas's forte." Shrugging, he wandered the perimeter of Corbin's hideaway much as Corbin sometimes walked the circle of his tower workroom. "I would have left your pretense of solitude undisturbed, but I don't have time to wait out your sulk."

Corbin opened his mouth on a biting retort but shut it again. David, for all his teasing, appeared uncommonly restless. The clench of his fingers in his robes was a plain indication that something was off, as was his trek back and forth between the two hearths. David, Corbin knew, preferred to keep his body leashed and rarely gave in to fidgeting.

"What is it?" Corbin slipped his knives back up his sleeve. He rose fluidly from his seat on the floor in the middle of the room and met his friend midpace. "David."

The scholar sighed. He ruffled his curls with both hands, digging bony fingers into his scalp. Then he pursed his lips in a moue of embarrassment.

"Nothing. Probably nothing. But even so." He reached into the pouch at his belt. Corbin heard the clatter of bones and beads. "I'd like to give this back to you. In fact, I'd like you to wear it."

Puzzled, Corbin reclaimed the necklace. The shark's teeth felt rough against his palm, the finger bones polished and smooth.

"If you've no more need of it—" he began, but David cut him off.

"I have need of it. Around your neck, if you'd be so kind. It's taken me some time to be sure, but I've concluded that is where it's meant to be. Put it on, now. Oh, don't look like that. Wear it under your shirt. No one will notice."

"Except for the rattling." But David's expression brooked

no argument, so Corbin fastened the gruesome thing around his throat. He paused in tucking it beneath his collar. "You've changed it. What's this you've added, a pebble?" The new bead was no larger than Corbin's thumb knuckle, gray and smooth but for a single inscribed rune.

"Fired clay." David replied, watching Corbin minutely. "Some of my people believe strong magic can be made with an angel's proper name. I've given you Michael's; he has a talent for slaying beasts."

Corbin squinted at the rune. It looked like nothing more than two squiggles and several dots. "Thank you," he ventured, securing the necklace under his tunic. "But why?"

David bit at his lower lip. Corbin, who also preferred to keep his body carefully under control, had to look away. It was somehow easier to count the knife sticks in the wall than watch David fret.

"Your father paid Thomas a merchant's fortune to prepare you for whatever lies ahead in the black forest," the scholar began. "And also to keep you safe until that day you meet the Littleton devil at his manor gate. Laurie's games and traps are one thing, as are misspent day trips with Affrodille away from the château. But now we've real danger on the hill, and it's my duty to see you have every protection available."

"You mean the soothsayer," Corbin hazarded. It wasn't a great leap. "That man, Rob."

"Yes. Stay away from Rob, Corbin. Stay out of the warren, if only for the time being." Just as Marc had earlier, David rose on his toes, forcing Corbin to acknowledge his fierce regard. It was Corbin's turn to fidget.

"I've better things to do than lurk about in the tunnels beneath the kitchens."

David's relief gusted against the hollow of Corbin's throat.

"Good. I have your promise?"

Corbin turned abruptly away. That David would require his word on any matter stung.

"Corbin?" the scholar pressed.

"Yes." Corbin stalked toward the door and freedom. "You have my promise. I'll stay out of the tunnels."

IT SOON BECAME apparent that David had extracted promises form the wrong student.

"Does he keep it up in that tower room of his?" Laurie asked Corbin as the two dueled with borrowed poniards in the courtyard one evening in early summer. It was a lazy game of swordplay, more a flexing of muscles and knowledge than real battle. Laurie was rarely so indolent, and Corbin didn't mind. Laurie, distracted or otherwise, always made bladework beautiful. By all accounts, his mother was a dancer in Paris, and Corbin believed it. Laurie was graceful even when he dodged Corbin's best upward thrust.

"*Pardon?*" Corbin murmured, blocking Laurie's answering feint.

"The scrying basin." Laurie jogged a stride away, twisted —and lunged. His poniard slid up and in under Corbin's guard. Corbin had to drop and roll on the flagstones to avoid blooding. As he came up, he flicked his own flexible blade to the side, aiming for Laurie's shins. It was a dirty move and illegal. Laurie hopped away before Corbin could score, whistling between his teeth.

"Filthy cheat." Laurie laughed. He executed a second hop then reversed midair, thrusting straight down toward Corbin's torso with all his strength. The point of his blade caught Corbin's sleeve between his armpit and ribs, punching a neat hole in wool before blunting on the flagstone below and flopping onto the ground. Corbin swore, but Laurie only laughed harder as he extended a hand.

"My fencing instructor would have you whipped for a move like that," he said, helping Corbin to his feet. "Very much not the gentleman's game."

"I'm no gentleman," Corbin reminded his friend, grinning as he did so. He retrieved Laurie's sword from the flagstone and returned it with a mocking bow. The afternoon was pleasant, warm but not yet sunk into the heat of summer. There was a breeze off the river below. It smelled some of old fish but cooled the sweat on his brow.

"So, Corbin?" prompted Laurie. "The basin?"

"If you mean the great silver bowl, I haven't seen it since the day I helped Sir Thomas haul the farmer into the warren. I've not seen it anywhere in David's tower. I doubt he has is."

"He does. I know it." Laurie wiped his mouth with the back of his hand. Fine weather had brought a scatter of new freckles across his nose and cheeks. Last of all the inglorious crew, his face was still round and soft as a lad's. "I've seen him with it, walking the warren and hanging about in the libraries."

"It's not in his tower. I would have noticed so much silver in one place," Corbin repeated, already dismissing the matter. He was due in the main hall where Affrodille planned to quiz him on Latin letters despite his regular protest that a working knowledge of the alphabet was unlikely to help him slay the Littleton Fiend.

"It's not kept anywhere in the warren, either," Laurie muttered, trailing Corbin back into the château. "I suppose that's sensible. A powerful tool like that, Sir Thomas will want it kept close to hand. The old knight probably sleeps with it under his pillow."

Considering the matter closed, Corbin shrugged agreement.

· · ·

But Laurie came to him again, waking Corbin in the dead of night not long after Midsummer's Eve. The moon shone bright through cracks in the roof above. Corbin had been sleeping with bedding pulled up over his face to keep the silver gleam at bay. When Laurie pulled the sheltering folds away from his eyes, he sat up in a fright, reaching for Da's sword.

"It's only me," Laurie whispered, although there was no real need for lowered voices. Sir Thomas hadn't yet found any new lads to fill the dormitory's empty cots; with Marc gone, Corbin and Laurie were the chamber's only occupants.

"What are you doing?" Corbin demanded, breathing past a spike of terror. He'd been dreaming and not of pleasant things. Littleton had been burning while all of his efforts to drag buckets of water from the Alevins had failed. "*Merde*, Laurie! I was sleeping."

"And now you're not," Laurie said. His teeth gleamed in the moonlight, but his sunny smile fell flat. "I need your help."

Corbin let go of Da's sword. He pushed blankets to the floor as he sat up. "In the middle of the night? Are you ill?"

"No, of course not. But one of Sir Thomas's clandestine ships has come in. He's ridden down to meet it, all in a furious lather, and he's taken David with him."

Corbin suspected he was doing a perfect impression of a startled owl. "I don't understand."

"Affrodille and the twins are well asleep, Corbin, I checked. Now's our chance."

"I don't understand," Corbin repeated. He glanced about the dormitory, suspecting he might still be caught in dreams but saw nary a wisp of smoke.

"Come on now." Laurie prodded Corbin, urging him to his feet and handing him his boots. "We haven't a lot of time. I just want a look, but God knows how long a thing like that takes, and if he misses the keys, he may as well turn right around and rush home."

Corbin dropped a boot in consternation. "You mean Sir Thomas. Laurie, what have you done?"

But Laurie was already out the door. Corbin shoved his foot into his boot, grabbed Da's sword, and ran after, catching his friend halfway down the spiral staircase. The moonlight followed them down the stairs and into the main hall; every window in White Hill was open to the warm night. The hearth was banked, the boards cleared until breakfast. A kitchen maid slept across the threshold, snoring gently. Laurie stepped over the lass, motioning Corbin to follow.

They hurried through the kitchen and out into the small herb garden kept in one corner of the inner bailey by Sir Thomas's cook. There lavender scrubs large as Mother's boxed in smaller plots of rosemary, thyme, and mint. Water onion grew in a small flat pond. In the light of the moon, Corbin could see pale fish darting from plant to plant. A makeshift wall of scavenged Rouen stone kept hares and foxes from the greens. After putting a finger to his lips, Laurie led Corbin around the pond and under the low hanging branches of an old lemon tree.

Rob the soothsayer sat on his haunches against the trunk of the tree, a cup of red wine cradled in both hands. When the big man saw Laurie, his weathered face split into an affable smile. He made as if to rise.

Da's sword was in Corbin's hand before he knew he'd reached for it, the point of the blade pressed beneath the soothsayer's chin, kissing flesh but not quite drawing blood.

"Oh," Laurie breathed, impressed. "You really have improved."

"If this is another of your tests," Corbin replied through gritted teeth. "I prefer the spider."

"Not a test." Laurie shoved at Corbin's sword arm. Corbin didn't yield. The soothsayer crouched without moving, face white in the moonlight. When the man swallowed, the apple in his throat bobbed, and so did the tip of Da's sword.

"*Jésus*, Corbin, let be. Rob's with me. Here, Rob, don't look so frightened. I've brought you a fish patisserie from the kitchen, just as I promised you."

Corbin heard the rustle of paper before Laurie tossed a small packet at the soothsayer. The offering landed in the grass next to Rob's shoe. Rob's small black eyes widened, but he didn't look away from Corbin.

"What do you mean, 'with you'?" demanded Corbin. "This man is dangerous. He's supposed to be locked in the warren."

Laurie's fingers closed on Corbin's wrist: a warning. Tiny sparks of pain fluttered along his sword arm. Laurie's expression as he bent close was open, almost pleading.

"Your fingers will go numb in a minute," he said. "You remember the trick, of course. It's one of our master's favorites. You've three choices: back away, drop the sword, or strike me through before you lose the use of your hand."

"I mean no harm, monsieur," Rob added. His voice was as high as a child's, ill fitted to his gigantic frame. "It's all a terrible misunderstanding. A mistake."

"Corbin," Laurie murmured, a deeper counterpoint, gentle even as his fingers ground Corbin's bones. "Don't you trust me?"

There were blue bruises forming beneath Laurie's fingertips, phantom bruises forming on Corbin's heart.

Corbin took the craven's lot. He backed Da's sword away from Rob's fleshy throat. Laurie's grip relaxed, but he didn't release Corbin's wrist until the afreet glaive was safely sheathed.

"Good lad." Laurie heaved a sigh of relief. "Didn't I tell

you, friend Rob? Corbin's not like the rest. He's a merchant's son; he hasn't any use for King Charles's favor."

"He means you're common," Rob told Corbin, reaching for the packet of food. He unwrapped the paper slowly then held the pastry up, studying it in the moonlight. "A farmer, like me. His kind, they've got romantic notions about our till and our scythe."

"He'd do better to recall the rope you used as garrote," Corbin retorted. "Or did you think Sir Bellamy hadn't warned us all? Five wellborn lasses, all strangled within days, and you stood panting over the last of them." Disgust and horror roiled in his gut.

Rob smiled around a mouthful of pastry. "That's naught but another romantic notion," he said, spitting crumbs. "I told this one, I did. His Majesty needed an excuse to keep me close under guard. Murder's easier to explain than magic."

"I've seen your magic at work. Sir Thomas is still recovering. Laurie!" Corbin wheeled, not quite turning his back to the soothsayer. "This man is dangerous. He's here because White Hill is meant to keep him out of the world, just like all the other dangerous things Sir Thomas has secured beneath the château."

"Every dangerous thing in this household is also advantageous, or haven't you realized?" Laurie returned coolly, smile dimmed. "Sir Thomas is an old worm sitting atop a pile of unimaginable treasure. Why should he care if I make use of a very small portion?"

Eyes fixed still on the soothsayer, Corbin started for the kitchens. Laurie leaped after, darting between Corbin and the château. He spread his arms wide as if Corbin couldn't easily knock him aside. They were well matched in swordsmanship and fisticuffs, but when it came to brute strength, Corbin had the upper hand.

"Not the gentleman's game, I confess, luring you out here

like this." Laurie spoke quickly, biting off each syllable with a click of his teeth. "But we've already established you're no gentleman, Corbin, and the truth is you're my last resort. If you go to Sir Thomas or David or—God forbid—the girls, I'm finished."

Rob grunted dark amusement. He finished his pastry and sipped from his cup. Moonlight speckled his bulky form silver through the shifting leaves of the lemon tree. He grunted again, paused, and peered thoughtfully into the depths of his drink.

"I'm in over my head, underwater, and sinking," Laurie continued in a rush. "I've lost it all, everything I had. It's a habit, a very bad habit, a *curse*. The gaming, you know, I know you know. Affrodille surely told you. She disapproves. She always has. I'm not good enough for her beloved chevalier. I'm smudged, besmirched, the most inglorious of all the crew."

Corbin began to feel cold in the warm night. He could make no real sense of Laurie's patter, but the desperate, self-pitying tune was one he'd heard many times before, years and years of the same song as he stood practicing bladework, batting the flat of his heavy wooden sword against Mother's lavender and roses, and Da spoke over and over again of things unfairly lost.

"I need your help." Laurie tried to smile as he begged. "You must understand. It's not my fault."

CHAPTER 14

*A*ffrodille was not the gossip Laurie believed she was. Corbin, having lived three quarters of a year among the inglorious crew, hadn't bothered to give his fellow students much thought past the necessity of day-to-day companionship. It wasn't that he was callous or even disinterested. But Corbin guarded his own privacy like a hound with one last bone to its name, and he accorded his new friends the same respect. He comforted Marc in the midst of night terrors but didn't press come daylight. Explanation enough was writ plain across the man's burned face and hands. He was often witness to Dot's sour humor but never thought to ask why the sound of her sister's voice lifted in idle song sometimes set her to weeping or why Mary-Louise locked herself in the lass's dormitory whenever fog off the Seine rolled up the hill and cloaked the château in cloud. Corbin knew even before Sir Bellamy rode in with the spring —from a word dropped here or there across the boards— that Affrodille and her mother were long estranged. Of all people, Corbin knew exactly what it felt like to mourn a parent, yet it never occurred to him Affrodille might appreciate any expression of empathy.

Corbin wasn't a cold man. He certainly wasn't cruel. He was so busy preparing to face the Beast he didn't pause to think that those around him might already be battling their own monsters. So while the rest of White Hill and, in fact, most of patrician France knew very well that the Duke of Spare suffered a heir sweet on games of chance and short on luck, and all of Fontainebleau had politely looked away when the duke had sent his beloved Laurent into service before the lad could lose the last of his inheritance in the cockpits, Corbin knew only that Laurie's boots were sore in need of cobbling, his weaponry was generally shabby if carefully kept, and that he sometimes came to bed quite late of night smelling distinctly of the river.

Addictions often run bone deep, and temptation will always rear its eager snout. Shrewder souls than young Laurent Spare have fallen prey centuries over to Honnefleu's moneylenders. The duke was a very stupid man to assume his son would let a little thing like a frozen allowance keep him from his pleasure.

Rob went willing back into the warren, but there was a slyness to his glance when he cast eyes Corbin's way. He moved with a quickness that belied his bulk and made Corbin nervous. It was easy to imagine him with his hands or a rope around a lass's throat, strangling. Sir Bellmany had said the soothsayer left his victims with blue faces and swollen tongues.

They strode quickly through the tunnels. Laurie implored Rob to hasten for he expected Sir Thomas and David back before moonset. Rob lengthened his stride obediently, his attention still on the cup in his hand. Corbin, bringing up the rear, knew all at once that the soothsayer didn't require a silver basin for his scrying. He knocked the cup from Rob's hand, sending wine onto the tunnel floor.

This time around it was Laurie who stood poised with sword in hand.

"It's not just spring water and a bowl he uses," Corbin said. They stood frozen, three in a line in the earth beneath the château, faces shuttered, muscles twitching. "He was doing something with the wine. I saw it. Some sort of…conjuring."

"I'm no sorcerer," Rob argued. He gave Laurie's sword the same cautious respect he'd given Corbin's under the lemon tree. "Reading the sediment, that's what I do. Can't much help it when I see a thing in the cup. Comes upon a man naturally, like noticing the weather or the state of the crop in the fields." His high voice cracked. "It's harmless."

"Move," Corbin grated, meaning both men. He wanted nothing more than to see Rob safely returned to his cell. Rob lowered his chin and trudged on. Laurie followed close on his heels. He didn't sheathe his sword.

They walked the rest of the way without speaking. Every underground echo and imagined sound made Corbin's breath catch. He expected to round the next corner and come face-to-face with the matched sisters on one errand or another even though he knew they were asleep in their beds several stories above. Once he thought he heard the scrape of footsteps in the tunnels behind them, but when he paused to listen there was only the pop of guttering torches.

The door to the cell stood open. The chamber beyond was black. Rob stepped over the threshold as if he could see in the dark as well as into the future. The rock in the corner sprang to life, flooding the space with yellow light. The cell looked exactly as Corbin had last seen it, uninhabited bare but for the cot and a single blanket folded neatly at one end of the mattress.

Rob sat on the floor at the base of the lamp, crouched again on his heels. He wagged his chin not at Laurie but at Corbin, black eyes twinkling. It wasn't a friendly scrutiny, but Laurie seemed blind to the soothsayer's malicious cast, smiling as he put away his sword, affable as a suitor bidding his latest conquest temporary farewell.

"Two nights," he said. "Maybe four."

"For this I will need my bowl," Rob mused as he bobbed his head. "Wine will do or snowmelt, fresh. Not well water or ale. And the coin."

"Of course," Laurie replied. He curved subtly toward the soothsayer, well and truly hooked. Corbin's heart sank.

"You friend needs convincing," Rob said.

"He'll come round." Laurie shepherded Corbin back away from the chamber. He strained to pull the sliding door from its pocket in the wall. Corbin, sneering over the top of Laurie's head at the soothsayer, didn't offer to help.

"He's stubborn like his namesake," Rob mused, nodding and nodding as he beamed at Corbin. "I saw it, in the dregs, I did, before he dared spill my wine. Stubborn, interfering crow. But the wolf will pluck your tail feathers, boy, keep you caged, and soon enough, you'll go willingly to perch on his shoulder. I saw it."

"What? What do you say?" Corbin tried to brush past his friend, but Laurie seemed to have gained strength with desperation. He shoved at Corbin with both hands. Corbin, startled, fell back a pace, and Laurie managed to pull the sliding door.

"Wait! What did he mean? Laurie, what did you tell him about me?"

"Absolutely nothing." Laurie's fingers shook as he locked the door. Sir Thomas's key ring looked wrong in his hands.

Corbin remembered that it was stolen and would soon be missed. "Whatever he thinks he knows he saw in the wine, just as he claimed. And he's good, Corbin, very good. Why, I've tested him thrice just to be sure. He's not been wrong once. I think I could try him a thousand times and never catch him out. He's genuine, Corbin. He's going to save my life."

"A LOAN," Laurie explained after he'd seen Sir Thomas's keys returned just in time to their place on a peg on the wall in the chevalier's chamber. He sat on the end of Corbin's cot, kicking his heels restlessly against the plank floor. "I know you're flush, Corbin. We all saw the state of your purse when David dragged you in that first day, half-dead. The master practically fell dead himself when he weighed all that coin in one hand."

Corbin threw his friend a dark look. "You know that was payment for my year on White Hill." He had one ear pressed against the dormitory door, straining to hear any footstep on the spiral stair, convinced that Sir Thomas would somehow know Rob had escaped his cell.

"I know David made sure the master took only what he was owed," Laurie replied. "Nothing stays secret long in this house. I even know where you've got it squirreled away." He looked pointedly at the floor alongside Corbin's cot.

Corbin set his back to the door. He took a long breath between gritted teeth. "I'd blacken your nose, Laurie, if I didn't think it would start the others asking questions."

Laurie's cocky grin dimmed. "Go ahead," he suggested. "If it means you'll help me. Better a broken nose than a broken skull. The Growler's men won't stop at one punch if I turn up short of funds again four days hence."

Groaning, Corbin stomped across the room. "How much do you owe?"

He knelt in front of his hidey-hole. Laurie's sigh of relief was loud enough to cover the scrape of the floorboard pulling free in Corbin's hands. After reaching into the narrow space, Corbin pushed aside the square of black wool, freeing his old purse. It was still bulky in his hand, despite Sir Thomas's missing portion and the handful of coins Corbin had given away in Honnefleu.

Laurie snatched the purse from Corbin's palm. He loosened the strings and turned it upside down over the cot. He counted the coins as they fell upon the mattress.

"More than thirty," he admitted sadly. But his grin had reappeared. He slapped Corbin on the back. "Luckily for my skull, thirty's more than enough to buy in one last game, and with Rob's divinations I shan't lose. All I need is the winning bird, two or three times, and I'll be back above water, right as rain."

"You'll be right as rain," echoed Corbin, watching as Laurie scooped coin back into the purse. "What about me?"

"Don't look so low. I told you; it's a loan. Once the Growler's satisfied and I've got my luck back—with old Rob's help—I'll be able to pay you back, with interest."

"It's not my purse I'm fretting over. It's Sir Thomas's temper when he discovers you're making use of his prisoner."

Laurie tucked Corbin's purse under his tunic. He stared at Corbin, his expression solemn. He had very green eyes and very long lashes, and all of White Hill knew how he used them to his advantage. But Corbin was unmoved.

Laurie laughed. "Stubborn crow. Rob was right about you. But Sir Thomas wouldn't want me dead, Corbin, would he? Over a streak of bad luck at the cockpit? And what he doesn't know won't hurt us. Rob's certainly not going to talk, is he? And I know I can count on you, friend." He widened his eyes again, chewing winsomely on his lower lip. "Can't I?"

Corbin plunked down hard on his mattress. After plucking his boots free one at a time, he hurled them at Laurie. "Go away," he snarled. "It's almost dawn, and I'm to meet Affrodille after breakfast. She'll know if I don't get some sleep."

"Fantastic," Laurie replied eagerly. "Mayhap she knows where David and Sir Thomas have hid the soothsayer's silver basin. Poke around, will you, but don't be obvious about."

"Why should I help you further? Isn't my coin enough? I know better than to mingle with a man like that, madman and murderer, enemy of the crown, even if you don't."

"You might reconsider," Laurie said, shameless in his cajoling. "He saw something of you in only wine dregs. What might he see in his basin, do you think? I imagine he could tell you a thing or two about how best to defeat the Littleton Fiend or how best to keep from dying while you try. Don't you think?"

Corbin, groaning again, turned his back to the room and pressed his fists over his ears.

A DAY PASSED, then one more. Laurie appeared subdued but undamaged. His skull remained in one piece, and as far as Corbin could tell, the Growler's men hadn't taken him to task. Corbin dared hope maybe the last of Da's coin had been enough to put his friend's debts right after all, but he was afraid to ask. Even if Corbin had found the courage, he would have struggled to find the time or place. Laurie was often away from the château on Sir Thomas's business. When Corbin did see the other man on White Hill, it was always at the boards or during drills and in the company of either Affrodille or one or both of the matched sisters.

Wherever Laurie was sleeping, it wasn't in the lads' dormitory. Corbin should have found his absence concerning, but he well knew Laurie preferred bed company whenever possible, and so he managed to convince himself Laurie had simply gone to ground in a kitchen maid's bed or snugged up with one of the lads in the stables.

David soon put that hopeful supposition firmly to rest. After returning to his tower late one evening and interrupting Corbin at another staring contest with the beastly portrait, the scholar tossed an armful of dusty scrolls onto the seat of his padded chair. Scrubbing both hands over his face, he peered through his fingers at Corbin.

"What's your bedmate up to?" David demanded. "I can't go down into the warren lately without tripping over the man, and he's never too fond to see me. When I came upon him this evening, he looked exactly like he'd seen a ghost, and as we've already discussed, White Hill is *not* haunted."

"Nor is Laurie my bedmate," Corbin retorted, taken aback.

"Isn't he?" In a fit of ire, David changed his mind and knocked the pile of scrolls from his toile cushion to the floor, then collapsed in their place. He spread his legs long, shoving an errant scroll aside with one foot. "It's not any of the kitchen lasses, nor anyone in the stables. He's been avoiding Honnefleu. It's not Affrodille, nor Dot or Mary-Louise; they *have* been to the stables. It's certainly not Sir Thomas, nor myself. I assumed he'd finally put his mind to seducing *you.*"

"I—what?"

"Oh, don't look so surprised." David pressed his knuckles against the bridge of his nose. "It's my business to know everything that happens in this château, I've told you so. Granted, I thought you had better taste than to fall for the Spare's errant heir, but recently it seems all my assumptions are in error."

Corbin bent to pick up one of the scattered scrolls. "I don't have a bedmate." He felt the unavoidable blush staining his cheeks and so busied himself with unrolling the parchment. Dust caught on the front of his tunic and made him sneeze. The writing on the scroll was faded, and while the letters were familiar, their groupings made no sense.

"It's in *latium vulgare*," David explained. "Italian vernacular. Sir Thomas has a client in Rome who believes he's discovered a nest of vampires." He sounded lighter, amused, but Corbin didn't yet dare glance his way. "And I'm sorry if I've offended you, Corbin. I can tell by the color in your face I have."

"I don't—" Corbin replaced the scroll and confronted David. He imagined he could feel the Beast's painted yellow glare burning on his neck as he summoned what he hoped was a reassuring smile. "I've never thought of Laurie...like that."

David's sour mien softened. "Believe me, you wouldn't be the first if you had. He draws lovers like flies to honey, that man." He folded bony hands in front of his nose. "But what is he about, lingering in the warren? He's always preferred fresh air to catacombs. He's up to no good, I think, and Thomas won't listen to my warnings."

Corbin was glad of his earlier blush to disguise new heat beneath his skin. David didn't seem to expect an answer, so Corbin returned his attention to the relative safety of the demon portrait. The devil looked down from the canvas, the moon shining over one shoulder, a pitiless sneer fixed forever on the wolfish snout. Corbin, as he often did, touched the dark fur, reminding himself that this version, at least, was paint and not living.

"You've stayed away as I asked, haven't you?" David sounded anxious. "The fortune-teller's been compliant since

I melted his basin to ingot, but a man like that will always be a threat. You've enough to worry about as is."

To ingot. Of course.

Corbin couldn't help himself. Standing still with one hand on canvas, he shifted sideways and let his gaze roam idly about the tower chamber. It didn't take long, now that he knew what he was looking for. The ingot sat atop David's oven, a rough lump of silver almost obscured by a collection of glass vials and a bundle of spotted feathers. It wasn't a pretty specimen. Half as large as a man's head, it was lumpy as a miniature mountain range, the silver dulled to black by whatever alchemy David had used to change its shape.

"Corbin?" David prompted. "Tell me you're not involved in whatever new mischief Laurie's stirring up. You've stayed out of the warren?"

"Yes," Corbin promised, unable to look away from the misshapen silver. What hope did Laurie have, he wondered, if the basin was destroyed? "Yes, it's nothing, David. Likely one of Laurie's strange games, you know how he is."

David seemed to relax. Corbin felt an unlooked for pang of disappointment. Not for Laurie's sake, he realized, abashed, but for his own. It struck him then that a small, secret part of him had wanted Rob to look into the silver bowl and tell him how best to defeat the Beast.

As if seeing the way through a demon's curse was as easy as auguring a cockfight.

Corbin shook his head, dismissing himself for a coward. When he glanced up at the canvas, he imagined he saw bitter amusement lurking in that painted snarl.

Laurie was already well into his cups when Corbin finally tracked him down at the Blue Goose Tavern. It was apparent he'd been warming the table and chair in a back corner for quite some time; empty platters and flagons littered the table's surface. Despite the pleasant weather, Laurie wore a long cloak over his White Hill uniform, the hood pulled up even inside to conceal his face. As far as Corbin could tell, the other man was without his sword, and doing his best to appear as unremarkable as possible.

"There you are." Corbin tugged an empty chair against the table and dropped into it. "I've been looking for you. No one knew where you'd gone to, and I was beginning to despair."

Laurie had both elbows planted firmly on the table. He clutched a tankard of cheap ale loosely in his fingers. He stank of old sweat, too much drink, and chicken grease.

"Despair." After setting the ale aside, Laurie leaned back in his chair. He regarded Corbin from beneath his hood. "I know despair, hiding out in Honnefleu's most humdrum tavern, playing dice for my keep, and scrubbing dishes for my breakfast and supper." He made a sour face across Corbin's shoulder at the skinny matron who tended the bar. "The proprietress is a friend, else I'd be out on my ear. And what does that matter? I've searched high and low for the fortune-teller's bowl, and I've found nothing. Rob's stopped speaking to me altogether, and the Growler's sent word he'll be coming for me himself soon as he's back from business north."

Corbin, peering nervously about the common room as though the Growler might pop up from behind the closest keg of ale, decided the Blue Goose was a pleasant sort of place in which to hole up, if one had no other choices. The rushes on the floor were clean, the suppertime patrons genial if loud. A flock of plucked chickens roasted on a long spit against the hearth, turned by a freckle-faced lad with a gap in his smile. Grease popped when it dripped from the spit into the fire, making the flames turn blue.

Laurie, scowling, kicked Corbin under the table. "Why've you come then?" He sat up suddenly. "Have you found it?" Hope erased the new lines on his face and made him young again. "Thank God. I knew I could count on you, Corbin. You've got more luck hanging about you than any other man I know. Quick! Give it to me." He crawled out of his seat and leaned over the table, grasping.

"No." Corbin held up a hand. "Stop, Laurie. No. I don't have the basin; I fear it's gone. I've come to urge you again—go to Sir Thomas or Affrodille for help. You must. You said it yourself: the chevalier won't want you dead, Laurie. He'll pay the Growler what you owe, I'm sure of it." As the words tumbled out, Corbin felt lighter. Of course Sir Thomas would put things right. "It will sting your pride, I know, but damaged pride is far better than a broken head."

Laurie, still spread across the table, thumped both fists hard on wood.

"Not," he said, face white, "when he discovers I've been selling pieces of treasure out of the warren the last two years in order to keep my tab clear." He pushed violently back into his chair, slamming two platters and a mug to the rushes with his fists as he did so. Then he wrapped his arms about his middle, groaning. "It's been a hell of a thing, slipping bits past David's gimlet eye, but now the good pieces—anything gold, it's only gold he'll take or French coin—is gone. Not even a single bloody gilded relic to buy me another week. It's *all* gone."

"Laurie," Corbin breathed, aghast. "Oh, Laurie."

"Exactly. You see it now." Laurie didn't hide his bitterness. "The master's as likely to strike me down as the Growler, if not more so. I'll have no friends left in Honnefleu or anywhere else, once the truth is out. Why, His Majesty himself will call for my head—White Hill's treasure belongs to the throne when it comes down to it."

Corbin fumbled at his belt. He dropped his coin purse on the table between them.

"Take this," he said. "Take it and run. You can't stay here, Laurie. Get off your ass and go."

Laurie stared at the fat purse in shock. "How?"

"I sold Da's ermine cloak." Corbin regarded Laurie earnestly. "Just this morning. It's very fine fur, that, and what need of it had I? *I've* friends now down on the docks, and they got me a good price."

"A very good price." Laurie snatched up the purse, weighing it in his hand. He licked his lips before glancing at Corbin, eyes wide and astonished. "Are you sure? This is… this is good. And too much. Corbin?"

"I'm sure," Corbin promised, even though he wasn't. He was frightened and horrified by the extent of Laurie's trespasses. "Just, please. Take it and go now, before it's too late. It'll get you a fast horse, I think, and a meal or two along the road."

Laurie laughed, a gasp of joy or relief. "Thank you! Thank you!" He stood so quickly his chair overturned. Then he bent and kissed Corbin on the mouth, quick and fierce and hard, before he was gone, over the fallen chair and out the door.

Corbin set a finger against his lips. His mouth tingled as if he'd been struck by nettles or been out in the sun too long, but the sting of Laurie's kiss left a wisp of pleasure unfurling low behind his rib cage, and the surge of surprised arousal felt like fire in his veins.

"Oh," he murmured, pressing his thumb against his lower lip until it bruised.

The matron behind the bar tsked, loudly unimpressed.

"He's run off without paying for half a fowl," she declared. "Will you be doing his share of the washing up?"

. . .

CORBIN WOKE BEFORE DAWN, disturbed from deep sleep by the howling of wolves. He rolled to his feet, grabbing up Da's sword. He wasn't at home in Littleton, the black forest pack running wild through Nell's herd, nor was he lying near death in the dirt near the king's highway listening helplessly as a few bloodthirsty monsters tore the Benedictine apart. Nor, as was his first mad thought, had the Beast come early across Normandy to collect his due.

He was alone in the lads' dormitory. A single banked cresset glimmered in one corner as he'd left it before retiring for bed. He knew it was near dawn only by the clock in his head and almost a year of sleeping in the windowless space. The clamor that had woken him was not a wolf's howl at all, but the baying of a madman. As he shook sleep from his head, Corbin recognized the high, childish cries: Rob the soothsayer out of the warren again, by the near sound of it.

Corbin knew better than to run headlong down the spiral staircase, but he descended much more quickly than was strictly safe, slipping on stone. Only natural dexterity and long practice kept him from falling. The shouts grew louder as Corbin ran toward the main hall then choked abruptly off. The hall was dark but for low flames in the hearth; the candles were snuffed for the night. The cook and her little maid cowered on the kitchen threshold. The cook clutched the sobbing maid against her ample bosom, muttering soothing nonsense. She flinched as Corbin.

"In the garden," she said over the maid's weeping. "He came up through the warren, broke all the crockery, scared my Anna half to death. Screaming the whole way and young lord Spare on his heels, looking just as addled."

"Laurie's here?" Corbin stopped.

"Of course he is. Where else would he be lately but at the center of every mess?" David appeared out of the darkness at Corbin's elbow, making the cook gasp and the maid shriek.

The scholar shushed the two woman with a stern look, then tugged at Corbin's sleeve. "If the fortune-teller's out, there's no telling what we're walking into. Let me go first. And if I tell you to run for Thomas, go at once, no questions."

"I'm the one with the sword," Corbin protested.

"And I'm the one with wit," retorted David. "Quietly now."

The kitchen was as dark as the main hall. Crockery crunched underfoot. The pungent smell of citrus and lavender made Corbin's nose itch dangerously. As his eyes adjusted to the predawn light filtering through open garden door, he saw why: the cook's collection of dried herbs were torn from their usual places tethered to the kitchen rafters and scattered over the floor, ground into packed earth as though by purposeful stomps and strikes. Sir Thomas's precious jug of olive oil—a gift sent all the way from Fontainebleau and opened only on the most celebratory of occasions—was sheared top from bottom. Olive oil puddled beneath the broken jug, spreading in a lazy river across the kitchen worktable.

David stepped silently out of the château and into the morning. Corbin followed, blade at the ready. The new quiet after such clamor worried him, but when they stepped into the herb garden, he believed at first that their caution was unnecessary, that they'd arrived late, and Rob was already contained, surrounded by Sir Thomas and the rest of his inglorious crew. Sir Thomas held the smoking remains of a long torch, while Affrodille stood astride a clump of rosemary, a knife in each hand. The matched sisters stood beneath the lemon tree, conspicuously relaxed, even as Corbin knew they were both poised to strike if need be.

Rob hadn't made it very far into the garden, collapsing instead onto his stomach just outside the kitchen between two lavender shrubs, arms outstretched across the ground, fingers just brushing the edge of cook's small water garden.

Tiny wavelets rolled from the center of the pond toward the shore where Rob lay. A fish arched from water to sky and back again, silver in the dawn. A second followed, and then another, and another, until all of cook's little school jumped into the air, and the entire surface of the pond seemed to boil with restless energy.

"Stop him!" David cried. "Don't let him get into the water!"

"He's well stopped," Sir Thomas answered grimly. "As I put out my torch in his eyes, and Affrodille knocked the basin from his hands. There it is, nearly sunk. Someone will have to wade in and retrieve the bloody thing, I suppose."

Corbin's nose, as if prodded by the chevalier's dry recital, finally awoke to the smell of burned flesh. He gulped to keep from gagging, turned his head to spit, and in doing so caught sight of where his friend Laurie crouched in spring grass near the kitchen's outer wall. Laurie's face was obscured by the gnarled branches of an old climbing rose, its blossoms yellow as the rising sun, but tension was evident in the tight coil of his body against Caen stone.

"This man's scrying bowl no longer exists." David, heedless of Sir Thomas's murmured warning, knelt at Rob's side. For the first time, Corbin realized the scholar was without both cap and robes. Instead David was dressed in dark trousers and a tunic, his curls run riot over his head. "I destroyed it myself."

He put both hands on Rob's shoulders and rolled him over. In the twilight, Corbin could clearly see the damage done to the soothsayer's face. From brow to nose, his flesh was blackened, his eyes naught but charred holes in his face. Rob's mouth opened and closed as he gasped and whimpered. David shuddered in sympathy.

"Dot," he ordered after one slow breath, looking up and around, "bring me butter and honey from the kitchen. As much of it as you can find, please." Dot dashed away. David shucked off his tunic. Affrodille tossed him one of her knives. David went to work on the fabric, cutting it quickly into bandages.

"Stay, Laurent," Sir Thomas barked. Laurie, having risen furtively to his feet beneath the yellow blossoms, froze. "No use running now, I think. The damage is done. The truth will come out. The cheap tureen floating in my cook's pond is your doing, I suppose?" He waded into the pond, grabbing up a simple silver bowl hardly bigger than a chamber pot. He held it up for examination.

"Cheap!" Laurie snarled. He struck aside thorny branches, stalked past Corbin without word or recognition, and glared between Sir Thomas and Rob. "It's silver through and through. I spent good coin on it, I did. He promised me it would work. And what did I get in return? Nothing at all!" Disgusted, he jabbed the toe of one boot into Rob's twitching thigh. Rob wailed. Laurie, muscles trembling in furious mimicry, kicked out again.

"Stop!" Sir Thomas crossed the pond in three great leaps. After tossing the bowl aside, he shoved one gloved hand up and into Laurie's jaw, squeezing as he pressed the young man back again into the trailing rose. Laurie staggered in shock. He reached up, trying to pry his master's fingers away, but the old chevalier would not relent.

"Did you think I didn't know? You should have run when you had the chance. Sneak, thief, snake in my house," Sir Thomas accused softly. Laurie panted, scrabbling for air. Yellow blossoms broke free and fell around them both. The sky above had brightened so that Corbin could see the concern on Affrodille's face as she skirted the pond and approached Sir Thomas.

"Strangling Spare's heir in our home will not help anyone," she cautioned. "He's Fontainebleau's problem now,

Thomas. We'll lock them together in a cell, and I'll ride at once for the guard."

Sir Thomas looked as if he'd like to argue, but Affrodille set a hand on his shoulder in quiet entreaty. The chevalier growled before relenting. He relaxed his fingers, allowing Laurie a whistling inhale, and started to pull away, turning to Affrodille, mouth still creased.

Corbin saw Laurie move before anyone else—Corbin who had been trained by Laurie himself to recognize unlooked for danger. Da's sword sliced forward and straight through before Corbin quite understood what he'd done, and even as he stared at his own hand in disbelief, that hand twisted the afreet glaive neatly once and then back again in Laurie's soft belly.

A woman screamed. Corbin, unable to look away from Laurie's wide, startled eyes, thought at first it was Mary-Louise. But it was Affrodille crying aloud in grief and horror as she caught at Sir Thomas's falling body. Corbin had been quick but not quick enough: Laurie's sharp little kitchen knife had, against all odds, managed to sever Thomas's throat lengthwise in an ugly, ragged smile. The chevalier was dead even as Affrodille pulled him into her lap. David, face gone the color of old bone, scrambled on his hands and knees across the grass toward his master.

Laurie wasn't dead. He writhed on the end of Corbin's sword, a fish thoroughly hooked. The weight of him pulled Corbin forward. He had to put a foot on Laurie's pelvis to keep from falling atop the other man, and that made Laurie open his mouth. Blood bubbled between his teeth, rising on his tongue, overflowing his chin. His eyes widened farther in terror.

"Finish him." It was Dot, standing steady at Corbin's elbow. "You're not meant to let them suffer, Corbin. That's a messy kill. Give him mercy."

So Corbin put all his weight on his foot and yanked Da's sword. He heard Laurie's pelvis crack as the blade pulled free. After that, it was only another twist of the wrist, and then Laurie wore a gaping smile bloody as Sir Thomas's, only more skillfully done.

There was a lot of blood. On Laurie's body, on Corbin's arms and hands and down his front, in the pond, and on the yellow roses. Even on Dot, who tugged Corbin away toward the kitchen. He followed without resisting even as he thought he belonged on the grass with Affrodille and David, mourning their murdered chevalier. Rob was screaming again—or maybe it was Affrodille—Corbin couldn't be sure without turning back, but his body continued to disobey his heart. He trailed after Dot, dripping gore, meek as newborn calf.

Dot shut the kitchen door on the garden. The cook and her maid stood pale as ghosts over broken crockery.

"Down to the stables," Dot said. She sounded gruff. "Mary-Louise will have your jennet ready by the time you get there. You can't stay, not now. Lord Spare will have you hanged for Laurie and Sir Thomas both to save his name. We won't be able to protect you, not without Thomas, not against Fontainebleau."

"You want me to run away." Corbin worked it out more slowly than he should have. His head felt full of cobwebs. He worried that he was dripping Laurie's blood onto the cook's floor, that she wouldn't be able to scrub it clean. "Like Laurie was meant to. Only he didn't."

"You will." While the cook and her little maid watched, Dot pushed and cajoled Corbin into the main hall. "Stay off the highway. Keep to the fields, and keep out of sight the best you can. They'll be sending men after you, Corbin. Use your head." Gently, she shoved him in the direction of the spiral staircase. "Clean your hands, grab your things, and ride."

"But where should I go?" That wasn't what he'd meant to say at all. The question slipped out, anguished.

Dot regarded him with pity. "Why, where you've always been meant to go. The king's guard won't easily find you in the black forest, I think."

THE FIEND IN THE FOREST

"When the devil grows old he turns hermit."

—Ariosto

CHAPTER 15

Corbin rode away from Honnefleu without incident.

He'd cleaned Laurie's blood from his hands and body. Then he'd stripped off his stained tunic and left it all in a heap on the dormitory floor, exchanging it for the more elegant version he'd had a chance to wear only once, during yuletide celebrations. It was a lighter weight and would do little to keep him warm in the night, but no one would stop him on the streets and call him murderer.

Mary-Louise met him in the stable just as Dot had promised. Jenny wore her bridle and a saddle Corbin didn't recognize cinched over her old blanket. Mary-Louise tossed him the donkey's reins before handing him a small packet of bread and sausage. Then she held out a square of carefully folded parchment.

"Sir Thomas would want you to take these," she said. Her eyes were red-rimmed, but her voice was steady. "He always said an educated soldier had every advantage."

Corbin knew the pages of the English king's book by feel. He unfolded the bundle anyway. The newly torn edges were ragged and raw against old illustrations of the Littleton

Fiend. He didn't have the heart to tell her he'd memorized every word in the short entry and could recite it forward and backward to even David's exacting standards.

"Thank you," he said instead, tucking the pages safely in his purse.

Mary-Louise stood on her toes to kiss him on each cheek. "Don't be frightened," she said. And then, just as her sister had: "Use your head, Corbin."

In the spring morning, Jenny was as fresh as Corbin had ever seen her. She tossed her mane, springing to the canter. All the way down the hill, she snorted at songbirds and shadows. Corbin let her have her head and stood in the stirrups to keep from jostling off her back. Even so, finger bones and teeth bounced on their string beneath the collar of his shirt in wordless reproof. Michael's bead chafed his sternum.

He knew he didn't deserve David's gift, not any longer. He had no doubt his friend must blame him now for Sir Thomas's death. But when he reached up, intending to rip the necklace from his throat, he discovered he didn't want to let it go. He let the necklace fall back beneath his shirt. The bead continued to rub the flesh above his heart, but that was the very least of his pains. Corbin focused on that small irritation as Jenny galloped off the hill, and he looked one last time on the château's fluttering pennants.

They paid him no mind on the city streets, thinking him just another traveler come from shipboard, or mayhap a village man riding out early on family business. It seemed impossible that no one knew he'd just killed a friend, turned his blade twice to ensure the deed was consummated.

It was done before I knew it. Too easily done. Da was right—I have a knack for it.

For the first time, and far too late, Corbin wished otherwise.

WHERE HONNEFLEU MET the king's highway Corbin urged Jenny off the road. They pushed south through Picardy fields, skirting hedge and cottage. Jenny slowed to a trot. Corbin lightened his hand on her rein. The spring crop was only knee high to the donkey, but he didn't want her to set foot awry in a gopher's hole or stumble into a dwarf's nest. Springtime dwarves were less dangerous, made lazy by warming weather, but Sir Thomas had lately taken to speaking aloud his increasing concern about their new boldness around Honnefleu. The old chevalier had meant to send his inglorious crew on a hunt come summer; now the city would have to deal with the growing infestation without White Hill's help.

"What will they do without Sir Thomas?" Corbin demanded of Jenny's pricked ears. "What will happen now?"

But, of course, he knew exactly what would happen next. He could see it in his mind's eye, just as Dot had described it. If the alarm hadn't already been raised by one of the household, perhaps even the cook or—a far worse truth to face—David and Affrodille, it soon would be. The château would send riders to Fontainebleau with word of misfortune. Within a day, two at the most, Honnefleu would be overrun with soldiers. Three days, possibly less, and those same men would storm the countryside, spreading Corbin's name and description from village to village.

He'd been lucky to reach Littleton ahead of the tale.

CORBIN DIDN'T STOP for rest until the sun was low in the sky, and then he did so only for Jenny's sake. Just behind a stony hedgerow he found a spot of bare sand beside a swift-flowing creek. He let Jenny drink her fill before cupping his hands and doing the same. The water was cold and sweet. The drink woke Corbin's stomach. It grumbled, reminding him that he hadn't eaten since the day before. He sat in the sand and opened Dot's packet of food. He ate methodically while Jenny grazed. As soon as the first mouthful of sausage hit his gut, he felt nauseous, but he continued doggedly.

Berries grew on patches of thorny briar along the base of the hedge. He recognized them, red and plump, for the blood currants Nan used to boil into jam. The currants tasted foul without added honey and spice, but they were safe to eat and portable. He picked several handfuls, bundling them alongside the last of his bread and sausage. By the time he finished, he was ready to ride on. Every shift of the breeze in the grass made him start and reach for his sword. Wiser to lay low until after dark, he knew, but he didn't dare waste a moment. Terror spurred him onward even as he dreaded the end of his journey.

When Corbin recalled the dead weight of Laurie's body on his blade, the crunch of bones beneath his foot, and the spray of blood in the dawn, he knew he'd rather fight the Beast in the black forest than draw blade again against another man.

THEY PASSED a farmer in his sheep pasture and a group of children playing hide-and-go-seek in the fields. The farmer paid Corbin no mind at all while the children called and waved. A hound barked in the distance, and after sunset, wolves sang. They were close enough to make Jenny snort and break from trot to gallop, but by that time Corbin was so steeped in dread, he barely noticed. When they stopped again beneath a copse of old scrub trees in the black of night, Jenny wouldn't leave his side even to investigate a nearby patch of dandelion. Corbin sat in the dark with his knees pulled under his chin and Da's sword unsheathed at his side. There was no point in chasing sleep. Every time he closed his eyes he saw Laurie laughing or dying. Unable to stomach the thought of bread and sausage, he nibbled at his collection of blood currants and watched the stars shift in the sky overhead.

Halfway through the second day, Jenny startled a pair of fat grouse from a nearby hedge. Dully, Corbin watched the birds take flight. It wasn't until they'd alighted in a neighboring sycamore that he thought of his empty stomach. Affrodille and her knives, he knew, would have had both birds skewered and on the ground before they reached sheltering branches. He still wore a knife up his own sleeve, but it seemed doubtful that he'd bring a bird down.

Use your head, Corbin.

He tried and missed three times. The birds watched him between wide sycamore leaves, confident enough in their position to stay put. When, on his fourth attempt, Corbin almost lost his knife in the undergrowth and had to go wading through grass and bramble to retrieve it, he gave up for fear of dulling the blade.

"See?" he challenged Jenny. "A fool's errand."

Jenny cocked an eye in Corbin's direction but didn't look up from the sweet grass she'd discovered growing nearby. She followed obediently when he walked on, loose reins catching on her long ears when she dipped her head to graze. It felt good to walk and stretch his legs. His thighs ached from riding. Corbin cast an apologetic glance the donkey's way, knowing her back must be as sore as his ass.

"You're a good lass," he told the donkey. Soft green crop

stretched to either side. Ahead another copse of gnarled trees bent beneath blue skies. Behind he could still hear the grouse shifting on the sycamore branches. "You deserve better than a hard ride and then take your chances in the black forest."

Jenny blew through both nostrils in agreement. For the first time since they'd fled White Hill, Corbin smiled.

THEY SHELTERED the second night behind the remains of a deserted cottage long ago burned to the ground. The thatched roof was gone the way of smoke and flame, but the blackened walls stood. There had been a barn once as well, now fallen and covered in swathes of thorny vine. Forgotten crop grew in tangles across a paltry field. The old well was still good, although Corbin had to rehang the bucket before he could slake his thirst.

Red hens roosted in the cottage. They squawked when Corbin chased them out only to boldly return once he'd bedded down in a corner. The chickens would make an easier meal than their wild cousins, but Corbin let them be. He found comfort in their contented mutterings and familiar, dusty smell. He lay on his back with his head on folded arms and counted stars to practice his numbers and keep from thinking of sorrows behind or ahead. He didn't plan on sleep. It caught him by surprise, the needs of his body outweighing two days' trepidation. Corbin felt himself falling. He struggled briefly then slipped under with a sigh.

He slept long. When he woke, the chickens were perched above his head atop the cottage's roofless walls. Afternoon sun streamed through the fluttering leaves of yet another ancient sycamore, warming his face. There were two unbroken eggs in the scratched dirt near his feet. Corbin gathered them carefully in one hand as he rose. Jenny, standing with a leg cocked beneath the sycamore, turned her head when he wandered out of the ruins. Her saddle lay where he'd left it the night before, tipped sideways in the grass. The abandoned farmstead was reassuringly quiet.

Corbin stretched, working kinks from his back. His eyes felt swollen, his head muzzy. Slowly he drew more water from the well. He scrubbed his face and drank. He choked down both eggs, shells and all, before drinking again. He reckoned on half a day's ride south and then west to Littleton. He didn't know Picardy as well as some, but he'd been blessed with a keen sense of direction and Mother's attention to botany. The smaller trees almost lost behind the sycamore would bear apples in the fall. When he picked a blade of grass from alongside the well and crushed it between his teeth, he tasted the same peculiar salt that made Littleton's cheeses so sublime.

"Nearly there," he promised Jenny, even as he wondered if he'd lost his advantage to sleep. Corbin couldn't guess what Da would do once he heard word of Sir Thomas's death.

He won't turn me in. Not so long as he still needs me to keep his bargain. He still needs me.

"We'll have to keep out of sight even once home," Corbin warned Jenny. "There are some in Littleton that wouldn't hesitate to hand me over for the king's favor."

It wasn't until he retrieved his saddle from the grass that he realized they'd had visitors in the night. There in the shadow of the sycamore, between Jenny and the cottage, the grass was pressed flat. Mayhap the jennet had lain down in the night or mayhap something else had trampled the blades flat into the soil. Corbin thought the second was more likely, as for all her remarkable attributes Jenny had never before presented him an offering of two grouse.

Corbin set the saddle back down on the ground. He

approached the grouse carefully, stepping cautiously onto the flattened grass. On White Hill he'd heard stories of pixies who sometimes lured a man to his death in the fields, trapping him in a circle of enchanted mushrooms before pelting him with tiny, poison-tipped darts. But there were no mushrooms that he could see—only the grouse, laid on their fronts, wings spread as if to show off glossy feathers. When Corbin examined them more closely, he saw that their necks were broken and their fat breasts punctured front to back as though they'd been caught in a huntsman's hinged trap.

Grouse in hand, Corbin scanned the abandoned farmstead, searching for signs of company. The barn and the cottage looked exactly as deserted as they had when he'd settled in beneath the stars. The hens scratched around the well, placid. It was a lonely, peaceful scene, but Corbin felt the hair rise on the back of his neck.

Corbin saddled Jenny as quickly as possible. He left the grouse behind in the grass. Whether or not they were the lure of pixies looking to trap a human servant, the birds were an unnatural sort of gift, and one he had no intention of accepting.

HE SMELLED the sea before he heard it and heard the crash of water against rock before he saw the cliff line. By the time they came upon Littleton's western edges, the sun was threatening to dip into the water below. He'd lost time again in late morning when Jenny picked up a stone in her frog. Corbin had cleared the pebble from her foot but not in time to prevent bruising. The jennet was off even at the walk, and Corbin didn't have the heart to ride her. They'd kept as far away from the highway and byways as Corbin could contrive, which meant clambering through a variety of thorny brush, over crumbling walls, and around day laborers at work in the rearmost cropland.

Corbin was scratched and insect-bitten. Jenny was sore, bored, and out of sorts. The evening promised to be cool. Corbin lingered briefly on a sandy precipice over the boiling sea as he'd been wont to do as a child, enjoying the sting of the salt air. The water below was painted scarlet and purple by the setting sun. The tide was going out. A child and its mother wandered the narrow strip of sand below, each laden with a long, pointed stick and a basket for crabs. Corbin watched them until they disappeared around a bend in the cliff, reminiscing. He'd had a talent for crab catching, once, and had kept Mother's cook pot full for days at a time. There was a joy to dodging wave and rock in pursuit of scuttling shellfish that he'd long ago put away as boyish entertainment, but now he thought he'd like nothing better than to walk the cragged shoreline again with stick and basket.

The setting sun flashed green in the sky. Corbin turned his back on the sea. He picked a resolute path through shale and scrub toward home. Jenny walked at his side, long ears folded flat against her skull. They crossed the boundary of Gaffer Julian's back pasture. The farthest edge of the black forest rose up between Corbin and the sea. Gnarled roots thick as his forearm pierced the cliff's outward face as if reaching for the freedom of the water below. Brown squirrels nested in the roots against the bluff. Those on the uppermost lip watched Corbin and Jenny as they limped past, wary of threat.

Bracken gave way to cobblestone. Corbin paused between the forest and the gaffer's property, racked by indecision. Littleton's lights were kindling in the twilight. The de Beaumont cottage was within shouting distance. He wanted desperately to see Nan and his sisters one last time before he braved the Beast, but the prospect of soldiers in the gloaming kept him fixed on the road.

"Look sharp, monsieur. The forest wolves have lately become bold after sunset."

Corbin whirled, startling a loud gasp from both the woman and her young companion. Silently he cursed himself for a fool. He'd been too lost in his own head to hear their approach. He knew them from the sticks they carried and from the heavily laden crab basket over the woman's shoulder. They must have taken the old path up the cliff face from the beach below as he stood thinking of home.

Exhaustion dulled his wits so he thought for a minute he was mistaken. She'd changed much in his short absence, butchered her shock of long hair so it fell barely past her ears and traded her skirts for a man's shirt and trousers. But her wicked smile was the same, and the smudge of dirt always across her nose. The child clinging to the tail of her shirt was just as grimy but brighter of hair and eye both.

"Nell," he said, gone light-headed with relief. He put a hand against Jenny's neck to keep from dropping like a stone in the road.

She was at his side in an instant, bucket and stick forgotten, the child clutched in her arms. She peered beneath the cowl he used to cover his head then clucked her tongue in dismay.

"Corbin. Stupid man! What are you doing here?"

"I came to see that Nan and my sisters are well." He reached to clasp her hand, but she batted his fingers. The little boy wrinkled his mouth in confusion but didn't fuss. Denied Nell's affection, Corbin put his hand atop the child's head instead. "He's grown."

"Babies do," Nell said. Then she swore and struck Corbin on the arm. "You can't be here, you great lout. There are men in town, and at the cottage, asking about you. King's men.

Saying things that made your da shout and your nan take to bed. Beauty's got the girls tucked away in the spare room above Henri's shop. Hope thinks the soldiers are here to take all of Littleton to the gallows." She stepped back to get a better look at his face, jostling the little boy from arms to hip. "Corbin, what happened? They're saying you killed two men, and one of them wore His Majesty's favor on his breast."

"I killed one man. He was my friend. At least, I thought he was. And it wasn't—" Corbin swallowed past the lump in his throat. "I didn't mean to."

Nell's expression softened. "You're an eyesore. Come and sit before you fall down." She pointed at a bit of flowering bramble alongside the gaffer's wall. "There. The soldiers won't come close to the forest, not after dusk. I meant it when I said the wolves have become uncommonly bold. Here, now." Without warning Nell put her son in Corbin's arms. "Sit down and have a cuddle while I think. This is a pretty jennet you've found—did you steal her?"

Corbin sat. The little boy was a warm weight on his lap, the gaffer's wall a solid foundation against his spine. The child, unusually bold, scrutinized Corbin with baffled fascination.

"I didn't steal her. She's mine. Nell, if the wolves have been roaming, should we be sitting like two spring lambs a pebble's toss from the forest canopy?" He peered over the boy's head at the line of trees. Shadows were catching in their branches, obscuring the thicket beyond.

"The wolves don't bother me." But Nell scooped up her sharply pointed crabbing stick. "Not since I grew tired of losing calves to their hunt and struck a deal with their master."

Corbin's jaw dropped. "What? With the Beast?"

"Aye, that's what you called the creature, isn't it?" Nell set about examining Jenny from nose to flank, tutting when she discovered the donkey's tender foot. "Of course, it wasn't himself I spoke to, but one of his odd messengers."

"Messengers?"

"The sort he chooses from those folks unlucky enough to get lost in his forest, like your da," Nell explained. She tugged Jenny's mane affectionately. "This time it was an accounting man, of sorts, on his way to court. Quite a sight he was, too, half-pissed with fright. I wouldn't have believed his tale, either, for all I know your own, but he carried a token for proof bundled all up with the contract."

Nell's son, growing restless, stuck a plump hand down Corbin's shirt. Discovering the pirate's necklace, he gurgled in delight and drew the bones from beneath Corbin's collar.

"Ugh, don't let him chew on that. You've gone white, Corbin. Whiter, I should say. Take a breath. *I* wasn't foolish enough to sign my life away. Three head of beef given freely every autumn is all he required to keep the wolves from my herd."

"I *am* dreaming," Corbin said as the child gummed David's bead.

"No." Nell didn't quite smile. "Though I imagine you might wish you were."

"Normal people don't make commerce with demons, Nell."

"Normal people don't trade a child to the devil, Corbin. I'm hardly the only one in Littleton sending trade goods into that forest. But more than victuals I'd never bargain away, nor would any other sane person." Now she did smile as she looked at the boy Corbin held. "A child is a precious thing, not given away lightly."

Abashed, Corbin looked away. "He's a solid lad. And canny, walking already. Beauty says you named him Jasper."

"For the color of his hair."

"I'm sorry." The apology felt stale. "I should have stopped in to say good-bye."

Nell shrugged. "That's past. The question is: what are we going to do with you now? You can't go into town, not with the soldiers hopping about like fleas on a dog."

Corbin hugged Jasper against his chest. "No, I suppose not," he said, contemplating the forest. "I've come too late after all."

SHE TOOK Jenny and Jasper back into town and returned with food and a flask of good wine and her father's old calving lantern. She made Corbin eat, the circle of light from the lantern a star in the night, and she listened while he talked haltingly of White Hill, of David and Affrodille, of Marc and the matched sisters, and lastly of Sir Thomas and Laurie. She exclaimed over his descriptions of the ships in Honnefleu but only shook her head over mad Rob.

"My grandmother was a dowser," she said. "It's why I'm so good with the fish, I imagine, and why Jasper's got his way with the sea. Water's like a living thing all its own, Corbin, and it makes a powerful magic."

Before White Hill, Corbin might have scoffed. Not any longer. "I think Laurie was ensorcelled. I think the farmer changed him, somehow." Corbin tried and failed to blink back tears. "He loved Sir Thomas. The soothsayer changed him into someone…different."

Nell didn't reply. She let Corbin weep himself dry then passed him her flask.

"*Qu'il repose en paix*," she said. "Drink."

While Corbin drank, Nell took the purse from her belt and shook its contents onto her hand. "This is yours," she said. "I think you should take it with you."

Corbin goggled at the tiny black faceted stone. "That's one of Mother's earrings."

Nell freed the earring from her collection of coin and seashells. She set it on his waiting palm. "I told you he sent a trinket, for proof. This is it. Everyone in Littleton knew your mum's bridal earrings. She was never without them."

The earring caught lamplight, sparkling. "Does Da know?"

"Naught but you and me and he who sent it."

"Thank you." Corbin had wept all his tears. He leaned forward and kissed Nell on the forehead in gratitude before tucking the earring safely away.

"Might bring you luck." Nell ducked her chin, embarrassed. "A bit of your mum to look after you."

They both looked at the forest. In the moonless night, it was visible only by the eddy of lightning bugs around trunks and low branches. Without breeze, the trees were deathly quiet. Corbin could hear the roar of the ocean beyond the cliffs.

"Follow the path for as long as you can," Nell instructed. "It will take you away from the water, south, before it jogs back again west again toward Caen. Step off the path and you'll be lost; the trees grow tight together and are the provenance of dwarves and deadlier things."

Corbin laughed bitterly. "It's the deadlier things I'm after, Nell. If I can find him."

"Oh. I imagine you'll have no trouble." She sounded resigned. "Soon, though. Once the sun's up, His Majesty's men will remember to be brave. They'll come this way and look for you on the back tracks. Best you're well in before they nose about the underbrush."

"Finish the drink and go." Now he heard the sorrow beneath her calm. "Get the business done. Cut off the monster's head and return safely to us, debt paid."

"His heart," Corbin corrected, swallowing the last drops of good wine.

"What?"

Corbin tossed Nell her empty flask and climbed to his feet. He felt steadier with rest and drink although the small portion of food he'd nibbled through sat like a rock in his stomach.

"It's the Beast's heart I'm after," he said. "Not his head."

CHAPTER 16

orbin slung Da's sword across his back, embraced Nell another time, and took her lantern with him into the forest. He didn't look back. The candle inside the lantern case was burning low, but not so low that he was yet worried. He held the light out in front of him so as not to trip over a tree root or fallen branch. Clouds of brilliant lightning bugs scattered at his approach. The path was wide enough for three men abreast or a wagon, but the cobblestones were broken and uneven in many places. Only a few steps in and the dark seemed to gather close, the late hour and the tangled branches working together to obscure Littleton behind.

Corbin walked softly, listening. He knew Da's tale by heart, having heard it recited again and again, awake and in his dreams. The Beast's slavering pack had attacked Mother and Da on their way home from Caen; an hour more and they might have exited the black forest unscathed. But Da couldn't say exactly where in the forest the devil made his home, whether his lair lay closer to Littleton or to the coast or somewhere in between.

"It's a great walled manor house," Da would explain as he taught Corbin how to correctly strop his blade. "Old as the cliffs and wreathed all in leaf and thorn. One minute I wept alone over your poor mother's torn body, keeping the wolves back with naught but kicks and curses, and the next the manor was just *there*, behind us where before—*Marie Mère de Dieu*—I swear to you, son, before we saw nothing but trees and stone."

Corbin hadn't quite believed it then. Da was frail and sick, addled by Mother's loss, consumed by thoughts of revenge, and mayhap exaggerating some. But Corbin believed it now, after more than a season spent on White Hill, witness to secrets more far-fetched than a manor house gone one moment and visible the very next.

Corbin made almost no sound as he ghosted along the path. Dot had taught him how to walk like a cat, and Marc had shown him how to breath softly through his nose instead of his mouth. Mother, with her garden, had demonstrated how best to love the plants and animals while Nell had warned him to respect the wild places for the dangers they concealed. He forgot to be afraid. His muscles warmed, loosening as he walked, until he felt supple and strong. He'd been raised on retribution and honed like the sword he wore on his back to his sharpest point. There was nothing left to do but kill the Beast or be killed, and the simplicity of it burned every other concern from Corbin's skull. He felt light and free and empty.

He heard dawn in the waking squirrels on the forest canopy above. The ever-present lightning bugs vanished seemingly all at once. The forest came to life bit by bit, in squeaks and rustles and calls. Colorful birds and tiny bats both swooped back and forth across the path, barely clearing Corbin's head before disappearing again into the surrounding trees. It was only when Corbin paused to admire a lurid, purple-plumed finch that he realized he no longer had need of Nell's lamp. Ribbons of sunlight filtered through the branches above, painting path and forest with soft yellow light. The rousing wildwood had the quality of a half-forgotten favorite dream: remote and yet abidingly sweet.

When Beastly Manor grew out of the trees with magical suddenness, wrapped in leaf and vine, Corbin didn't so much as blink. He wasn't sure how long he'd been walking. He was no more or less weary than when he'd left Nell behind. It felt as if he was the only person in the gold and green world. Even the manor appeared to be suffering form protracted desertion. The tall stone wall was crumbling along its highest point. And there was the manor gate, just as Da had described it: a rusting iron monstrosity wrapped round with chains and secured with a heavy lock. Da had struck the gate with his fists as he screamed for help, as the slavering wolf pack closed in.

Corbin, much younger and stronger than Da, ignored the gate and climbed the wall, using ancient shanks of moss and cracks in the stone as leverage. He paused at the top to take stock of his surroundings from the greater height. The trees seemed less threatening in the morning. He could glimpse patches of blue sky past the woven canopy. Exactly in front of the rusting gate the cobblestone path veered sharply north and west toward Caen. Corbin, who'd seen the manor materialize where before only trees stood watch, suspected the way home would soon be lost to him. Nevertheless, he turned his back on the road to study the edifice beyond the wall.

The devil's manor was not as impressive as the château on White Hill. The house lacked turrets, pennants, even crenels. It was large, certainly, but square and plain. There were windows—eight that Corbin could see from his perch

—two to either side of the front door, six more in a row above. The windows were each fitted with real glass—a luxury Corbin couldn't comprehend—but most of the panes had broken into shining jagged teeth. The manor facade was stone, but a stone Corbin didn't recognize. The color of sand, striated in places with veins of ivory and scarlet, it wasn't good Norman rock or even Rouen limestone. The slanted roof was a miracle of blue ceramic tile but patched in places with Littleton thatch. Curling white smoke rose from one of three chimneys. The smoke was the only indication Corbin saw that the house might be occupied.

He hopped gracefully down from the wall and onto manor grounds. In the bailey, a garden slept, near death but for a scattering of Littleton violets along the base of the wall. A thick carpet of old leaves concealed the ground. Statues, many missing limbs or faces, stood guard among dormant hedges. A giant, three-tiered fountain anchored the court-yard's center. It dripped flags of moss instead of water.

Corbin waded through vine and leaf. He climbed wide, blue-tiled steps to the entry. Debris shifted under his feet, crackling. The sound was loud in the hushed garden. Corbin paused, glancing around anxiously, but if he was expecting the Beast to leap from behind a hedge or statue, he was disappointed.

A tarnished brass knocker in the shape of a wolf's head watched Corbin from the center of the manor door. Corbin didn't bother with knocking. He tried the latch, found the door unlocked, and pushed his way over the threshold, blade now in hand.

The inside of the manor was as forsaken as the bailey. White sheets wrapped what furniture remained. A large chandelier over the grand stairway wept disconcertingly enormous spiderwebs. Another dusting of leaves covered the floor.

Corbin took several more steps farther into the manor, wondering if he should go up the staircase or venture deeper into the near shadows. He could smell mold and rot, but nothing like the pungent, sulfurous scent the English king's book had warned him to expect. He had just about decided "up" might be the best option, and had one foot on the curving staircase, when a gust of wind kicked up leaves and slammed the door closed. Corbin froze, holding his breath.

The wind had come not from outside the building but from within.

Corbin felt the Beast's approach, heavy footsteps like a pulse deep in the stone heart of the manor. He whirled, Da's sword raised in defense.

"You've come ill-equipped." The Beast stood just inside the threshold, against the manor door. He looked Corbin very thoroughly from head to toe and back up again. "Or improperly educated. The curse says I'm ended not by blade or stone or fire, but of a broken heart."

Corbin didn't waver. He studied the Beast just as assiduously as the Beast studied him. He'd expected the monster from Da's memories—all fang and fur and wolfish claws—or even the flame-eyed devil he knew from David's canvas. The eyes were there—yellow as the sun and so very bright—but they belonged to a dapper young man dressed in breeches and a clean white shirt beneath a dusty velvet coat. He wore his long black hair in a neat braid. His fingers were long and elegant, nails short and clean. His polite smile showed only white, even teeth against dusky skin.

Demons, Corbin knew from hours of David's tutelage, were tricky creatures. They delighted in surprise and confusion, and fed upon a man's terror.

"I carry an enchanted afreet glaive," Corbin replied evenly. "One of only four blades made sharp enough to pierce a devil's breast."

The Beast's smile spread wider. He laughed.

"You're the cheese monger's get. You've his temper and his naïveté." The Beast left the door. He approached Corbin carefully, circling in and then away. "But you're two seasons too early, and although you've your mother's delicate features, you're certainly no girl. I was promised the merchant's heir. What was her name?" He paused, head tilted, yellow eyes narrowed to burning slits. "I was promised *Beauty*."

"You'll not have Beauty," Corbin proclaimed. "Da only let you think Beauty was the oldest. She's not. I am. I'm the heir. And I've come to have your head, devil!"

"I thought it was my heart you were after," drawled the Beast. He stopped moving no more than three paces from Corbin's side. He didn't stink after all. He smelled of rain on grass and the forest at dawn. Corbin could feel the heat off his skin and the uncanny warmth of his regard.

"The merchant was wiser than he appeared," the Beast conceded. "Wise indeed. You'll be little use to me as housekeeper, but you're handsome enough to look upon. It happens I'm in need of a companion."

Concubine. It was Laurie's voice in Corbin's head. He bristled, offended.

"I'm not yours to keep, devil! I've come here to kill you!"

Still smiling, the Beast lowered his chin.

CORBIN WAS OUTMATCHED from the first feint. The demon fought not in beastly form, with tooth and claw, but with a narrow sword conjured from thin air. The clash of blades became a dance: back and forth across the foyer, up a step and then down. Corbin knew his worth as a swordsman. The Beast matched him at every turn. Corbin lunged. The Beast turned his blade. Corbin pivoted and struck out. The Beast dodged. It was apparent the devil was king in his manor house. He waltzed Corbin around and around seemingly without effort.

Minutes seemed to stretch into hours. Corbin grew weary. His arm grew heavy. For the first time since he'd entered the forest, he remembered to be afraid. He'd imagined himself the hero of this tale for so long, but now he thought his bones would end up on the Beast's dinner plate.

"Finish it!" Desperate, he swung with renewed energy. The Beast blocked him easily—once, and then once again. "Kill me and be done!"

In answer, the demon's sword kissed the hollow of Corbin's throat, drawing blood. The Beast backed Corbin sideways until he fetched up against a wall. Da's sword wobbled in Corbin's grip before falling with a clatter to the floor. He gasped for air, the Beast's blade a tooth against his heart vein.

"Your clever papa made me a bargain," the Beast said. "And unless you want me to send my hungry wolves into your brave little hamlet, you'll keep that bargain. You'll serve me until I grow bored of you, or I'll feast upon Littleton entire."

Corbin slumped. His head spun. So quickly it was over— years of preparation all to no avail.

"Yes," he conceded. "Just let them be."

The Beast's sword bit more deeply.

"Swear it," he commanded. "You'll serve me until I say you need not, and you won't attempt escape. I have your loyalty. Swear it. You are mine. *Swear it.*"

"Yes," Corbin repeated, even as he wanted to rend the demon's velvet coat to pieces. "I swear it."

"Good."

The blade fell away. It disappeared the way it had come, back into the air. The Beast brushed down his sleeves.

"It's growing late," he said. "And it's best not to be about these halls after dark. Choose a chamber to sleep in. Bar the door and don't open it till dawn. Meet me in the kitchen after sunrise. Bring your magical sword."

"How will I find the kitchen?" Corbin asked dimly.

Scorn shone in the demon's yellow eyes. "You found me. Hunting the larder should be less difficult than hunting the Manor Beast. Use your wits, if you have any about you."

The Beast disappeared in a puff of white smoke, and now Corbin did smell sulfur. Coughing, he retrieved Da's sword. Dully, he climbed the grand staircase in search of shelter for the night. His heart beat fast, not now with fear, but with hatred.

CORBIN SLEPT RESTLESSLY. He woke to loud birdsong. He sat up, reaching for his blade. It was where he'd left it the night before, at his right hand. The birds were directly above his head, perched high on a massive armoire across the room and also on the tattered remains of the bed canopy.

They watched him with clever eyes as he slid from the four-poster bed. He watched them back as he strapped on Da's sword. Never before had he seen such colorful plumage: wings and breasts of red and purple and green. David, he thought, would be agog.

The chamber had been dark when Corbin stumbled into it. Now he could see that it was a disaster. The windowpanes were smashed. Pieces of glass littered the floor. One of the bed bolsters was torn apart. Mice made nests in the horsehair stuffing. Faded paper peeled in strips from the walls. The floorboards were stained by snow and rain.

Corbin ventured out into the hall. Pink dawn streamed through more broken panes. A carpet he hadn't noticed the night before ran the length of the corridor. It was patterned with roses and worn through in spots. He followed it to the staircase and found himself at eye level with the old chandelier. He could see from the landing that it had once been beautiful, fashioned all of silver and horn, but the spiders had dulled its splendor with their webs and snares. It made him think of David's Rouen pulley in White Hill's spiral staircase.

Corbin braced himself. He took a deep, steadying breath—

And smelled breakfast: cooking meat and freshly baked bread and the faint tang of citrus. His stomach fisted. Corbin cursed his gut as a traitor but followed the perfume down the staircase and through a dank servant's hall to the manor kitchen.

"Wasn't difficult after all, was it?" asked the Beast from his place on a stool by the hearth. "Sleep well? Come. Eat." He spread his hands, revealing a feast laid out on a high serving board. Corbin saw sausages and oranges and porridge and black bread and real butter. His mouth flooded.

"I won't eat demon fare," he said.

"It's human fare," corrected the Beast. "Perfectly mortal, carried to me by merchants like your papa. I give them gold; they give me provisions. Except for the bread. The bread I bake myself. I've a talent for it."

Corbin stared. The demon smiled back, feigning patience, but he tapped long fingers restlessly on one thigh. He was wearing the same velvet coat over breeches and shirt. His black hair was loose about his shoulders. He chose a pitcher of ale from the serving board and poured out two cups.

"You're mine, recall?" He pointed at the stool across from his own. "Sit. Eat. Drink. Cover your sword or I'll banish it permanently from my home."

Corbin didn't remember drawing his blade. He sheathed it cautiously. The Beast loaded a trencher with food.

"Take it," he ordered. "And tell me your name."

Corbin sat. He selected an orange and took his time peeling it. Then he shook his head.

"I owe you my service," he said around a mouthful of the tart fruit. "Nothing more than that."

The Beast's dark brows rose. His mouth curled.

"Red, then, for your hair." He took a healthy swallow of his own ale, humming in pleasure. "Today, Red, you are going to teach me how to use a sword. I have one, somewhere in this mess of a house. I'll find it; you'll teach me."

"But you're a swordsman," Corbin blurted around a mouthful of orange. "You bested *me*."

The Beast laughed. "That was sorcery. Easy. I want a challenge. I want to fight like a man."

WHEN CORBIN FELL onto his mattress the second night in Beastly Manor, he was decorated with bruises and cuts, and his muscles were cramping protest, but his honor was better satisfied. The Beast had proved to be hardly more than a novice with real steel. Corbin had given far better than he got. It didn't matter that every wound he'd dealt the demon healed over near instantaneously; the chagrined expression on the other man's face was as valuable as any lasting scar.

Almost as valuable; it didn't escape Corbin's notice that the Beast was careful to ensure the afreet glaive never once came near his heart. When Corbin did break past the devil's guard too near breast or backbone, Da's sword was sharply turned away, jarring Corbin's hand and arm as if he'd run the blade up against a wall of ice.

"Cheating!" Corbin accused through gritted teeth. "Like a man, you said. No magic."

"You've an enchanted sword in hand," the Beast replied, panting. His white linen shirt was soaked through, but his velvet coat remained impeccable. "Do you take me for a fool?"

They'd sparred almost the entire day long, taking breaks only to feast on more bread and sausage, and to drink more of the Beast's sweet ale.

"You've more stamina than I imagined," the demon purred when he paused to wipe sulfurous sweat from his brow.

"I've trained since I was a small lad," Corbin returned. "For one purpose."

"To kill me." Recovered, the Beast danced in, his two-handed sword swinging. He had strength and grace and temper to match Corbin, in spades.

"To save my family," corrected Corbin. He easily blocked the Beast's blow.

Now, as he pulled an ancient coverlet up over his shoulders and stretched out upon the mouse-chewed mattress, he thought of Beauty and wondered if mayhap all was not yet lost.

The Beast woke Corbin before the birds, lighting the chamber with a shard of green demon fire he held like a jewel in his hand.

"There are soldiers sniffing about the edge of my forest," he said. "Care to explain?"

Corbin smothered a groan. Even as he rubbed sleep from his eyes, his right hand was on his blade. His muscles and sinew pulled, overused.

"What makes you think they've to do with me?"

"Who else?" The Beast loomed over the bed. Demon light flickered in Corbin's face. "You're the most interesting thing to happen beneath the trees as of late."

Corbin sat up. The birds perched on the furniture were

still asleep, their heads tucked beneath colorful wings, not at all disturbed by the Beast and his light.

"*Mon Dieu*," Corbin complained without thought. "The sun is still abed."

The Beast smirked. In the unnatural light, he looked very young and very eager, younger even than Corbin, although Corbin knew that was impossible.

"You belong to me," he said. "Day or night, it makes no difference. The soldiers will have to return home unsatisfied. Get up, Red. I have something to show you."

Corbin rolled out of bed. Grumbling, he trailed the Beast from the room and down the long corridor. They turned left and then right, then left again, and again, until Corbin knew he was lost. The rose-covered carpet was the same in every hall. Every window was broken. Paper peeled on every wall.

The manor cannot be this spacious, Corbin thought with some anxiety. *This must be more sorcery at work.*

"What happened in this house?" he asked uneasily. "Has it been through storm or siege?"

"Both." The Beast flicked his fingers. "A battle against time, and time won, as it is wont to do."

"I don't understand."

"You'll come to," the demon promised. "Time unwinds even as we stand outside it. Every century or two, I lose interest and sleep. A long sleep, while the manor crumbles and falls."

Corbin shivered. He thought of the fragile pages torn from the English king's ancient tome. "How long have you lived here?"

"Lived?" The Beast stopped. He turned on the heel of his shining black boot. "This is not *living*," he said, yellow eyes wide. "I but *reside* waiting for the day my heart finally fails and I may *end*."

He wheeled, sorcerous light flaring, and stormed away. Speechless, Corbin followed.

"There." The Beast pointed. "That. Play it."

They stood in a cavernous ballroom. Torches burned in sconces on the walls, shedding light but no smoke. The walls themselves were gilded. Cracks and corrosion ran through the delicate detail. Chairs waited on the sidelines in rows and stacks. Someone had spread heavy cloth across the floor, obscuring most of the glossy wood. Someone had also left a large pile of bones in a far corner. A grinning skull topped the grisly collection.

"Sometimes I grow tired of mortal fare," the demon admitted, catching Corbin's horrified look. "Ignore them."

"They're human bones." Corbin's fingers itched to draw his sword, but prudence and something in the demon's desperate expression made him leave the blade strapped to his back.

"Not every idiot who knocks on my gate is as lucky as your papa." The Beast grabbed Corbin by one wrist, tugging him forward. The demon's long fingers were very warm. They heated Corbin's skin beneath his tunic and made the blood in his veins begin to pulse pleasurably.

"What is *that*?" Corbin shook his arm free. He knew it was the way of demons to seduce, but he didn't like the way his flesh responded to the Beast's touch.

"It's a music box," the Beast announced. "All the way from Sainte-Croix."

"A music box?" Corbin examined the thing with trepidation. At first glance, it appeared to be nothing more than a wooden coffer set atop a three-legged table, but when he peered close, he saw that it was topped with more glass. The box contained an impossible metal cylinder attached to a protruding handle. The handle was tipped in more gold.

"You'll play it for me," the Beast confirmed. "I want to dance. It's been so long since I danced to real music."

"Play it?" Corbin studied the box. "What nonsense is this?"

The Beast sighed. Gently, he opened the glass lid, exposing the box's complicated innards. "I had a magnifying horn, but I've lost it. You'll have to be very quiet while you turn the handle."

The Beast snuffed his light. He took Corbin's right hand, placed it on the end of the lever, and demonstrated. The lever turned without resistance. Immediately music spilled from the box, muted but sure. Corbin froze.

"Don't stop!" the Beast scolded, gripping Corbin's hand painfully. "Don't stop until I say you may."

Corbin glanced over his shoulder. The Beast was uncomfortably close, almost pressed against Corbin's spine. His hot breath caressed Corbin's cheek.

"And if I won't?" Corbin challenged, more baffled than properly afraid.

"Then I'll tear off your head and add it to my pile," the Beast growled into Corbin's ear. The gruff sound drew an involuntary shiver across Corbin's entire body. He stiffened.

The Beast stepped away. He threw his hands in the air as he snarled.

"Play!"

Corbin closed his eyes and turned the lever. Music unspooled from beneath his hand, thinner than a human voice and yet just as evocative. The tinkling notes rose and fell, burbling like the Alevins in springtime. Corbin, grudgingly impressed, opened his eyes to ask the demon what manner of magic produced such sounds, but the question caught in his throat.

The Beast danced alone in the empty ballroom with only his shadow for company. The flames on the wall dipped as he passed before them, snapping back into place only once he'd moved on. He advanced with a sinuous agility that was more bewitching and alarming than anything Corbin had ever seen before. His yellow eyes were so tightly shut they drove wrinkles into his brow.

Tears glittered on his dark lashes and ran unrestrained down his cheeks.

THEY TOOK their supper in the ballroom, seated together on the floor. Corbin had turned the handle from dawn until dusk. When the palm of his hand began to blister and bleed, the Beast healed it with a touch, and when Corbin's strength began to falter, the Beast renewed his energy with a sorcerous word.

"Harder than swordplay, was it?" the demon asked over spring berries and sparkling wine. "You've got calluses in the wrong places."

"You could play it yourself," Corbin retorted for the sake of his pride.

"I can't play it and dance at the same time, Red," scoffed the Beast. "And I enjoy dancing even more than I appreciate your stubborn scowl. It's been a very long time since I've had musical accompaniment. Thank you."

Corbin choked on his wine. "It wasn't my choice."

"Wasn't it?" The Beast leaned forward. He laid his fingers on Corbin's brow, light as a butterfly. "I may play with time, and I may threaten and cajole, but you, Red—you played your fingers to the bloody bone for my pleasure, by your own will."

Corbin didn't pull away. He stared into those yellow eyes

and saw a truth he'd suspected since Da first returned home with tales of the devil in the black forest.

"You're bored. And lonely. Lonely unto death."

The demon straightened. "Unto death? Oh, I hope so." He popped a berry into his mouth, crushing the red fruit between his teeth. "I dearly hope so. Tomorrow, I'll teach you chess."

BUT THE THIRD day in the Beast's lair brought the clang of a fist on the rusting gate and the cries of a familiar, beloved voice.

"Beauty!" Corbin rose from the swaybacked chair he'd commandeered in the Beast's enormous library, overturning chess pieces. "That's Beauty!"

"Ah!" The demon followed Corbin to the library window. Together, they peered through the cracks at the garden below. "Perhaps your papa is regretting his choice and she's come in your stead?" He hummed. "Lovely little thing, isn't she?"

Corbin felt a shock of something that felt like jealousy. Furious, he squashed it away.

"Something's amiss! Let her in!"

"I think not," the Beast demurred. "This is our home. As it turns out, I'm well pleased with my side of your papa's bargain. Let my wolves eat her."

When Corbin swore, reaching for his sword, the Beast rolled his eyes.

"Very well." He snapped his fingers, and they stood in the sleeping garden before the gate, buffeted by Beauty's cries.

"Don't tarry long," said the Beast. "I want to make croissants for lunch and I've decided after we'll clean the chandelier." He strode away into the garden where he pretended to examine the damaged fountain.

"Corbin!" Beauty gasped through the bars. She tugged on the padlock and chains. "There you are! You must come home! Da's ill. Those soldiers—the things they said! They called you a murderer, brother, and accused us of harboring an outlaw. Da stood up to them, he did, but once they'd gone he just…stopped. I think you broke his heart."

Corbin flinched. "I'm sorry, Beauty."

"You should be. Haven't we enough sorrow? Didn't I always say that temper of yours would ruin us? A murderer, and by all accounts they were two good men!" She shook the chains angrily. "Nan's grown thin as a rail, and Da's hasn't left his bed for a fortnight."

Corbin felt a shock of horror and disbelief. "A fortnight? But I've been here three days, no more."

Beauty shook her head. She stamped one foot. "Corbin. It's deep spring. You've been gone so long we thought you lost, in the forest or to the fiend. But here you are, fine and fit." She lowered her voice to a whisper. "Why haven't you killed him yet? Kill him and come home!"

Over by the moss-hung fountain the Beast made a noise of mirth or mockery. Corbin shot him an accusatory glance.

"You led me to believe only days had passed."

"My dear *Corbin*, I told you. Time and I war." Suddenly back at Corbin's shoulder, the demon smiled at Beauty. His smile had fangs. Beauty gasped. She reared back away from the gate. Then she squared her shoulders.

"I'll stay here, in the manor," she decided. "You go, Corbin, and help Hope with the firewood and with carrying water from the well. We're all hungry, but I can't catch Daisy for butchering. Come home and make good, and mayhap Da will get better."

Corbin stared at the Beast. The Beast stared back.

"No doubt," the demon said, "your papa is plagued by embarrassment. Even I know it's the bull you butcher, not the milk cow. Seems the wily merchant put all his eggs in one basket and sent the basket to me. It appears I win, twice over."

Beauty stomped her foot again in the mud. She grabbed at the padlock with both hands, twisting ineffectually. "Give me back my brother, fiend!"

"So you can take his place, stay forever at my side?" asked the Beast. "There are rats in the larder and bones in the ball-room, and the plumbing gave way long ago, but it's true I have stacks of gold buried about...somewhere."

He reached behind Corbin's ear and drew forth a gold medallion. Both Beauty and Corbin gaped. The medallion was thicker than a slice of meat. It was also studded with brilliant gemstones.

"Impressive, isn't it? I grew bored counting treasure many centuries ago. Gold is of little use to a man who can't leave his home." The Beast leaned forward until he was almost nose to nose with Beauty through the bars of the gate. Corbin thought he saw those inhuman yellow eyes flicker.

"It's yours. Take it." The Beast started to extend the medallion then snatched it back. "Wait. Either, or. Choose. Stay and I'll release your brother. Or take this marvel instead. You, your wily papa, and your sisters can live like royalty for the rest of your lives on this tiny piece of my treasure. But Corbin stays here, and if any of you come knocking at my gate ever again, I'll pick my teeth with your bones."

Corbin stood very still. He knew Beauty's choice before she made it. She loved him; of that he had no doubt. But she'd never wanted to do the hard work.

He tried not to blame her when she grabbed the medallion through the bars, hugging the gold to her chest. Still, he couldn't suppress a small sound of dismay.

Beauty didn't meet his eye. Clutching her prize, she

turned and fled back along the cobblestone path toward Littleton.

"It's not too late," the Beast said after a moment of shared silence. "Do you want her eaten?"

"No!" Corbin turned his back on the gate and on the demon both. "She's kin. She's my sister."

"She seems to have forgotten that."

Corbin didn't bother with a reply. He looked down at his fists, surprised to find them clenched. His knuckles shone bloodless through his skin. The demon inhaled loudly, then exhaled through his nose in a snort.

"You're no good to me in a sulk, Red." He held out a hand. "Come. The chessboard awaits. I've yet to teach you the knight."

Corbin frowned through the gate at Beauty's muddy tracks then back at the Beast. For once he was spared that yellow gaze. The demon stood partly turned away as if bored with talking. But his waiting hand trembled the tiniest bit. His elegant shoulders were stooped.

This is not living. I but reside, waiting for the day my heart finally fails.

Corbin took the demon's hand. The shaking fingers closed tight around his own.

"I've come to kill you," he reminded the Beast, part regret and part promise.

"Try," the Beast returned, smiling wide.

$\mathcal{B}$eastly Manor contained a dungeon. The Beast used it to store wheels of imported cheeses and barrels of fine wine from the north.

"Lovely," Corbin complained, swiping aside flags of spider silk with his elbow as he followed the Beast down rough-hewn stairs. A few lone strands of sticky web caught in his hair and his nose. He sneezed.

"Can't you just"—Corbin wiggled his fingers—"magic us up the proper wedge? Do we have to go hunting about in the bowels of hell?"

"This isn't hell," the Beast replied. He held a glowing shard of demon light on his palm, lighting their way. The light was a soft orange this evening, the color of sunset. Corbin had only recently discovered the hue of the flame changed alongside the demon's mercurial moods.

"And I could snap my fingers and summon us a bit of chèvre, but it's not the same. It never is. You of all people should know the value of a well-chosen cheese."

The narrow stairway ended in an arch. The Beast lifted his light high. Corbin got a wavering impression of abandoned stone cells piled floor-to-ceiling with shadowy clutter. A layer of frost glittered on the floor, but the air was surprisingly dry. Corbin smelled dust and cedar. He sneezed again.

"Lurgy?" the Beast asked, deadpan. "Shall I make you a posset?"

"It's freezing down here." Corbin shivered. "Let's find your cheese and get out."

The Beast shrugged. "This way."

Their boots left footprints in the frost. The Beast murmured a word. His light expanded to fill the entire cavern. Corbin counted more than one hundred barrels of wine, most of them as tall as his hip, piled in unwieldy stacks along the walls. Dust and spiderwebs covered the collection like a second skin.

"Gone to vinegar, most likely," the Beast said, answering Corbin's unspoken question. "I keep the newer vintages in the back."

He led Corbin to the westmost corner of the room then held his light against the floor.

"There," he said. "Open it, will you?"

"A trapdoor?" Corbin's brows rose, but his curiosity was piqued. An iron ring graced the center of the square door. The metal was cold and slippery. It took Corbin three tries to pull the door up and out of the floor.

A burst of musty air rose from below.

"There's a ladder." The Beast indicated. "Do you mind?"

Corbin met his captor's yellow stare across the hole in the floor. It wasn't impossible the demon was playing one of his eccentric and sometimes frankly frightening games. Corbin had learned very quickly that the Beast required endless entertainment. The devil also had a wicked sense of humor.

Corbin found himself thanking Laurie almost daily for the lesson on self-control.

The Beast smiled. His aristocratic face was too pretty to

be human, his smile charming. Dust coated his black hair and his white shirt. His breeches and coat remained immaculate.

"Yes, it's an oubliette, one of many in this place," he said. "And no, I don't intend to lock you in. I use them to store *cheese*. Here." Quick as a striking snake, he grabbed Corbin's wrist and turned Corbin's hand upward. He set the demon shard on Corbin's palm. "Take this; the ladder may be slipper, and I want the *correct* slice of Le Roule."

The shard pulsed in Corbin's hand, warming his flesh. The sensation was pleasant. Corbin's skin goose-bumped in response. The Beast's smile grew.

"Like that, is it?" he purred. "Interesting."

Corbin flushed. "Don't flatter yourself," he snapped. He held the light over the oubliette until he could make out the lines of a metal ladder secured to the cavern wall.

He sat on the edge of the hole and swung his legs into the damp, twisting until he found purchase on slippery rungs. Carefully, he inched his way down into the cavern, one hand on the ladder rails, the other cradling the demon's light.

"The one I want will be to your left," the Beast called down. "Wrapped in brown paper. Make sure it's the one in *brown* paper, Corbin. I don't want Wensleydale tonight."

The oubliette wasn't as deep as Corbin had imagined. It was only as tall as a man, and then half a man again. He tried not to wonder about the wretched prisoners who had met their end in the depths. When he stepped off the ladder and turned around, he saw that the oubliette was shaped like a teardrop: wide at the bottom while the shaft above was a narrow funnel.

The walls were rough stone and hand hewn. Rounds of cheese, most wrapped in paper, took up most of the space.

"Brown, Corbin! Unwrap the paper carefully. I want a largish slice. Half for the bread and half for the potatoes. It's what I liked best about your papa, you know. He did so appreciate a good cheese."

Corbin rolled his eyes. He turned in circles until he located a round dressed in brown parchment. He pulled his belt knife, approached the cheese, and clumsily unwrapped one end with his free hand. The paper crumbled between his fingers. The sudden, tart smell of cranberries and goats' milk made his stomach growl.

It was difficult to carve cheese single-handedly, but he was surprisingly loath to set the Beast's light on the damp ground. When the cheese finally separated, it fell, tumbling to the floor. Corbin sighed and squatted to retrieve the rogue slice. When he did, the shard of light in his hand flickered and the floor of the oubliette lit up in response.

"Corbin?" the Beast called down petulantly.

"There's something down here."

"What?" The Beast's voice grew louder as he leaned over the opening.

"On the floor." Corbin moved the light back and forth. More bits of the floor began to glow in response. "There's something on the floor!"

There was a weighty silence before the Beast spat a sharp curse. The light in Corbin's hand turned from rosy to purple. The lines on the floor burned red. They were pieces of a whole, Corbin saw now, part of a design: fragmented runes.

"It's a pentagram." He'd studied one before, in one of David's books. "And letters. Etched into the rock." Corbin bent and spread his fingers over a glowing channel. Heat rose off the stone. The demon shard in his hand pulsed.

"Corbin!" the demon roared. "My cheese! Now!"

"TRUTH IS," the Beast admitted later, frowning. "I'd forgotten it was there."

Corbin's scowled in disbelief.

"You've a sorcerous pentagram in your dungeon—"

"Wine cellar."

"In your *dungeon*, Beast, and you'd forgotten?"

They were sitting together in the manor garden, watching the sun set pink over the top of the forest, nibbling on slices of rescued Le Roule and sweet rolls the Beast had baked a day earlier. The Beast perched on the edge of the dry fountain, legs crossed, a half-empty bottle of wine open by his side. Corbin sat in the dirt at his feet, quietly enjoying the mix of wine and cheese on his tongue. The combination reminded him poignantly of home.

"Of course I hadn't forgotten it *existed*." The Beast refilled Corbin's glass. "How could I? It's what ties me to this land. I'd simply…misplaced…it."

Corbin rolled a swallow of wine over his tongue. When he'd stumbled upon the fiery runes etched into the floor of the oubliette, he'd felt more curiosity than fright. He'd spent a season on White Hill studying stories of similar sorceries, of foul curses and demon spells, all in preparation for killing the Beast. Strange things that might once have made him uncomfortable had become near commonplace.

"What's on the other side?" he asked. "If it's a summoning circle, what's on the other side?"

The Beast's mouth curved in a half smile. His yellow eyes gleamed down at Corbin.

"Sleep," he replied. "Deep, dreamless, dark. The sleep of the dead, or those who wish to be."

Corbin had begun to know the Beast tended toward drama. He studied the demon, trying to read his aristocratic face. The Beast's smile widened, but his eyes were wistful.

"Who cast the sorcery?" Corbin demanded. "That bound you here?"

The Beast uncrossed his legs and hopped up off the fountain, taking the bottle of wine with him, rudely jouncing Corbin's shoulder with his foot as he did so. The demon lifted the bottle in a toast to the fading sky then gulped down the last dregs.

"What does it matter?" He glared at a piece of dead shrubbery. Corbin knew the Beast's distaste was meant for the question and not the poor plant. "Hardly important at all now. The trap was sprung long before your father's father's father squalled aloud his first breath, Red. Why should you care?"

Corbin finished his own glass of wine and rose, stretching. He plucked up the final sweet roll, juggling it between his hands as he approached the Beast.

"Da often speculated," he said. He split the roll in half and handed one portion to the Beast. "No one in Littleton knows. In fact, no one at all seems to know. You've inhabited the manor always, it's said, as long as the trees have rooted the forest."

The Beast grunted. "It's also said I require the blood of a virgin every one hundred years or I'll send my wolves to ravage Littleton entire." He took a bite of bread and sighed in pleasure. "Be careful who you believe, Red."

"That last may be true," Corbin said, remembering the pile of human bones he'd discovered in the manor ballroom. The Beast smirked.

"You don't remember," Corbin continued on a guess, "who tied you here. Who drew the circle and spoke the curse. It's been so long, you've forgotten. Haven't you?"

"Of course I haven't," the demon replied sharply. But he kept his back to Corbin and his shoulders were rigid. He'd finished the last of the bread. His empty hands flexed at his side, elegant fingers clenching and unclenching. The setting sun sparked on his dark hair.

"Tell me," Corbin suggested. "Mayhap there's something I can do…to help."

The Beast whirled, looming as he did when he wanted to frighten, throwing an oversize shadow across Corbin. Corbin held his ground.

"You?" the Beast mocked. "Cheese monger's heir? *You* can break the enchantment that's bound me here for centuries?"

Corbin scowled. "What I do know might surprise you. I didn't come here unprepared, Beast."

The Beast snorted. "My hero." His hands came up to tug at his velvet collar. "Oh, please, Corbin, save me, do. I've waited so very long." He leaned in until his nose brushed Corbin's own.

"My champion," he breathed, fluttering dark lashes.

Corbin struck out. The Beast danced away, insubstantial as smoke, laughing. The sound wasn't at all pleasant.

"Look to your own imprisonment," the demon warned. "You're bound here as irrevocably as I."

Then he vanished, leaving Corbin alone with the sunset and the sleeping garden.

Corbin waited until the sky outside his broken windows was a heavy gray, the forest beyond the manor sleeping in shadow. The flocks of birds perched above his bed and on the wardrobe barley stirred when he stood; just one turned a bright eye his way.

He found his boots on the floor and laced them tightly. He slung Da's sword across his shoulders, grabbed the beeswax taper he'd claimed from a dusty kitchen pantry for reading, and took the candle with him out into the hall.

Outside his room the air was cold. Corbin cupped the candle flame with his palm, shielding the light, as he padded quietly down the corridor. He took the grand stairway one step at a time, afraid the ancient architecture would squeal in protest.

A single torch lit the foyer. The large front door hung open, explaining the unwelcome draft. Corbin smelled summer in the air, but desiccated brown leaves still littered the garden and much of the entryway. He shut the door softly. The Beast, he'd learned, had an absentminded tendency to leave the manor open to the world.

Corbin paused, listening. The ancient home vibrated with the scratch of shifting foundation and scrape of old stone. He was used to that also. Beastly Manor was never completely still. It was as full of sorcery as White Hill, but where Sir Thomas's château was an open repository for strange magic, the manor house seemed loath to give up its secrets.

He waited long enough to make sure the Beast wasn't alerted to his wakefulness. Corbin preferred to stay abed until well after dawn, while the Beast tended to spend nights in the manor's kitchen, slaving over loaves, pastries, and the occasional soufflé.

He held his breath for a long moment before exhaling in relief. Nothing untoward stirred in the shadows.

Still sheltering the candle flame, Corbin turned under the stairs and crept away from the foyer. He trailed the fingers of one hand along the wall so as not to miss a turn. He'd practiced the way in his head for several days now, even going so far as to sketch it in the dirt in the garden. He wasn't easily frightened, but the thought of becoming lost in the Beast's lair made Corbin's skin prickle.

Beastly Manor was as changeable as its lord. Time ran fluid inside its cursed walls.

But luck was with him. Corbin found the wooden door he remembered without too much difficulty. It was unlocked. He took the narrow stairway down. A narrow thread of spider silk caught against the wick of his candle and burned, smoking.

The passage ended in a low arch. Abandoned stone cells loomed, guarding a random collection of crates and barrels. Footprints broke the layer of frost glittering on the floor. Corbin muffled a sneeze.

He followed the footprints to the west corner of the dungeon. There he set his taper on the floor, using both hands to haul the lid from the oubliette. As it had before, the cold metal stung his flesh. The lid scraped loudly as he pulled it across the flagstone. He held his breath, waiting.

Silence.

He didn't suppose he faced death if caught mucking around were he wasn't wanted, but he did think the Beast would be very displeased.

Corbin retrieved his candle and slid into the hole, again climbing one-handed. He smelled cheese and cedar and mold. His boot soles slipped a little on the ladder, but he was sure-footed and quick and didn't fall.

He dropped the last three feet into the hole, sword bouncing against his shoulders. He ignored the frankly astounding selection of cheeses piled in wheels against the wall. He took half a step forward, then dropped to his knees, holding the candle out just above the floor, searching.

He didn't have to search long. The pentagram carved into the bottom of the oubliette sparked in welcome. Red light spread like molten liquid across etched symbols and runes, racing faster and faster until the summoning circle burst fully to light, sparking eagerly.

The blood in Corbin's veins leaped in echo. His heart began to race. Something like lust coiled in his belly. He couldn't help himself. Licking his lips, he stretched out one hand, fingers spread a hair's breadth above the glow.

Nothing happened.

Corbin held his fingers above the flickering runes until his arm began to cramp. Disappointed, he withdrew his hand, flexing to ease his aching muscle. The tips of his fingers buzzed with a pleasant warmth. His body felt languid. He regarded the pentagram. He wasn't fool enough to step into the spell or even to touch the liquid flame directly, but he couldn't help but wonder from whence the Beast came and if it was indeed possible to send the devil back.

For a time, the Beast left Corbin rather pointedly to his own devices. Corbin, who understood a good sulk, spent the first morning wandering the manor in search of his captor but quickly gave up the task as impossible. Even if the Beast wasn't hiding, many of the house's rooms and corridors swapped regularly, changing place in accord with some internal rhythm Corbin hadn't yet deciphered. It wasn't exactly dangerous to go roaming the manor during daylight hours, but it was possible to lose an entire day trying to return to the start.

If the Beast didn't want to be found, there wasn't a thing Corbin could do about it.

Undeterred, Corbin used his newfound solitude to explore the manor gardens, and soon discovered that—like the house—the grounds were much larger than they first appeared. The hedges seemed to meander this way and that, hiding a myriad of alcoves and in one case a decaying gazebo. He found a dry fishpond, an overgrown rose trellis complete with fading blossoms, and what appeared to be an evergreen maze.

The maze was taller than Corbin's head and guarded by a fearsome-looking stone gargoyle. Corbin peered into the entrance but wasn't fool enough to step foot in the labyrinth.

A house with bones in the ballroom and a pentagram in the wine cellar wasn't likely to shelter something innocuous in a hedge maze.

In some places, the garden was impassible. Thorny bramble or piles of crumbling stone blocked off sections great and small. Once Corbin stumbled across a mound of silver treasure piled forgotten around the base of a broken stone monolith. The monolith was snapped in two, its fallen upper half barely visible in the tangled briar beyond. The treasure was tarnished; vases, candlesticks, tableware, and even pieces of armor all gone black with neglect. A basin large as the soothsayer's divining bowl had at some point tumbled free of the collection. It lay on its side in the bramble, shining in the sun.

Corbin left the treasure untouched. In its own way, the forgotten silver seemed as subtly perilous as the evergreen maze.

So when on the fourth day he discovered a one-room stable tucked away behind the manor he couldn't help but explore. The stable, with its solid limestone walls and thatched roof, seemed so unlike Beastly Manor as to be safe. Inside Corbin found two empty box stalls, a perfectly kept carriage, a collection of molding tack, and a rack full of rusting weaponry. The stable smelled of leather but not of animal. He thought it had been a very long time since any horse had slept under its roof.

With nothing else to occupy his time and comforted by the hominess of the place, Corbin decided to put the stable to rights. He started with the tack, culling pieces of harness from fragments of bridles and cavesson. So engrossed was he in the simple, palliative task that he failed to notice encroaching evening until the Beast stood in the doorway with a candle in hand.

"Dark soon," the demon warned softly. "Come back to the house."

Corbin set aside the cheek strap he'd been examining and regarded his captor. If the demon had indeed been plagued by a sulk the last few days, he appeared to have gotten over his temper. His smile was placid as he studied the inside of the stable. His yellow stare seemed muted; he'd piled his long black hair atop his head in a messy warrior's knot.

The Beast stepped into the room, handing Corbin the taper even as he looked about. "I see you've been exploring. One of the more extraneous pieces of my holdings, I'm afraid. I've no use for horses. Although"—he poked at one of Corbin's carefully constructed piles with a long finger—"handy for storage, as you can see."

"Some of this is still workable," Corbin said. He shook his head, baffled. "There's enough here to kit a regiment. Where did it all come from?"

The Beast's smile turned enigmatic. "Oh. Off visitors, some of it. And some of it I trade from the tinkers who brave my gate." He rummaged in the weaponry rack, chose a sturdy-looking bow from the assortment of rusting armament, and held it up close for study. "You may have noticed I enjoy pretty things."

Corbin had to admit the bow was a handsome example. Crafted all of glossy dark wood, its limbs were as smooth as glass and flexible beneath the Beast's fingers. Its string was long frayed.

"This will do you well in the forest," the Beast decided. He bent over the rack again. "If I recall correctly, it came with a full set of beautifully fletched arrows. It's been a long time since I've tasted well-prepared venison."

"I'm no deer stalker," Corbin cautioned, reluctantly amused. He could see the Beast licking his lips in antic-ipation.

"Not with a sword, of course not," the Beast agreed. He whistled low in triumph as he pulled a petite quiver from the rack. A jumble of weaponry caught on the quiver's strap, spilling onto the stable floor. The Beast ignored the mess. "Teach yourself to shoot and catch me a buck."

"I can shoot," Corbin replied absently. His eye had caught on a gleam of brilliance among the metal on the floor. "Just not well. Dot despaired of my aim." Ignoring the bow and arrows thrust in his direction, he stepped around the Beast and squatted by the jumble of fallen metal.

"Practice makes perfect," the demon replied. He watched Corbin, brow wrinkled. "What are you doing?"

"This." Corbin drew a knife from beneath the pile. The jeweled hilt fit in his palm as if he'd never lost it. "This is mine."

"Is it? Interesting," the Beast said, eyeing the little knife with a distinct lack of enthusiasm. "Are you sure?"

"Of course I am!" Corbin stood. He wiped the knife clean on the edge of his shirt. "Mother gave it to me, when I was a lad. It's one of a kind and very precious." He frowned at the Beast. "I last had it near Honnefleu. There was a thief, you see, dressed in Dom's robes. He meant to kill me, because—"

"Because?" Prompted the Beast, brows quirked high over impossible yellow eyes.

Corbin set his jaw. "Because my family made truck with demons. But how did it end up here?"

The Beast only shrugged his shoulders. "Possibly I traded it off a tinker. It *is* a fine piece. No matter. It's yours again, and this bow, and these arrows." Before Corbin could further protest, the demon set the bow and quiver into his arms. "Tomorrow I'll give you a few pointers on shooting. *I* used to be quite good. But for the nonce"—he retrieved the candle, beckoning—"come home and tell me about the Dom who wasn't. I love a good story."

CHAPTER 18

"*A* treasure hunt," Corbin echoed, frowning in the Beast's direction. "You've already got enough gold squirreled away to pave the king's highway to the coast and back."

"There's never such thing as too much gold," the Beast retorted, eyes bright. He sat on a rotting hay bale in the manor's empty stable, knees drawn up beneath his chin, long fingers laced about his shins. "A moot point, however, as it's not gold we're after."

"Right." Corbin set aside the pieces of leather harness he'd spent the morning mending and oiling. The Beast claimed horses wouldn't willingly pass the manor gate, but Corbin hated to see good equipment go to waste. He thought the old tack, now clean and repaired, might fetch him a few coins when next one of the Beast's regular tinkers called at the gate.

"If not gold..." He dusted the palms of his hands on his tunic, transferring dirt from flesh to fabric. "Then what?"

The Beast smiled wide, showing pointed teeth. He hopped from his perch, stretching long until Corbin could hear his supple joints crack. The demon had braided back his long hair into a warrior's knot, confining the wild dark strands neatly at the nape of his neck.

"Come, Red. Hunting's best when the sun's high in the sky. Bring your sword. We may need it."

"Lovely." Corbin grunted but complied, grabbing up Da's sword from its place on his workbench. He shot the leather tack one wistful glance—he'd planned to spend the afternoon at work—then followed his captor from the stable.

Outside the sun was at its highest point, burning bright against a clear blue sky. The air smelled of late summer. The Beast's garden was empty of squirrel or any other animal. Only the birds would venture past the briar hedges. But new flowers grew among the brambles, brave roses in bright colors, and patches of green grass struggled up between flagstones.

The manor fountain, recently repaired, burbled and chuckled as it sent a spray of clean water into the air.

"This way." The Beast took Corbin's elbow and steered him east along the manor's perimeter, between smooth foundation and towering hedges. The hedges scraped at Corbin's tunic and trousers. The manor wall was warm against his left shoulder, the strange, sandy rock rough.

"We're hunting in your back garden?" The space between manor and hedge narrowed, and they were forced to walk single file to avoid briar scratches. The Beast walked at Corbin's back, steering him with one hand, occasionally stepping on the backs of Corbin's boots. "There's nothing back here but thorn hedges and old herbs run wild."

The Beast didn't reply. Corbin knew the quality of that silence far too well for comfort. He stopped, wary, and turned.

"Is there?" he prompted. "Something back here other than thorns and rosemary?"

The Beast tilted his head and awarded Corbin a fond half smile.

"Betimes things fall up through the pentagram in my cellar," he said. "Interesting things, beautiful things, dangerous things."

"*Mon Dieu*," said Corbin, briefly closing his eyes. "Not dwarves?"

The Beast laughed. His breath was warm on Corbin's mouth, warmer than the stone against his shoulder. When Corbin opened his eyes again, the demon was very close, his nose almost bumping the tip of Corbin's chin.

"Dwarves are a local problem. *This* is far more exciting." He prodded Corbin in the hip with one sharp finger. "Keep walking. It's not far now."

Corbin didn't move. "In that case, you go first."

"You're the one with the sword."

"You're the demon," Corbin retorted. "And the bloody treasure hunter. What's back here, devil?"

The Beast didn't answer. Instead he slid past Corbin, wriggling to avoid thorns. His front was long and lean against Corbin's own pressed chest and thigh, and near hot as hearth coals. A shiver of pleasure shook Corbin from his toes to his scalp. He bit the inside of his cheek to keep from gasping.

The Beast seemed unaware. Once past Corbin, he stalked ahead. Corbin took a deep breath, reaching for composure, and strode after.

"What's back here?" he repeated. The Beast was following a narrow trail away from the manor, and now there were tall brambles on both sides, strange evergreen hedges with waxy green leaves as big as Corbin's palms and long thorns. "Beast!"

"Worm," his friend hissed, low, without looking round. "Hush, now. They've excellent hearing, worms."

"Worm!" Corbin strangled a shout. He struggled to lower his voice. "You don't mean a dragon."

"It's not native, certainly," the Beast agreed in an easy whisper. He turned a corner in the hedge maze, briefly disappearing. "Up through the oubliette, as I said. Lucky for me."

Corbin increased his pace, then nearly ran the demon down. The Beast had stopped at the edge of two turnings. He crouched low, examining a break in the hedge. Corbin's blade was in his hand. His heart raced.

"Hah," the Beast breathed, nearly inaudible, obviously pleased. "It's as I hoped. She's gone through there, made a perfect nest in the hedge. Fantastic, Red. Are you ready?" He looked up at Corbin, yellow eyes merry. "She'll be quick, but not terribly bright. Avoid the fangs. They're poisonous. Time to test the worth of your enchanted sword, I think. Aim for her eye, as they say one good strike to the brain will kill a worm at once. And whatever you do, don't break the eggs, or I'll have you for my supper."

"Eggs?" Corbin mouthed, horrified.

The Beast nodded. He made an impatient gesture with his hand, pointing at the hole in the hedge. Corbin glared.

"Not afraid, are you?" the Beast asked, to all appearances honestly curious. "No time for that. Put it off, and soon she'll have a family to feed, and we both know she'll head straight to Littleton. Delicious." He licked his lips, pink tongue delicate. "Go on. Cold steel to the brain—that's the only thing for it."

"And what will you be doing?" Corbin whispered, furious. "While I'm slaying the dragon?"

"Gathering her clutch, of course," the Beast replied. "The shells, ground, make an *egg-cellent* poultice against burns."

Corbin gaped. "Did you just...?"

"No," the Beast said. He stood all at once and grabbed

Corbin around the waist, then tossed him headfirst into the worm's nest.

The demon was inhumanly strong and dangerously self-indulged. Corbin tumbled through the narrow tunnel, long thorns ripping clothes and flesh, tearing at his curls and at his knees. He managed to shield his eyes with his arm and to retain Da's sword even as briars caught at the blade, tugging.

He rolled to his feet and staggered upright. The worm had indeed hollowed out a nest in the hedge, round as a small pond, wide as a tall man. The prickly roof brushed the top of Corbin's head, but he had room enough to swing his blade and space to edge from side to side.

Afternoon sunlight filtered through the hedge, warming the nest and the worm who lay basking atop her jeweled eggs.

"Ah. Good," the Beast said from behind Corbin. "It's as I hoped. She's been napping. The heat makes her sluggish."

"Hells take you," Corbin said, and set his feet wide, striving for balance between leaf and thorn. "If I die here because you wanted a chance at eggshells."

The worm stirred. She unwound her tail from about her eggs and blinked eyes the color of underwater rainbows in Corbin's direction. She wasn't much larger than a sheep or one of the Beast's wolves, which would have been reassuring if not for the dripping fangs in her mouth. She had claws long as the hedge thorns, but sharp as needles, and her body was an overlay of green and yellow scales. There were feathers on her long tail, more yellow and green, and stubby pinions furled close to her body.

"She's just an infant," the Beast said in clinical tones. "Through the eye, Corbin. I'll keep her skeleton, I think. What a catch!"

The worm hissed, uncurling more. She stood over her eggs, shaking each of her legs one at a time, lashing her tail sideways in the small space. She looked from Corbin to the Beast and then at Corbin's afreet glaive. When she snarled a fetid, boiling fog rolled in oily waves from her snout. Her multicolored eyes gleamed hatred.

"*Merde*," Corbin breathed. He lowered his head against the awful heat and stepped forward, sword raised.

Afterward the Beast soothed Corbin's burned hands with a poultice made from crushed worm shell and bound them with soft linen.

"More dangerous than I remembered," the demon conceded as Corbin winced and cursed. "Still, that was a lovely strike you managed, straight up the nostril. Not quite as effective as the eye, obviously."

"She was about to close her jaws around my neck," protested Corbin. "An inch to the right and I'd be dead."

The Beast only smiled. He brushed an errant feather from Corbin's scratched cheek. Corbin yelped, then sighed through his nose.

"You were right. Eventually she'd have been large enough to take Littleton apart. You got all the eggs?"

"I did," the Beast said, patting Corbin's thigh in reassurance. They sat on Corbin's mattress in Corbin's room. The songbirds were returning through the window, away from the afternoon heat.

The Beast's warrior's knot had come undone. Worm fire had scalded away one of his eyebrows, but it was slowly growing back to normal, even as Corbin watched.

"That was quick thinking," Corbin said grudgingly. "The bit with the thorn between her breast scales."

The Beast giggled. His hand flexed on Corbin's thigh, kneading. "Distracted her, didn't it? Just enough."

"Just enough," Corbin agreed. The Beast's cheeks were

dark with amusement, his unnatural eyes bright. Corbin found himself staring at his mouth. Sudden heat pooled low in his belly. He swayed forward.

The Beast let go of Corbin's thigh and leaped upright off the mattress. He paced toward the door, coat tales flapping, near bouncing on his toes.

"You must be starving," he said. "I know I am. I've got ragout in mind, with that brown bread I put to rise just last night." He paused in the doorway and smiled once. "We make a good team, don't we, Red?"

"Yes," replied Corbin thoughtfully, even as new emotion, poignant and sharp as hedge thorns pricked his heart. "I believe we do."

Much later Corbin watched the moon rise through the manor's open door. The throbbing in his hands had kept him from sleep. He thought that might be a good thing; he suspected the worm would haunt his dreams for years to come. Not for the first time, he wondered how David and Affrodille fared on White Hill, whether the soothsayer had been allowed to live, and if Dot and Mary-Louise had yet been inducted into the royal army.

The silver moon rose in its usual track above the forest. The hours ticked off as expected in Corbin's head, but he couldn't be sure how many days had passed outside the boundary of the Beast's prison.

Mayhap I'm forgotten, Corbin fretted. *Or worse, they've aged a lifespan in my four days, and they're all but bones in the ground.*

He set his bandaged hands palm-up on his knees. The step he'd commandeered was cold through his trousers but not unpleasantly so. He reminded himself that the outside world was no longer his concern. Even if he could somehow convince the Beast to free him, there was no guarantee he'd find home as he'd left it.

Something of distress must have been on his face because when the Beast wandered into the front hall he stopped short, regarding Corbin in consternation.

"Is it your hands?" he asked. "I promise you, the poultice should have them healed by morning."

Corbin grunted. "What's that you have?" he demanded, hoping to steer the Beast's attention from his wretchedness.

"The last of her eggs." It was difficult to tell in the light of the moon, but Corbin thought the demon fidgeted a little. "I wondered, you see, if I could hatch it. It would be a tricky endeavor, but not hopeless."

"No!" Corbin exclaimed, aghast. "You can't mean it."

"I don't," agreed the Beast, chortling. "That way madness lies. In truth, I was wondering if I could somehow preserve the specimen alongside its mother's skeleton, once her bones are bleached. But the look on your face was worth it."

Corbin groaned. The Beast came to squat on the staircase at his side. The worm's colorful egg seemed muted against the glow of the demon's yellow eyes.

"It's not just your hands making you look like your favorite hound just died," he diagnosed. "Give me a moment. Ah! Sleeplessness, moping about under the moon. Yes, I see it now. I know exactly what ails you."

"Do you?" The Beast was too close. Corbin would have pushed him away if not for his stinging hands. Instead he shifted away along the step.

Cradling the egg in one arm, the Beast reached down and ruffled Corbin's short curls. The caress was not dissimilar to the pets he'd had as a child with Nell and his sisters, Corbin thought bitterly.

"You're facing immortality," said the Beast. "And finding it loathsome. I could tell you it gets easier, but it doesn't."

"I'm not immortal," Corbin argued. The Beast's fingers in his hair made his scalp tingle. He had to steel himself to keep from leaning into the gentle touch.

"So long as you live in my house, you are," promised the Beast. "Assuming I don't choose someday to kill you."

"Or I, you."

"Yes, about that." The Beast's fingers stilled. "You've had plenty of opportunity. Why haven't you?"

Corbin hesitated. He could claim he was but biding time, but he suspected the Beast might see through the lie, so he settled on the simple truth.

"You're not what I expected."

The Beast removed his hand from Corbin's hair. "Would it be easier if I were eight feet tall and more wolf than man? A monster in form as well as function?"

"Mayhap," Corbin admitted. "But I can't say for sure. I don't have much heart for killing, if you must know."

"But you're very good at it."

"Yes," Corbin said. "I am."

"Come with me," the Beast demanded abruptly. "There's a thing I want to give you."

Corbin climbed slowly to his feet. He gazed askance at his captor. "Your gifts are often dangerous, I think."

"The bow served you well enough, didn't it? Stop fussing and come along."

IT TOOK SOME DOING, but eventually the Beast found the right corridor. Corbin, wearier than he'd realized, had trailed the demon through the shifting manor without taking much notice of his surroundings. He was confident the Beast would set them right again if they got lost. It occurred to him that over the past weeks the Beast had somehow gained his trust without Corbin quite realizing how thoroughly things had shifted.

"Here!" the Beast caroled finally, extravagant in his excitement, as he threw open a wooden door. *"Voilà!"*

Outwardly the door was like any other in the manor. The chamber beyond—dusty bed, moldy desk, broken chair —was also unremarkable but for the square looking glass hung on one wall where by all indications a window should be.

Corbin took careful stock of the room, saw that the mattress seemed to be inhabited by a family of voles instead of the usual mice, and then gave the Beast a blank look.

"I like my chamber," he said. "It rarely moves around, and I've managed to sweep out most of the bird droppings."

"Red." The Beast sighed. "If you were any less observant I'd have to wrap you in cotton to keep you from breaking your face on my walls. Did Thomas Chevalier teach you nothing? The mirror!"

He advance across the room and stood in front of the framed oval. The glass was hung at the Beast's eye level, which meant when Corbin came to stand in front of it, the frame cut off the very top of his head. The last time he'd examined his face so closely had been in David's much smaller glass. He saw now that he'd changed much since fleeing White Hill. There were lines at the corner of his eyes that made him look older than his seventeen years and a stubborn set to his jaw that made him appear far more resolute than he felt. His curls had grown out longer than he usually kept them but not so long as to be a dangerous disadvantage in a fight. A night's worth of ginger whiskers shadowed his face.

The Beast's reflection was dark and somber next to his own. The demon was at least half a head shorter than Corbin, a fact that Corbin rarely recalled; the Beast's vivid personality made him seem impossibly large. Corbin, blinking into the glass, started.

"*Are* you in truth eight feet tall, more wolf than man, with claws long as daggers?"

The Beast smiled his white smile. "You've seen my painting."

"You spoke just now of Sir Thomas."

"A good man come to a bad end. I was sorry to hear of his loss. Pray tell, how exactly did it happen?"

Shoulder to shoulder they watched each other in the looking glass. The Beast's smile didn't falter, but Corbin thought it became a trifle stiff. Corbin's face was drained of color but for two mortified spots of pink on his cheeks.

"You knew," he accused after a long moment of prickly silence.

"That Jean de Beaumont played a long game with his only son? I knew," the Beast said quietly. "Of course I knew. How do you think your papa came to have in his possession a very rare and powerful afreet glaive? Did you think he'd found it by chance at market in Caen? Of course not! I made sure it came into his hands."

Corbin turned from the mirror, nonplused. "But, Beast. Da found his sword when I was just a babe."

The Beast tilted his head. His long fingers stroked the egg he still held. "I did tell you time and I are at war. Occasionally I win a skirmish. I knew of you, Red, long before you knew of me. And I decided you'd need every advantage I could engineer."

"Advantage?" Corbin's ears rang. "Your wolves killed my mother! *You* set this in motion! What have you done to me to make me forget?" Corbin grabbed the Beast by his shoulders and shook him until his dark head wobbled. His burned hands throbbed protest. The Beast, for once, didn't try to defend himself. "Is it more enchantment? This?" Releasing the demon, he waved a hand up and down the other man's lithe body. "An illusion? What are you really? Show yourself, devil!"

"You see me clearly," the Beast replied, chin lifted. With one hand, he smoothed the creases Corbin's grip had left behind from his coat. "Even if I desired to pull the wool over your eyes, I couldn't—not with Michael's sigil on your breast."

Corbin had become so used to the feel of the bone necklace around his throat he rarely paid it any mind. Now he drew it from beneath his collar, running a thumb over the fired bead.

"Yes, that," agreed the Beast dryly. "The bones are powerful enough in themselves but whoever made the sigil knew what he was doing. I'd like to meet him. He's effectively shielded you from magic more powerful even than mine, so long as you wear that charm."

"David," Corbin said, closing his hand over the bead. "It was David."

"One of Thomas's, I suppose," said the Beast. "It's clear he values you. And you, him?"

Corbin nodded. His anger had fled as quickly as it had come, leaving an empty spot behind his breastbone. If not for the starkness of the Beast's expression he would have suspected enchantment for certain. How else could he look at the demon and feel something so very close to pity?

"Ah. Well, as it seems to be a night for honesty, I'll tell you that I tried to save your mother, at the very end. But things went wrong too quickly, and *that* was a skirmish I lost."

Corbin felt sick. The Beast sighed and lowered dark lashes over yellow eyes, then gestured at the square on the wall.

"I promised you a gift," he said. Then lifted his voice. "Mirror, mirror..."

Fog gathered on the surface of the glass like mist settled just above a still pond. Corbin took a hasty step away, but the Beast nudged him back into place.

"Look deep," he explained. "It will show you whatever you desire to look upon, true things, not trickery. It's my window into the wider world. But think of a place and you'll see it as it is."

"Anywhere?" Corbin tipped forward until his nose almost brushed the surface of the glass. The bead still clutched in his hand hurt his blistered palm, but he couldn't quite let go, not yet.

"Anywhere and anytime," the Beast affirmed. "Just make a wish. I'll leave you to it."

CORBIN IS NOT A COMPLICATED MAN.

Once the Beast was gone, he peered into the looking glass and wished with all his heart for home. He expected Littleton, of course, and that is what he saw first when the fog cleared. Littleton as he remembered it but changed in small ways. Da's cottage had a new roof. There were brown and white cows in the de Beaumont pasture. Faith ran through dormant fields beneath a winter sky, a barking dog at her heels, much grown but not yet old enough to abandon pigtails for braids. Hope walked behind, bundled in a shawl. Her breath smoked against blue sky as she called after Faith, laughing. He saw no sign of Beauty or Da or Nan.

When he squinted, concentrating harder on *home*, the looking glass fogged again, shifting scenes. His heart leaped behind his breast when the mist shredded and he looked upon, not Da's cottage and not Littleton, but White Hill and David's cozy tower chamber.

Here it was not winter for the tapestry was pulled back from the window and sunlight streamed across David's worktables, shining on vials of bubbling liquid and limning the scholar's books with gold. David himself was bent over the old oven, poking with a long fork at something that bubbled in a pot atop the hot surface.

Corbin must have made a sound. David stilled over his concoction, shoulders stiffening. He turned from the stove, pot forgotten, and looked square at the tallest table where Corbin knew he kept his own small looking glass. Behind his spectacles David's eyes were fierce and expectant. He wore a new cap on his head: black instead of white and almost flat against his skull. There were strands of silver among the black in his curls.

"I know you're there," he said evenly as he came to stand at the table, bending close until Corbin could see every sparse hair on his chin. "Who is it? Reveal yourself."

"David," Corbin said. Mortified when his voice cracked on the second syllable, he tried again, with more force. "David! It's me, Corbin! Can you hear me?"

But David couldn't, even when Corbin shouted and pounded on the surface of the glass with one fist. The frame swayed dangerously against the wall. Corbin reared back, then forward again, grasping filigreed edges lest the glass fall and shatter. His pulse ran ragged in his veins. When he was sure the glass was no longer in danger, he dared look back into its depths. The surface was black. Corbin couldn't summon either reflection or mist when he concentrated desperately again on David.

Home, he thought, willing the shadows to part. *Show me home.*

A silver glow softened the matte surface. As Corbin watched, the light coalesced into a fat moon shining high in a starry sky. Corbin recognized the stars and the moon and the spreading forest below. He knew the untamed garden and the square manor house, and he couldn't fail to recognize the lithe young man who sat just outside the rusting iron gate, knees pulled up beneath a sharp chin, yellow eyes half-closed against moonlight. His dark hair hung loose, tangled in knots as though it had been buffeted by strong wind, and for once he was without his velvet coat.

CHAPTER 19

Corbin was rereading the pages from the English king's book in his bedroom, holding the parchment up to his broken window as if the morning could reveal new secrets, when the Beast wandered through the door. The demon cast a yellow glance Corbin's way before throwing himself onto Corbin's mattress.

"About time you woke." The demon yawned. He lay on his back, hands behind his head, regarding the busy birds on the bed canopy with distant interest. "I've a job for you."

Corbin blinked. Carefully he refolded the pages and set them on the chair he'd brought up from the ballroom and now used as a catch-all. "A job?"

The Beast's feet were bare, which was a first as far as Corbin could recall. The demon's toes were long and brown. He wiggled them as he grinned.

"A job," he confirmed. "Up! I've packed you breakfast. You'll have to leave now if you intend to be back before dark."

"Leave?" Corbin stiffened. "We're leaving the manor?"

"You're leaving." The Beast pulled one hand from behind

his head. He waved it gently in the air. "I'm not allowed, remember? Five or ten steps outside my gate and I'm useless as a mewling infant."

Corbin squinted. The Beast stared back, expression mild. Corbin didn't like feeling a fool. He scowled.

"You're sending me back to Littleton?" he asked. The thought brought a knot to the pit of his stomach. He told himself it was anticipation but feared it was disappointment.

"Don't be droll." The Beast leaped off the bed. He landed on his toes, light as a cat. "You're mine. I'm not giving you up. And it's not to Littleton you're headed." He darted back into the hall then returned with a worn journey bag that he tossed at Corbin. Corbin caught it automatically. "The edge of the forest, west. Crofter's cabin. The crofter's called Roland, and he has a thing that belongs to me. I need you to bring it back."

Corbin peeked into the bag then shook his head, sighing. He stuck his feet into his boots and tightened the laces.

"What 'thing'? Will it bite?"

"It won't." Very gingerly, the Beast passed Corbin his sword. "The crofter's daughter might. Enjoy yourself and don't open the casket."

Corbin scrubbed a hand through his curls, trying to chase sleep from his skull. They'd been up half the night playing chess. The Beast had lost more rounds than he'd won, and now Corbin wondered if this sudden errand was some manner of punishment.

"The edge of the forest, west?"

"There's only one path. Follow it." The Beast slapped Corbin between his shoulder blades. "Better start; it's a long walk."

The forest beyond the manor was unusually quiet and that was Corbin's first inkling that something was off. Common sense said a safe wood was a busy wood, full of birds and squirrels and rodents. The silence made the back of his neck itch. He kept his sword in hand instead of strapped to his back.

Then he saw the wolf and relaxed. It was one of the Beast's pack. The animal quite clearly meant to be seen. It followed him at an easy lope between the trees, tongue happily lolling. It was a big wolf, all black fur and strange white paws, and eyes with absolutely no color at all.

He supposed the wolf could have decided to eat him on the Beast's whim, but they'd left their last chess match unfinished, which meant it was unlikely the demon would kill him this day. The Beast never left anything unfinished for long.

Corbin sheathed his sword. His journey bag was heavy with a croissant and jam and sausage. He ate the croissant himself before tossing the sausage over his shoulder to the wolf. The wolf snapped it up, greedy.

There's nothing to keep you from running free. The tiny thought surprised him when it popped into the back of his skull. *Go, now. Start a new life somewhere beyond the forest.*

"Nothing," Corbin told temptation, "but my word given, and the toothy black guardian on my heels."

He reached the edge of the forest just after midafternoon. Beyond the canopy, the sun burned white in a blue sky. The path meandered past the edge of the woods and onto razed fields. The crofter's cottage squatted beneath the spread of a flowering tree. Smoke curled from two chimneys.

Whistling, Corbin picked up his pace. The wolf skulked after. There were spotted milk cows in the crofter's fields. They kicked up a fuss when they scented the wolf.

"I'll be the one blamed if you eat them," Corbin warned his companion. "Damaging a man's livestock is a hanging offense. Stay off."

The wolf ignored Corbin. It sniffed thoughtfully the air.

It wasn't the crofter who met Corbin at the cottage door,

but a woman. Not much older than Corbin himself, she was all softness and curves beneath a thin robe. Her golden hair fell down her back, unbound.

"Lovely afternoon," she said, smiling. She had a dimple in one cheek and silver rings in her ears. She was also barefoot and damp with sweat.

"Bit warm," Corbin replied politely, trying not to stare. "I'm looking for Roland the crofter."

"He's out. I'm his daughter, called Valentine." Her lashes were as gold as her hair, but tipped with black. She held her robe closed with one tiny hand. Corbin couldn't help but notice that her nipples had turned to pebbles beneath the thin cloth. He looked politely away.

"Is that your dog?" Valentine asked.

"No." Corbin hesitated. "I mean, I suppose so." The wolf sat in the dirt five strides away, tail thumping. Corbin had the distinct and uneasy feeling the animal was laughing.

"What do you want with my father?"

"Oh." Corbin blinked. "I've come on an errand. From Beastly Manor."

"Oh, aye." Valentine grinned. She mimicked Corbin's accent well. "I've been expecting a call, thought not a pretty lad with curls the color of fire. Come in, I've what you want."

Corbin felt a blush rise along his neck. He wasn't a stranger to female charm; the girls of Littleton had admired his skill with a sword. As a boy, he hadn't lacked for stolen kisses near the old mill, but as he'd grown, the lasses seemed to sense his uneasy disinterest. Eventually they'd abandoned pursuit.

The inside of the cottage was larger than Corbin expected. Hooks and bundles of drying herbs decorated the walls. A clutch of fossilized fetal pigs hung on a string from the rafters. A preserved owl watched from a stone mantel. Several fist-size crystals made a tiny stone forest on the floor in one corner. Corbin thought the flayed skin tacked behind the door had once belonged to a dwarf.

Valentine gathered a heavy tunic from a hook by the cold hearth. She shrugged the tunic over her head, dropping the thin robe beneath as she did so. Corbin caught a glimpse of pink flesh and shapely legs before the woman was properly and modestly covered.

"If you belong to the Beast, I'll not be expecting the usual payment," she said, knotting her hair at her neck and securing it with a bit of bone. "Although I can't say as though I would have regretted tasting you, lad. What's your name?"

"Corbin."

She'd left the cottage door cracked open. Corbin thought he could hear the wolf breathing on the other side.

"Well, Corbin." Valentine dug beneath a cot spread out alongside the crystal forest. She pulled forth a small silver casket and blew dust from the lid. "Here it is. Don't drop it on your way home. And whatever you do, don't open the bloody thing."

Corbin realized his hands were tucked behind his back.

"What is it?"

"Woe," Valentine said. "But nothing a strong young man like you can't handle, Corbin from Beastly Manor." Still holding the silver box, she stood on her tiptoes and gifted Corbin with a chaste kiss on one cheek. "Lovely lad. Next time you come calling, bring me a spring flower and a single uncut ruby and I'll change your mind."

She shoved the casket against Corbin's chest. He took it carefully. "Change my mind?"

"Oh, aye, village boy." She showed her dimple. "I like the look of you. Ask the Beast for a ruby from his treasure pile and bring me a tulip in the spring. I'll lie with you then in a form you'll like—all beard and hard planes and a fine prick between my legs—and you'll never forget."

Then she shoved him out of the cottage and into the heat, shutting the door firmly at his back.

The wolf was definitely laughing, probably at the bulge in Corbin's trousers.

The walk back through forest was less pleasant than the journey out. Corbin's blood sang of spring even as he dripped in the muggy heat. He worried over the puzzle in the silver box. Birds were singing in the dusk, and squirrels called their children to bed. Corbin realized that his guardian had vanished.

When he reached Beastly Manor, it was almost full dark. Corbin climbed the wall. He trudged through the dormant gardens, bypassing the singing fountain, and stomped up the entry steps. The great front door was unlocked as always. Corbin shoved it open with his booted foot.

"Beast!" he shouted. "Where are you, Beast? I've returned."

There was no answer. Corbin growled. He tromped up the curving stairway and down the long hallway to his room where he dropped off his sword and journey bag. Then he took the silver casket with him farther into the manor and wandered room by room, growing more irritated, until he finally found the demon ensconced by a roaring fire in the library.

"Beast," Corbin snapped. "I've been looking for you."

Most of the books in the library had rotted, and most of the shelves were crumbled to kindling. A single sagging sofa remained, ripped and stained. The Beast sprawled across the sad furniture. A candle burned in a silver stick on the floor, even though faint light still shone through floor-to-ceiling windows.

The Beast lay on his stomach, knees bent and bare feet dangling above his spine. He held pieces of parchment in his hands.

"What are you doing?" Corbin asked, thrown by the spectacles. They made him think sharply of David.

"Reading. Obviously." Yellow eyes rolled behind lenses. "I believe I've discovered an excellent recipe for treacle tart."

Corbin arched a brow.

"Did you bring it?" the Beast asked, setting aside the sheaf of papers.

"Must you have a fire burning midsummer? It's hot as hell in here." But Corbin held out the box.

"I get cold." Shrugging, the Beast rose. He took the casket carefully from Corbin's grasp. "Did you enjoy yourself? Valentine kept you properly entranced, I imagine?"

"You needn't have sent your wolf after," Corbin chided. "I gave you my word. I'll not leave your service unless you first grant me permission."

"I know." The Beast fiddled with the casket. Latches clicked. He lifted the lid. "The wolf was purely for my own entertainment." He peered above wire spectacles and into the box. "Oh, excellent."

Corbin couldn't help asking: "What is it?"

The Beast smiled wide. "Roland always sends me the best tithes, he does." He tilted the box. Corbin blanched and backed away.

"The heart of Valentine's last lover," the demon said. "And still beating, too. Isn't it *delicious?*"

"*Mon Dieu*, Beast!" Corbin backed away, hands raised.

The Beast laughed. He set the casket on the floor then shoved it under the sofa with his foot. He yawned and stretched, indolent as a cat. Then he smirked at Corbin.

"So. Valentine?"

Ignoring the demon's impertinence, Corbin snatched at the papers on the sofa. "These are mine."

"No," corrected the Beast. "Those pages are torn from a book that once belonged to the descendants of one Abu al-'Abbas as-Saffah, and as far as I can determine only recently found its way into Edward's treasury. Shall I hazard a guess as to how this chapter was separated from the binding and subsequently ended up across the water in your possession."

Ducking his chin to hide the flush on his cheeks, Corbin folded the pages again into their neat packet.

"Did you send me to the crofter's daughter to be bedded and disemboweled?" he demanded. That he could feel guilty at being caught out with the Beast's abbreviated history in hand made the question harsher than he intended.

The Beast laughed. "Valentine only keeps a lover's heart. The rest goes to her pigs for slops. And, no, I didn't send you away to your death. She wouldn't dare touch one of mine." He returned to the sofa, sitting cross-legged on the cushions. "Still, there's very few who can resist that witch's specialized appeal. She's quite good at what she does." He pursed his lips in exaggerated thought, tapping his chin with a knuckle. "You've been low lately, Red. I but meant to provide you some entertainment. Lift your…spirits…if you take my meaning."

I've a particular house I enjoy. It's clean and safe. I'll take you, if you like. I'd say you've earned it.

"She's not to my taste," Corbin replied coldly even as his face burned. "And I'll thank you to stay out of my business. I'm hardly in need of a whore's *specialized appeal.*"

"Valentine's no whore." The demon's eyes sparked secret amusement. "But I've only known one other who avoided her net, and he eschewed the finer sex when it came to bed play. Is it the same with you?"

"Stay out of my business," Corbin repeated through gritted teeth. Somewhere along the way he'd forgotten the Beast was his enemy. The demon's smug grin brought bitterness rushing back. "Isn't it enough you keep me here at beck and call? I'll play your games, devil; I'll even run your convoluted errands at risk to life and limb. But *my* heart is *mine own,* and you'll not spend your idle time testing it."

"Heart?" the Beast drawled. "Who said anything of your *heart*? I sent you to Valentine for the sake of your cock."

Corbin punched him in the face.

The Beast got his hands up in time to deflect the first blow from nose to chin, but the second blackened his right eye. The twitch of awe across the demon's face before blood spurted from his lip might have made Corbin laugh another time. It was apparent he hadn't expected fisticuffs, and possible he'd never before in his very long life been struck so.

He fell back on the sofa, hand against his mouth, staring at Corbin in disbelief. His eye, Corbin saw with satisfaction, was already beginning to swell.

"I also am not a whore," Corbin enunciated coolly, "and you'd be wise to consider my heart and my *cock* of similar mind when it comes to bedding."

The Beast's undamaged eye grew round. Blood dripped from beneath his hand, staining the front of his shirt. He crouched on the cushions, preternaturally still but for the rise and fall of his chest. Corbin, who had seen many a wolf poise in the crop the same way before springing to take down cow or calf, braced himself for attack.

But the Beast surprised him. He took his gory hand from his mouth, smiling small.

"You're a romantic," he breathed around his split lip. "A romantic with an unhealthy temper, but a romantic all the same."

"My temper is improved." Corbin studied his reddened knuckles, shamming calm. He wanted nothing more than to run from the library and lock himself in his chamber away from the Beast and the demon's bold curiosity. But that was a lad's solution and one he could no longer afford. "Once I would have reached for my blade."

"I am grateful that you did not." Slowly the Beast relaxed. After scooting to the edge of the sofa, he tugged his shirt from his breeches and used the hem to staunch the trickle of blood over his chin. "I owe you an apology."

Corbin's brow creased. He couldn't tell what the Beast's mouth was doing behind the fold of his shirt. "More mockery," he guessed bitterly.

"No," the demon promised. Corbin, seeing the shine of honesty in those yellow eyes, realized the Beast spoke true. "I am…I am sorry. If you must know—it's been so long—I'd forgotten what chivalry looks like."

"I'm no knight," Corbin warned, thinking of Sir Thomas. "Nor would I be. But I'll thank you to stop setting me tests just to see how I might react, Beast. I'm a man like any other: prone to homesickness, daunted by worms in the garden, vexed by temptation, and capable of making mistakes. I'm a man. I will be your companion. But I am not your plaything."

The Beast took his time with answering, so long that Corbin thought he might not. But then the demon straightened his spine and shook his whole body like a dog after a swim. The split in his lip was healing itself as his wounds always did. His right eye had swollen shut, bruised flesh the color of a ripe plum.

"I see I have misjudged you," he said quietly. "Will you forgive me?"

"Not everything," Corbin said. "Never everything. Not Mother, nor what you did to my da. Not your threats against Littleton or that you keep me imprisoned here out of my time. But for misunderstanding me: this once, yes."

"Thank you," said the Beast in an uncommonly small voice before he excused himself to the kitchen to tend his battered face.

. . .

AFTER THAT, things began to change and not in slight ways. New blankets appeared overnight on Corbin's bed—clean, heavy quilts and pillows stuffed with goose feathers. The mice in the mattress were understandably overjoyed. The tattered canopy repaired itself in front of his disbelieving eyes. The armoire became good as new while Corbin dined with the Beast one pleasant evening. When he returned to his chamber for bed, half-drunk on good food and wine, and threw open the cupboard doors in astonishment, he discovered that the shelves were stocked with shirts and trousers in a multitude of fabrics and weights. The clothes were cut to fit him as if by the most skilled of tailors. There were new boots—three pairs—and a heavy fur cloak for encroaching winter.

The cloak was better made than the one Corbin had sold in Honnefleu for Laurie's sake, fit for a king. It made him think of Beauty and her gold medallion. He hoped she'd had the sense to use the treasure wisely. He fretted that she hadn't.

"What is this?" he demanded of the Beast, dragging an armful of bedding all the way down the grand staircase and into the kitchen. The Beast, busy boiling worm bones in a gigantic pot on the hearth, looked at Corbin askance.

"A striking example of Coptic needlework," said the Beast, poking at his bones with a wooden spoon. "Puts the *Bayeux* to shame, I think, but then I'm partial."

Corbin shook a bolster pillow in the demon's direction. "But where is it all coming from?"

The Beast made a dismissive noise, lowering his nose almost into the pot to get a better look at his grisly stew. "How should I know? The house has a mind of its own. Surely by now you've noticed the erratic floor plan."

Next came piles of food: veritable feasts set out in the most unlikely places. Scones and clotted cream arranged on a silver tray beside his bed in the mornings when Corbin awoke, fruit pies and sparkling wine in the library after dusk, and the tiniest of chocolate cakes on a three-tiered severing stand in what Corbin had come to think of as the Mirror Room.

"Are you feeding me up?" Corbin asked the Beast after he'd discovered a roast pig, complete with apple compote, spread on a platter in the stable.

The Beast only peered at Corbin over the book he was perusing in the sunlight on the manor's front steps. A flock of gaudy birds watched from the peek of the roof while a single brown starling bathed itself in the bubbling fountain.

"You don't eat enough," he said mildly. "What did you think of the compote? That recipe is, quite literally, older than Moses."

Corbin stared at the Beast. The Beast stared boldly back.

But it was the roses that drove Corbin to distraction. As summer waned and what few flowers graced the walled garden withered again, inside its walls Beastly Manor grew buckets and buckets of white roses in the hours between dusk and dawn. The wood-slat buckets were unremarkable but for their sheer number. Corbin had seen their like in Littleton and Honnefleu and everywhere in between. The blossoms, white as virgin snow, he'd seen only one other place, and then in childhood.

"These are my mother's roses!" he accused the Beast from atop the manor staircase. There were two budding buckets for every step between the floors. The Beast, caught at the foot of the staircase, stood frozen in a veritable forest of fragrant white blossoms, watching Corbin with wary yellow eyes. "What magic is this?"

"The house betrays me," the demon conceded reluctantly. Then he sighed. "Do you like them?"

Corbin was struck by an unwelcome thought. Mother's first white rosebush, like the jet earrings, had been a gift from Da in celebration of their betrothal.

"Beast," he ventured as his stomach knotted, "is this a *courtship?*"

The Beast met his gaze unflinchingly. "What if it were? You warm to my touch and yearn toward my flame. Did you think I didn't notice from the beginning? At first I thought it was the usual way of things, but I was wrong. You wear Michael's rune; my seductive nature, like Valentine's, is diminished before it. Therefore your responses are more genuine than I deserve."

Corbin opened his mouth before prudently shutting it again.

"You tolerate my company even as you appreciate my body," the Beast continued. His fingers danced restlessly along the seams of his jacket. "That's more than any man has done since..." He looked briefly down and away. "For more years than I care to remember."

"No," grated Corbin. "You're wrong."

"Am I?" challenged the Beast. He placed one booted foot on the first stair but paused when Corbin raised a hand in warning. "Can you say you haven't wondered, mayhap in the dark of night, what it might be like to quench your loneliness in my heat?"

"I haven't," said Corbin. A pulse low in his gut made the words a lie. He grimaced at his body's betrayal. "And I won't."

The Beast narrowed his eyes to yellow slits. "Not because I lack bosoms and a skirt. Not because I'm a man."

"But you're not," answered Corbin in his coldest tone. "Are you? No matter how lovely you are in daylight, you'll always be the Littleton Fiend beneath."

CHAPTER 20

*A*utumn brought rain and a new breed of problems.

"Did you think you were the only one who wants me dead?" the Beast demanded, sharp teeth bared in a grin. Blood spattered his face and hair, but his trousers and coat remained clean.

Corbin swallowed convulsively.

"I hadn't given it much thought," he admitted, eyeing the three fallen men in their garden. "Did you have to tear them to pieces?"

The Beast shrugged. His yellow eyes gleamed as he considered the splatter of gore across the fountain, gate, and garden. He wrinkled his nose.

"Messy, but efficient. They came to kill me, Red, and I've better things to do than play victim. Clean it up, will you?"

"No," replied Corbin, crossing his arms over his chest. He wasn't a stranger to blood or bared muscle and organ. Since coming to Beastly Manor, he'd butchered his fair share of game. But this wasn't fresh-killed rabbit steaming in the kitchen, and those were human intestines hanging from the lowest garden branches.

The Beast snarled. "They're not from Littleton," he said. "They're no one you know. Mercenaries, likely, sent by the Huntsman. Although he's not my only enemy by far, only the most predictable."

"The Huntsman?" Corbin inquired cautiously. Since the incident with the roses the Beast has been at turns reserved and short-tempered. Corbin didn't blame the demon. He was suffering his own share of sleepless nights and was hardly in the mood for pleasantries.

Blood stained the demon's mouth. He licked it away with a delicate swipe of tongue. Corbin shuddered. He had to swallow again to keep from losing a late breakfast of tea and scones.

"The Huntsman," the Beast confirmed. "He sends a group or three every autumn, as soon as the weather cools. He wants my head for his trophy wall, you see. I believe it's a matter of inflated ego. And stupidity. As it's not by siege I'll end, but by a heart shattered."

"I'm not entirely sure you have a heart." Corbin sighed. "I'm going back to bed. Get rid of *this*." He waved a hand, hating the unsteadiness of his fingers. "It's horrific, and it's *murder*."

Corbin hid in his room under a mountain of embroidered quilts until sunset. When the brightly colored birds returned through the broken windows and settled for the night on his armoire, the Beast came with them, only properly through the chamber door.

"It's not murder if it's self defense," he argued, climbing onto the mattress by Corbin's bolster. "I didn't track those men down because I was desirous of a snack, Corbin. They breached my gate. They attacked *me*!"

Corbin groaned. He rolled his head on the pillow. He cracked his eyelids, squinting up at his captor. The Beast was clean again, his dark hair braided back. He smelled of yeast and baking. Corbin wished he wasn't so beautiful against the setting sun.

"You should have sent them away," Corbin said. "Frightened them or bribed them, as you did Beauty, or let your wolves chase them back through the forest. You didn't need to strip their flesh with your fingernails."

"I promise you, they meant to do the same to me." The Beast studied his hands. "I can't show my enemies mercy. The softer I appear, the more will coming hunting the *Littleton Fiend* and his legendary treasure." He huffed a breath. "A few good harvest massacres and they leave me alone until first thaw comes again."

Corbin jerked back, burrowing farther under the quilts.

"Go away," he said.

The Beast sighed again. He touched Corbin's back briefly through the bedding. The mattress squeaked as he hopped to the floor. He hesitated.

"Have you yet killed your first man, Corbin?" he asked.

"Go away," Corbin repeated, thumping a fist into his pillow. This time the Beast complied.

DAYS PASSED, sinuous and sleepy. The Beast's garden fell back into the earth. The water in the fountain froze over. Four more parties of foolish men and women came hunting the Beast. The demon killed them all with relish. A knot settled behind Corbin's ribs and wouldn't be soothed by food or drink or sleep. He took to walking his nerves out beneath the forest canopy. He spent most of his days wandering away from the manor, shadowed always by one or more of the Beast's watchful wolves.

At night he dreamed of Laurie.

He spoke to the Beast little if at all.

· · ·

CORBIN RETURNED EARLIER than usual one afternoon, a brace of rabbits over one shoulder, legs made leaden by the increasing cold, yet still stepping so lightly across frozen grass that he heard the voices long before he laid eyes on the manor. He slowed, holding his breath, and reached automatically for his blade.

"Leave here." Corbin recognized the Beast's flat, bored tones. "Tell your master to give up the hunt. He'll not have my head or any other piece of me. This game has grown tedious. There's no distraction left in it."

Corbin slipped from the forest. He set the rabbits on the ground and pressed his spine against tree bark, safe in the wedge of shadow. The Beast, standing casually outside the unlocked manor gate, a branch of holly in his hand, didn't appear to see him. Neither did the squat, muscled man who held a glittering dirk against the demon's side.

"No game, this," the man said in a thick accent. He was dressed in strange, heavy mail. Blue tattoos decorated his face. "This is livelihood. You are very valuable."

The Beast's fine, dark brows rose to his hairline. His eyes sparked.

"The Huntsman must be growing desperate or suffering embarrassment. I've plenty of gold myself, you know. I'll pay you to leave me be."

The mercenary laughed. "Fool," he scoffed. "I'd but take your gold and kill you anyway."

"Yes," the demon said. Then he looked straight at Corbin. "I thought you might. Here, then, let's get it over—ah!"

The gasp was pain and surprise, as the tattooed man's knife slipped between the Beast's ribs. The Beast dropped his holly. He collapsed back against the gate, pressing trembling fingers against his bloodied shirt.

"Very powerful knife." The mercenary laughed again.

"Charmed by an old wise woman on my island. You're stupid; the others were stupid. I am not."

He lifted the knife in a shining arc to finish the Beast, but Corbin cut the man down before the blow could fall. The mercenary's strange armor caught at Da's sword, sticking, and Corbin had to throw his entire weight into the cut, using the ground as leverage.

For an instant, he was back on White Hill, Laurie dying on the end of his blade. Corbin's grip loosened. He let go of the pommel.

The man groaned. Then he fell, taking Corbin's sword with him. Blood bubbled from his nose and mouth. He twitched, coughing, but didn't rise.

Corbin caught the Beast where he stood clinging with one hand to the gate, patting desperately at the smiling cut on his side with the other.

"Are you—?"

The Beast shook his head, eyes wide and startled.

"Hurts," he admitted, in a liquid whisper. "It will heal. They always do. He was right." Dark lashes fluttered as the demon glanced over Corbin's shoulder at the mercenary. "I *was* stupid." He breathed low, leaning hard against Corbin. "I should have ripped him to bits immediately. Chatting him up was a mistake. Don't know why I bothered."

Corbin scooped the Beast into his arms. He stepped over the dying man, shoved the gate open with his knee, and strode into the manor, through dusty halls to the library. For once he had no trouble finding it. The Beast's blood dripped on rotting carpet. Corbin put the demon to bed on the old sofa, stripped away his coat and tunic, daubing at the cut with wadded velvet, then watched in disbelief as the deep wound sealed itself. The Beast closed his eyes and appeared to fall into a faint, but when Corbin checked the demon's pulse in a panic, it was strong. Unable to help himself, he brushed his knuckles across the other man's brow in quiet reassurance. Then he covered him chin to toe with the counterpane the Beast kept near the hearth against increasingly cold nights.

While the devil slept, Corbin went back to the edge of the forest. He retrieved Da's sword from the dead man's back. The blade grated against bone. Already a thin layer of frost covered the corpse. Corbin spat the sour taste from his tongue, wiping moisture from his nose and eyes with the back of his hand.

He cleaned Da's sword against the dead grass and took the blade with him back into the library, where he balanced it across his knees as he sat on the floor against the sofa. He rested his head back against the Beast's thigh and closed his eyes.

The Beast slept past moonrise. When he woke, it was with a gasp. Corbin stirred, groaning at the crick in his neck.

"He *wasn't* your first," the demon said after a moment, voice like rough stone.

"No," replied Corbin. "He was my second. The first was a friend."

He could almost hear the Beast thinking. Then: "Did you vomit after? Did you weep for your friend?"

"Yes," said Corbin. "I weep for him still." He hesitated. "Did you…did you know…was that purposeful?"

"Did I know you would come when you did? Was it a lesson taught?" the Beast said gently. "No. But I saw you there, and in the end it worked out rather well for me that you came in time."

"Yes," Corbin said, staring at the cracks and stains in the library ceiling. The manor no longer conjured bouquets of white roses in every room, but he could still smell their perfume when he least expected it. He closed his eyes again.

The Beast dropped one warm hand to Corbin's shoulder.

Corbin reached up and found those long fingers, and squeezed.

HUNTING WAS GOOD THAT FALL. Corbin became more practiced with the black bow and arrow, although he would never be as skilled at shooting as he was at swordplay, and he hadn't yet managed a doe, let alone a buck. His aptitude with track and snare also increased. The Beast, become again less likely to snarl in Corbin's direction, taught him which plants were poisonous and which were safe for eating. He began to think he could live off the forest forever if need be.

CORBIN WAS HANGING a white-tailed deer from the rafters of an unused bedchamber when the Beast shouted. Corbin jerked in surprise. He wobbled on his unsteady prop, nearly dropping the rope he'd finally managed to loop around a thick beam. The rope slipped, and the doe's back legs jigged briefly against the floor.

"*Boules de Dieu!*" Corbin snapped. The chair he'd used for elevation wobbled on delicate spindles. The doe wasn't quite heavier than Corbin, but it was a close match. Corbin fought for balance, hauling hard on the rope. His shoulders pulled uncomfortably, but the chair stopped rocking, and the rope scraped back along the beam, winching the carcass into the air.

The chamber door slammed open, rattling the walls, the floorboards, and Corbin's chair. The Beast launched himself across the threshold, all but thrumming in excitement, long black hair festooned with cobwebs and dust.

"Red!" he said, bouncing on the toes of his boots much like Faith had on a fidgety day. "Didn't you hear me call?"

"I heard."

Corbin bent his knees, anchoring the rope with his right hand, feeding out slack with his left. He tossed a second loop over the beam and tied a quick farmer's knot. The doe on her tether swayed idly, but she would keep.

The Beast paused midbounce. He slitted his yellow eyes at the carcass, patrician nose wrinkling.

"What's that?"

"Dinner for several nights, once she's hung long enough for proper butchering." Corbin slapped his palms on his trousers before hopping to the floor. "Found her just this morning, killed in a dwarf trap, poor thing. Not dead long and only a little gnawed. She'll do. I thought you'd be pleased."

"Ugh." The demon put his hands behind his back. "Must you string it up in here?"

Corbin glanced around the chamber at peeling wallpaper, moth-eaten linens, and disintegrating furniture. He shrugged.

"Closest room to the front stairs and it's the perfect temperature. Weather's cold enough she might do in the garden, but I don't trust your wolves to let her be."

The Beast pulled a face. "This was the princess's chamber once."

"Really? It looks the same as all the others. Which princess would that be?"

"How would I know?" The Beast shifted impatiently. He waved a slender hand. "Never mind. I need you."

"Right." Smothering a sigh, Corbin plucked his hunting pack from the floor and slung it over a shoulder. "What is it now?"

Despite unfeigned irritation, Corbin felt a flicker of interest. He'd spent the last few days quietly. The Beast had disappeared in his own chamber behind locked doors, as he was still wont to do. Corbin knew better than to disturb the demon when those doors were latched tight. The sounds and smells seeping beneath the jamb were repulsive enough to give him nightmares for a year.

"What's happened? Is there news from outside?" They'd had a family of tinkers earlier in the week. Corbin, overjoyed at the company, had convinced them to stay overnight and to his great surprise they'd accepted without hesitation. The Beast had proved to be a gracious host while the tinkers had seemed untroubled by the manor's eccentricities. Corbin couldn't help but wonder what they would have said had they known about the bones in the ballroom or the pentagram in the wine cellar.

"No. Not news." The Beast stopped halfway through the door and glanced back over his shoulder at the doe. "It's not going to…drip…on my floors…or anything similar?"

Corbin placed the flat of his hand between the Beast's shoulder blades and shoved, none too gently.

"Because the rest of your floors are so clean? I've seen what you do in the kitchen, remember?"

It was a long-standing contention, but this time the Beast didn't rise to the bait. Instead his yellow eyes lit with an emotion that could only be joy. Corbin felt a surge of affection at that glimpse of uncommon warmth. He couldn't help but grin.

"What is it, devil?" he demanded again. "What's happened?"

The Beast bounced in place. Corbin couldn't quite contain a snort of amusement. Recently the demon tended toward sulk and temper rather than joy, and Corbin had lately begun to hoard the other man's smile as dearly as the Beast had once treasured gold.

"I've found it! Finally found it." The Beast grabbed Corbin by the cuff of his sleeve. He pulled him down the corridor toward the curving stairway. "I thought it was lost, and it nearly was, buried beneath an atrocious mid-nineteenth-century chaise. It's broken but just bent, really, and I know you can fix it, Corbin. You were so handy with my fountain, once I showed you how to work the plaster."

"Did you say mid-nineteenth-century chaise?" Corbin blinked. "Beast?"

There were leaves on the steps even though the garden beyond was sleeping under snow. The Beast hopped over the debris. His hand had somehow slid from Corbin's sleeve; his fingers somehow become tangled in Corbin's own. Corbin felt a lurch of dismay or desire or both at the realization, but he couldn't bring himself to pull away.

They ducked flags of new spiderweb trailing from the old chandelier above. Corbin sighed.

"We should clean that, don't you think? There are a few saplings out back I've got my eye on for making a ladder."

"Or I could witch you weightless," the Beast said, tugging Corbin to a halt at the foot of the staircase. "Wouldn't that be fun. Later. Right now: *look*." He released Corbin's hand, pointing.

Corbin frowned, puzzled. He squatted next to his friend on the marble floor, squinting suspiciously at the Beast's treasure. At first glance, it didn't appear very impressive: a wide metal flower blooming from a rectangular wooden box.

But Corbin knew better than to trust his eyes. It was likely as not the flower could suddenly expand and swallow him entire or sprout metal tentacles and drag him down to the very depths of hell.

"Is it another music box?" he hazarded cautiously. It was similar in construction.

"Better. It's a *phonograph*." The Beast snorted when Corbin didn't speak. "It *records* music. Captures them. Music and voices. And it mimics the sound back."

"Ah." Corbin nodded wisely. "Magic then."

"No!" The Beast laughed. He sounded a little wild, a little desperate. Corbin stared at him. The Beast stared back.

"It's science," the demon explained. On his knees, he bent over the "phonograph." He caressed the metal flower then tapped a shiny cylinder. "This, this roll, there's music etched upon it, much like in the other box, yes. But set the roll to motion, and the stylus vibrates, turning etchings into sound."

"And?" Corbin prompted.

"Can't you see?" His friend snarled, shifting from starry-eyed to sour in a heartbeat. "Didn't I say? The stylus is *bent*. It won't work. I need you to fix it, Corbin. Make yourself useful, for once."

Corbin ignored the implied insult. He was growing inured to the demon's frequent mood swings, God help him.

"We have music," he reminded the Beast. "I turn the handle. You dance. Endlessly."

"Yes, yes." The Beast tugged on the ends of his own hair in apparent frustration. "But I've gotten weary of dancing alone, Red. I want more. I want to dance with *you*."

"I can't dance," Corbin replied, carefully bland. "I know farming and some hunting and a good deal of swordsmanship, but not the rufty tufty."

"I'll teach you," the Beast returned, quick as a serpent. "Fix my phonograph. And we'll dance."

Corbin glared. The Beast glared back. Then his mouth softened and those yellow eyes grew wide.

"Please," he said.

Corbin's heart turned over behind his ribs. He relented.

"But tomorrow," he cautioned, "we are cleaning the chandelier. All right?"

"All right," the Beast echoed. Distracted, he bent once again over the music maker. "After we dance, Corbin. After we dance."

· · ·

IT WASN'T any more difficult than repairing tack. The Beast held his shard of flame over the phonograph while Corbin used the tip of his jeweled knife and a pair of slim iron tongs to straighten the stylus. It took much of the rest of the day and many adjustments before the Beast was satisfied that the instrument was as it should be. By then evening had come and gone and the demon's red flame was the only light in the foyer.

"Oh, excellent," the Beast breathed when he gave the cylinder a gentle nudge and a sprinkle of musical notes fell like soft rain trough the metal flower. "Hold this while I tune it, if you will."

The demon flame was in Corbin's palm before he could protest. It flickered scarlet, licking at his fingers, and Corbin was hard pressed not to groan aloud at the delicious sensation. As it was, the Beast shot him a surprised glance, then smiled as he adjusted the phonograph. When the music flowed a second time, it was less a trickle than a river. Corbin was staggered by its beauty. He exhaled in shock.

"Ravel," the Beast explained, taking his flame from Corbin's hand and sending it floating overhead. "Come here. Let me teach you the waltz." He held out his hand.

Time grew slow, waiting on Corbin. He knew he stood on a precipice as clearly as if he saw the rocky shore far beneath his feet. He'd never been afraid of heights as a lad, had climbed up and down Littleton's cliffs without a thought for his own safety. Now, a grown man, he closed his eyes as he slipped over the edge.

The demon's hand was hot against Corbin's cooler flesh. The Beast intertwined his fingers with Corbin's own then tugged him forward until they stood slotted front to front. The Beast, half a head shorter, put his other hand on Corbin's hip.

"I'll lead," he said into the hollow of Corbin's throat. "Do as I do, and you'll be fine."

Corbin forced his eyes open again just as the Beast sent them into a spin across the floor. The footwork was not terribly difficult. The Beast was a patient tutor, and Corbin was naturally graceful. Before he knew it, he was learning by feel rather than observation. The Beast was a burning coal against his front, setting every nerve to light where flesh brushed flesh through fabric. Corbin licked his lips and swallowed.

"This 'waltz,'" he managed, "is a very unseemly sort of dance."

The Beast laughed deep in his chest. "Why do you think I chose it? If only you knew how many chambers I've over-turned looking for this music. The third floor will never again be the same."

"We don't have a third floor," Corbin said. Then the Beast shifted his hips, moving deliberately against Corbin's front, making him moan. "Beast—"

"Good," the demon agreed. Then: "You should kiss me now, Red."

I'm not on the precipice at all. I'm falling, Corbin realized. *I've been falling all along.*

He dipped his head. The Beast's mouth opened eagerly beneath him. It wasn't at all like kissing lasses behind the old mill or Nell across her father's fence or even Laurie there at the end of all things on White Hill. *Those* had been hollow, a blunted taste of something meant to be sharper and hot. *This* was velvet flame and drowning in yellow heat and the race of greed through his veins until his toes curled in his boots. He fisted his hands on the Beast's shoulders, dragging the other man up hard against his chest, groaning.

The Beast went boneless against him, sighing into his

mouth. Then he pulled reluctantly away, looking up at Corbin through lowered lashes.

"To answer your question: yes."

"Yes?" Corbin couldn't think past the ache in his groin. "What do you mean, yes?"

"Yes, this is courtship," the Beast said, and stood on his toes to kiss him again.

THEY ENDED up in Corbin's bed, atop a spread of quilts. Corbin's strangled moans sent the mice scurrying beneath the mattress, and the Beast's growling sighs chased the birds away through the window. Corbin learned this new dance as quickly as he had the waltz, although the Beast had to teach him patience when he tried to race to the finish.

"Corbin," the Beast teased even as his breath caught and he arched, stripped naked in the candlelight, against Corbin's eager tongue. "You're ardent as a neophyte." He gasped again then grabbed Corbin's hair to pull him up and meet his eye. "Surely you don't mean to tell me—"

But Corbin shut him up with a blistering kiss, and soon enough the Beast forgot his astonishment as they writhed and grappled and bit and scraped until all at once everything lined up perfectly. Corbin finished first with a shout. The Beast followed soon after, head thrown back in a rigid paroxysm of controlled pleasure.

They lay tangled and sweating beneath the canopy. Corbin was beyond blushing, but he buried his nose in the Beast's shoulder, inhaling the demon's faintly sulfurous scent, trying to calm his pounding heart. He felt as though every muscle in his body had been stretched to breaking and then soothed to a languid simmer. The Beast's fingers wandered absently up and down his spine, counting heels of bone.

"That was very nice," the devil ventured once he'd got his breath back. "Much nicer than I anticipated. But surely—it seemed—" He cleared his throat. "Do you mean to tell me I'm your first?"

"Is it so hard to believe?" Corbin demanded, meeting luminous yellow eyes boldly. "When I've spent every hour of the last ten years training to kill you? What freedom did I have for dalliance? Besides," he relented, "it was only the lasses in Littleton who paid me any attention, and I had no interest in their flirtations."

"Poor lasses." The Beast smirked. He cupped his hand at the nape of Corbin's neck, wriggling impossibly closer. "Now they'll never know your charms."

Corbin couldn't help but snort. "Won't they?"

"Of course not." The demon's smile turned dangerous beneath Corbin's seeking mouth. "As it happens, circumstances ensure I'm not only your first but your last."

CHAPTER 21

It was deep midwinter, and snow was falling in a blizzard over the garden when the Beast woke Corbin from dreams of summer with a kiss and a pinch.

"There's a child scaling our gate," the demon said, irritation plain on his face. He'd been distracted for days with secret business of his own. Whatever it was that demanded all his attention Corbin had chosen prudence over curiosity. It was enough that when the Beast came to bed at night—if only for an hour or two of rest—he clutched Corbin as if he were the most precious piece of treasure in all the manor's collection.

Corbin yawned, chivvying himself from the sofa's embrace. A fire crackled merrily in the hearth. A single rosebud, fat and white in a tall silver vase, decorated a pile of the Beast's books left near the sofa. Corbin smiled when he saw the flower.

"What do you expect me to do? Is it one of the tinkers' lads?"

"Last I looked the tinkers' get were all brown as nuts." The Beast's velvet jacket had gone missing. His shirtsleeves were rolled to his elbows, and his fingers were coated with something that might be blood or berry preserves. "This child has hair red as your own. Go see what he wants before my wolves grow tired of playing."

So Corbin tied on his boots and wrapped a warm cloak about his shoulders and left the library for the storm outside. The snow blew over the manor wall at a slant, stinging Corbin's face as he stood on the wide steps. He had to squint to make sense of the spectacle below. He saw the wolves first: six of the great hairy beasts, black and brindle against the white. They ringed the gate between the wall and the forest, snapping and snarling at both the falling snow and the lad balanced across the rusty bars.

Corbin whistled. The wolves, being their master's creatures, ignored him. The boy on the gate looked sharply his direction.

"Hurry!" he cried. "Please hurry!"

Corbin grunted. He took the steps carefully so as not to slip on ice. After scooping up a handful of snow, he packed it in his hands as he descended and then tossed it into the wolf pack. The wolves went silent. They looked his way, tongues lolling. Corbin threw two more balls to oblige their sense of mischief, landing one nicely between the eyes of a large female. She growled insult before taking off in the direction of the forest, biting at the undergrowth as she ran. The rest of the pack turned tail and scattered. They disappeared back into the trees.

Corbin peered up at the lad. "I used to hate them, too," he said. "But they've their own sort of morality. In their eyes, you're just a pup. They might scare you, but they probably wouldn't eat you." He reached out a hand to help the boy over the top of the gate.

"What, them?" the lad scoffed. Ignoring Corbin's offer of help, he twisted lithely over the gate, landing on his feet in front of Corbin. "I'm not afraid of them. My mum has an old bargain with the lord of the manor. They won't hurt me, not ever."

Corbin frowned. The lad, for all his bravado, was breathing hard as if he'd run hell for leather through the forest. His ginger curls were damp with sweat, his upturned nose dripping snot. Wherever he'd come from, he'd come in only a thin tunic and boots. Goose pimples stood pink on his bare legs.

Corbin's scowl deepened. He recognized the nose and the hair, but not the rangy young body.

"Jasper," he hazarded, ignoring fleeting sadness. "You look like your mum. How old are you now?"

"Ten come spring," Nell's son replied. "Are you Corbin? Mum says I'm to tell you to hurry and hide yourself away."

"Did she now?" Corbin threw an arm around Jasper's thin shoulder, drawing him toward the manor and out of the snow. "And why's that?"

"His Majesty's sent an army after you, sir," the boy said, eyes wide. "Mum said to tell you they're ranging in the village square, and they'll be at your gate before the day is out."

"AN ARMY?" the Beast drawled as he set a slice of tart in front of Nell's child. "Bit of an overreaction, I should think. An entire army just for Corbin?"

Jasper blushed over his tart but didn't relent. "I counted fifteen men myself, my lord. And William the innkeeper's boy says he counted ten more coming down the highway. They want his head on a pike in front of the palace, my lord."

"Innkeeper?" Corbin mused aloud, ignoring the Beast's affronted growl. "Does Littleton have a proper inn then?"

The boy nodded as he shoveled food into his mouth.

"Two, sir. Used to be three, but the Wattle Rat burned down last time we had lightning. I was six. I remember the flame and how mum got even the gentry to carry buckets from the river, but it was too late."

Corbin sat on his stool next to the kitchen hearth. Speechless, he watched Jasper eat. He didn't miss the Beast's covert yellow glance, but he did refuse to acknowledge the demon's quiet concern.

"Five years," Corbin said. "Five years at least and I've been beneath this roof—how long?"

"Not yet one year," the Beast conceded. He cut another slice of tart and shoved it in Corbin's direction. "I'm sorry," he added more quietly.

Corbin quirked a brow at the rare apology, but the Beast was watching Jasper avidly.

"They used to say he looked like me, in Littleton, before I left," Corbin said, smiling a little in amused recollection.

"They still do say," Jasper agreed. He had sugar all over his lower lip. The Beast offered the boy a hankie from the pocket of his velvet coat. "They all say I'm yours, sir. Your lad."

"You are not," replied Corbin somberly. He couldn't help but squirm. The Beast hid his laugh behind a polite cough.

"Oh, I know," said Jasper with the serenity of the very young. "But we let my aunties pretend because it makes them happy to think I'm your bastard, sir."

This time the Beast couldn't quite smother his hilarity. But Corbin was intent on Nell's son.

"Your aunties? My sisters, you mean? Faith, Hope, and Beauty?"

Jasper nodded. Then he shook his head. "Auntie Faith and Auntie Beauty, but Hope's been gone a very long time, sir. She ran off to Fontainebleau after your da passed—I'm sorry, sir—and no one's heard a word of her since."

"He's dead then? My da?" Corbin had expected as much,

had known that it was inevitable. He sat rigidly, waiting for grief or even relief, but he felt nothing at all.

"Corbin." The Beast was at his side, one hand on his shoulder. "I'm sorry."

"This time it's hardly your fault," Corbin retorted lightly. He touched the Beast's fingers before rising to his feet. Jasper's plate was cleaned of every crumb. Corbin set his untouched slice in front of the boy, wondering if it was a child's natural appetite for sweets or if he need be concerned for Nell's little family. "Now. Tell me why the crown is after my head—again."

"Oh, not again, sir." Jasper wiped his mouth with the Beast's handkerchief, a prim little gesture that reminded Corbin not at all of Nell. "Still. There's a new king, you see, and mum says Lord Spare's convinced the new one you have a thing that belongs to him." He looked at Corbin, puzzled. "A magical sword, sir. Everyone knows you keep it close at hand to stop the Littleton Fiend from biting off your head— begging your pardon, my lord. But where is it?"

"Spare's relentless as a mastiff," Corbin complained as he opened the chest usually kept beneath their bed. "No wonder Laurie feared the man. He holds a bitter grudge."

The Beast, standing at the broken window, looked down on the forest below. "They mean to take you as well as the sword," he said. "Your head on a pike in front of the palace."

"They won't find me." The afreet glaive was heavy in Corbin's hand as he drew it from the chest. He fumbled with the straps and buckles. "The forest is vast, and I daresay by now I know it better than anyone. Once you let me go, I'll keep hidden until they give up on beating the bush as a lost cause." He looked at the Beast. "You *will* let me go?"

The demon's hands were folded tightly behind his back as

he regarded the garden with a small frown. "This winter is especially cold," he mused. "Do you remember the dwarves you found, frozen in their barrows?"

"Of course I do." Corbin finished securing the blade across his back. He crossed the room and looked out the window himself. "It was only last week. You threatened to make a pie of their kidneys." He essayed a dramatic shudder, but the Beast didn't smile.

"Fifteen, possibly twenty soldiers," the devil mused. "If Jasper is correct in his count. My wolves alone can take down maybe half that many."

Corbin snaked an arm around the other man's waist. He pulled him close, squeezing a warning. "And then you'll have war. An outlaw is a passing distraction. But whoever this new king is, he's not likely to forgive twenty men murdered in his own realm. He'll only send more, until he has you overwhelmed."

"My realm, this," the Beast corrected, wriggling free of Corbin's embrace. "And how little you think of me, Red, if you believe I'm easily overwhelmed."

Corbin crossed his arms over his chest to keep from reaching for the Beast again. He didn't like the way the demon chewed worriedly on his lower lip or the lines bracketing his yellow eyes. Those lines had been increasing since autumn, Corbin realized, etched deeper as each day passed.

"What is it?" he ventured. Coaxing answers from the Beast was a tricky thing. Corbin never knew whether even the most innocent of queries would provoke sweetness or sparks. "What's wrong?"

The Beast whirled away from Corbin, presenting his unyielding back. He gripped a bedpost in both hands, glaring up at the birds ranged on the canopy instead of meeting Corbin's eye.

"Other than you are mine and another has come to steal

you away?" the demon hissed. Smoke curled in wisps around his fingers. Corbin smelled charring wood and sulfur.

Corbin refused to be cowed. "Tell me."

"It's nothing." But the Beast in turn refused to meet Corbin's stare. "This house has its moods. Generally I find them tolerable. Of late I find them difficult."

"You'll soon set our bed afire," Corbin pointed out mildly as the birds on the canopy began to hop about in alarm. "I wish you wouldn't. I've become rather fond of it."

The demon snatched his hands from the bedpost. Dark streaks marked the wood where his fingers had been. He paced from armoire to bed—once, twice, again. Then with a vicious, fanged snarl, he kicked the bedstead, hard.

"It will not obey when I am desirous of a change of scenery." Again the Beast kicked at the furniture and again, fractious as a child. "Bloody, feckless scrap of stone and bone! Uproot yourself! Take us deeper into the forest, away from danger and distraction! What use are you to me if you will not *move*?"

Corbin, quite certain that even the Beast ought not taunt their capricious prison, grabbed for the demon, but too late. Before the Beast could land another blow, the manor began to shake.

THEY FOUND Jasper at the foot of the grand stairway, small face creased in amazement.

"Was that sorcery?" he asked the Beast hopefully. "It felt like a sneeze and a bee sting all at once." He was flushed with excitement and not at all afraid. "You made the forest disappear!"

The Beast ran to the door, pulling it open. He paused an instant before slamming it shut again. His eyes were molten as the sun, his face gone completely blank.

"What is it?" Corbin strode across the foyer, sidestepping the demon when the Beast blocked his path. "What's happened?" He yanked the door open and peered out into the snowy garden.

"The forest hasn't disappeared," the demon replied without infliction. "It's only moved. Behind us, you see. Excitement may have addled young Jasper's brain, but I imagine you recognize the scenery."

Corbin did, despite small changes. The fence line showed signs of recent repair, and there were goats in the mare's field. But the distant cottage was unchanged.

"Gaffer Julian's land," Corbin agreed, stunned. "Littleton."

"Close and latch the door," the Beast growled. "Immediately."

Corbin glanced at the demon and saw that even he recognized the futility of that request.

"If you love me, as I think you do," Corbin replied, ignoring the Beast's twitch of surprise. "You'll stay hidden, inside. I can't protect us both. Convince the manor to take you back, if you can. I'll find you again, when *I* can." The Beast's face looked carved of stone. His mouth was set in a flat line. Corbin bent and kissed him softly in farewell. The Beast stood unmoving under his caress. "Jasper and I are going home. Do I have your permission?"

"No," said the Beast.

"I see mum!" Jasper cried from the door. "Mum and Auntie Beauty and all he king's men!"

"Please," Corbin said, grazing a thumb along the Beast's cheek. Tears overflowed the demon's dark eyelashes, threatening to scald. "Trust me."

"And what of Lord Spare?" the Beast demanded, choked. "Shall I trust him not to take your head?"

Corbin summoned a smile. "He's but an old man, Beast. I've been trained to slay demons."

The Beast snuffled once. Then he drew himself up, dashing tears from the tip of his nose, drawing brittle arrogance about his slight form like armor.

"Fine, then," he said. "Go." And then, in a booming voice that shook the manor walls once more, he yelled, "Be gone!"

WHEN THEY STOOD outside the manor gate, Jasper plucked uneasily at Corbin's sleeve.

"I was supposed to make sure you hid safe," he fretted. "Now mum will worry."

"You did your very best." Corbin folded the lad's fingers in his palm. "Now I shall do mine. Come, now. Reintroduce me to your mum."

The years had changed her, he saw at once. She galloped ahead of the approaching soldiers. He laughed when he saw it was Jenny she rode. She threw herself off the donkey, gathering Jasper close, looking first at Corbin before staring past his shoulder at the manor. Her hair was glossy, though still cut short as a boy's. For once her face was clean, and her clothes, although worn, were also well kept. She wore trousers, a long shirt, and boots on her feet.

"Jasper." She kissed her child once on each cheek. "Brave lad. But this isn't quite what I had in mind when I sent you to warn Corbin away."

"Nell." Corbin embraced his friend warmly. Resting his chin atop her head, he closed his eyes, breathing in the scent of home. He'd glimpsed her once or twice through the looking glass in the Mirror Room, but never for long and always out of time. Once, when he'd found her, she'd been gray-haired and crooked, happy in her home, surrounded by people he would never know. Family, he'd assumed. At the time, he'd wondered if it was jealousy making his throat tight. Now, as he held her close, he knew it had been pride.

The sound of many hooves on cobblestone grew loud. Corbin set Nell gently aside. "Take your son away from this," he warned. He drew Da's sword from its scabbard on his back and stepped forward to meet his would-be captors.

There were not fifteen men, or even twenty-five, but thirty. Ten soldiers rode astride fine black horses. The rest of the regiment jogged on foot. Their livery was bright against the wintery background. Their weaponry gleamed even in the cold gray light.

Corbin picked out Spare from the group for his face, so like Laurie's despite the ravages of time and sorrow. He wore blue as well, but in a finer cloth. Two swans were emblazoned on his tunic in silver. There were ribbons on his sleeve and on his horse.

Beauty rode at his lordship's side. Her horse was fat, her tack polished to a dull gleam, her gown as richly fashioned as Spare's, and her cloak was good wool. She wore rings on her fingers and a silver circlet in her hair. When she saw Corbin her lovely mouth trembled, but as soon as she caught him looking, she lifted her chin, glaring haughtily down her nose.

"Nell said you weren't dead and eaten," she said, pulling up a cautious horse-length from Corbin. "I thought it unlikely you'd held the devil at bay for five long years, but I see she spoke true."

"And hello to you, sister," Corbin replied. It broke his heart just a little to see how very much she resembled Mother now that she was grown. "Will you introduce me to your friends?" Smiling grimly, he passed Da's sword from hand to hand.

Beauty was visibly unimpressed. "Lord Spare has come all the way from Fontainebleau with a warrant for your arrest, brother. My lord desires recompense for his heir's murder, while His Majesty requires you return that sword that belongs in the throne's armory. Littleton has promised them both satisfaction."

"Not all of Littleton," Nell said. She had thrust Jasper behind her back but refused to leave Corbin's side. Silently Corbin blessed her for a loyal fool. "Only those few more concerned with the king's approbation than honor."

"Honor?" Lord Spare barked a caustic laugh. He looked down at Corbin from his horse, one hand resting on the dirk at his belt. "The de Beaumont line knows nothing of *honor,* not since this man's sire made alliance with the Littleton Fiend and grew wealthy off that demon's favor. *Honor* belongs to the pious. Men and women who bargain with the devil or his minions deserve to be drawn and quartered."

Corbin glanced at Beauty. She sat her horse untroubled, mouth pursed, head held high.

"My lord." One of the mounted soldiers urged his horse close. "You recall, I hope: so long as Corbin places the glaive at once into my keeping we'll return him to Fontainebleau to face the king's council on the question of Laurie's murder. It is why we are here, my lord. To ensure this man's *safe* return to court."

Corbin, astonished, stared up into Marc Saulniers's seamed face. His friend smiled back, though his eyes were grave. He wore the blue as if it sat lightly on his shoulders. Age had changed him not at all.

"I'm very glad to see you still alive," his friend said. "Shall we keep it that way? Hand over the king's sword. It is my duty to see it reclaimed."

"This sword was my father's," Corbin said evenly. "Passed to me so I may kill the demon that holds my family in thrall."

Marc folded his hands on the pommel of his saddle as he regarded Corbin. "And did you?" he asked. "You stand here in one piece, and for that I'm very grateful." He looked past

Corbin at the manor. "Did you slay the monster? Is celebration in order?"

"My son is dead," grated Lord Snare. "Years in the grave. The good chevalier, Sir Thomas of White Hill, fell also to this man in Laurent's defense. Celebration is not in order."

"The Littleton Fiend is vanquished," Corbin said. His fingers tightened around the pommel of Da's sword. "The demon is not a threat. Nor am I, Marc. Nor was I ever."

"My son would say differently!"

Ignoring his lordship, Marc swung down from his horse. He tossed the animal's reins to the nearest foot soldier. He extended a hand in friendship.

"You have my word, Corbin. The king and his council will hear you out. Affrodille and David, Mary-Louise and Dot—each has over the years given testimony before the throne. We wait now upon you for closure. Laurie deserves that much, don't you think?"

Corbin could read nothing of intent on Marc's face. Out of the corner of his eye, Nell rocked from heel to toe; she looked as if she had just swallowed something sour. He had to squelch the urge to glance back toward the manor.

"Corbin," entreated Marc, taking another step forward. "Recall the garlic under my pillow to keep away the nightmares? Yes? Well, then. It's my turn. Let me help you now. Hand over the glaive."

It took all of Corbin's courage to give up Da's sword. It was almost physically impossible; his fingers cramped around the pommel at the last moment, and Marc had to pry it from his hand. But Lord Snare's derisive snort kept Corbin from pulling the blade away. He would not let Laurie's father see him falter.

"Thank God," Beauty said once the sword was safely in Marc's possession. "Exile may have done you good, brother; I was certain you'd fall prey to temper and kill more innocent men today." She pressed a hand against her breast in fluttering distress. "Nell, take Jasper home at once. He shouldn't have to watch his father bound."

Nell swore with such creativity that the nearest soldiers blushed. Corbin was hard pressed to keep back a hysterical giggle. Thirty soldiers watched impassively as Marc finished securing Da's sword to his own belt then returned to Corbin, a twist of thick rope in hand.

"I'm sorry," he apologized quietly. "But you understand; I must keep up appearances for his lordship's sake."

Corbin acquiesced with a shrug. Marc tied his wrists deftly behind his back, testing the knot three times before he was content it would hold.

"Walk with me beside my horse," he directed in a kindly tone. "At least until town where we'll see to it you have a mount of your own. Shall we stop at your home along the way? Is there anything you should like to collect before we ride for Fontainebleau?"

"No," replied Corbin. Everything he had left of home was locked behind the rusting manor gate.

"As you wish." Marc set a hand on Corbin's elbow, guiding him toward the waiting horse, but at that moment, Lord Snare kicked out with all his strength. The toe of his boot connected solidly with Corbin's chin. Corbin staggered. Pain turned his vision spotty. He would have fallen if not for Marc's supporting hand.

"You pompous little *shit!*" cried Nell. Corbin meant to tell her to hush before she made everything worse, but he thought his lordship's boot had shattered a tooth and lacerated his tongue, and he couldn't bring his hands around to staunch the gush of blood.

"Oh, no," said Beauty suddenly. "No. The wolves! Look what you've done!"

Corbin wasn't sure whether his sister meant her scold for

himself or his lordship. It was the very same tone she'd used when he'd ruined one of Da's cheeses by mistake or accidentally overturned Nan's butter churn. He did laugh then, for the absurdity of it all. The taste of iron clogged his throat. He spat, which hurt, and also made him forget to feel sympathy for Lord Spare when six very angry wolves rushed around the manor wall and toward his lordship through the snow.

Thirty stoic soldiers reached for their best artillery in the face of oncoming fang and fury. They pointed sword tip and arrow point not at the rushing pack but at Corbin. The wolves, called to heel by some inaudible signal, stopped in their tracks. Corbin's heart sank, and not because death pointed its finger at him from every angle.

Lightning split the air, making the ground quiver. Falling snow hissed as it turned to vapor. Sulfur made the air fetid. Beauty screamed. Jasper buried his face against his mother's side. Several of the nearest soldiers began to back away. The wolves moved again, slowly, crouched low to the ground, creeping toward their master.

"You said he was contained," Marc muttered through his teeth. Setting his feet wide, he drew Da's sword. "Fuck me, that's an old and ugly specimen. Sir Thomas would die again to see one like this."

Corbin couldn't help but agree. He'd seen the Beast's image recorded in ink on the English king's pages and spread tall across David's painted canvas. Neither rendering did the demon justice. He was far more wolf than Corbin had guessed; from snout to slavering tongue to splayed, hairy feet. He traveled on all fours like his pack but rose, human-like, to two as he approached the gathered army. On four feet he was larger than any horse. On two he towered over them all.

"No wonder your da went mad," Nell murmured. She

kept Jasper caged protectively in both arms. "To live with that for so long. And you—how have you stood it?"

Corbin looked past the stippled pelt and wolfish features into angry yellow eyes. The Beast, wetting his snout with a long tongue, stared back.

"Stay away, fiend!" warned Marc, brandishing the afreet glaive. "We've no quarrel with you."

"Haven't you?" When the Beast spoke, it was like thunder breaking. The king's horses began to sweat and dance. Jenny sat down on her haunches in the snow. Jasper stuck his fingers in his ears. "Then return to me what is mine. At once."

"This sword belongs to the king of France!"

"Not the sword." The Beast stretched clawed fingers. He swiveled his head, looking from Lord Snare to Marc and then to Corbin. "The man. Corbin de Beaumont belongs to me."

Lord Snare, whey-faced, drew his own thin blade. "Come closer, devil, and you'll see him dead. I've thirty men sworn to my command, and I *will* have justice. By blood right, de Beaumont belongs to me. I intend to take him to Fontainebleau."

"You're a very popular man," Nell said to Corbin under her breath. "But then, you were a popular child. *What* is your sister doing?"

Corbin had been watching the play of muscle along the Beast's barrel chest and coiled haunches. The Beast, having notice Corbin's attention, was showing a good bit of disdainful fang. They turned as one just in time to see Beauty snatch a staff from the nearest soldier and club Lord Spare across his skull. His lordship crumpled, pitching slowly from his horse into the snow. No one moved to stop his fall.

"He's not well liked at court," Beauty said, returning the bloodied staff to its gaping owner. "No one has forgotten how he ruined his heir. If not for Charles's inexperience, none of this"—she gestured about—"would have come to pass. How dare he bloody my brother! Is he dead?"

"Not quite," rumbled the Beast. Possibly only Corbin heard the reluctant mirth beneath the monster's timber. "But that's easily fixed." He stalked forward.

"Hold!" Marc called. "This changes nothing." He barked a command. The king's soldiers split their attention between Corbin and the Beast. Corbin, seeing blade and bow pointed at the demon, felt a frisson of rage shiver along his spine.

Spare, lying stunned on cobblestones, began to whimper.

The Beast gnashed his teeth. "I'll tear you to bits," he threatened Marc, lashing his tail in the snow. "I'll make you into blood pudding. I'll strike this hamlet from the map and then ravage Fontainebleau until the sky rains red!"

"But you can't," retorted Marc. "Can you? I've studied you very thoroughly, fiend. All of us on White Hill did, for Corbin's sake. I know you're tied to the manor; I suspect your powers wane beyond its walls. I wager you're struggling to hold form as it is." He clicked his tongue. Two blue-clad men broke ranks to scoop Lord Spare off the road. They gave Beauty a wide birth.

"I'm not wrong, am I?" continued Marc. "Ah, look at you! So angry! How long have you been trapped beneath that roof? Can you even recall the taste of freedom? Or have you grown so used to confinement you cower beneath the blue sky?"

The Beast's howl sent Nell and Jasper to their knees. The manor quaked. A handful of soldiers let their arrows fly in fear. Four struck the Beast about his head and shoulders. They stuck in his pelt like porcupine quills on a hound. He snarled. His wolves circled restlessly in circles around him, gnashing their teeth.

"I've not Corbin's natural skill," Marc admitted. "But I'm a fine swordsman. And this is a magnificent sword. I'll lay odds I can cut your heart from your chest before you rip my head from my shoulders."

"Stop." Corbin slid in front of Da's sword. The fickle blade pricked his chest. It hurt his mouth to speak, but he persevered because he'd seen a foreign mercenary's charmed knife slip between the Beast's ribs, and he knew Marc spoke true. The Beast, a king in his manor, was terribly vulnerable outside its walls. "Both of you—stop!"

The Beast whined low in his throat. He curled and uncurled his wicked claws. Marc lowered his blade.

"He holds your family hostage," the burned man said. "He strangles you with your father's ill-made promise."

"Not anymore," corrected Corbin. "He's given me leave to go free."

Beauty put her hand over her mouth. Nell gasped. Jasper looked up and around at Corbin, eyes wide. Even Marc appeared taken aback.

"But?" he demanded.

"Because he's my friend," said Corbin simply. "And he because he trusts me. Now get me to Fontainebleau."

CHAPTER 22

No one was surprised when Lord Spare insisted Beauty be taken into custody. She accepted her fate calmly, although she insisted on renting the cooper's cart for the long journey from Littleton to Fontainebleau.

"I am a lady," she reiterated icily. "And not fit for many hours on horseback. Besides which, my brother is injured and just barely escaped from the demon's clutches. He needs rest. He needs *me*."

Only the pain in Corbin's mouth kept him from laughing aloud at her insistence. Beauty was no more the nurturing sort than she was a lady. But he kept his thoughts to himself. If Marc saw Corbin's aborted amusement, he was still wise enough to send ahead into Littleton for two wagons: one for the de Beaumonts and the second for Lord Spare.

The Beast had vanished, but the manor remained on the edge of the forest. Gaffer Julian's goats were not impressed by the change in scenery. Nor was Julian's grandson who soon came across the pasture to see what the fuss was about. The young man was as frightened by the sight of Corbin returned from the devil as he was by the lingering pack of wolves. He set about throwing stones and snowballs at both the animals and the soldiers until his lordship, barely recovered from his faint, screamed at him to stop.

The wolves, blessed with a good deal of sense, returned to the forest. Marc, patience obviously worn to a nub, quickly got his regiment turned about and headed back into town.

"God save me from women and children and the peerage of the realm," he muttered under his breath, stepping into his stirrups. Corbin, walking alongside Marc's horse with his hands bound still behind his back and the blood on his mouth sluggishly drying, fought a smile.

He couldn't help but look over his shoulder one last time at the receding manor.

"Don't scowl so," Nell said from four paces behind. "You're free."

Jasper snorted. "Mum," he lamented in carrying tones, "you said yourself the new king wants Corbin for his dungeons."

Nell scoffed. "Beauty will never let that happen. Now run along to Faith. Tell her to come and kiss Corbin safe journey."

They passed Mother and Da's cottage along the way. Snow blanketed sleeping rosebushes. Nell turned Jenny through the pasture gate. Tallow candles burned in the windows, but if Faith was there, she refused to show herself, even when Beauty called her name. Of Jasper there was no sign.

"They've dashed ahead," Beauty hazarded when her summons went unanswered. "Faith's grown headstrong since Hope left and Nan died. We buried her beneath the lavender, just two summers past." She pointed vaguely in the direction of Mother's small garden. "Papa, too, although he fell in early autumn, and we had to wait on the thaw to dig his grave. That's why Hope ran, I think; she couldn't stand the thought of Da's corpse in the cellar while we pretended everything was bearable. It never really was, not after you left."

The cottage seemed smaller than Corbin remembered. There were signs of fresh thatch under the snow and panes of glass in the front window.

"I've made improvements," Beauty said archly, seeing Corbin's consternation. "It's warmer now. Comfortable. I've a man to work the fields and another to press Mother's apples into brandy. We're the wealthiest family in town again. Faith will have no lack of beaus once she's of age."

"The Beast's gold." Corbin shook his head. "I thought you'd spend it away on fripperies."

"Of course not," retorted Beauty from atop her fat horse. "We sold you twice over, brother. Did you think I'd waste your blood money on silken hose?" The rings on her fingers sparkled when she laughed.

All of Littleton turned out to see Corbin and Beauty loaded into the cooper's wagon. Corbin glimpsed many faces he recognized, and many more he did not. Farmer and gentry alike gawked from buildings where before there had been only hedgerow and grass. Henri's bakery was under new ownership. The innkeeper was loathe to part with his cart and horse for Lord Spare's comfort but too cowardly to voice protest in the face of so much blue. Corbin couldn't blame the fellow.

Nell helped Corbin into the wagon after Beauty. She kissed him lightly on his smarting mouth.

"You're a good man, Corbin," she said into his ear. "And don't you forget it."

She hopped off the wagon. A young soldier took her place, gathering up the long reins and clucking the cooper's horse forward.

"Lay your head on my lap," Beauty said. "You've gone a bit

green. And better for us if you keep your poor battered face out of his lordship's way."

"You're the one who knocked him off his horse. He'll not forgive you that anytime soon." But Corbin did as she asked, stretching out on his left side along the narrow bench. He had to bend his knees in the small space. His shoulders pulled uncomfortably and the rope around his wrists chafed, but neither plagued Corbin as much as the empty scabbard still strapped to his back. Beauty spread her cloak about them both, smiling as she ruffled his hair.

"I paid mind, you know. When Papa schooled you over and over again. It was hard not to, he shouted so loud. But I paid attention, learned a few things. I dare say I know how to look after myself." Her smile faded. "I suppose he taught us all that much, didn't he? Damn him for a fool."

THEY WERE ALMOST out of Littleton when Faith and Jasper caught up to the regiment. Beauty saw them first. She sat up straight, startling Corbin out of a light doze. He reached for Da's sword before recalling he'd lost it.

"Wait!" Beauty ordered the driver. "That's my sister. Hold the horse!"

Only Beauty, Corbin thought as he peered muzzily through increased snowfall, *could order about an entire regiment by force of will.* Although he suspected the driver's obedience had as much to do with Beauty's ample charms as her imperious command.

The driver slowed the wagon. Jasper and Faith scrambled up the board and over the side. Both children were grinning ear to ear. Jasper clutched an armful of blankets while Faith carried one of Nell's buckets over her arm. Corbin's littlest sister was grown from babyhood into a winsome and merry young lass. She dropped the bucket on the wagon floor, launching herself into Beauty's arms and making the driver yelp protest.

"Here, now! You'll frighten the horse!"

"Send them back, Corbin." Marc appeared alongside the wagon, looking cold and irritable despite the blue cape tucked around his throat and spread over his horse's haunches. "The King's council is no place for children."

"We're not to stay," agreed Jasper solemnly. "But mum says they'll likely freeze in this weather, with naught but their everyday togs. I've blankets and hot coals and brandy and fish pie."

"Bless Nell for thinking of it," Corbin said. "And bless you two for running all this way." For Jasper was red-faced and panting.

"Faith," Beauty cajoled. "Look, here's your brother who saved us from the Littleton Fiend. Do you remember? It was Corbin's pony you first learned to ride on, and his dolls you played with on the beach. Give him a kiss, now, for luck."

But Faith shook her head, mouth crumpling in distress, and turned her head away.

"It's fine." Corbin sorted through blankets to hide his sorrow. "She was just an infant, Beauty. Barely walking on her own."

Beauty, for once in her life, was silent and stricken. Marc glanced at Corbin, regret writ large across his scarred face, but it was the young soldier driving the wagon who broke the pained silence.

"Pass me one o' them pies," he said. "And a coal or six for my feet. Why His Majesty had to send thirty good men through a storm unto nowhere I'll never understand. All for a sword. It's not as if you're one of them *English* spies." He paused. "Come to think o' it, though, it was worth it to see the wolf man for myself. Something out of my gran's bedtime stories, wasn't he?"

"Yes," Corbin agreed. "He is."

It wasn't until after they'd said good-bye to the children—Corbin with an ache in his breast for Faith's distrust—and finished Nell's pies and most of the brandy that Corbin noticed the odd quilt among Littleton wool. Beauty, always appreciative of lovely things, had the quilt already wrapped around her head and shoulders. Corbin, bundled beneath plainer blankets, brushed a finger across Coptic embroidery.

"It's very unusual, isn't it?" Beauty murmured. She yawned. The sun had dropped low on the horizon. "It's not at all to Nell's taste. It's so very soft and warm—and it smells like Mother's roses."

They reached Fontainebleau Palace on the fourth day.

By the time they arrived, Beauty was stiff and quiet from too much time on the road. Corbin was little better. The regiment had stopped five times along the way, to rest the horses and to replenish supplies. Each time Corbin and Beauty were allowed to stretch their legs and empty their bladders. Beauty had made the most of her limited freedom, finding friends among the soldiers, but as the days stretched long and the snow continued to fall, her energy flagged. When Corbin pressed her to she ate, but she preferred to take refuge in sleep, wrapped tightly in the Beast's quilt beneath a pile of Littleton blankets. Corbin could see the strength leaching from her bones.

He was very glad to sight the palace. Whatever Spare and the new king had in store, Corbin knew for Beauty at least it would be easier than a regiment's grueling pace.

Marc saw them both into a double chamber on the west end of the palace. Corbin, who had marveled at White Hill and then again at Beastly Manor, hadn't the energy to spend on Fontainebleau. He caught a brief impression of vast ceilings, shining floors, and impossible archways before Marc secreted them away.

"A lesser wing, but you're better off here, away from the daily bustle." There were two servants standing attendance. Marc sent them scurrying with a clap of his hands. "Hot water! Masses of it! And wine. My lady, shall I send for a physician?"

Beauty demurred but didn't protest when a maidservant shepherded her away to bathe. Marc watched until the door between chambers was shut, before turning concern Corbin's way.

"She looks ghastly," he said. "I apologize. It would have been better had we left her behind in Littleton, but Spare will not see any sense. He's waited a long time for this."

"For me, you mean." The room was full of overstuffed furniture. A massive bed, hung with curtains and dressed in velvet and linen, made the space feel further cramped.

Corbin chose the closest chair and sat. Wincing, he massaged a shoulder. Marc had cut the rope from around his wrists on the second day after Corbin had shown no inclination toward escape, but the muscles still protested abuse.

Marc looked as travel worn as Corbin felt. Mud and snow plastered his hair to his scalp. His livery was soaked through. He closed his eyes briefly as he nodded.

"To clear Laurie's name. No man, especially one so well known as Lord Spare, wants to count his son treasonous and a murderer to boot. Much easier to blame a cheese monger's son."

For Marc, Corbin knew, Sir Thomas's death was years past. For Corbin, the loss was a raw wound yet to form a scab. "What happened to the soothsayer?"

"Affrodille has never said. Put back in the warren, I

suppose. Although mayhap better if she hacked him to bloody bits. She runs the place, now, did you know? She and David. Together they've filled *his* shoes. For better or for worse, White Hill continues." He scratched his chin. "Are you cold? Bit of a fancy blanket, that. Bedouin, is it?"

Corbin blinked down at the quilt folded in his lap. Beauty had kept it wrapped tight about it even as they'd left the wagon for the palace. Unlike everything else, the fabric was impossibly dry despite days exposed to cold and wet. Corbin didn't remember picking up the blanket. Now he was unwilling to let it go.

"I'll build up the fire, shall I?" Marc suggested, hastening to the hearth. Da's sword on his belt was long enough to scrape the floor when he crouched over the basket of kindling. "Nasty business, this weather. You'll want to bathe and rest yourself, Corbin. You'll see His Majesty tomorrow morning and the council after. I know it's quick, but best to get these things rolling, you understand."

A silver badge, similar to the one Sir Thomas had worn on his own breast, shone on Marc's tunic beneath the fold of his cape: the king's favor. Corbin hadn't noticed it earlier while his friend had been bundled tight against the snow.

"You've done well for yourself, Marc. I'm glad."

"Thank you." Marc slapped soot from his hands. "It's a dangerous business, but it suits me. I've a wife now and an infant daughter. You'll meet them, of course, once this mess is cleared."

"I'd like that." When Corbin smiled, he tasted blood.

After Marc made his excuses, three page boys popped into the chamber with hot water and a tub for bathing. Corbin sluiced himself down, shivering, then crawled naked into bed. He folded the quilt under his head for a pillow, ignoring the many bolsters scattered across the mattress. Exhausted and sore, he fell immediately into sleep.

. . .

THE NEW KING of France was just a boy. Corbin, on his knees before the royal dais with his hands bound once again behind his back, didn't know what to make of the thin lad sitting the throne. Dark of hair and fair of skin, King Charles VI peered at Corbin with somber curiosity. The heavy robes and tall crown he wore made his body seem fragile.

Beauty, skirts spread wide, directed her low curtsy first to His Majesty and then to the four dukes ranged at Charles's side. Marc managed to include all five men in his attention while looking only at the king. He held Da's sheathed sword flat on his palms as he bent one knee.

"Your Majesty," he said. "The afreet blade."

"Thank you, *Capitaine,*" the king of France replied. "We are pleased by your successes." His brown eyes weighed Corbin thoughtfully. "Was it very difficult?"

"No, Majesty. The weather was trying, but de Beaumont came at once to your summons and gave the sword into my keeping without protest."

But the king, for all his size, was no fool: "What happened to his face?"

"He fell, my king, on the snow and ice." The lie tripped off Marc's tongue.

King Charles leaned forward. The tendons in his slender throat stood out beneath the weight of his crown. "Did you stumble, monsieur? Did Spare's boot catch on your mouth as you went down?"

It was a test. Corbin weighed his response. The four dukes, without paying overt notice, waited carefully upon his answer.

"Yes, Your Majesty," Corbin answered after a moment. "It did."

Corbin didn't think he imagined King Charles's relieved exhale.

"We will return the glaive to its rightful place in our treasury alongside its sisters," the king said.

"And, Majesty, the small matter of White Hill and Lord Spare's quarrel with de Beaumont?" Marc prompted.

The boy king folded his hands on his robes. "A matter for our council," he said. "At a later date. We'll wait upon Spare, who has taken to his bed with a concussed head. As you know, he also fell prey to the weather when his horse tripped on snow and threw him."

CHARLES'S unspoken pardon did nothing to ease Beauty.

"Of course they would not dare punish me for Spare's stupidity," she railed. "I am a wealthy woman without husband—they'd rather marry me off. The Duke of Burgundy likely has a list of eligible allies already on the table. They won't be subtle about it. I'll be lucky if I see Littleton again."

"Isn't it what you've always wanted?" Corbin asked. He poked listlessly at the late breakfast set on a table beneath the chamber window. Ignoring eggs and ham, he poured sweet wine into a goblet. "A life of circumstance and leisure?"

"It's what I wanted until I went out and took it for myself," Beauty retorted. "Littleton is home; I've no patience for court life. Besides, Faith would be miserable, trapped always inside palace walls."

Corbin drained his goblet in one swallow and then took himself back to bed.

"Wake me when your banns are posted," he said, pulling bedclothes over his head.

· · ·

WHEN HE WOKE to piss and to drink more wine, the chamber was dark and cold, the tapestry pulled across the window. Beauty was nowhere to be seen, the door between rooms shut. He rekindled the hearth for warmth and went back to bed.

When he roused a second time, the tapestry was drawn, but it was night outside. Dinner was cold on the table, the flagon refilled with red wine. The fire leaped high. Bath water warmed in a bucket on the hearth. Corbin drank four glasses of red and fell back into bed.

The third time he woke it was to bright sunlight and angry voices.

"I don't care who you are!" Beauty hissed from somewhere past the foot of the bed. "He's resting."

"He's sulking," replied David loudly. He pitched his voice at the mattress. "And from the smell of it, in his cups. Or didn't you know he's prone to dark moods?"

Corbin sat up. Beauty, gowned in teal and wearing silver in her ears, looked fresh and lovely as a flower. David, rumpled and wet from travel, was as angry as Corbin had ever seen him. They both turned blinding scowls in Corbin's direction.

"Ah, there he is. Sleep well?" David asked, viciously polite. "I can't say you look refreshed."

"You're covered in mud, and your spectacles are bent," Corbin replied, wincing at the light through the window-pane. "It must be worse than I hoped, if Marc sent for you. Is it to be a hanging or my head on a pike?"

Beauty blanched. Marc unslung his dripping pack from his shoulders. He tossed it onto the breakfast table alongside fresh oranges. After yanking at the laces with trembling hands, he retrieved a small oval glass from within.

"Marc didn't send for me, though I'll be having a strong word with him for that," David said. He slid the glass across the bedcovers. "No. It was your other champion, the one who prefers sorcery to messenger."

It was Corbin's turn to recoil.

"No, take it." Visibly furious, David gave the looking glass another poke. "You may find it surprising, but I dislike being indebted to your family demon. Take the glass and end the bargain."

Corbin took the glass. He pulled his knees up beneath the bedclothes and propped the shining oval on his thighs. It took only a heartbeat for his reflection to fog and reform.

"By God," spat the Beast, yellow eyes narrowed to slits. "I'll have his balls on a platter. Did he break your jaw or just your nose?"

"Only some teeth." But Corbin, who'd caught a glimpse of his own bruised face before the mirror shifted, lifted a hand to shield his mouth. "It's fine. What have you done to David? How did you find him?"

"Give me some credit." Behind the Beast, the Mirror Room was littered with books and scrolls and candle stubs. The white rose in its vase had opened its petals. "It's my mirror in my house; I know on whom you spy when you're revisiting the past." His black hair was a bird's nest atop his head. He'd shed his velvet coat, and there were brown stains on his shirt. "The Jew is the only one of your friends who isn't useless."

"Meaning I had a looking glass at hand," explained David in a dry voice. "Which aided in conversation."

In the mirror, the Beast waved a dismissive hand. "As I said, not useless. Red, he'll spring you from Spare's snare. You'll be on your way before you know it."

"What did you do to David to make him come?" Corbin demanded.

The Beast's brows rose almost to his hairline. He set his fingers on the other side of the glass, but David spoke first.

"Corbin, he only had to tell me what was happening. He wouldn't explain all of it until I swore to bring my glass with me to Fontainebleau." David's face twisted. "Did you think I wouldn't come, once I'd heard?"

"Red," said the Beast softly from the glass. "Get out of bed. Wash yourself. Eat something. It's time to fight."

IT WAS a strange collaboration around the hearth. Corbin, clean and dressed, picking at bread and fruit, sat on his legs in an overstuffed chair as around him his companions conversed. David, also tidied and fed, sat across the table from Marc. Corbin couldn't hear what they were saying, but Marc looked chastened. Beauty, elbows propped on a chair cushion, was whispering to the Beast's reflection. Corbin worried the two were becoming—if not friends—then cohorts. Or partners in mischief.

Outside the chamber, snow continued to fall. Fontainebleau was blanketed so thoroughly in white Corbin couldn't tell where the palace ended and the grounds began. The landscape was deserted; no one dared go out in the storm.

Corbin stood, stretched, and excused himself for the chamber pot. After that, it was a simple matter to escape through Beauty's adjoining room. He expected guards outside, but the hall was empty. He walked quickly, knowing it would only be a matter of minutes before Beauty or the Beast noticed his escape.

Fontainebleau was a maze. Only once Corbin left the west chambers behind did he understood how they'd been kept from the center of it all. The main palace buzzed with frenetic energy. There were more people, Corbin thought, in a single foyer than he'd seen in Honnefleu in one afternoon. And these were the peerage of the realm, men and women with the king's ear, or at least business with his dukes. They wore their wealth in vibrant display and spoke in rapid, stilted syllables. There was no likelihood at all that he could pass unremarked among them.

"Do you plan on running?" David asked, easing alongside Corbin. "You won't make it far. Just because you didn't notice the guardians don't mean they didn't notice you. If you hadn't been still wearing Michael's rune—of which I am very glad—you would have been struck unconscious before you left the hall."

Corbin squinted at his friend. "You don't mean ghosts."

"White Hill may not be haunted. Fontainebleau most certainly is. And by unnatural creations more dangerous than ghosts." David took Corbin's elbow. "Thomas gave House Valois every advantage."

"I'm stifled in there." Corbin set his heels stubbornly in plush carpet. "I'm not ready to go back."

"We're not going back. I've made up my mind. We're going to see Lord Spare."

SPARE LOOKED at Corbin's damaged mouth and laughed.

"Not as pretty now," he said from his chair by the fire. He wore a lap blanket on his knees and a bandage around his head. His lordship's chamber was better appointed than those in the west end of the palace, warmer and richer both.

Spare had sent his attendants away. Now he looked between Corbin and David with acid curiosity.

"How did you bypass my men? I'll have someone whipped for negligence."

David grimaced. "I've been warned you're a very stupid man," he said. "I see it's true."

"Laurent, I suppose. He hated me at the end."

"My lord," cautioned David. "White Hill has kept the

details of Thomas Chevalier's death close, for Laurie's sake and for our own. And because we believed Corbin safely out of it. But now you've made issue of what we prefer kept quiet. I can't allow it."

Malice glittered behind Spare's lashes. "I'm not afraid of White Hill."

"Then you're the only one in this palace who is not," David returned. He adjusted his spectacles on his nose. "Will you test us? I think you would regret it."

Spare threw off his blanket, made to rise, then faltered beneath David's regard.

"What is he to you that White Hill promises him protection?" Lord Spare challenged.

"Family," replied David. "Just as Laurie was, and Thomas. Keep away from my family, Spare, or I'll see to it you never sleep a peaceful wink again."

"You thought we blamed you," he said later as they shared supper over the boards in the soldiers' barracks. "All this time, you thought we blamed you. I should have listened to Affrodille and somehow sent word."

Corbin's appetite had, predictably, returned with a vengeance. He'd sated himself on bread, cheese, and apples. Now he snuck a glance David's way, trying to catalogue the many and few ways his friend had changed.

"Time behaves unexpectedly in the manor," Corbin said. The silver he'd glimpsed on his friend in the Beast's mirror had yet to appear. The crooked white hat was the same, but there were more lines around David's mouth. He'd traded short scholars' robes for longer vestments. There were new white scars on both his wrists, up and down his forearms, like scratches or knife marks. Corbin, knowing the secrets caged in the warren, hesitated to ask what had caused them.

"It hasn't been so long as you assume," he added. "For me, Laurie died in the spring."

"You're still mourning," David realized. He reached across the boards and, in his own way, squeezed Corbin's shoulder.

Did you weep for your friend?

"Yes," said Corbin. "I think I will always. Whether or not anyone else believes it was my fault; I know it was. I should have come to you, David, when it started. I could have stopped it from happening. He needed me to do that for him, and I didn't."

David nodded. "What will you do now? You've nothing constraining you; your life is at long last your own. Where will you go?"

Corbin's slow smile stretched into a lopsided grin. "Home."

EPILOGUE

Once upon a time in faraway land a very wealthy merchant lived on a good piece of property just west of the hamlet we now call Littleton. He was the sort of man who made much of his luck to whomsoever would listen and didn't often stop to think of others less fortunate. His gentle wife called him Roux because of the color of his hair, and also in secret because of his temper that sparked like wildfire when least expected and sometimes sent her young son to cowering in the garden behind the white roses.

"He'll kill that child by accident if you're not careful," the lad's nan warned his mother. "Corbin looks too much like you, daughter, and too little like your husband. Jean's a canny man. He knows something's amiss. Be more vigilant."

The merchant's wife went into the black forest for help as she had three years earlier when for all her husband's rutting her womb would not bear fruit. It was the way of her mother, her grandmother, and countless generations of Littleton's women. She made correct offering to the forest fay: milk and sugar and blood from a needle prick on Corbin's finger. She asked for the forest's protection and mayhap, in the darkest recess of her heart, she asked to be rid of her husband.

The fay took due note, but not only the fay. There was a wolf hidden in the briarwood that day. The wolf carried word of all she had seen and heard back to through the trees to an older denizen of the forest.

I'll admit to it; my interest was peaked.

It was a simple thing to spy on the merchant's cottage. The subtle brutality I saw there made me wake to rage. I'd not felt such affront for centuries. In the east, we treat our children and our wives with care; this Picardie man used his small family no better than chattel.

I sent her the sword, first, for the boy's sake, and for her own. I thought she could use it against his ebony cane. She was growing round with her second child by then. It was de Beaumont's get, but still I worried. He'd developed a taste for the sound of his stick against innocent flesh.

It was an easy thing to see the afreet glaive into Caen on the same day one of de Beaumont's ships came into port. Valentine's father knows how to entice coin from a man. De Beaumont paid willingly; the glaive is an unusual and beautiful blade. I should know. I remember when it was forged in Saracen fires.

I thought she'd use the glaive to strike off his head in the way of my people. She didn't. He exchanged stick for glaive, and after that was rarely parted from the sword. He wore it on his hip and slept with it under his hand, and I hated him all the more.

He passed through my land a dozen times, Corbin's Da. He never knew I watched. I think *she* knew, in the end. When she died in my lap because she got in the way of the wolves meant to savage her husband, she laughed at our combined hubris.

"All of us make mistakes," she said. And then, awed: "You're weeping."

De Beaumont groveled in the dirt. He scratched at my gate as my wolves circled. I smiled at him through the bars, her blood on my hands and on my shirt.

"I'll bury her on my land," I promised. "But I'll leave you out here to rot once they're finished."

I've said in the beginning that the merchant was a canny man. Before my wolves pounced, he dared to bargain.

"Let me live!" he screamed. "I'm a rich man! Only let me live and I'll give you whatever of mine you so desire!"

Simplicity itself to make him believe he'd tricked me. I wasn't in need of a concubine and certainly not a wife. I only wished to take from the man what he didn't deserve.

Corbin's been away longer than he knows. The white rose finally dropped its petals several nights ago; now they're drifting brown on the library floor. I wasn't certain he'd find his way back in time. I didn't doubt his intent. But the house has been intransigent as of late, and the Jew—David—would have kept him longer if he could. Possibly forever.

"Beast!" he calls, stamping his boots on cabbage-rose carpet. "Where have you got to? The kitchen smells of rotted meat!"

I roll my eyes behind heavy lids. The wolves brought me plenty of kill while he was gone, but there's only so much one can do with coney and grouse. I got quickly bored.

"*Mon Dieu*, this place is a disaster." But he's glad to see me, there on the sofa. I can hear it in his voice, past the slur of his injured tongue. "Worse than usual. What happened?"

"Time," I say. Opening my eyes, I prop myself on one elbow. He's right. The library looks a sight, covered in a layer of dust and cobwebs. I've been asleep longer than I realized.

"You look the same." I'm both surprised and angry. His poor, battered face makes me want to howl. Spare will pay for that, just as soon as I marshal inspiration. "How long were you gone?"

He moves my legs and settles on the sofa. I set my bare feet in his lap. He doesn't shove them off. His strong thighs beneath the pads of my toes are enough to make me lick my lips in anticipation.

"Ten days," he says. "Give or take. Nell wanted to feed me up again. Then it took me longer to track the manor than I liked." He studies me. "How long was I gone?"

"Nine weeks, give or take," I say. Then I shiver. "I admit I'd begun to worry you weren't coming."

He flushes up pink when he's embarrassed or angry. The color clashes with his hair and the stubble on his face, but I don't care. I think he's the most beautiful thing I've seen, and I've walked Wadi Rum.

"Why wouldn't I?" Not embarrassed but angry. "I told you I'd find you again."

"You're without your blade," I say to needle him further because I'm weaker than I like and I don't want him to see. "You're no threat to me any longer. My heart is quite safe."

"Yes," he agrees, growling like one of my wolves. Then he lifts me into his arms and launches us both up off the sofa. He's a big man, which I like, but gentle with his strength, which I respect. "Quite safe now. Why didn't you warn me? If I'd known my leaving would take you so, I would have found a way to stay, damn Spare and the king's army both."

"I didn't know. Not for certain." I brush my palm against the whiskers on his chin. They're rough as a cat's tongue. I shiver again and bury my face in his neck so he won't see my mouth twist. "I've never bothered with love before. I think it's worse than loneliness."

He puts me tenderly to bed and wraps himself around me

and breathes. I grow healthier in his presence, heartbeat by heartbeat. The old curse has redoubled. I'm tethered to the pentagram in my dungeon and now again to this man. The sorceress who bound me so would rejoice had she not drowned in the Tigris generations ago.

Corbin shifts on our mattress. He looks into my face. I could happily drown in the sea of his stormy blue gaze.

"Beast," he demands. "Are you laughing?"

"Yes," I say. Then I turn in his arms and tenderly kiss his bruised mouth. He sighs his pleasure and draws me close, and I think that a thousand years more might be too short.

SPUN

A BEASTLY FABLE - BOOK TWO -
SUMMER 2018

In the bowels of the earth, pausing to rest his feet and adjust the lantern he carried in one hand, David heard White Hill's catacombs exhale.

He froze. The flame on the candle affixed in front of the mirrored lens bowed almost horizontal in the swell of musty air, shivering orange and yellow on a black wick, pointing back along the tunnel from where David had most recently come. He licked dry lips, heart thumping in his breast, but although the flame smoked angrily the light did not go out.

The unwelcome and unnatural breeze reversed itself - an inhale - and the flame flickered briefly in the opposite direction before settling again where David much preferred it stay: upright on the candle wick.

His fingers cramped on the lantern's handle; he made them unclench one by one, setting the lantern on the floor, smooth stone to match the curved walls and ceiling. Eyes fixed on tunnel ahead – pitch black beyond the cheerful glow of the lantern – hand settled now on the hilt of the smallsword he wore on his belt, David waited.

La Tarasque, the ancient wyrm that had once burrowed

beneath White Hill, leaving behind a system of tunnels so vast even David's predecessor hadn't been able to explore them all, was presumed long dead, nothing now but dust and bone and memory.

But other, equally dangerous, creatures had come to inhabit the warren in more recent centuries, most of them unwilling prisoners, compelled by the old magician who had kept White Hill's secrets in the name of Charles the Wise and King John before him. The old magician's eclectic menagerie had once been the envy of every scholar who dared dabble in supernatural studies; the royal purse and House Valois' implicit approval meant White Hill need spare no expense when it came to research or instruction.

The kings of France relied on White Hill to produce a very special breed of champion, an elite variety of soldier prepared to defend both the throne and the empire from evils the average person preferred not to acknowledge. Vampires, sorcerers, fay and demon, witch, basilisk and brownie to name only a few – there were more monsters above and below the earth than most men could face and still retain a shred of sanity.

The students who managed to graduate White Hill's hallowed halls in one piece and go on to don a hero's blue and silver livery were of stronger character than most. And by the time they left Le Château for court many understood that sanity was a small price to pay for the continued safety of France.

But the old magician had been gone for decades, the royal purse – thanks to Philip VI's war against England's Black Prince – was running dry, Le Château was all but empty of students, and White Hill's underground warrens were maybe not quite so secure as they had once been, aging cells crumbling into disrepair, their contents neglected.

La Tarasque might be long dead and the old magician's

menagerie essentially dismantled, but that did not mean the tunnels David braved as part of his daily routine were, by any stretch of the imagination, safe.

The flame on its wick in David's lantern burned merrily upright, undisturbed by surprise subterranean breezes. Nothing stirred the stale air. Whatever trouble had lurked there in the darkness outside the lantern light must have moved on.

Or so David fervently hoped.

An anxious sweat dripped between his eyes. Briefly snatching precious spectacles from the bridge of his nose, David used the sleeve of his robe to wipe his face. Anticipation heated his blood, flushing his cheeks and loosening his muscles, threatening to fog glass lenses when he returned his spectacles to his nose. So deep into White Hill the tunnels were cold. Frost filmed the floor and ceiling, diminishing the sparkle of the striated gold and green mineral that ran throughout the warren. David had spent his first few months on White Hill half in love with the swirl of shining color in the tunnel walls, had looked for any excuse to walk the labyrinth, enchanted by the glimmer or underground starlight.

It didn't take long for the novelty to wear off. The stars in the heavens might be more commonplace, but at least above ground a man better escape prowling monsters. And David had learned soon after settling in as Sir Thomas Chevalier's in-house scholar-cum-alchemist-cum-physicker that when it came to supernatural threat judicious retreat was much preferable to close combat.

But like *La Tarasque* and the old magician, Sir Thomas was dead, murdered six years earlier in his own garden by a much-beloved student wielding nothing more remarkable than a kitchen knife, and David no longer had the luxury of hiding behind books or potions in the face of danger.

By order of King Charles, Le Château's recruits were David's responsibility now, had been since the day Sir Thomas' body was sent in a wagon to Paris for burning. White Hill's secrets – the good, the bad, the magnificent and the execrable – were his to shepherd. David still relied heavily on the comfort of his books and potions, but now his hands also bore the callouses of a practiced swordsman. His body had traded the awkwardness of youth for the muscled confidence of a soldier in his prime; he was yet the scholar but in taking over White Hill he'd had to turn teach his body how to be equally as deadly as his mind.

The lantern sputtered. David sighed. Reminiscing would do nothing to make the task ahead lighter, even as it was the task ahead that stirred memories best left buried.

Drawing his sword with his left hand in case whatever had been breathing in the shadows returned, David picked up the lantern and walked deeper into the earth.

The door was like any other door in the warren: old wood bound in iron, latched and locked. None of the underground cells were marked in any way. He was relying on the map he kept in his head, a piece of ink-marked vellum he'd memorized on Sir Thomas' insistence. Even so, there was no guarantee the room on the other side of the door was the room he'd spent half a day chasing. David need only read a thing twice or thrice to remember it later in perfect detail, but experience had taught him Sir Thomas' map was not entirely accurate. He supposed even the steadiest mapmaker might become disorientated in *La Tarasque's* warren.

He set the lantern down again while he fumbled at the heavy ring of keys he wore on his belt but he wasn't so foolish as to sheathe his smallsword. The back of his neck prickled as he fit key after key into the hasp; his spectacles were beginning to fog once again. It took him eight tries, eight different bronze keys, before he found the one that worked.

The lock clicked open, the snick of the tumblers bouncing against the tunnel wall. David cleaned his spectacles a second time before shoving at the door. It opened grudgingly, not into the room but sideways into the stone wall along an iron track. The track needed oiling. The door and the small cell beyond hadn't seen a visitor for a very long time, possibly since before the old magician's death.

David stepped over the threshold, leaving his lantern behind on the tunnel floor. Once inside the cell there was no need for candlelight. Every cell within the warren was enchanted for warmth and light; as soon as he set foot in the room a large cluster of natural crystal burst into yellow light, making David blink.

His predecessor's enchantments still lingered, more helpful than not. The light could be quenched with a touch, David knew, and summoned again with another. When activated, the crystals provided warmth as well as illumination. And the old magician had been thorough. David had yet to encounter a room in the catacombs not fitted with the luminous mineral.

"Bless you, *rabbi,*" David murmured, fingers restless on the hilt of his sword, turning this way and that as he waited for his eyes to adjust to the yellow light. "For your wisdom and your foresight."

Wooden chests of varying sizes filled the narrow cell, stacked one atop another on the floor. A few of the half-hazard piles reached the ceiling. Most ended at shoulder-height, the top-most coffers leaning dangerously against curved stone walls. Time or the quaking earth had sent two of the larger trunks smashing onto the floor. Pieces of wood slat lay in pieces amongst a scattering of straw.

Whatever treasure the boxes had contained was lost to

time as well; shards of broken glass and pottery winked from beneath straw and wood.

The chests were neatly catalogued in the old magician's eccentric hand, a mixture of letters from the Hebraic alphabet and alchemic runes burnt into the wood. A quick glance over the inscriptions reassured David he'd found the room he needed.

"Blood magic," he confirmed out loud, suppressing a shiver of distaste. The alchemic runes indicated the contents of each chest were tuned to human blood, the most powerful of all bodily fluids and, in David's opinion, the most repugnant of alchemic ingredients.

The short Hebraic phrases seared alongside the runes provided more specific clarification as to nature of the artifacts packed inside each chest. *Divination* or *contamination, transmutation* or *conservation. Strength* and *nourishment, poison* and *protection.*

Human blood was a precious fluid indeed, blood magic a potent – and explicitly forbidden – alchemical tradition.

An-cold eddy crept suddenly through the open door and into the cell, plucking at the hem of David's robe and sending a violent shudder through his bones. He whirled, sword raised, braced against attack, but whatever was hunting him – and he had no doubt that something *was* – did not deign show itself.

Playing cat and mouse, David thought with rising dismay. *Trying to frighten me useless. It's working.*

And then, when chill fingers wafted against the back of his neck, a lover's ghoulish caress: *What in God's name is loose down here this time?*

"Begone!" he commanded the room at large in confident tones that belied the pounding of his heart. "White Hill and the treasures within are mine to guard and you are not welcome!"

He waited, eyes darting from shadow to shadow. There was no response, either from vigilant shadows or unexpected breezes. He did not fool himself that admonishment would scare whatever it was away. Banishment properly worked on the preternatural only when strong spells were involved.

Not a revenant. Keeping his front to the cell door, David backed carefully through the accumulation of chests, reading labels with a rapidity born of desperation. *Despite the ghostly freeze.*

White Hill couldn't be haunted; the old magician had seen to that.

Not dwarf nor troll nor vampire. Even as he sorted through wooden coffers he sorted also through the lore in his head. *They're none of them subtle.* His gaze caught on a chest smaller than most of the others, wedged between a tilting stack and the stone wall. No bigger than a loaf of bread, the chest was the right size, but turned sideways to the floor so David couldn't make out any inscription.

Basilisks can't disappear. Step by step he edged his way toward his goal. *A troll would leave behind a very obvious mess. And a gnome – Gnomes stink. I'd know at once if it were a gnome.*

As close as he could get without turning around, unwilling to relinquish his sword or defensive stance, David wedged the toe of his boot under corner of the chest and dragged it away from the wall, causing the nearest coffers to wobble precariously as he did so.

"Careful, lovely. They'll all come down atop your head if you're not more circumspect. And then where would you be?"

Oh, thought David as the sound of that familiar voice made his mouth go dry. *Incubus.* Lifting his chin, appraising the monster now standing just inside the threshold and wearing the form of an old friend as disguise and entice-ment, David couldn't help but grin.

"Child of Lilith," he acknowledged, sword and stance unwavering. "This place is not your home. Get thee gone."

The incubus smiled Corbin de Beaumont's white smile. Corbin's blue eyes widened, guileless, beneath a tousled ginger fringe. David knew the ginger fringe as intimately as he knew his own darker curls; David had tended Corbin's battered body more than once as White Hill's resident physicker, seen Corbin in every state of undress and several times gravely wounded, and not once had David looked upon that well-made form with anything other than aesthetic appreciation.

"I've missed you," protested the creature in a perfect mimicry of Corbin's gruff tones. Pink stained Corbin's cheeks as he slipped across stone toward David. He licked his lips as if in anticipation of a good meal after long starvation, the tip of his tongue shining briefly in the yellow light.

It was meant as seduction: the children of Lilith were born to feed off sexual stimulus, to milk lust until the monster was satiated and the victim a desiccated corpse. That an incubus was wandering loose in White Hill's catacombs was disturbing in more ways than one. That it had snatched an imaged of David's true love from the recesses of his mind was expected. That it meant to make a meal of his carnal desires, a dark joke.

"Keep back!" David warned, blocking the monster's advance with the blade of his sword. Lilith's lesser children – succubi, incubi, the Will o' the Wisp - were more easily killed than a full-blooded demon. A true fiend wouldn't be cowed by something so mundane as David's iron small sword.

The incubus went still, staring from the weapon to David's face, Corbin's features twisted in confusion. By now David should be showing signs of the enchantment, becoming addled by wave after wave of desire, made clumsy by the body's overwhelming appetite.

Instead David watched the creature coldly, unmoved.

"I thought you missed me, too," it complained, mouth turning petulant. Corbin's head tilted in disbelief as the monster eyed David's sword. "I thought you loved me."

David knew better than anyone that love and lust were too very different things. The incubus had made a fatal mistake. Almost, he felt sorry it. Mayhap the demon could not easily distinguish between the heart's desire and the body's. In the end it mattered only that Lilith's children could not make a meal of sentiment, nor could they ensorcel a man immune to sexual urgency.

Without lust to draw upon, the lesser demon was powerless, a shade throwing deception. Even as David pressed his advantage, crowding the monster with sword edge and revulsion, the illusion frayed. Corbin flickered, as tenuous as the flame in David's lantern, and behind ginger hair and wide blue eyes something squat and black angrily flexed a multitude of wizened tentacles.

David's breakfast turned uneasily in his gut, threatening to rise. Now that he could see the creature behind the disguise he could also smell it: wet fur and sulfur, worse than any gnome.

He could not think how the monster had ended in up in White Hill's warren to begin with. He and Sir Thomas had cleaned the catacombs of any artifact related to demonology when they'd decided to aid Corbin de Beaumont in his quest to kill the Littleton Fiend. David did not think it possible they'd missed something so obvious as a living specimen lurking beneath their home. Nor had the old magician listed one of Lilith's offspring in the extensive catalog he'd kept of his trophies.

David should know. He'd spent more hours than he liked to admit reading over the artifact lists.

"There's nothing here for you," he told the incubus. Logic

said he should kill it immediately. A demon, even the lesser variety, couldn't be allowed to continue. But curiosity stayed David's hand. Except for in pages of White Hill's many books, he'd come face-to-face with only one other devil, and that with the silvered glass of a scrying mirror as protection.

The scholar in David hesitated as a deerstalker might before a ten-pointed buck. He couldn't quite help making the moment last, even as he knew only a fool would delay.

"Nothing *here*," the incubus agreed after an instant of similar hesitation, running Corbin's stare once again along the iron blade, then over David and the assortment of wooden chests before it shrugged and dropped false semblance. "I've made a mistake." An abomination of feeler and fang, it used Corbin's voice still, and that was somehow worse than the original deception. "The juicer meal calls to me from upstairs, from Le Château." Dismissing David and his sword, it scuttled toward the door, but, being Lilith's offspring, it could not resist one last taunt.

"You, you're not good to me, mortal. You're flawed." Corbin's voice, dripping disgust, was as injurious as poison.

Incubus, succubus, Will o' the Wisp – they were used to being the hunter, not the hunted, and they were not terribly clever when it came down to it.

"No," said David.

"No?" the demon was almost out the door, unnatural appendages twitching as it reached for the threshold. It glanced back at David, yellow eyes shining in a noseless face.

"You've made two mistakes," corrected David before his sword took the incubus through the middle. The blade caught on bone and gelatin. The incubus shuddered. David twisted until black ichor burst across floor, wall, and ceiling. "The first was in breaching White Hill. The second was in discounting me."

The incubus shrieked as it fell, tentacles whipping back

and forth in paroxysms of agony. David leaned hard on the sword, gripping the pommel with both hands, using all of his weight to keep the demon pinned. The devil's true form was – despite an overabundance of angry feelers – roughly the size of a billy goat, but David's smallsword was meant for sparring with students or defending against the infestation of dwarves that ran amok in the forest below White Hill, and not at all the weapon he would have chosen to face down a demon, even the lessor sort.

Weakened by starvation, still the incubus struggled to the very last, several times landing a solid blow across David's legs. A single thorny tentacle managed to encircle his knee, squeezing. Pain blossomed where the thorns punctured his trousers and scraped his flesh, but the creature died before it could gain a solid hold. The tentacle quivered and then went lax, leaving a smear of blood as it fell away.

He stood gasping, weight still on his sword, until he was certain the incubus was dead. The stink of sulfur increased to noxious. Splashes of ichor ate away at stone, leaving permanent scars. When at last David tugged his weapon free of the demon's body, he saw that its yellow eyes had gone milky white in death.

Backing away, he wiped what ichor he could off his blade onto the floor, knowing that the iron blade was likely already ruined, pitted by the incubus' poisons. He could not sheath it for fear of damaging the leather sheath he wore, nor would he leave the sword behind and walk the tunnels back to White Hill without defense.

"A demon in the cellar," he muttered, holding the still-wet sword point away from his body as he retrieved his temporarily abandoned prize from the floor. "Sir Thomas is rolling over in his grave." He tucked the chest under one arm then edged carefully around the incubus' slowly dissolving corpse, sidestepping a spreading puddle of ichor and gore.

The sink of immediate decomposition made his eyes sting and water.

Once safely outside he closed and locked the cell door. The room would have to be cleaned and quarantined, the coffers moved to a new location. The incubus' death made the space unusable. Lore said the demon-stain endured long after the ichor was invisible to the mortal eye, and was unlucky.

Grabbing up his lantern, David hurried back the along the tunnels the way he'd come. The cleansing would have to wait. David had more pressing business, specifically one of the king's most trusted dukes waiting – by now no doubt impatiently – upon his return. John of Berry seemed a tolerant man, but also a man of action, and in the face of supernatural threat David supposed he could not expect Berry be contained indefinitely. Affrodille would do her best to act as distraction, but David feared sooner rather than later the duke would grow desperate and take off for Littleton's black forest all on his own.

And *that* would surely mean the duke's death, as the Littleton Fiend tended to eat unexpected visitors before they had a chance to state their business.